OCEANSIDE PUBLIC LIBRARY
330 N. Coast Highway
Oceanside, CA. 92054

CIVIC CENTER

My Unfair Godmother

Also by Janette Rallison

Playing the Field
All's Fair in Love, War, and High School
Life, Love, and the Pursuit of Free Throws
Fame, Glory, and Other Things on My To Do List
It's a Mall World After All
Revenge of the Cheerleaders
My Fair Godmother

YA

My Unfair Godmother

Janette Rallison

Walker & Company
New York

Copyright © 2011 by Janette Rallison
All rights reserved. No part of this book may be reproduced or transmitted in any form
or by any means, electronic or mechanical, including photocopying, recording, or by any
information storage and retrieval system, without permission in writing from the publisher.

First published in the United States of America in April 2011
by Walker Publishing Company, Inc., a division of Bloomsbury Publishing, Inc.
www.bloomsburyteens.com

For information about permission to reproduce selections from this book, write to
Permissions, Walker BFYR, 175 Fifth Avenue, New York, New York 10010

Library of Congress Cataloging-in-Publication Data
Rallison, Janette.
My unfair godmother / Janette Rallison.
p.   cm.
Summary: A fairy godmother-in-training is sent to help angry seventeen-year-old Tansy, who
reluctantly is staying with her father and his new wife while her mother and sister are
traveling, but the unfortunate result of this intended help is chaos and confusion.
ISBN 978-0-8027-2236-2
[1. Fairy godmothers—Fiction. 2. Magic—Fiction. 3. Time travel—Fiction. 4. Middle Ages—
Fiction. 5. Stepfamilies—Fiction.] I. Title.
PZ7.R13455Mz 2011   [Fic]—dc22   2010025482

Book design by Nicole Gastonguay
Typeset by Westchester Book Composition
Printed in the U.S.A. by Quad/Graphics, Fairfield, Pennsylvania
2 4 6 8 10 9 7 5 3 1

All papers used by Bloomsbury Publishing, Inc., are natural, recyclable products
made from wood grown in well-managed forests. The manufacturing processes
conform to the environmental regulations of the country of origin.

3 1232 00895 4028

To my husband, who became a superparent while I shut myself in a room and worked long hours writing this book. Car pool, grocery shopping, dinner—he did it all. (Actual comment overheard at my daughter's softball practice: "Does Arianna have a mother?")

To my children, who lived on frozen dinners, pizza, and Dad's cooking while I wrote—and especially to Faith, who checked my computer every day when she came home from school to see what I'd written on the story. You kept me going!

And lastly to my editor, Emily Easton. I don't know if you believe in magic, but I'm glad you believe in my fairy, Chrysanthemum Everstar.

My Unfair Godmother

Dear Professor Goldengill,

Thank you for another opportunity to raise my semester grade with an extra-credit project. As you read my report I hope you'll see that I'm more than ready to enter Fairy Godmother University.

I have mastered fluttering, flitting, and twinkling. My wand-waving technique is excellent, and I can out-sparkle just about anybody. But, most important, I totally relate to teenage girls and all their woeful little problems. During this assignment, whether the trouble was with boys, fashion, or evil megalomaniac ex-fairies trying to kill my teenage charge, I was always completely understanding.

True, there were a few glitches along the way, and maybe a mortal or two got misplaced in the wrong time period, but I would like to point out that no one died during the assignment. And the stuff that went wrong was pretty much my assistant's fault anyway.

When I found out I had been assigned Clover T. Bloomsbottle as my assistant, I reminded the coordinator at the Fairy Godmother Affairs office quite pointedly—and maybe even with a little bit of hysteria—that I had already said I never wanted to work with another leprechaun—especially and specifically Clover T. Bloomsbottle. But she got all uppity and told me the FGA is trying to find a position for Clover that best uses his talents. Considering that his main talent is his amazing ability to spread incompetence around, I suggest you relegate him to a cereal box somewhere.

Here is my nine-page report, complete with side notes, to show you how much I've already learned about human culture.

Sincerely,
Chrysanthemum Everstar

HOW I USED MY FAIRY GODMOTHER SKILLS TO FIX ANOTHER LUCKY MORTAL'S DISMAL LIFE

by Chrysanthemum Everstar

Subject: Tansy Miller Harris, age seventeen
Place: Queens, New York, early twenty-first century

Mortals are always going on about how important family is to them. They even believe it's true. When Tansy Miller was seven, her father used to tell her he wouldn't trade her for a mountain of gold. Of course, she should have been suspicious of this claim, since it was hard to prove. Very few gold-mountain owners are interested in bartering for little girls. But still, Tansy believed him.

Tansy suspected her mother liked Kendall, Tansy's two-year-old sister, best. Kendall was as petite and delicate as newly sprouted rosebuds and would cry if it was too dark, or her clothes were too prickly, or if she spotted something frightening like cockroaches or broccoli. Kendall clung to their mother, following her from room to room like the train of a wedding gown. Their mother was constantly cooing and caring for Kendall, forever making things cooler, hotter, or more pink. But Tansy didn't mind because she had her father. Mr. Miller took her on bike rides, called her his princess, and pointed out faraway places on the map with odd-sounding names like Ulaanbaatar, Kathmandu, and Sacramento.

Every day, Tansy sat in her bedroom window seat, covered in jelly stains, grass stains, and whatever other stains she managed to acquire, and waited for her father to come home from work. She would color pictures and watch the trees outside her window rustling at each other while they ignored the pedestrians on 159th Street. Tansy liked to pick out books for her father to read to her, and the later he was, the more stories went on the stack. Perhaps he knew this. He was never very late.

Often, he brought home new books. That was one of the perks of working at the Brooklyn Public Library. Mr. Miller was rich in glossy picture books, even if he wasn't rich in the other kind of printed paper—the green variety with portraits of stern-looking presidents.

"Don't just read words," he would tell her as he held up the latest story, "devour them. Let the words create new worlds."

By the time Tansy was twelve, she had worlds without number enfolded in her heart. And each one of them was built with the scaffolding of her father's voice. She couldn't read without hearing him narrate the story in her mind.

A week before her thirteenth birthday, he rearranged her life with one short word. Divorce. It had started with a lot of other words, accusations, and fights that Tansy didn't understand. It ended when he decided to take a job in another state.

"I'm leaving your mother, but not you and Kendall," he told her. "I'll always be your father."

Fairy's side note: Even mortals with the best intentions will tell a devastation of lies.

Because he did leave Tansy and her sister. The very next day.

Mr. Miller left a stack of boxes by the front door for the UPS man to pick up, then took a battered suitcase and went outside to wait for a cab. Tansy watched him from her window seat, willing with all the magic she possessed to make him turn around, come back inside, and decide to stay.

Fairy's side note: Mortals are woefully lacking in magic.

He didn't come back inside. He didn't even look up at Tansy to notice she'd rested her head against the window, her face streaked with tears.

The cab pulled up. Tansy's father put his suitcase in the trunk, shut it with a clang of determination, then climbed into the backseat. He settled in and let out a sigh, of relief probably. Why else did one sigh alone in a cab? It wasn't a sigh of regret or sadness, she knew, because he never looked back at their apartment. Not once. She watched him growing smaller, disappearing from her life, until the car turned and went down another street.

And every one of the worlds in Tansy's heart crashed together like a book being closed. He moved across the country to a place he'd never pointed out on a map: Rock Canyon, Arizona. A land of parched earth and cacti with thorns so thick and fierce they could draw blood. It was a fitting symbol in this new world of pain. Even the plants in Arizona wanted to hurt you.

Tansy threw away most of the books her father had given her. She vowed never to read another story again. She didn't want to hear her father's voice narrating in her head.

Instead, she heard more keenly her mother's voice. Tansy remembered every criticism her mother gave her, as though she were engraving a monument of her mother's opinion.

You're so stubborn. Why won't you listen to anyone? You're as bad as your father.

That one was engraved with deep, sharp edges.

You're as bad as your father.

She wondered what her father would have said to that criticism. He wouldn't have let it stand. But he wasn't around to defend either himself or Tansy. True, he called on the phone, but Tansy, when she talked at all, only gave brief answers to his questions. She was cutting herself out of his life as thoroughly as he had cut himself out of hers. And so there they were, both of them cut.

The next year, Tansy only saw her father for one month in the summer when she and Kendall went west for a visit. During most of that month, Mr. Miller was busy at work—Rock Canyon had opened a new library branch, and he was in charge of it. Being in charge meant staying late every night.

Fairy's side note: At that point, Tansy probably should have asked if he'd acquired a gold mountain somewhere.

When she was fifteen, Tansy's father married Sandra, one of the other librarians at the branch. Perhaps it wasn't only his work ethic that made him put in late hours even when his daughters were visiting. New love for an auburn-haired woman with a quick smile and the ability to quote both Shakespeare and romance novels easily trumps time with one's resentful teenage daughter.

In what was possibly the tackiest wedding reception ever to grace Rock Canyon, Mr. Frank Miller and the newly crowned Mrs. Sandra Miller greeted friends, neighbors, and avid readers right next to the checkout desk in the library lobby.

Tansy and Kendall got a stepbrother who was just a few months younger than Tansy, and on those occasions when they came from New York to visit, Tansy got to watch firsthand the zeal her father put into parenting him. He proofed Nick's school papers, went to his swim meets, and played some fantasy computer game where they both went around hacking trolls to pieces.

Every time Tansy saw them at it, happy in the new world they'd created, she gritted her teeth.

But because she was a teenager, her father couldn't tell the difference between her sullenness and normal moody teenage behavior. Sometimes it's hard to tell with mortal girls. Besides, Kendall had enough love inside her that their father didn't go without hugs and affection and chatter. She was young enough that she hadn't learned yet to ration love out.

When Tansy was seventeen and happy for the most part with her life among the skyscrapers, good fortune struck Kendall— and bludgeoned Tansy. Kendall was chosen to play a main part in a Broadway play. She would travel across the nation singing in the spotlight, fed by caterers and applause. And since she was only twelve years old, her mother needed to travel with her.

Tansy was shipped off to live with her father in a land of palm trees but no ocean. To a new wardrobe of shorts and sandals, but nowhere to wear them. And to a high school full of kids, but no friends.

She met Bo on her first day of school at Rock Canyon High. She was in the office registering, and he was in the office getting in trouble. He wore clothes that said he didn't care what other people thought. His stance said the same thing. His hair, if interviewed, would have given a different story. His hair had been fussed over and grown to the perfect length to show off his features. The skulls on his T-shirt and the holes in his jeans might proclaim he was a bad boy, but his hair asserted he was a bad boy with a standing monthly appointment at Lenora's Uptown Style Salon.

While Bo and Tansy waited in line to speak to the secretary, he looked at her from underneath brooding bangs and said, "What are you in for?"

"The time of my life, according to my mother."

Bo laughed. "Do you listen to your mother?"

"Hard to do since she's in"—Tansy checked her watch—"Chicago right now."

"What's she doing in Chicago?"

"Taking care of my sister." Tansy looked at the school office with a sigh, wondering yet again where her well-being rated on her mother's list of priorities. Not very high, probably.

"Ahh," Bo said, as though he understood. And maybe he did. Bo was the type of guy who was close friends with anger and roommates with resentment.

Tansy looked him over thoroughly now, for the first time appreciating these qualities in a guy. Why care what other people thought? Why try to be good? She had done that her whole life and all it had gotten her was a trip to Small Town, Arizona, and a father who knew everything about his stepson but nothing about her.

Bo didn't miss her hungry gaze. "So you're a new kid?"

She nodded. She had just realized there were all sorts of new things she could be. She didn't have to be the smart girl, the good girl. She could be rebellious, dangerous.

"You're pretty," Bo said. "You want to get together later and do something?"

Fairy's side note: Bo wasn't the best at pickup lines.

Tansy smiled and said, "Sure." Sometimes the allure of rebellion is more attractive than a good pickup line. She gave him her phone number, and, when he thought to ask for it, her name. Tansy Harris. She had stopped using her father's name when he left New York.

That day at lunch, instead of eating with her stepbrother, Nick, and his honor student friends, Tansy skipped school with Bo and rode on his motorcycle to a fast-food place.

The first week of school, Bo came over to Tansy's house twice—coming over meaning sitting in front of her house on his motorcycle wearing mirrored sunglasses and a bored expression. She climbed on his bike and he took her to his older brother's band rehearsals. They called themselves Indestruction and played music that sounded like trains crashing into each other. It was usually too loud in the room to talk, and when Bo's brother wasn't singing, he was saturating the room with cigarette smoke. Still, Tansy felt a certain exhilaration being around Bo's friends. No one told her to look on the bright side of anything. No one told her to give her new school a chance. No one made her promises they weren't going to keep. And as an extra bonus, every time she came back home, her father looked irritated and worried about her.

That hadn't happened for years. And although she wouldn't have admitted to it, it gave her hope. Hope he still cared.

Nick didn't approve. He'd known Bo since junior high, back when Bo cared enough about school to cheat on his exams. Bo had stolen Nick's lunch and tripped him in PE and . . . there were several more ands.

But in Bo's defense, he was handsome.

Fairy's side note: Mortal girls will overlook a piñata full of faults if a guy is considerate enough to be handsome.

Things might have continued between Tansy and Bo for quite some time. After all, she had lived with the scales in her heart tipped to one side for so long it was hard for her to judge situations with accuracy now. For example, when Bo told her he loved her, she actually believed him.

Fairy's side note: The only things you can truly love after such a short time are ice cream flavors and comfortable shoes.

Then misfortune struck. Misfortune, in this case, carried with it the same sorts of travel plans her cousin Fortune had brought to Tansy earlier.

Misfortune and Fortune are eerily identical, although Fortune is a better dresser and much more fun at parties.

The mayor of Rock Canyon announced that due to a budget shortfall, the library branch where Mr. and Mrs. Miller worked would close in December. Not only would the memories of their courtship be torn down with the shelves, but in a few months, they would be out of jobs.

The community took the news with only a whimper of protest. Very few people in Rock Canyon stood up to the mayor, and he listened to even fewer. Unfortunately, none of the people he listened to liked to read.

Frank and Sandra Miller talked about petitions and appeals, but when they thought the kids were asleep, they talked about where they could go. Sandra's sister lived in Los Angeles, and they could move in with her for a while. Nick could share a room with his cousin John, and Tansy . . .

And Tansy . . .

Well, the only place for Tansy would be the couch. And who knew how long it would take for them to find jobs again. They wouldn't be able to buy another house until they were settled someplace. Perhaps it would be best, more stable, if Tansy went to live with her grandmother in New Jersey and finished school there.

Tansy wasn't thrilled with this solution. Her grandmother was not especially fond of children, and she had a few quirks. For example, she liked having vacuum-cleaner lines in the carpet proclaiming its spotlessness and revacuumed if someone messed up the pattern. She wanted anyone who ate at her table to keep their silverware laid in parallel lines, and she didn't talk much during dinner because she was busy counting how many times she chewed her food.

As her father and stepmother discussed the matter, they said things like, "We don't have a lot of choices," and "Tansy has only been to school at Rock Canyon High for a month; it won't be hard for her to move in December," and "It will get her away from that jerk of a boyfriend."

In Tansy's dark moments, she wondered if her father had ever at any point really wanted her around.

To his credit, Bo was angry about the library closing, or at least he was angry about Tansy leaving. He took her to city hall to settle the score.

Which only made things worse.

Fairy's side note: Mortals often do more damage than good when attempting to fix things. They also firmly believe that problems can be solved with money. Mortals think if they stack up enough dollar bills, they can buy happiness.

Happiness, of course, is more expensive than that. Which is why people need magic.

As Tansy's fairy godmother, I helped her learn these things. Please accept this extra-credit project as proof I am more than ready to enter Fairy Godmother University.

From the Honorable Master Sagewick Goldengill
To Mistress Berrypond

Dear Mistress Berrypond,
    I'm in receipt of Chrysanthemum Everstar's report on Tansy Miller Harris, but it seems to be missing some crucial details. Can you have the Memoir Elves look into the matter and write their own report so I can better assess Chrysanthemum's role as Tansy Miller Harris's fairy godmother?

    Most magical thanks,
    Sagewick Goldengill

From the Department of Fairy Advancement
To the Honorable Sagewick Goldengill

Dear Professor,

The Memoir Elves submerged themselves into Tansy's mind while she slept, and, after several nights of observation, have composed her story in her own words. I remind you that sending Memoir Elves into teenage girls' minds is unhealthy for the elves. Even after short amounts of exposure to the jumble of impulses and hormones that make up a teenage girl's mind, the Memoir Elves are apt to pick up bad habits, grow obsessive about their hair, and giggle when boys pass by.

All the elves involved in Tansy's case are in detox and are recovering well—except for Blinka Ruefeather, who refuses to give up her iPod and keeps belting out Taylor Swift lyrics. But then, Blinka always was susceptible to love songs. She may need stronger intervention.

At any rate, you should be able to see Chrysanthemum Everstar's role as Tansy's godmother from the following memoir.

Flitteringly yours,
Mistress Berrypond

Chapter 1

Bo's text message to me was short: "I hope you like surprises."

It was all he would say about our date tonight. He was probably trying to be romantic, but that's the thing about guys. They don't understand that it takes girls some thought and effort to get ready. Was I supposed to wear heels? Tennis shoes? Waterproof mascara? A parachute? He could have at least given me a category for the night's activity.

After changing outfits three times, I decided on dressy casual—it worked for most things—then went out to the living room to put on my shoes. My shoes were in the closet by the front door because Sandra, my stepmother, insisted we take off our footwear as soon as we came inside. It was better for the carpet.

Sandra was one of those immaculate housekeepers that I hope never to be. I'm all for cleanliness, but I draw the line at immaculate. Sometimes it's okay if the light fixtures have streaks.

My stepbrother, Nick, was sprawled out on the couch reading a book. He has reddish blond hair and so many freckles that Sandra refers to them as "the stars dotting the sky of his features." Nick just calls them the freckle convention that showed up on his face.

Out on the street, Bo honked his motorcycle horn. At the noise, Nick looked up from his book. "Classy way to signal the beginning of a date."

I grabbed my shoes and slipped them on. "If he rang the doorbell, he'd have to turn off his motorcycle."

"And?" Nick asked.

I rolled my eyes, like Nick was making a big deal out of nothing, but to tell the truth, it was starting to bug me too. I stopped at the entryway mirror to check my appearance. I had pulled my long blond hair back in a french braid, which is one of the few hairstyles you can wear on a motorcycle and not look like you're impersonating a sea anemone at the end of the ride. Since I started dating Bo, my hairstyles have become all about wind control.

Behind me in the reflection, Nick stared at me. Slowly he said, "The problem with dating a guy to tick off your father is you end up having an idiot for a boyfriend."

"I'm not dating Bo to tick off anyone." This was partially true. Ticking off my father was an added benefit. "Bo accepts me for who I am. He cares about me."

The horn blared again.

"He cares about you, but not enough to get off his motorcycle?"

Despite my best intentions to hate Nick for becoming my replacement—he was, after all, the kid my dad had lived with for years—I actually liked Nick. He felt like a brother.

Nick was still staring at me, waiting for some response. Really, he should have been happy I was dating Bo. Bo's friends had become downright nice to Nick lately. They would nod to him in the school hallways like they'd always been on good terms.

I asked Bo once why he had picked on Nick before I'd moved in. Bo had looked surprised at the question. "Guys mess around," he said. "It doesn't mean anything."

And it probably didn't to Bo. It means a little more if you're the one getting messed around with.

The horn honked again. Nick went back to his book, shaking his head. "Have a fun time. If that's possible while you're out with a troglodyte."

Nick liked to throw around vocabulary no high school student should know. It was his way of winning arguments. People couldn't dispute anything he said when they needed a dictionary to figure out what he was talking about. But I had a vocabulary that rivaled Nick's. It came from reading hundreds of novels back before Dad left.

Despite sounding like something that should hang in caves with stalagmites and stalactites, a troglodyte is a stupid brute. They show up a lot in time-travel novels.

Sometimes I missed reading.

"Bo isn't as bad as you think," I said.

"Probably not, since I think he's devil spawn."

"You should have an open mind," I said. "Bo does."

Nick flipped a page of his book. "You're confusing open with empty."

I ignored the comment, tucked a stray strand of hair back into my braid, and went outside. Even though it was 9:00 p.m., the Arizona air was still so warm it felt heavy against my skin. Dad said it would cool down in October, but I didn't believe him. Arizona only knew two temperatures: hot and hotter.

Bo was sitting on his motorcycle, casually fingering the handlebars. His dark hair swept across his forehead and a shadow of stubble dotted his jaw. On most guys, I wouldn't have thought that looked good. But on Bo it worked. He watched me walk up to his bike and smiled.

Nick was wrong about him. Bo wasn't bad—just misunderstood. He was the kind of guy who didn't play by other people's rules. I could respect that. Bo handed me a helmet, and even though he never wore his, I strapped mine on. I wanted to rebel a little, but I wanted to do it with my head attached.

"So where are we going?" I asked. Judging from the paint splatters on his jeans and T-shirt, it wasn't going to be any place fancy. I hoped I wasn't overdressed.

He gave me a secretive smile. "You'll see when we get there. I'm taking you to do something you've never done before."

That could be a lot of things. I climbed onto the back of the bike, wound my arms around his waist, and we sped down the street. As usual, I tried not to think about the fact that Bo and I were wider than the motorcycle wheels, which would seem to make us an unbalanced load. Especially since the wheels were spinning. Very fast.

Real rebellious girls didn't worry about those sorts of things.

We drove out of the neighborhood and headed downtown. As the buildings went by, I tried to guess where Bo was taking me. I hoped it wasn't some concert his brother's band was putting on. I had already spent hours listening to them practice, and lately every time I heard the band's name I wanted to snap, "There's no such word as 'indestruction.' You can either be Indestructible or In Destruction although I don't know why you'd want to be the last one." Actually, the only things they were destroying were chords, notes, and probably their hearing.

I held on to Bo a little tighter and resolved to act delighted if the surprise turned out to be a whole night of listening to indiscernible lyrics. Indiscernible, that would work as a band name too. Or maybe Indecipherable, Inconceivable, or Insufferable.

We drove through downtown and at last pulled into the city hall's empty parking lot. It was a boxy two-story building that the architect had tried to dress up by throwing a few columns onto the front. But the columns only made it look like a post office with pretentions.

I was surprised Bo had taken me here. And even more surprised that four of Bo's friends stood beside their motorcycles at the far end of the parking lot.

"Why are we here?" I asked. If Bo had planned to stage some sort of demonstration, it wasn't going to work. The building was closed.

Bo pulled up to the other motorcycles and turned off his ignition. "Revenge."

He got off his bike. I stayed on, eyeing the trash bag his best friend, Steve, was holding. "What are you talking about?"

Bo held out his hand to help me off his bike and kept his fingers twined through mine as he led me over to the others.

Steve opened up the trash bag. "It took you long enough to get here."

Bo half nodded in my direction. "You know how girls are. They're never ready when you pick them up."

I glared at Bo, because it hadn't taken me *that* long, but he wasn't paying attention to me. Steve reached into the bag and took out two cans of red spray paint. He threw one at Bo and one at me. "Well, hurry. This ain't the most private place in town."

The spray can felt cold in my hands. A ball of dread formed in my stomach. "You're not going to vandalize city hall, are you?"

Bo laughed and propelled me closer to the building. "I told you I was taking you to do something you've never done before."

Yes, he was, and it turned out I was way overdressed for our date. If he had told me the category for tonight was committing a crime, I could have worn a ski mask. Or better yet, not come at all.

I pulled my hand away from his. "We can't do this."

He pointed toward the broken street light in front of city hall. "Don't worry. I came here before and knocked out the lights. No one will see us."

The other guys were already beside the building. They took the lids off their cans and sprayed red streaks across the wall. The night hissed with the sound as the smell of fresh paint drifted back to me.

Bo shook his can and popped off the lid. "Go ahead. Let the mayor know what you think." He stepped forward and sprayed a red slash on the pale stucco wall. It looked like a bleeding wound.

"This is not a good idea." I tried to keep my voice low, but it spiraled upward. "We'll get in so much trouble if we get caught."

"We haven't been caught yet."

We'd only been here for a few minutes.

One of Bo's friends, Mike, wrote, "Close this dump not the libary!"

Which meant even though I hadn't uncapped my spray can, this was my fault. Bo's friends were risking getting in trouble to support me.

But it was wrong, and not only because Mike had left an *r* out of "library." I had to push away my sudden urge to spray paint an extra *r* in to correct the word. Or to add the comma the sentence needed. You're not supposed to edit graffiti.

Bo tapped the can in my hand with his own, clicking them together like he was making a toast. "Write something. It'll feel good."

I stared at the wall. Hadn't I wanted to be the rebellious type? This was it. Rebellion. Danger. And it would feel good to let the mayor know people were upset, to mess up his building like he was messing up my life. I didn't move though; I just gripped the can.

Steve walked over to us. "Hey, Bo, I bet you can't hit that upper window."

Bo leaned down and picked up one of the river rocks lying in the landscaping. "Ten bucks says I can."

Breaking windows was worse than spray painting. You couldn't fix windows by painting over them. "Don't break it," I said. "That's serious."

My comment caused a wave of laughter to go through the guys. A guy named Brandon, who had earring holes so big you could shoot marbles through them, nudged Bo. "Dude, you've gone serious on us."

Steve made kissy noises. "He's a serious boyfriend."

Bo shrugged away from his friends. He didn't like their ribbing, didn't like that I'd spoken up. He shot me an aggravated look. "Loosen up and have some fun."

Bo sized up the distance to the window, then flung the rock upward. It bounced off the wall and shot back to the ground. Brandon stepped out of the way and swore. "Are you trying to kill us?"

Steve rubbed his thumb against his fingers and smirked at Bo. "You owe me ten, man."

Bo stretched his shoulders. "Stand back. I get more than one try."

I stepped away from Bo and the rest of them. My palms were sweaty against the spray can, and I couldn't relax enough to stand in one place. Obviously, I wasn't cut out to be the rebellious type, because I couldn't do this. I didn't know whether to try again to make Bo stop or walk away from the building and find my own way home. How upset would Bo be if I just left? He and his friends were doing this for me. For the *libary.* Maybe I was ungrateful to get upset with them.

Everything was happening so fast that I couldn't sort it out in my mind. I needed advice, and the only one I could think to call was Nick.

"I'm going around the back of the building," I said. None of the guys paid much attention to me since they were watching Bo pick up another rock.

He held it in his palm, testing its weight. "You do that, baby. You write a whole novel back there."

I hurried to the back of the building. Another smack sounded against the wall. Bo's friends snorted with laughter.

Bo said, "Hey, in baseball you get three strikes—that's only two."

I took out my cell phone and dialed Nick's phone one slow number at a time. I had just gotten the phone and hadn't programmed the speed dial yet. I leaned against the wall while the phone rang. An angry crash sounded from the other side of the building. Apparently Bo's aim wasn't that bad after all.

"Perfect hit," Bo said, his voice filled with strut and confidence.

"That was the wrong window," Steve said. "You still owe me a ten."

Nick picked up. "Hey, Tansy."

"Bo and his friends are vandalizing city hall and I don't know what to do."

Nick paused. "They're what?"

"They're spray painting stuff and they broke a window." Another crashing noise came from the other side of the building. "Make that two windows."

Nick's voice sounded incredulous. "On your date?"

"He's doing it because he cares about me."

"Sheesh, couldn't you find a guy who would just give you flowers?"

I paced along the back side of the wall, not even caring that I could hardly see where I was going. "How do I make them stop?"

"Start walking toward our house and I'll drive down and get you."

"If I make a big deal about this, Bo will be angry. What if he breaks up with me?"

"And the downside of that would be?"

"I don't want to be dumped." My voice choked. "Bo is the only person in the world who cares about me."

"Tansy!" I heard Bo yell, but I didn't answer him. I didn't know what to say to him yet.

Nick's voice came over the line. "You know what Bo is doing is wrong or you wouldn't have called me. You can't go along with this."

I let out a whimper, but I knew he was right. I would have to tell the guys to stop.

"I don't want to deal with those miscreants when I pick you up," Nick said, "so ditch them."

Miscreants: troublemakers or wrongdoers. In this case, not only an insult but an accurate description.

Nick was right. It was better not to involve him. "You don't have to pick me up." I let out a sigh of resignation. "I'll make Bo take me home. I guess we need to talk about this."

Motorcycles started up and peeled out of the parking lot. Some of the guys must have left. Good, less damage to worry about.

"Your dad is going to freak," Nick said.

"No, he won't, because he's not going to find out." As soon as I said it, I knew he would. The guys had painted stuff about the library closing onto the side of the building. Was there any way to buy tan paint and cover that up before people got to work in the morning?

I laughed at myself. I hated the mayor, but I would have to spend the night painting city hall in order to cover the graffiti. I was *so* not cut out to be the bad girl.

I walked slowly back around the corner of the building, trying to phrase what to say to Bo.

Immediately I noticed flashlight beams running across the

side of the building. Two guys stood by the wall, illuminating the graffiti—checking their work, I supposed. Using flashlights was a stupid thing to do since we didn't want to be seen by people on the street. I wondered where Bo had gone.

I kept walking. Then I realized the two figures weren't Bo's friends. Bo and the others were nowhere around. The two figures were policemen.

For a moment I stood frozen to the spot. Every curse word I knew—and some that I made up just for the occasion—went through my mind. Should I run for it or stay frozen and hope the officers didn't notice me?

I took a slow-motion step backward. Before I could try another, one of the policemen swung his flashlight beam on me.

I dropped the spray can, turned, and fled back the way I'd come.

"Hey!" a policeman barked. "Stop!"

I ran faster. I had no idea where I was going, where I could go, but panic pushed me forward. A cinder block fence edged the back of city hall's property. It was too tall to climb over. I kept running.

Where had Bo gone? Had they captured him already?

And then the pieces fell in place in my mind. The way he had called my name. The sound of the motorcycles. The fact that I hadn't seen any motorcycles in the parking lot just now.

Bo had seen the police coming. And he'd left me.

While I was back behind city hall telling Nick that Bo was the only person in the world who cared about me, he'd deserted me. He'd left me to the police.

I was too stunned to even feel angry.

I had nearly run the length of city hall when another policeman stepped around the side of the building, blocking the path in front of me. His flashlight beam trained in on me, blinding me. "Hold it right there," he panted out. "You're not going anywhere."

He was right. I couldn't get around him, and his partner was coming up behind me.

I held my hand up to shield my eyes. The policeman in front of me became a blur against the light, but I could tell he was shaking his head in disgust. "You're in a heap of trouble. You know that, don't you?"

I did. I was in trouble. And Bo didn't care about me.

Chapter 2

The police car was parked close to the street. The officers made me walk to it with my hands on the back of my head. I thought this was the most humiliating moment in my life, until they had me stand, feet apart, with my hands pressed against the side of the car. Then one of the police officers frisked me with the back of his hands. Which is still pretty much like being felt up by an old man. All this while a stream of cars drove by. I could tell the drivers were watching me because they slowed way down. I prayed none of them were kids from school.

In the reflection of the car window, I noticed my french braid hadn't worked to keep my hair in place. A big strand had pulled loose. Well, that was going to look great in a mug shot.

After Officer A-little-too-eager-to-frisk-teenage-girls made sure I didn't have any weapons shoved in my clothes, he handcuffed my hands behind my back and made me sit in the police car. He had a bulge of fat underneath his chin and only the suggestion of hair draped over the top of his head. Leaning into the car to look at me, he said, "So did you do this by yourself, or did your friends help?"

I had no friends. I didn't say anything, just looked straight ahead.

"What's your name?" he asked.

I didn't answer. The handcuffs were too tight and bit into my wrists. I opened and shut my hands, trying to ease the pinch.

He had taken my cell phone from my pocket when he frisked me, and he flipped it open. I wondered if he was going through my text messages with Bo. He wouldn't find my name from that. Bo called me Babe.

The officer snapped my phone shut. "Your parents will need to come pick you up. If you don't give us your name, you're going to be at the station for a long time."

I still didn't say anything. I had the right to remain silent.

He sneered and leaned closer. I caught the smell of stale coffee on his breath. "You hoodlums always think you're so tough. Takes a lot of guts to break windows. You're real brave coming out after dark to spray paint buildings." His voice gained momentum. "You're nothing but a messed-up punk who can make this easier, or who can sit there glaring and make it harder."

I wasn't glaring; I was in shock. I was trying not to shake, not to cry.

"Fine then," the man said. "Let's go to the station." He slammed the door and got in the front of the car.

Well, Bo was right about one thing. Tonight he took me to do something I'd never done before.

• • •

When I got to the police station, Officer Cop A. Feely marched me through the lobby, past the receptionist, or sentinel, or whatever you call the lady in the police shirt who rules over the lobby. Then he took me down the hall to a holding room. He strutted during all of this, like I was some elk he'd bagged.

I've always been a law-abiding citizen. Once when I bought a pair of jeans, I picked up a keychain from a countertop display and absentmindedly walked out of the store with it. I was only a few feet down the street when I realized I still had it, but I totally freaked out. I was convinced the store manager would rush through the doors after me and no one would ever believe I hadn't purposely shoplifted it. I hurried back to the store, holding the keychain out like it was about to burst into flames.

But now with an officer marching me through the station, I felt like scum. And I hated him for making me feel that way. I also hated the receptionist/sentinel for looking smug and unconcerned, and just for good measure, I hated anyone in the world who happened to be wearing a dark blue shirt at that moment.

The officer led me to a room, took off my handcuffs, and motioned for me to sit down. "You ready to tell us who you are?"

I sat down and shook my head. Once I told them my name, they would ask other questions like who had been with me tonight. I didn't know how to answer that yet.

He walked back to the door and sent another threatening look in my direction. "The detective will come talk to you in a minute." Then he shut the door.

A two-way mirror lined the wall in front of me. I wondered if there was anyone behind it, or if the police only spied on hardened criminals. A black camera sat perched in the corner of the ceiling. I might be recorded. Great. I would have to be careful about what I said.

The minutes ticked by. I wasn't sure if the detective was busy or whether this was part of my punishment—making me sit here and worry about my fate as a guest in Hotel Convictland.

Actually, I appreciated the time to think.

I was seething at Bo. He had taken me to vandalize the city hall on a date, and he didn't listen when I told him we shouldn't do it, and worst of all, he left me there.

You didn't do that to people you loved. Romeo wouldn't have left Juliet with a spray can clutched in her hand. But Bo left me. He left me to take the fine or jail time or whatever punishment I was going to get.

Would I have a criminal record now? My stomach clenched at the thought. Job applications always asked if you had ever been convicted of a crime. Colleges probably asked the same thing. This could change my whole life.

So maybe the things Nick said about Bo were true. Maybe he wasn't a misunderstood, brooding bad boy; maybe he really was a jerk.

Should I show him the same loyalty he'd shown me and turn him and his friends over to the police? But I hardly knew anyone at school. If I told the police the truth, I would be known as Narc Girl. And Snitch Girl. And Fink Girl. And as many other synonyms as there were for Girl Who Lands Her Boyfriend In Jail. No one at school would want to speak to me, including Bo.

Although right now I wasn't sure if I was ever speaking to Bo again anyway, so maybe that part didn't matter.

My stomach felt like a lid someone had screwed on too tight. There wasn't a good solution to this. My dad would flip, and my mom—wherever she was on the road—would flip too. I glanced at the mirror again, at the strand of hair that had come loose from my french braid. I couldn't leave it like that. When my dad finally came to pick me up, I didn't want to look like one of those half-coherent criminals who stumbled around on cop shows. Besides, it was easier to fix my hair than think about everything else.

I looked at my reflection and tried to tuck the strand back into the braid. When that didn't work, I took the braid out and combed my fingers through my hair the best I could. Which wasn't all that well. My hair had still been a little damp when I braided it. Now it was wavy and looked wild and tousled.

A middle-aged man opened the door and walked in. He held a coffee cup in one hand and a file folder in the other. Barely glancing at me, he settled into the chair on the other side of the table. "When the criminals are so bored they're doing their hair, it means it's time to talk."

They *had* been watching me. I felt myself blush. I wanted to say, "I wasn't trying to make myself look nice for you, if that's what you're thinking." But I had already decided not to say anything. Instead of meeting his eyes, I scrutinized his tie. It was pale blue with little cacti on it. Arizona: not just a place, a fashion statement.

"So, Tansy, do you want to tell me what happened tonight?"

I let out a gasp. I had no idea how he'd guessed my name. No, guessed wasn't the right word. If he were guessing, he wouldn't have come up with Tansy. In my entire life, I'd never met another Tansy. My father chose the name from some old book he loved.

The detective smiled at my reaction. "You're not in Queens anymore. People talk in small towns. They know things about each other."

How did he know I was from Queens? I had never seen him before in my life.

He tapped his pen against the table impatiently. "Who was with you tonight?"

I clutched my hands in my lap and didn't answer.

"Are you saying it was only you?" he asked. "Because if you're taking responsibility for the damage, replacing those busted windows will run you between fifteen hundred and two thousand dollars. Hiring someone to repaint the side of the building will cost a few hundred more. If you want us to send the bill to someone else, you need to tell us who."

I tried not to let him see me flinch. I didn't have that much money and my dad was about to lose his job. Still, I didn't want to let this guy intimidate me into turning over my boyfriend. Or ex-boyfriend, probably. I hadn't decided yet. After all, Bo might show up on my doorstep with flowers, begging for my forgiveness. He might offer to pay the fine.

"You know, this isn't the first building that's been vandalized in the last month." The detective held up a folder to show me the proof. "We've got a dentist's office, a gas station, and a McDonald's. Same sort of handiwork we found on the city hall. We've been searching for the vandals, and tonight we caught you." He leaned back in his chair, his hands folded smugly in his lap. "It would be a shame if these got pinned on you too."

My stomach lurched. Bo hadn't vandalized those other buildings, had he? Tonight had happened because he was mad about my father and stepmother losing their jobs. He had thrown those rocks for me.

"You're making that up about the other buildings," I said.

Without a trace of emotion, the detective flipped open the folder, took out a picture, and slid it to me. "Look familiar?"

It didn't. The photo showed a gas station with red slashes across the side of one wall, like a giant cat had scratched it. Why would Bo have sprayed graffiti on the other buildings?

The detective put the picture back in the folder. "I don't think you realize how much trouble you're in, so I want your parents to come down and talk with you. Then you can decide what to tell me." He pushed himself away from the table. "If you're a smart girl, you won't take the rap for someone else."

He stood up and motioned me to follow him out of the room. When we reached the lobby, he said, "Take a seat. It will be a while before Mary gets around to calling your parents. It's been a busy night." He glanced over at the waiting room's other occupant, a teenage guy. He sat in the middle of the only row of chairs, flipping through a magazine without paying attention to it. Before the detective left the room, he sent me a humorless smile. "Hope you're not out past your curfew."

I sat down on the last chair in the row. I had remained outwardly calm so far, and I'd been proud of myself for staying tough. But now my hands shook. I wasn't tough. And I was alone sitting in the police station. The last thing I wanted to do was cry, but the tears ran down my cheeks without permission. The most I could manage was to choke back the sobs that pulsed in my throat.

I hadn't noticed the teenage guy move, but he sat down on the chair next to me, holding out a box of tissues.

"Thanks." I took a couple and blew my nose. I had never blown my nose in front of a stranger, let alone a guy who was my age and good-looking. And he was good-looking. I wouldn't have even glanced at his face, except I wondered if I knew him from school, and once I saw him, the handsome thing was sort of hard to overlook. He had wavy brown hair, tanned skin, and dark brown eyes that made him look like he'd stepped off a movie set somewhere. He wore a pair of faded blue jeans, the kind that have been worn comfortably thin, and an olive green T-shirt that fit snugly across his broad shoulders.

I hoped he had already graduated from high school, because the fewer people from Rock Canyon High who knew about my trip here, the better. Then again, he was here too, so he couldn't look down on me for being hauled into the police station.

"Are you okay?" he asked, his voice a soft lull in the large room.

I nodded, then laughed at my automatic reaction. I clearly wasn't okay. I took another tissue from the box and wiped tears from my cheeks, trying to pull myself together. I must have looked like a mess. "So what brings you here?" I asked.

He grinned like it didn't matter. "Same thing as usual. Being in the wrong place at the wrong time. You drive your truck through a park, do a few spinouts, and these guys get all bent out of shape." He stretched out his legs. "What about you?"

I let out a grunt. "I should use my one phone call to contact *The Guinness Book of World Records*. Because I've just had the worst date in history."

"A date, huh?" The guy looked around the lobby. "So where did he end up? Do they have him in the back?"

Now that the police were gone, I suddenly wanted to talk about what had happened. I wanted some sympathy before my father came down to the station and ripped into me. "No, he left with his friends when they saw the police coming. At least, that's what I assume. I was around the back of a building making a phone call."

"Oh." The guy nodded philosophically. "Girls using cell phones while on dates. I see your boyfriend's point."

I smiled despite myself. "That's not how it was."

"Just joking." He held up a hand like he was taking a pledge. "Personally, I would never leave my girlfriend talking on a cell phone while the police closed in."

Hmm. I guess that made him a loyal criminal. I shouldn't have found that attractive in a guy but I did.

He surveyed me, his dark eyes resting on mine. "So what was so important that you had to make a phone call while your boyfriend was out committing a crime?"

"I was asking advice on how to make my boyfriend stop committing the crime."

"Ahh." The guy drew out the sound. "That's irony. Or bad timing."

"That's my usual luck."

He raised an eyebrow at my statement. "Do you come here often?" Then he smiled. He had gorgeous straight teeth. "That sounded like a pickup line, didn't it? Hey, if your boyfriend is the jealous, violent type, forget I said that."

"I've never been here before." I glanced around the lobby at the gray plastic chairs. "And somehow I don't think it will make my list of favorite date destinations."

The guy lowered his voice. "So how did a date with your boyfriend turn into a crime? Did he say, 'Hey, do you want to catch a movie, and then we'll hold up a convenience store?'"

"He didn't tell me where we were going," I said. "And I thought he was doing it for me—taking on city hall, or at least breaking their windows." That didn't make sense, so I added, "Bo wanted to get revenge for me."

I hadn't realized I said Bo's name out loud until the guy said, "Bo Grimes?"

"You know Bo?" I asked.

"Oh yeah, Bo and I go way back."

It figured I would run into one of Bo's friends in the police station. I wondered why I hadn't seen this guy at Indestruction's practice. On second thought, I didn't really wonder that. He probably had some musical taste.

"Let me guess who his friends were." He ticked the names off his fingers as he spoke. "Gibbs Johnson, Mike Hunsaker, and Steve and Brandon Hart."

"Yes," I said, with as much surprise as if he'd done a magic trick. "You know them too?"

The guy leaned back in his seat, trying to hide his smile. "Of course."

Of course. The detective had told me everyone knew each other in small towns. Apparently it was true. He had also said that people talked. And judging by the fact that the police knew who I was, people hadn't been saying good things about me. This night would just give everyone more to talk about.

I wadded the tissue in my hand. "This is a stupid hick town. I can't wait to move back to New York."

"Right," the guy said with a slow drawl. " 'Cause the police don't hassle teenagers in New York."

The guy had a point, but I didn't concede it. I glanced at the front door. Dad and Sandra would be here soon and I still wasn't sure what to tell the detective. It was a desperate thing to do, asking advice from a stranger in the waiting room of the police station, but he was the only one around. Besides, looking into his deep brown eyes, I felt he would understand my predicament.

He knew I was in trouble, but he was also cut from the same cloth as Bo—he was someone who bucked the system. I whispered, "The detective said if I don't tell them who was with me, they'll pin everything on me—including a bunch of other vandalism jobs. Can they do that?"

The guy shrugged. "They'll try all sorts of things to mess with you. Sometimes it's best to give them what they want."

"But I can't turn in my boyfriend and his friends. How low class is that?"

"Not quite as low class as leaving your girlfriend to be arrested for your crime." He sent me an incredulous look. "Do you still want Bo as your boyfriend?"

The reminder stung. "Maybe not. But that doesn't mean I want him dragged in here by these minions in blue shirts and charged with a bunch of stuff he didn't do." I glared down the hallway where I'd last seen Officer Frisky McFriskerson. "The police are a bunch of power-hungry jerks."

"Jerks," the guy repeated mockingly. He probably would have chosen a stronger word.

I looked down at my wrists, still seeing the handcuffs that had been there earlier. "I've only gone to school here for a month; if I turn in my friends, I'll never get any new ones."

"Maybe you should just try hanging out with guys who aren't criminals," he said.

This is when I realized that even though the guy had said he knew Bo and his friends, he'd never said he liked them.

My gaze went to his eyes, trying to read his expression. He wasn't looking at me, though. He waved at someone across the lobby. I turned to see who it was, but the only one in the room was the lady behind the desk. She motioned to someone behind her.

I didn't understand what it meant. I turned back to him with a question on my lips. It never got past my lips because the detective opened the lobby door and walked over. I expected him to come talk to me. I braced myself for it, but he barely looked at me. He went over to the guy. "Well?"

I waited for the guy to scowl at the detective. Instead his voice came out casually. "It's who we thought and she named them all." He reached into his pocket and pulled out a small, thin box. A recorder.

My mouth dropped open. I felt like I had been punched. "You work for the police?"

His gaze flickered back to me. "When I have to." He turned to the detective. "She didn't know they were going to do it beforehand, and she didn't get away because she was behind the building calling someone to ask how she should stop Bo. The guys saw the police coming and took off without her."

The detective let out a short dismissive laugh. "What a great catch Bo is." He took the recorder from the guy and slipped it into his breast pocket. "We'll send some officers out to see if we can track down our missing artists. Thanks for your work." He turned to me almost as an afterthought. "Be glad you decided to cooperate with us, Tansy. It would have gone much worse for you otherwise. Your parents will pick you up soon."

I couldn't process much of what the detective said. He walked back across the lobby, and I stared at the guy who I had thought was my age, but was obviously some sort of undercover police officer. I had trusted him and he betrayed me. Why hadn't I seen that coming?

I wanted to call him a string of names. Instead I slowly said, "You lied to me."

"And you were an accessory to a crime. Which of us has had a worse night?" He stood up and wiped his hands on the front of his jeans as though to say he was finished with this job. I turned sharply away, erasing him from my line of vision. I didn't want to look at him.

"You made the right choice to tell us, even if you don't know it yet," he said.

I clenched my teeth. "Drop dead."

"And they couldn't pin the other crimes on you," he said as if I hadn't spoken. "They couldn't even pin this one on you. You don't have any traces of spray paint on your hands or clothes. Anyone could tell you weren't involved in the graffiti."

Which made this that much worse. They had known I hadn't done it and had bullied me anyway. "You are such a jerk," I said.

He laughed, and I hated the sound of it. "You know, Tansy, you've got the good guys and the bad guys confused. Your life will get better once you figure them out."

He turned, walked across the lobby, and disappeared through the same door the detective had gone through.

I hated him. And I hated that as he walked away, I noticed how nicely his jeans fit across his muscular thighs. You shouldn't notice that about a person you hate.

Chapter 3

My dad didn't say anything as we climbed into our car. He had been tight-lipped and angry the entire time he was at the police station. He pulled out of the parking lot going about twice the speed limit, which was sort of careless considering where we were.

His silence didn't last long. "Do you have any idea how much trouble you caused tonight?" He didn't wait for me to answer. "The only person in Rock Canyon who is worse to have on your bad side than Mayor Rossman is Police Chief Gardner. If there was ever a chance of saving the library, it's gone now. All because you had to spray paint commentary about the library on city hall."

My father should have known I didn't do that. I know how to spell "library."

"The police chief has been in a bad mood for a long time and is just looking for people to take it out on. You put us front and center in his sights."

I wanted to say I was sorry, but I've always been lousy at

apologies. Somehow I couldn't say the words while he was yelling. Eventually he would ask why I had gone along with Bo, and then I would explain that I hadn't known, and had called Nick to ask for advice.

Dad gripped the steering wheel with increasingly white knuckles. "This is the end of it, Tansy. No more rebellious friends, no more attitude. If Bo says hi to you in the hallway at school, you are to walk by him without so much as a nod. Do you understand?" He still didn't wait for me to answer. "You're grounded until further notice, and from here on out, any friends who can't produce proof that they're on the honor roll will not have access to your phone number."

I didn't point out that none of his punishments mattered because I wouldn't have friends now anyway.

He went on berating me about everything I had done ever since I moved in with them. He had a whole list. I wondered why he didn't come out and say he didn't want me. It was more than obvious. By the time we reached our house, tears pinched the back of my eyes.

When the car stopped, I opened my door and choked out, "What gives you the right to tell me how to live my life?"

"I'm your father," he shouted, emphasizing every word. "And that boy deserted you at a crime scene!"

"Yeah, and you deserted me a long time before that!" I slammed the car door, ran into the house, and didn't stop running until I reached my room.

For a while I lay on my bed, hugging my pillow to my stomach and crying. The real problem behind all of this, I decided, was that I kept looking for someone to love me. My father. Bo. All those guys I dated in Queens—I had gone out with some gems there. The guy who hit on my best friend. The guy who wanted me to do his math homework. The guy who was always too busy playing computer games to talk on the phone. Actually, that described a lot of them.

When was I going to learn that trying to pry affection

out of people just made me vulnerable? I always ended up getting hurt. Love was a liability. I wouldn't look for it anymore. I would give up on love and become one of those high-powered career women who crushed people beneath her stiletto heels.

My mom called. She yelled at me about being involved with vandals and then for telling my father he deserted me. I took it stoically. It was par for the night.

A half hour later my cell phone beeped. I opened a text from Bo. His message consisted of four-letter words—except for the part where he said he never wanted to see me again. I supposed that meant the police had found him.

I put my face back down in my pillow and tried to fall asleep, tried to stop the emotions that squeezed me. I made myself think of the positives: having no friends would make it easy to move to my grandma's in December.

Well, not really. Grandma didn't want footprints, let alone boarders, in her house. After she found out about tonight, she was going to harp on my criminal past for as long as I lived with her. She would probably count her possessions every night to make sure I didn't pocket something.

There were no positives to this.

I heard a noise, like something tiny clearing its throat. I looked up. The room had a dim glow that hadn't been there before, and when I glanced at the end of my bed I saw what looked like a six-inch leprechaun doll standing there.

A voice with a thick brogue accent said, "I must be at the right place. There's the damsel crying her eyes out, but no bloomin' fairy. I should have known that dosser would be late."

My first thought was that Nick had come into my room and was hiding at the end of my bed with a puppet in an attempt to cheer me up. He used to do that sort of thing with Kendall when she came for visits. Her Beanie Baby cat would have conversations with her about his plans to conquer the world. I wasn't twelve though, and I wasn't in the mood for these sorts of games. Even if I was glad that Nick cared.

"Just what I need right now," I said dryly, "a leprechaun."

"I'm short on gold," he said, "so it won't do you any good to ask for it."

"Of course you are. You wouldn't be my leprechaun if you weren't broke." I picked up my pillow and chucked it toward the end of the bed.

The leprechaun ducked as the pillow flew over his head, which was pretty amazing considering I didn't see Nick's hand holding the doll anywhere. Were there strings somewhere?

The leprechaun stood back up and pointed a finger at me—a perfectly formed, movable finger. "Attacking a magical creature is grounds for a curse, you know."

"What . . ." I leaned closer. The doll's eyes and mouth were actually moving. It was impossible, but I was watching it happen.

"Just because your life is right pathetic doesn't mean you're excused from good behavior." The leprechaun reached up and straightened the tiny green bowler hat perched on his head. "I've turned people into pebbles for less."

I blinked at him. He was still there. I blinked again. "I'm asleep."

The leprechaun surveyed me with furrowed brows. "I don't mean to contradict you, but you seem fairly awake—moving around and talking and all." He kept watching me. "The constant blinking is a little odd though."

"No, I'm pretty sure I'm asleep." I dug my fingernails into the back of my hand to prove my point. In dreams you didn't feel pain. But I felt it now. Insistent sharp jabs.

The leprechaun frowned. "Are you away in the head, lass?"

I let out a shrill gasp and sat back so hard I banged my back into my headboard. "You're a leprechaun!"

He folded his arms. "Yeah, real observant, you are."

"Leprechauns are real?"

"That logic would follow, wouldn't it?" He huffed and cocked his head at me. "You're not the brightest star in the constellation, are you, lass?"

I shrunk back on the bed, glancing around to see if there were more of them in the room. My dresser and bookshelf were clear. Nothing sat on the carpet but my shoes. "What are you doing in my bedroom?"

"Wasting my time, apparently. Aye, fairy godmothers are an unreliable bunch. And yours is worse than most." He sat down on my bedspread with a thump and kicked his legs out in front of him. His green suit was embroidered with leaves, but a couple of buttons were missing and the sleeves looked worn. Scuff marks lightened the front of his boots, and one heel was chipped.

A down-and-out leprechaun was sitting on my bed.

"You wouldn't have something to eat around here, would you?" he asked. "A Ding Dong, perhaps? I'm partial to those."

Then the other thing he said clicked in my mind. "I have a fairy godmother?" I could barely wrap my mind around the idea. I would have asked more questions, but a fountain of sparklers erupted in the middle of the room.

My fairy godmother was coming. With my luck, she had probably come to yell at me like my parents had.

The sparklers winked out with a puff, and a teenage girl with long pink hair, sunglasses, and translucent wings appeared in my room. She wore a violet miniskirt and thigh-high black boots. She held a silver wand, and a lavender sequined purse hung from her shoulder. I could already tell she was stunning even before she slipped her sunglasses onto her head. Somehow I hadn't expected my fairy godmother to be so young. Or to be wearing frosty purple eye shadow.

Instead of yelling at me for my police encounter, she smiled, and when she spoke, her voice had the same tinkling sound as wind chimes. "Greetings, Tansy. I'm Chrysanthemum Everstar, your fairy godmother."

"*Fair* godmother," the leprechaun called from the end of the bed.

Chrysanthemum's gaze shot over to the leprechaun, and her eyes widened in unhappy surprise. Her voice was no longer sweetness; it was as sharp as glass. "Clover, what are you doing here?"

The leprechaun crossed his arms. "I'm your assistant. I'm assisting."

Chrysanthemum thrust her wand downward in agitation. A stream of glittery lights shot across my floor and flashed up the length of my wall. For a moment the room lit up like a glowing candle.

Chrysanthemum walked toward Clover, her hand on her hip. "I told you I didn't want your help."

"Which means for once we agree. I would rather play nursemaid to a viper than help you, but unfortunately the Unified Magical Alliance scheduled me to be your assistant. Again." He shook his head in disgust. "They couldn't just punish me for abandoning my last assignment and be done with it. No, they had to resort to slow, aggravating torture."

Chrysanthemum turned back to me, her smile decidedly forced. "Ignore that bitter little man on the bed. He's of no consequence."

Except that he could turn me into a pebble if he was mad. My gaze ricocheted between them.

"As I was saying," Chrysanthemum continued, her voice like wind chimes again, "my name is Chrysanthemum Everstar, but you may call me Chrissy. My assistant, on the other hand, is only allowed to call me 'The Most High Boss' or 'Your Excellence of Fairyness.'"

"You don't have to worry about supplying names for me," Clover called to her. "I've plenty of me own for you."

Chrissy flicked her wand and sparks flew around the room, a couple of them nearly hitting the leprechaun, but she kept her gaze on me. "Since I'm your fairy godmother, I've come to grant you three wishes—"

"She's technically only a *fair* godmother," the leprechaun called, "because her grades in fairy school were only average." He folded his arms across the front of his worn green suit. "Go ahead, ask her if she can prolong time properly. She can't."

Chrissy turned and glared at him. "Which doesn't matter since very few mortals ever wish to prolong time." She flung her wand hand in my direction, and sparks zinged past me. "Do you really think Tansy wants this moment to go on forever? Look at her. Her eyes are bloodshot, her face is swollen—she basically looks like something a troll regurgitated. Who would want that every day for the rest of their lives?" Chrissy took a deep breath and her pale wings fluttered. She tapped the end of her wand into her palm and turned back to me. Her voice was softly lilting again. "Now, back to spreading happiness. You're allowed three wishes. Well, at least you will be once you sign the paperwork." She shot Clover a challenging look. "I assume that since you're my assistant, you have a copy of the contract?"

He stepped toward us, reaching into his suit pocket. "Of course I do." Not finding it in the first pocket, he checked another, then another, until he pulled out a tiny roll of parchment. He stepped to the end of the bed and handed it to me. "There you are. All in perfect order. Just sign at the bottom."

I took the scroll from his hand. It was no bigger than a stick of gum. "I'm supposed to sign this?"

Clover nodded and lowered his voice. "A word of warning, make sure you read the fine print."

I unrolled a bit of the scroll with one finger. "It's all fine print."

Chrissy took the contract and tapped it with her wand. "Which is why my assistant should have maximized it before he gave it to you." It grew until it was nearly the size of a roll of paper towels. Chrissy studied the top of the scroll for a moment, wiping her finger disapprovingly against a dark spot on the paper. "Clover, you spilled something on the contract."

"I've a weakness for chocolate. I can't help it."

"You've a weakness for too many things." Chrissy pulled a pen from her purse and handed it and the scroll to me. "You can read through this if you want, but quite frankly I have a job interview in ten minutes, so I'm in a bit of a rush."

"What?" Clover called from his side of the bed. "I thought you already had your dream job." He laughed while she narrowed her eyes. As though to let me in on the joke, Clover said, "She's a tooth fairy lackey. Works nights stealing teeth from wee little tykes."

"I'm not a lackey," she snapped, "I'm a team member. And I don't steal teeth, I grope around under pillows until I find the discarded ones." To me she said, "It's *so* revolting. I would quit in a second, but hey, it's expensive to accessorize when you have high fashion standards. I need some sort of part-time job." She pushed a strand of glossy pink hair behind her ear. "I'm hoping Muse Incorporated will hire me. I could totally flit around inspiring art and music. I mean . . ." She waved a hand over herself. "I'm completely inspiring."

Clover let out a snort. "Oh, right. That's what's causing me head to ache right now. It's all the inspiration."

I fingered the scroll, feeling awkward for interrupting them, but I had to ask the question that had been on my mind since Chrissy popped into my bedroom. "Why do I get a fairy godmother? I've never had anything good happen to me in my life."

Chrissy and Clover stopped arguing. Clover pursed his lips, then muttered, "Well, you certainly didn't earn one because of your overwhelming gratitude for all the good things that have happened in your life."

Chrissy stepped toward me. "I'm glad you brought that up.

It's true most maidens earn their fairy godmothers by doing good deeds or by helping poor beggars who turn out to be fairies in disguise. But to tell you the truth, I've never been big on dressing up in rags and waiting around in the snow to see if someone offers me their coat. If I'm out in the snow, it's because I'm skiing with some buff elf guys. However . . ." She reached into her purse and pulled out a disk that was a little larger than a CD. "I needed an extra-credit project, and your life qualified according to the pathetic-o-meter."

She handed me the disk, which had a picture of me in the center of a pie-shaped graph. A large portion of it was colored blue, a small portion was yellow, and little lines dotted the circumference like minutes on a clock. At the edge between the blue and yellow, it read: *Dated a hoodlum. 78 percent pathetic.* Beneath this line, in smaller print, was the sentence: *Willingly listened to dreadful band music.* And underneath this, in even smaller print: *Refuses to read novels, simply to aggravate her father.*

I couldn't read the other sentences. They were too small. "That's really . . . nice," I said, staring at the disk. "You've got a pie chart of all the ways I'm pathetic."

"You can keep it," Chrissy said. "That way you can track your progress."

"Great," I responded, without enthusiasm. How can you be enthusiastic when you find out your fairy godmother thinks you're 78 percent pathetic?

"Since you didn't technically earn your fairy wishes in the traditional way," Chrissy went on, "you should know about the dishonesty clause." She took the scroll and unrolled it to a place in the middle. The ends of the scroll lay across my carpet like lolling tongues. "Here, read this."

I squinted at the elaborate lettering. *Until the terms of thy wishes are met, if thou shalt tell an untruth, in consequence of such an act, a reptile or amphibian shalt grow upon thy tongue until such instance when thou spittith it out. Or if thou art an animal rights activist and considereth such an act to be inhumane to reptiles or amphibians, thou mayest choose instead to have flashing lights above thy head declaring thou art a blasted liar.*

"Oh," I said.

"The animal rights option is new this year," Chrissy said. "The UMA is very progressive." She waved her hand, showing a set of lavender fingernails. "Personally I've always thought telling the truth is overrated. Lies make the world a happier place, but rules are rules. So until I'm done being your fairy godmother, you need to choose. Which will it be—frogs or lights?"

"Lights," I said. I couldn't bear the thought of spitting out a frog.

She checked a box by the clause, and I skimmed through the next few paragraphs. Between the long sentences and old-fashioned phrasing, I couldn't make sense of them. "What does the rest of this say?"

"Telling lies is really the only thing you need to watch out for," Chrissy said. "The rest basically states that all wishes you make are permanent and binding, their consequences lasting. Also you may suffer certain side effects, such as drowsiness, headaches, lethargy, or an intense desire to eat bugs if, during your magical journey, you're turned into a frog." She didn't even pause for a breath before she went on. "You can't wish for more wishes or for vague generalities like happiness that are impossible to grant. Your wish has to be something specific enough that I can use my wand to make it happen. Oh, and recently there's been a ban on inserting yourself into the *Twilight* series. The Cullens are tired of different teenage girls pinging into their story every time they turn around."

Chrissy opened her lavender sequined purse and pulled out a quill. "It's your standard fairy godmother contract. You make a wish, and I watch over you. Sign where it reads, 'Damsel in distress.'"

I hesitated. It seemed risky to sign a magical contract I hadn't read.

Chrissy glanced at a diamond-studded watch on her wrist. "Now I have four minutes until my job interview."

I found the signature line and signed my name. Chrissy was my fairy godmother. She wouldn't ask me to sign something that could hurt me.

Chrissy took hold of the end of the scroll, yanked it downward, and the whole thing rolled up like a window shade. It must have shrunk back down to its original size, because as she put one end into her purse, it disappeared. "All right then, on to the first wish. What will make you happy?"

The way she phrased the question made me stop and think. I had been about to wish for a huge bank account—enough money to not only keep the library open but to name it in my honor. Would that make me happy though? It wouldn't change being an outcast at school on Monday morning. It wouldn't change my father's disappointment in me. I'm not sure what money would change, except instead of moving in with Grandma, I could stay here and live with people who thought of me as a snitch or a criminal.

For a moment I considered wishing for Kendall's play to close so she, Mom, and I could go back to living in New York. But I couldn't bring myself to take away my sister's dream.

I sat down on my bed. "I'm not sure . . ."

Chrissy glanced at her watch again. "Wealth is always a popular wish."

I picked at my pillowcase dejectedly. "Money won't buy me friends."

"If you wish for enough, it will," Chrissy said brightly. "People like to say they can't be bought, but they really can."

It sounded sort of horrifying when she put it like that. I didn't want friends who were only interested in me because I was rich.

I shook my head.

"Revenge, then? You can wish to change city hall and the police station into toadstools."

I laughed at the image that presented. I could see Officer Frisk-meister, a half-eaten doughnut in one hand, staring with a baffled expression at what used to be the police station. Better yet, I could see Mr. Handsome Undercover Cop trying to figure out who'd stolen the building.

Unfortunately, if I zapped away the police station and city hall, it would mean the mayor would have to take money from somewhere else to rebuild the buildings. Maybe they would close more programs.

"I could change a few police officers into ravens," Chrissy chimed. "Then they could be jailbirds."

Clover looked at the ceiling. "As if the world doesn't have enough birds with enormous egos."

Chrissy waved a dismissive hand at him, but I didn't want to hurt anybody. And with that realization, thoughts of revenge fizzled in my mind. So how did I fix things? "The problem is we have a mayor who doesn't care what we want. How do we fight the system?" As I looked around my room, my eyes rested on my bookshelf. I had a copy of *The Adventures of Robin Hood* sitting there, nestled among a few other novels Dad had put in my room. He had given me that one because it had been a favorite of mine when I was little. I had always loved the way Robin Hood stood up to the Sheriff of Nottingham to help the oppressed people.

I was only thinking out loud, trying to figure out a solution to my unhappiness. I spoke so quietly that Chrissy shouldn't have been able to hear it. "I wish Robin Hood were around today. He would know what to do."

"Good choice," Chrissy said. "He's totally hot." She swept her wand in my direction and a flurry of sparkles surrounded me, hundreds of tiny lights zinging everywhere.

"Wait!" I sputtered.

"Oh, don't worry," she called, her voice sounding far away. "I wouldn't let you meet him looking like that. I'll throw in a free makeover."

When the light cleared, she and Clover were gone. And there in my bedroom stood a dozen scraggly-looking men.

Chapter 4

For a moment, I just stared at the men. They wore tunics and leggings, with bows and arrows slung over their shoulders. A couple were older, with gray in their hair and beards, but most were young with muscled arms and tanned faces. I guess I had never considered what a bunch of men who lived in the forest and never showered would smell like, but in the confines of my bedroom, the smell of sweat, dirt, and unwashed clothes hit me with nose-curling strength. I tried to breathe through my mouth.

The men looked around my room, drawing swords and knives, then turned to me with fierce expressions.

"Chrissy!" I hissed, both panicked and elated—panicked because a dozen scary men were brandishing weapons, and elated because—talk about superstar sightings—Robin Hood and his Merry Men were in my bedroom.

Chrissy didn't come back.

"What devilry is this?" one of the men demanded.

"This has the look of magic to it," another said.

Actually my room had the look of the JCPenney teen department. Sandra decorated it before I moved in. "I'm sorry. I didn't mean to bring you here," I said, gulping. "There's been a mistake."

A young man with shoulder-length blond hair, a pointed green cap, and a dark green tunic stepped toward me, sizing me up. His features were sharp and flawlessly handsome. His eyes were startlingly blue in his tanned face. Chrissy hadn't been exaggerating when she said Robin Hood was hot.

His gaze ran over me, and he raised an eyebrow. I glanced at my reflection in my closet mirror to see what he was looking at. I wore a velvet green dress that swept around my ankles. My hair was pulled up into a bun with loose ringlets. No sign of tears or mascara streaks remained on my face. In fact, I wore bright red lipstick and smoky green eye shadow. This apparently was Chrissy's idea of a makeover. I looked like I was about to go to the prom.

"Who are you?" Robin Hood asked, his voice cautious. "Why have you brought us hither?"

"I didn't mean to." I lifted my hands up to show them I didn't have a weapon. "It was an accident. I'm trying to get her to come back and fix it." I glanced around the corners of my ceiling, hoping Chrissy might be floating around up there. "Chrissy, this isn't what I meant!"

Robin Hood sheathed his sword and folded his arms, but the other men kept their swords and knives drawn, which made them seem more menacing than merry. A burly man with a thick brown beard stepped forward. He stood at least six and a half feet tall, towering over everyone else. Little John, I guessed. "Who be this Chrissy you call for?"

I took a step back from him. He didn't seem to have any concept of personal space. Or hygiene. "Chrysanthemum Everstar. She's my fairy godmother."

This caused a round of grumbling from the Merry Men. "I knew it was magic," one of them growled, and then spat on my carpet.

"Hey," I said. "You're inside my bedroom. Don't do that."

Robin Hood fixed me with a look. "And why, pray tell, did your fairy godmother bring us to your bedchamber?"

"Well, you see, I had a run-in with the police tonight." When I didn't see any recognition on Robin Hood's face, I added, "The police work for the sheriff."

"The sheriff!" another man snarled, and spat on my floor.

I could see it sitting there all gooey and gross. I turned to Robin Hood. "Would you please make your men stop spitting on my carpet?"

"What dost thou mean by a run-in?" Robin Hood asked.

I ignored the spit soaking into my carpet. I would clean it up later. "Basically, it's where they hauled me into their head-quarters and threatened me." And then, because I really wanted someone to understand what I'd been through, I told them about the whole ordeal with Bo and the officer who tricked me.

Robin Hood and his men listened intently, and when I'd finished, Robin Hood nodded. "I see."

"Then while I was talking to my fairy godmother about it, I sort of wished that Robin Hood was around."

"To give the sheriff bigger game to pursue?"

"No," I said, blinking. "I wouldn't have wished you into the twenty-first century for that."

Little John's jaw dropped open. "*The twenty-first century?*"

I shrugged apologetically. "It's where I live."

The men turned their attention from me to my bedroom, examining it more closely. One used his sword to push the com-forter off my bed, checking to see if it was hiding anything. Several others picked knickknacks off my dresser. They flipped through books, poked at my iPod, opened my drawers. Friar Tuck lifted a necklace out of my jewelry box.

"If you don't mind," I said, shutting my underwear drawer and standing in front of it, "this is my personal stuff. I don't want anyone touching it."

Little John pushed back my curtains and eyed the houses on the street with interest. "Robin, cast your eyes at those buildings. And behold the torches that light the road. They stand as tall as trees!"

Robin Hood strode over to the window while I tried to keep the Merry Men from tossing things they found uninteresting onto the floor. I was able to rescue my cell phone. My box full of nail polish wasn't as lucky.

A man the others referred to as Will—I assumed Will Scarlet—took a book from my shelf, opened it, then held it upside down and shook it. His dark hair hung in greasy strands around his shoulders and his beard ended in a sharp point. "What odd, useless things you have in the future."

I snatched the novel from his hand before he could drop it. "It's a book, and that's not how you treat it."

This is what happens when you're raised by a librarian. Even though I had refused to read books for years, I still couldn't stand to see one ruined. I reshelved it with a forceful thud. "Chrissy," I hissed toward the ceiling. "We really need to talk." My giddy-fan feelings for Robin Hood were fading fast. These men didn't belong here, and they had to go back before my dad or Sandra discovered them here.

A car passed by our house, and Robin Hood and Little John simultaneously gasped.

Little John leaned into the window until his nose touched the glass. "What strange manner of beast was that? Lights streamed from its face."

"A car," I said. "They're one of the twenty-first century's very useful things. They're faster than horses and easier to take care of."

Robin Hood put one hand on the glass and peered farther down the street. "Are they friendly?"

"They're not alive. They're machines, like . . ." but I couldn't think what machines they had back in the Middle Ages. "They're tools. When you turn the key, they start up so you can drive them down the street."

Friar Tuck had finished going through my jewelry box and stuffed several rings and necklaces into the pockets of his robe. None of them were expensive, but still. "Hey, stop that," I said walking over to him. "You can't take those."

He smiled a nearly toothless grin. "I'm simply admiring them."

"Well, admire them in my jewelry box, not in your pockets."

Another of the Merry Men had thrown open my closet and pulled out shirts. "Behold the finery," he called to the others. "Her wardrobe puts the king's to shame." And then he looked at me accusingly, as though I had been hoarding shirts.

"Everyone has a lot of clothes now," I said, and went to take the hangers from his hand. "I'm not one of the rich, if that's what you're thinking. Far from it."

Robin Hood still scanned the street. "Wench," he called to me, "how can I procure one of these cars?"

Wench? "My name is Tansy," I said. "And will you please tell your men to stop pawing through my stuff?"

Robin Hood glanced lazily around the room. He let out a bird whistle and the men grudgingly turned their attention to him. I winced. If Dad and Sandra heard weird noises coming from my room, they would come in. How was I going to explain the presence of a dozen smelly men dressed in ratty clothes and wielding swords?

"Unhand the wench's things," Robin Hood said. "I want to go forth and discover what the world has become. Who is with me?"

The men let out a shout of agreement, still clutching shirts, knickknacks, and scented candles.

"Shhh," I called to them. "My dad and stepmother are down the hallway."

"How many men at arms be at your castle?" Little John asked.

I vaguely remembered from my reading days that men at arms were soldiers.

"This is a small house," I told him. "Only my family lives here."

Will Scarlet took hold of my doorknob and opened the door a few inches. I nearly threw myself against it. "You can't go out there. Someone will see you."

Robin Hood gestured out the window to the neighbors' homes. "And the other buildings nearby, are they small houses as well?"

"Yes," I said. "Mostly."

Robin Hood and Little John exchanged a look and grinned. Robin Hood, unlike so many of his men, had straight, beautiful teeth. Still, his smile made me uneasy.

I stepped away from the door and held my hands out to Robin Hood, pleading. "Look, you need to stay put until I can get hold of my fairy godmother. She had a job interview to go to, which is probably why she's not answering me, but that can't take long. Then we'll get this straightened out and she'll send you back to your home. In the meantime, you need to be quiet."

I had barely finished speaking when I heard Nick at the door. He knocked then said, "Dad says to turn off your iPod and go to sleep."

I didn't have my iPod on. "Okay," I called back.

I hoped he would go away, but he opened the door instead. "What are you listening to anyway? It sounds like—"

He stared at the occupants of the room with wide-eyed surprise and then took in my long dress and hair. His voice dropped to an indignant grumble. "You're having a costume party in your bedroom? Aren't you in enough trouble already?"

"It's not what it looks like," I said.

He rolled his eyes in disgust. "Whatever. It's your life. Who am I to stop you from wrecking it?"

He shut the door harder than he needed to.

I turned back to Robin Hood. "That was my stepbrother, Nick."

"He bore no weapons," Robin Hood said.

"People around here don't carry weapons. It's illegal, and it's not polite either. Which reminds me, could you ask the Merry Men to sheath their swords?"

"The who?" Robin Hood asked.

"Your Merry Men," I repeated. "That's what history calls them."

Robin Hood chuckled at his men. "Did you hear that? History knows us, and thinks we are merry."

"We've been called a far sight worse," Friar Tuck said. He was standing by my jewelry box again.

Another man snorted. "I'd be merrier if I had a spot to eat."

"I can get you food," I said, then wondered what to serve them. In the movies, the Merry Men always ate fire-roasted rabbits and stuff like that. I would find something. "It will take me a few minutes," I told Robin Hood. "Can you control your men until I get back?"

"Of course," he said, like it was a ridiculous question.

As I put my hand on the doorknob, Robin Hood took hold of my elbow. "One question before you go. What does history say of me?"

With his blue eyes staring down at me, and his hand touching my elbow, I felt like a giddy fan again. "You're a hero. You robbed from the rich to give to the poor."

"Ahh." He nodded, processing this. "History has been kind."

"I've got a book about you. You can have it if you want." I went to my shelf and took down *The Adventures of Robin Hood.* "My father read this to me when I was a little girl." I put the novel in his hands and felt myself blush. "I've admired you for a long time."

One of the men laughed and in a low voice said, "As have many women."

I hadn't meant it like that, but there was no explaining that now. Besides, Robin Hood had smiled when I said I admired him. He flipped open the book, first looking at the pictures, then the text.

"I'll be back soon," I said, then slipped out the door.

Down the hallway, Dad and Sandra's door was shut. The TV blared from their room. They had probably turned it up in an effort to drown out my "iPod." Good. I hoped that meant they would stay put. I took hold of my skirt and lifted it so I could hurry down the hallway without tripping over it. If my parents saw me, they would wonder why I was wearing a long dress and my hair was in a bun.

But I didn't have a choice about my wardrobe right now. It was better to keep the men busy with food until Chrissy came back.

I was microwaving chicken nuggets when I heard the crash. It was a familiar enough noise since I had already heard it twice that night—the sound of a window shattering. I left the kitchen and ran back to my room. When I opened the door, Little John pointed a sword at me and yelled, "Halt!"

I did, not because of the sword, but because of what the Merry Men were doing. They had not only broken my window; they'd laid my comforter across the remaining shards in the window frame and were proceeding to climb outside.

"What are you doing?" I walked over to them, hands in the air. "Do you know how expensive windows are? You could have just opened it."

Robin Hood sent me a half smile and bowed slightly. "Though we appreciate your hospitality, we must be on our way."

Friar Tuck heaved himself out of the window. I was so agitated I made little steps toward it, then toward Robin Hood, then back to the window. "You can't leave. You have nowhere to go."

Robin Hood remained unworried. "We shall live off the land. It is our way."

"You're in the middle of a neighborhood," I protested.

"There's no land to live off of." I motioned for the men outside to come in. Not only did they ignore me, but more climbed out. "You won't find any deer," I told them. "We don't have wild animals roaming around unless you count stray cats." The men kept going out the window without regarding me. As I watched them leave, frustration rose in my throat. "Robin," I said, "don't go."

He smiled and tucked one of my ringlets behind my ear. His voice took on a silky tone. "I regret I cannot stay and fulfill your wishes in that regard."

His men chuckled, and a few made comments about my wishes.

I flushed in embarrassment.

" 'Tis true your beau, Bo, has failed you," Robin Hood said, stroking my cheek, "but I'm unready to stand up with any woman, even one as beautiful as yourself."

"That wasn't why I . . . I'm not . . . ," I sputtered. "Don't you want to go back to Sherwood Forest?"

Robin Hood's hand slid from my cheek to my shoulder. "You brought us to a new land—a fortuitous event, indeed. The sheriff's men have death warrants on our heads, and they recently took to setting dogs on our trail. So, no, returning to Sherwood is not a pressing matter." He took one of my hands in his, then lifted it to his lips and gave it a brief kiss. "And now I must bid you farewell." After dropping my hand, he gestured to Little John. The big man left his place guarding my bedroom door and climbed out the window with more agility than I expected.

I blinked at Robin Hood, unbelieving. "But what about the poor villagers who depend on you?"

He laughed, which surprised me, then held up *The Adventures of Robin Hood* for me to see. "You are as amusing as your history." With the book still in his hand, he swung himself out the window and onto the rocks that bordered our lawn. The first few Merry Men were already running down the street.

I watched them disappear and sighed. I supposed they would come back when they realized what the world had become. They weren't going to be able to forage for food. Once you left town, the only things around were cacti and a bunch of scrub brushes that were waiting to dry up and turn into tumbleweeds. I hoped the Merry Men's survival skills would help them remember which house I lived in. That way, when they had second thoughts about living off the land, they would be able to find their way back.

I took some clothes into the bathroom and changed. Then I picked up the things the Merry Men had thrown around. Thankfully, most of the broken glass was on the outside of the window, so I didn't have to clean up much of that.

I couldn't even mutter angrily about them trashing my stuff. Not after I had just been to the police station for trashing city hall. Mr. Handsome Undercover Policeman would probably find it fitting that I was finishing up the night on my hands, wiping up spit from my carpet.

When I finished, I sat on my bed calling Chrissy. No one showed up except for a few bugs that flew through the broken window. I shut my eyes to rest them, and the next thing I knew, it was Saturday morning.

• • •

Sandra opened my door and called out, "Rise and shine. Time to do your chores." My dad usually woke me up on Saturday mornings, so the fact that Sandra had done it meant he was still mad at me. I was probably in for something horrendous like scraping pigeon poop off the roof.

I pulled the sheet over my head.

Sandra walked over and sat on my bed. "Come on, look on the bright side: today has to be better than yesterday."

Sandra was one of those optimistic people who not only saw the glass as half full, but figured it was half full of her favorite drink.

I tossed the sheet off and sat up—not from optimism, but because I suddenly remembered the rest of last night. My fairy godmother. Robin Hood. I didn't want Sandra to see my astonishment, so I tried to keep my expression calm.

She wasn't looking at me though. Her gaze zeroed in on the gaping hole in my window and she let out a shrill gasp of alarm. "What happened?"

I didn't think she'd believe me if I told her a bunch of Merry Men broke it. In fact, I wasn't sure I believed it myself. Could that stuff have really happened? Fairies and leprechauns didn't pop into people's bedrooms. Robin Hood and the Merry Men weren't real.

But nothing was left of my window except for jagged shards. That part was real enough.

I chose my words carefully. My lies might have magical consequences. "I was in the kitchen, and I heard a crash. When I got back to my room, the window was broken."

"Why didn't you tell us?"

"It was late."

She walked to the window, shaking her head. "You didn't see who did it?"

"No." Which was true. I didn't know which of the Merry Men had shattered it.

"It must have been Bo." Sandra's jaw clamped tight. "Well, he can pay for this window along with the ones he broke at city hall. I'll call his parents and tell them so."

"Don't," I said. "I'll pay for it." I hardly had any money to my name. I would have to find a job. I supposed that didn't matter, since I wasn't going to have a social life now.

She put her hands on her hips, watching my curtain flutter in and out of the frame. "I'll ask your father to put a board across it for now. I doubt anybody will be able to come out to fix it until Monday anyway."

Sandra left, muttering about Bo, and I stood in my room staring at the window. "Chrissy?" I called.

No one came. Had she been a dream—the product of an overstressed, overemotional brain? I walked to the closet tentatively. Last night I had hung up the long green dress. If it was still there, it would be proof I hadn't imagined everything.

I opened the closet, but the hanger I'd put the dress on was bare. I flipped through every shirt, dress, and skirt hanging there. No green dress. I threw up my hands. "It's official. I've lost my mind."

That's how the day started. It didn't get any better.

My chore list included hauling everything out of the garage, sweeping it out, and hauling everything back. Then I had to clean the bathrooms, mop the floor, and do laundry. Every once in a while, I whispered, "Chrissy?"

No twinkling lights erupted anywhere. I wasn't sure whether to be relieved or disappointed. The more the day wore on, the easier it was to convince myself none of the magical things had happened. I had dreamed it all.

Dad and Nick spent the day doing landscaping and painting the trim on the house, fixing it up for when we had to put it on the market. Nick had the radio on and sang along, but Dad worked with a stern expression, his eyes hard as stone.

Fine, I told myself. Let him think about what a disappointment I've turned out to be. He had chalked up a lot of points in the disappointment category himself.

It wasn't until eight o' clock that night when I was putting away my clean clothes that I saw the pathetic-o-meter sitting on my dresser.

I had completely forgotten about it, and I dropped the clothes on the floor and stared at the disk. The blue area had grown, and a new sentence read: *Thinks criminals are cool. 82 percent pathetic.*

I did not think criminals were cool, but that was beside the point. I hadn't dreamed the pathetic-o-meter into existence. It was real. And a fairy had given it to me.

Granted, the dress had disappeared, but then, Cinderella's dress had disappeared at midnight. So maybe fairy fashions just did that.

Still only half believing in my sanity, I picked up the pathetic-o-meter, walked to Nick's bedroom, and knocked. He opened the door. He wore a T-shirt that had pi written on it down to a thousand digits, but thanks to today's chores, a lot of them were now paint splotches.

I held the disk out to him. "You can see this, right?"

He squinted at my hand. "You think criminals are cool? Well, then it's not surprising that you're eighty-two percent pathetic."

"Did you see me wearing a long green dress last night? And there were a bunch of medieval men in my room?"

"Yeah, where did you find those guys anyway? They made Bo look downright normal."

I stepped into Nick's room, shut the door, and leaned against it. I wasn't sure whether to be happy or horrified about what had happened. "I *really* have a fairy godmother."

Nick gazed at me, unimpressed with this pronouncement. "If you're not careful you'll *really* have a parole officer too." He waved a hand in my direction. "Are you purposely seeking out every criminal you can find? Was there some sort of membership drive at the police station?"

Robin Hood and the Merry Men were real. And that meant they were out wandering around Rock Canyon somewhere. "This is going to be a problem." I put my hand against my chest, trying to stop my panic from spreading. "I accidentally wished Robin Hood and his Merry Men here. I need to find them."

"Yeah," he said, "you and every police officer in town."

Chapter 5

You and every police officer in town?

That was not a good sentence to hear Nick say. I clutched the pathetic-o-meter so hard its edges cut into my palm. "Why would the police be looking for them?"

Nick crossed his arms, which were paint splattered too. "Haven't you listened to the news today?"

I had only listened to my iPod. I shook my head. "What happened?"

Nick walked over to his computer. "I'm sure it's on the Internet by now." He clicked a few links and then a newscaster popped up on the screen. She had a cheerful expression even though she spent most of her time doling out information about disasters.

"The usually uneventful town of Rock Canyon is experiencing a bizarre crime wave today. A gang wearing medieval garb carjacked a pickup truck, then robbed a Pizza Hut and two gas stations at sword-point." The screen switched to a grainy surveillance tape that showed Robin Hood flanked by most of his men. He walked up to the checkout counter and drew his sword while his men went along the aisles emptying things into their sacks. They grabbed whatever was on the shelves— candy bars, chips, and lots of AA batteries. I had no idea what they were going to do with those. It was really too bad they didn't hit a deodorant or soap aisle.

The surveillance tape ended and the screen went to a reporter, who stood next to the store clerk. He was a scruffy, overweight college-aged guy with spiky hair and a goatee.

"Can you describe the attack?" the reporter asked.

The clerk leaned close to the microphone. "It was freaky. Sort of like a bunch of Renaissance festival actors turned bad. First the head dude asked for our gold and silver. When I told him we didn't stock that, he said to hand over my jewelry." The clerk shrugged. "I don't wear any jewelry except my nose ring, and I never thought anybody would want to steal that, but I gave it to him. Then the dude asked for money. I opened the cash register drawer and tried to give them the twenties, but they threw those aside and demanded the coins." The clerk scratched behind his ear. "They made off with about four dollars in change."

That didn't make sense until I remembered that paper money didn't exist in the Middle Ages.

On the screen, the newscaster smiled sympathetically. "Unfortunately the robbers caused more than four dollars' worth of damage to the store, didn't they?"

The clerk nodded. "Yeah—while they were swiping things off the shelves, one of them tried to yank the hot dog warmer off the counter. When that didn't work, he hit the glass with the back of his sword and busted in the side." The clerk shrugged again. "Not what I would call smart thieves."

"They're certainly a danger to our community though," the reporter said brightly. "Anyone with information about these crimes is urged to call the anonymous tip hotline."

I sat down with a thunk on Nick's bed. A tight ball of dread bounced around inside me. "This is awful."

"I didn't call the hotline," Nick said, turning so he faced me. "At least not yet. It might push your dad over the edge if he knew you were friends with those guys too."

I stared at the computer. It didn't make sense. "They were only supposed to rob from the rich."

Nick's eyes narrowed on me. "I get the whole teenage rebellion stuff to a point. You're mad that your dad left your family. I felt the same way when my parents split." He held up one hand to emphasize his point. "But instead of dealing with it, you want to drive everyone crazy."

I pressed my arms over my stomach as if this could keep it from hurting. "The books, the movies—they all said Robin Hood was a good guy."

Nick looked up at the ceiling, contemplating. "What happened the first time you came out for a visit? Oh yeah, that's when you pretended to be anorexic and wouldn't eat anything."

The accusation momentarily snapped my mind off of Robin Hood. "I wasn't pretending to be anorexic. Your mom was going through a tofu and bean recipe craze."

"And the second time you came, you had that tattoo of snakes coiling down your arm."

"It was just henna," I said. "It washed off."

Nick leaned against his dresser. "Yeah, but you didn't tell your dad that. You stepped off the plane and said, 'How do you like my new tattoo? My boyfriend and I got matching ones.'"

"If my dad had called and talked to me at all beforehand, he would have known I was joking. I didn't have a boyfriend at the time."

Nick drummed his fingers against the top of his dresser. "And since it wasn't enough to have a fake idiot boyfriend, the first thing you did when you moved here was date Bo, the genuine article."

That was the thing about Nick. He thought my dad was great, so he was bound to take his side on everything.

"You're a smart girl." Nick waved his hand at me like it was an accusation. "You get As in math and physics, but what is your grade in English?"

I didn't answer. He knew as well as I did that I had pulled nothing but Ds in English since my dad left us. It went along with my refusing to read books. I wasn't about to excel in anything Dad loved.

"And now you claim to have conjured up Robin Hood from the past," Nick went on. "I admit I don't quite see the angle on this one. How is this supposed to make your dad nuts?"

Robin Hood. The reference brought my mind back to the problem at hand. I stood up. "I've got to get ahold of my fairy godmother." She would be able to put a stop to this medieval crime spree. "Chrissy!" I looked for an eruption of sparkles, but nothing happened. "Chrysanthemum Everstar!" I called.

Still nothing.

"Clover?" I asked, remembering the leprechaun's name. No one appeared in the room.

Nick pressed his lips together, still questioning me. "Great fairy godmother you've got."

Clover had said she was only fair. I was beginning to see his point.

"Well," I said, "this means I've got to find Robin Hood myself. He thinks we have poor villagers who need his help. He's probably out somewhere wondering why no one is thrilled to be the recipient of nickels, pennies, and a used nose ring."

Nick went through the stack of clean laundry on his dresser, putting some socks into a drawer. "Your dad isn't going to let you go anywhere for a long time."

"Then I'll have to sneak out. This is important."

Nick let out an overlong "Ohhh . . ." as he turned back to me. "Now I get the whole Robin Hood angle. You have to sneak out to stop the Merry Men." He picked up his jeans and put them into one of the drawers. "You're creative, I'll give you that. And you have a really impressive knack for getting guys to take revenge for you. First Bo vandalized city hall, and now the Robin Hood dude is messing with the police. But as your little Frisbee there says, you think criminals are cool." Nick shoved his T-shirts into another drawer. "I bet the city council totally wishes they hadn't ticked you off now."

I didn't appreciate his sarcasm, but what could I say? He didn't believe me about the magical stuff, and the only proof I had was a pathetic-o-meter. "You won't tell on me when I sneak out, will you?" I asked.

He grunted. "I'm not going to mess with you. You might set your battalion of evil boyfriends on me."

"Thanks," I said, and walked out of his room.

It wasn't hard to sneak out. I went to my room and turned on my music loud enough so it seemed like I was in there, but not loud enough that my dad or Sandra would knock on the door and demand I turn it down. I didn't know what to take with me, so I slung a small purse over my shoulder and put my cell phone, wallet, and the pathetic-o-meter inside. Since it was magic, I vaguely hoped it would be able to do something to help me, like contact my fairy godmother if my pathetic reading went high enough. At any rate, I didn't want my dad to find it in my room. He would not be cheered by its pronouncement that I think criminals are cool.

Dad had bought a sheet of plywood and leaned it against my window. It moved easily enough, and I slipped outside into the warm September night. I went around to the side door of the garage. I couldn't take one of the cars. I had grown up in New York with its subway systems, so I didn't know how to drive very well. This left a bike as my only means of transportation.

Bike riding isn't the fastest way to track people, and it was probably a hopeless venture from the start, but I had to at least try to find Robin Hood and his men. I had brought them here, and if I didn't explain things to them, they would keep robbing people, and someone would get hurt.

I set out through the neighborhood, peering at people's lawns as I rode by. Would Robin Hood try to find a place like Sherwood Forest? We didn't have any forests around, but a lot of trees grew in yards. Maybe the men had climbed some and were hiding there. I looked up at every tree I passed but I didn't see them. Maybe they had found a deserted building. I headed toward the center of town, riding through street after street, searching for any sort of clue.

Everything seemed normal.

Navigating around downtown was hard. Cars zipped past me impatiently, driving by so closely that I kept jerking away from them. After a while, I headed into another neighborhood. There was nothing unusual there either, except for me, riding aimlessly around in the dark. I was getting tired. I stopped my bike to rest and took the pathetic-o-meter out of my purse. "Look," I told it, "I need to find Robin Hood before he runs somebody through with a sword or the police shoot him. Can you help me?"

As I watched, the lettering changed on the dial. I held my breath, thrilled for the magical help, until I read the new sentence: *Talks to inanimate objects.*

I was now 83 percent pathetic.

"Great," I said. "Just great." I shoved the pathetic-o-meter back into my purse. "See if I ever speak to you again."

I didn't check to see if yelling at inanimate objects had made the pathetic-o-meter go up. I might as well head home. I didn't have the stamina to keep pedaling for much longer.

I rode back to town sullenly, mumbling Chrissy's name every once in a while. I wasn't sure how her job interview as a muse had gone, but she certainly wasn't inspiring anything but stomach ulcers for me.

As I passed a Walgreens I saw them. I was so used to looking up in the trees that I scanned the roof without thinking about it. One of the Merry Men lay up there, bow drawn back, ready to shoot anyone who threatened him. My gaze dropped to the parking lot. There, crouched among the parked cars and moving in, was Robin Hood and the rest of his men. He should have looked ridiculous—a guy in a tunic squatting behind a parked car—but somehow with his muscular frame and handsome features, the tunic thing worked.

I rode my bike slowly up to them. "Robin!" I whispered.

He turned and saw me. "Not now, wench, we're about to liberate some wealth from the gentry."

I climbed off of my bike and wheeled it over to him. "My name is Tansy, and you can't hold up this store."

He raised an unimpressed eyebrow in my direction. "I read your Robin Hood book, but I refuse to believe it."

"Yeah, well, I'm having my doubts about it too."

"It says I die because a nun poisons me. A nun."

I had forgotten about that, but he glared at me as though I had written it into the book myself. "So avoid nuns from now on. They're easy enough to spot—long black dresses and wimples. Very few of them sneak up on people."

He went back to staking out the parking lot. "Women," he said with disgust. I wasn't sure whether he was referring to me or nuns.

I lowered my voice. "We need to talk. You see, you don't need to rob anyone here. We have agencies that take care of the poor, and if you keep holding places up, someone will get hurt."

He didn't look at me. He waved at some of the men, and they ran forward, still crouching and darting between cars. "Never worry, no harm shall come to me. I am more than a match for the menfolk here. My arms will remain unbound and will hold you in their embrace soon enough, just as you wished."

Several of the men chuckled knowingly at that.

My cheeks burned from embarrassment, but I kept my voice even. "I'm not worried about *you*—I don't want you to injure anybody *else*. You're attacking people who don't carry weapons."

"Such foolishness is astounding," he said. "But a fool and his money are soon parted. Our swords only speed the process."

The first two of Robin Hood's men had reached the Walgreens' front entrance. They pressed themselves against either side of the door, looking inside.

"Robin, this isn't stealing from the rich and giving to the poor; this is just stealing."

Robin Hood glanced at the building behind us, a Laundromat. On the top of it, a Merry Man lay on his stomach, a bow in his hands. "Ah, but you're wrong. Everyone here is rich, and my men and I are poor. It's fitting we should relieve your village folk of some of their goods." He motioned to the men nearest him, and then he and the men left their hiding places and sprinted toward the store doors.

They timed their surge wrong, piling up at the entrance, and had to wait for the automatic door to open all the way before they rushed inside.

I leaned my bike against a car and strode after them. When I walked into the store, Robin Hood already had his sword drawn and held it only inches away from a startled store clerk. He was a thin teenage boy who'd gone completely pale. The Merry Men walked along the aisles, dumping things into their sacks. A small group of shoppers were lined up, hands in the air, by the photo counter.

Maybe some stories have more sway than fact. Maybe they carve themselves into our minds and slant the way we see things. Because even then, I saw Robin Hood as a hero, as someone who cared about right and wrong. I marched over and tried one more time to make him understand. "You've got to stop. This is wrong."

Robin Hood didn't take his eyes off the clerk. The muscles in his arm flexed. "Hold your tongue, wench. I asked not for your blessing." He moved his sword tip close to the clerk. "Your jewelry, my good man, hand it over forthwith."

The teenage boy held his hands up higher. "I don't have any jewelry," he croaked.

I took a step closer to Robin Hood, frustration banging around inside of me. "You were supposed to be the good guy, the defender of the common people. But you're not—you're terrorizing innocent shoppers."

"Your beauty notwithstanding," Robin Hood said, glancing at me for a moment before he turned his attention back to the clerk, "you had best hold your tongue before I'm tempted to hold it on the blade of my sword."

I let out an incredulous gasp. "You're threatening me?"

Friar Tuck snorted as he dumped a box of Snickers into his bag. "The lady is quick-witted as well as beautiful."

I opened my mouth to say more, but someone took hold of my arm and yanked me sideways. I turned, expecting to see one of the Merry Men. Instead Mr. Handsome Undercover Policeman had a hold on me. In his jeans and T-shirt, he had blended in with the rest of the shoppers who stood over at the photo counter, and I hadn't seen him before. The police guy towed me over to the counter, keeping his gaze not on me but on Little John, who stood nearby. He held a sword loosely in our direction while he walked along an aisle, shoving Doritos into his bag.

I hated that I noticed, at a moment like this, that the hot police guy was every bit as tall and good-looking as I'd remembered. He was probably six foot two. His wavy brown hair looked mussed, and his deep brown eyes were intent, serious.

"What are you doing here?" I asked.

"I'm being held up like everyone else, and I suggest you leave the crazy men alone."

That's when the reality of the situation hit me. I was as powerless to stop Robin Hood as everyone else who was being held at sword-point. "This can't be happening," I said numbly.

The police guy's gaze slid over me. "You're brave; I'll give you that. But right now it's better to stay still. I know these guys' MO. They'll take a few things and go. There's nothing here worth risking your life for."

Of course he knew their MO—modus operandi, or method of operation—the police had studied the surveillance tapes. They'd been searching for these men. I noticed an open cell phone lying on the disposable cameras behind us. I whispered, "You called the police, didn't you?"

"Everything will be okay," he said.

Two older ladies dressed in polyester outfits stood by my side. One of them whimpered, and the other pressed her lips together in an angry grimace. Next to them, a teenage girl shivered. She was blinking back tears.

Everything would not be okay. I was already processing the outcome. Robin Hood and his men had never seen firearms. They wouldn't care when the police pointed guns in their direction. Robin Hood wouldn't listen when the police told them to drop their swords. And the police wouldn't expect archers on the tops of buildings. Even if the police somehow did capture the entire group of Merry Men without bloodshed, what could Robin Hood tell them that would make sense? And what would happen when the Merry Men told detectives that I had brought them to Rock Canyon?

The police were probably not going to be particularly understanding about that part.

Robin Hood and Friar Tuck strolled up. Robin Hood smirked at us. "Now, if you good folk would be so gracious as to take off your jewelry and any coin you have on you. Put them in the good friar's sack and we'll be much obliged."

Friar Tuck held out a rough-hewn sack to the girl. From the look of it, they had brought the sacks with them from the Middle Ages. It figured. They must travel with them. After all, you never know when you're going to meet someone you want to rob.

The teenage girl pulled off two earrings shaped like ice cream cones. She dropped these and a pinkie ring into the sack, then pressed herself as far away from the men as she could get. Friar Tuck turned to the older ladies. The first trembled as she put her wallet into the sack. The second sneered. "You remind me of my ex-husband, except he didn't smell quite as bad."

"I'm flattered, I'm sure," Friar Tuck said, then pointed to their rings. "We require those lovelies as well."

As the first woman tugged off her rings, I turned to Robin Hood, pleading, "You shouldn't take their wedding rings. They have sentimental value."

He laid his hand against his chest. "And I assure you they will have sentimental value to me as well."

I glared at him, but didn't argue anymore.

Next to me, the hot guy took off his watch and a class ring. I barely noticed it was Rock Canyon High's color—bright blue—before he dropped it in the sack.

I pulled off the one piece of jewelry I wore, an opal ring my mother had given me when I turned sixteen. It also had sentimental value, but it was pointless to bring that up.

This was such my luck. I was being robbed by the guy I had wished here.

Robin Hood held out his hand for my ring. I dropped it in his palm, but instead of putting it into the bag, he took hold of my hand and slipped it back onto my finger. "Your ring is not what I will steal from you." Still holding onto my hand, he slowly pulled me into an embrace. I looked up to ask what he was doing, and as our eyes met, he bent down and kissed me.

As soon as his lips touched mine, I put my hands on his chest to push him away. It was like pushing a wall. He was much stronger than me, and after a few moments, I quit struggling and let him kiss me. I figured once he made his point, he would stop.

He didn't.

History had never mentioned that Robin Hood was an exceptional kisser, but it should have. It was clearly one of his more impressive talents. I might have enjoyed the kiss if he weren't an outlaw and if I hadn't been in the middle of a hold-up in Walgreens. Even as it was, when he lifted his head from mine, I felt breathless.

Will Scarlet walked up to us. "Robin," he said with exasperation.

Robin Hood didn't let me go. He stared into my eyes, his smirk back again. His fingers made a slow trail down my back. "I suppose yours was not such a bad wish after all." He bent his head to kiss me again, but the break was enough to restore my sanity. This had to end.

"The police—the sheriff's men—they're on their way," I said.

Robin Hood stiffened, then dropped his hands away from me. "Are they?" He didn't ask how I knew, just stepped away and whistled to his men. "We best be off. The law is on our trail."

Most of the men flung their sacks over their shoulders and fled out of the door. With his sword still drawn, Will backed away from us. When he was far enough away, he turned and ran to the door as well. Robin Hood was the last one out. Before he left, he winked at me and said, "Until we meet again, fair Tansy." Then he was gone.

The woman beside me put a hand over her chest and let

out a stream of words that was too jumbled to understand. The other woman leaned against the counter, taking deep breaths. The teenage girl pulled her cell phone from her pocket with shuddering hands and dialed someone. The hot police guy turned to me, unshaken. He put his hands on his hips and narrowed his eyes. "You warned that thug the police were coming."

I flushed. I couldn't explain. "It was the best line I could think of to discourage him from a make-out session."

"Well, judging from your last boyfriend, I can see why that line would pop into your mind first. But to tell you the truth, you didn't look like you minded the make-out session all that much."

"I didn't have a choice about kissing him," I said. "He had a sword."

"He knew your name," the guy said. "Why is that?"

I refused to let him ruffle me. "It's a small town. Apparently everybody knows my name. Even random police detectives."

I turned toward the door. He reached out and grabbed my arm. His grip was firm, but not tight. "You need to stay to make a statement for the police. And we all need to file reports about what the robbers stole from us."

"I don't," I said. "He only stole a kiss from me, and I don't want it returned."

The guy's dark brown eyes turned piercing. "Tansy, you need to stay and talk to the police."

I pulled my arm away from him. "I think we've already established that I don't like talking to the police."

"It will look worse if you leave," he said.

"No, it will look worse if my father has to come down to the police station two nights in a row to pick me up."

I walked out the door without looking back at him.

• • •

I don't know why I thought Mr. Hot Police Officer would keep my name out of it. When I got home, a police car was parked in front of my house. I should have stayed at the Walgreens and saved myself the bike trip back. My thighs burned from all of the pedaling. I groaned and leaned my bike up against the side of the house. An officer sat in the car. He reported something into his car radio, then climbed out and followed me up the walkway.

When I got inside, my parents and another officer were standing in the living room talking. My father's face was taut with anger, his hands clenched into fists. He spoke to me, shooting each word out sharp and whole. "You were grounded. You were supposed to stay in your room."

I couldn't very well tell him I had been out trying to stop Robin Hood from plundering the city. I also couldn't tell him, with the police officers staring at me, that my fairy godmother had zapped them here on my command. "Sorry," I said.

He waited for me to say more. I didn't. It was pathetically lacking as an apology, but I didn't know how to spruce it up without ending up in a padded cell.

The younger of the two police officers stepped forward. His red hair had been cropped short in what was nearly a crew cut. He held up a clipboard to take notes and regarded me suspiciously. "You were at the Walgreens that was held up?"

I nodded.

"Do you have any idea where the criminals are now?"

"No."

"Have you ever seen them before?"

I nearly told them no, then remembered Chrissy's warning that I couldn't lie or lights would go off around me announcing the fact. It would be hard to explain that sort of thing right now. "I saw them on the news earlier today," I said. It was, after all, the truth.

"Why did the men know your name?"

"I ran into them in the parking lot before they went inside, and I told them my name." Also the truth.

The police officer raised an unbelieving eyebrow at me. "You saw a bunch of men you knew were dangerous criminals, and you went up to them in a parking lot and told them your name?"

"I was trying to convince them not to rob the Walgreens," I said.

"Uh-huh." The police officer pursed his lips, and I could tell this wasn't going well. "We'll need you to come down to the station so we can get a formal statement."

Chrissy was right. Telling the truth was way overrated.

I shook my head. "I'm not going with you."

Sandra said, "Tansy, I think—"

I wouldn't let her finish. I'd had enough of the police. "I'm not saying anything else. It isn't illegal to talk to people in a parking lot, so they can't arrest me for that. I didn't do anything wrong tonight."

The older officer crossed his arms. "Maybe you folks need to have a talk with your daughter about cooperation and then get back to us." He sent me a slow, intimidating stare. "Armed robbery is a felony. This isn't a game, young lady."

The officers turned and went to the door. Sandra followed them, apologizing for my behavior, telling them I normally wasn't like this. "Our family is going through a hard time right now," she said.

My father didn't move. He shook his head as though answering some question only he heard. "You didn't do anything wrong tonight?"

"I'm sorry," I said again.

"You were grounded and you went out consorting with criminals."

I didn't answer. I wasn't sure what consorting meant. Maybe it was time I started reading again. My vocabulary needed some refreshing.

"I don't even know who you are," my dad went on. He said the words quietly, but so forcefully it felt like he'd yelled them. "Just go to your room."

I turned and walked down the hallway. He was right. He didn't know who I was.

Chapter 6

On Sunday, a repairman came and put in a new window in my bedroom. Then another guy came over and set up an alarm system in the house. The weekend rate had probably cost my dad extra. He didn't tell me the alarm code, and I didn't ask. I knew he had ordered the alarm so I wouldn't be able to leave the house at night without setting it off.

Dad hardly spoke to me all day, and Sandra sent me disappointed looks that didn't change no matter how many times I said I was sorry. And I said it a lot. Apparently repeating the word multiple times didn't make me any better at apologies.

Nick, fortunately, was nice. When he saw me checking the Internet for news of more hold-ups, he told me he had a friend who had access to police scanners. Nick called his friend, then gave me the update: that afternoon the medieval bandits had robbed the Village Inn and made off with several boxes of sausages, all the pies in the dessert case, and an assortment of silverware. Robin Hood probably didn't realize it wasn't made from real silver.

I was glad no one was hurt, but it was just a matter of time. I had to get things straightened out with Chrissy.

• • •

Monday morning, instead of riding on the back of Bo's motorcycle to school, I sat in the passenger seat of Nick's beat-up old Camry. As we went through the school lobby, I was glad for his company. He was proof I had one friend. Even if Nick had been forced into the position when our parents married.

Everyone stared at me. They probably knew about my weekend. I tried not to meet their eyes. I especially didn't want to see Bo or any of his friends. I was mad that Bo wasn't sorry for what he'd done and mad that he hadn't given me a chance to explain, but mostly I was mad that after all my debating as to whether I should break up with him, he had dumped me first.

Eventually Nick and I split up to go to our lockers. As I walked down the hallway, I picked up bits and pieces of the conversations around me. Someone said the word "criminal." Were they talking about Robin Hood, Bo, or me? Or perhaps the homework load our teachers gave us?

It was going to be such a long day and such a long week.

I rounded the corner and saw Bo leaning against my locker. He was scowling, which probably meant he wasn't there to apologize. I let out a sigh. I wasn't in the mood for this.

I walked up and slid my backpack off my shoulder. "Hi, Bo."

He stepped close to me, leaning down so his face was inches away from mine. His eyes flared with indignation. "Why did you turn us in to the police?"

I spun the first number on my locker combination. "Oh, I don't know. It had something to do with the fact that you left me at a crime scene, and then the police handcuffed me, dragged me down to jail, and threatened to pin the whole thing on me." I could have told him the police tricked me into telling his name, but suddenly I didn't want to. His anger made me wish I had turned him in on purpose.

"You're such a—" He finished the sentence, but the word was muted when he punched my locker. "We did it for you, and this is what we get? I have a two-thousand-dollar fine and a court date."

I turned to face him. "You did it for me? Really? Because I remember asking you to stop. And what about the other buildings you vandalized? Those weren't for me. You just like to destroy things."

"Maybe I do." He punched my locker again, this time so hard I jumped. Then he put one hand on either side of me, trapping me against the lockers.

My pulse hammered. *He's not going to hurt me*, I told myself. *Bo isn't like that.* But as I stood there with the locker handle pressing into my back, I wasn't so sure what he was like anymore.

Bo's lips twisted into a snarl, and he opened his mouth to speak. Before he did, someone grabbed hold of his shoulder and pulled him backward, hard.

My first thought was that it was Nick—who else would stand up for me? A wave of dread ran through me. Bo would turn around and flatten him. Then Bo's friends would make Nick's life miserable.

When my eyes connected with my rescuer though, it wasn't Nick. The hot undercover police guy had pulled Bo away from me. He stood by my locker along with several beefy members of the football team.

"Is there a problem here?" Hot Police Guy asked. His jaw was set. His brown eyes flashed fiercely.

Bo stepped away. "Get off of me, freak!" His gaze went back and forth between the guy and me. "Is that what you did at the police station, Tansy? You got friendly with the police chief's son? What sort of interrogation was it?"

The police chief's son? I stared at the hot guy. I didn't know whether to be happy he'd shown up here or horrified that I would be running into him at school.

One of the football players stepped toward Bo, clenching his fingers into a fist. "Shove off, Bo."

Bo flinched away from me, rolling his shoulders as though to shrug off the entire situation. "You aren't worth my time," he said, then turned and sauntered back down the hallway, disappearing into the river of students.

I leaned against my locker and took a couple of shaky breaths.

The football players talked with the hot guy for a few moments. They did that boy thing where they bumped their knuckles together, and then the football players left.

The police chief's son stayed, surveying me. His brown eyes were softer now that Bo was gone, his stance more relaxed. "Are you okay?"

"Yeah. Thanks."

"I figured Bo might be a pain today." He looked down the hallway checking to make sure Bo didn't come back. "Hopefully that'll take care of it."

Some of my gratitude for my rescue vanished. Police Chief Junior had known Bo was going to react this way, but he'd still tricked me. He didn't care what it was going to do to my life or that I was going to be some sort of pariah at school now.

"So you're the police chief's son?"

His gaze returned to me. "My name is Hudson Gardner."

"You go to school here?" I asked.

"I'm a senior."

A senior—like me. I didn't have any classes with him, but we were bound to know some of the same people. Rock Canyon High wasn't that big. "So it wasn't even your job to wring a confession from me on Friday night; you did that for fun?"

He gave me an exasperated look. "When you wouldn't tell the police your name, my dad called me to ID you. I know everybody at school."

"You don't know me." I hadn't seen him before. I would have

remembered him. Guys that good-looking stick in your mind. "How did you know who I was?"

"Nick and I are friends. He's pointed you out."

I should have put my backpack away. I needed to get ready for first period, but I didn't move. "You're Nick's friend and you tricked me? Do you have any idea how traumatic that whole stint at the police station was?"

Hudson rolled his eyes. "Yeah, I could tell how traumatized you were by the way you used the two-way mirror to do your hair."

I blushed. He'd seen me do that. Stupid two-way mirrors. "I meant making me betray my boyfriend."

"Oh, your boyfriend." Hudson's gaze went to my locker. It had dents where Bo had hit it. "I hope the school doesn't make you pay for that."

I let out a sigh and finished my locker combination. With my luck not only would I have to pay for it, but the door would be stuck shut and I would be late for first period.

Hudson leaned against the locker next to mine. "Speaking of boyfriends, how come you won't tell the police anything about that Robin guy who held up Walgreens?"

My locker didn't stick, just creaked in protest as I opened it. "He's not my boyfriend, and thanks for telling the police I was there when it happened. You can imagine how happy my parents were when a squad car came to my house. I'm now officially grounded until I graduate."

Hudson was unperturbed. "If I hadn't told them, they would have still seen you on the surveillance tape . . ."

I drew in a sharp breath. I hadn't thought about the surveillance cameras. Not only would that footage be studied by the police, it might be played on the news. Then the world would see me kissing Robin Hood in the middle of an armed robbery.

". . . and your voice is on the 911 recording."

"The 911 recording?" I repeated.

"I called the police. Those calls are always recorded."

Even better. They had soundtrack of the whole thing too. I leaned my head against my locker. Did surveillance tapes ever end up on YouTube?

"You obviously knew those guys. Who are they? Friends from New York out here to visit you in the hick town?"

I ignored him, pulled my books out of my backpack, and put them on my locker shelf.

"Why the swords?" he asked. "What are they trying to prove?"

I hung my backpack on its hook, then took my history book from the shelf. I went to shut my locker door, but Hudson put his hand on it to force me to look at him. "If you cared about those guys, you would help us stop them before a few get shot. That's how a lot of armed robberies end up: with the bad guys leaking blood onto the pavement."

"You wouldn't believe me if I told you what I knew." I pulled my locker door away from him and shut it. "And I was trying to reason with them, trying to get them to stop robbing places. But I can't do that anymore, thanks to you. My father is keeping me under lock and key from now on."

Hudson ignored my complaints. "What wouldn't I believe?"

"I just need a little time to take care of them," I said. Surely, Chrissy would check in on me today. I still had two wishes left. She had to come back sometime to grant them. "Could you talk to your father and make sure the police don't shoot anybody before I can get rid of them?"

"What wouldn't I believe?" Hudson asked again.

I hesitated, then told him. "It's Robin Hood and the Merry Men."

"Robin Hood?" Hudson ran a hand across my locker door, tapping it in annoyance. "Sure he is. But what did I expect from you? You girls all think the guy is dreamy."

"I wouldn't exactly describe him as dreamy." I tucked my book under my arm. "Buff, yes. Handsome, I suppose. Daring . . ."

I thought of the way he'd kissed me. It made me smile. "Okay, he's dreamy."

Hudson shook his head in disbelief. "Your taste in men is pathetic."

Only if you believed what the pathetic-o-meter said.

Without saying good-bye, Hudson turned and went down the hallway, weaving between the rest of the students with a purposeful stride. I watched him go and my spirits sank. They shouldn't have. I shouldn't have cared what he thought—he was the guy who tricked me at the police station.

Hudson was right, really. My taste in men was pathetic.

As I made my way to class, I thought of Hudson's phrase. *You girls all think the guy is dreamy.* What did he mean by that? I wondered about it until I sat down in first period and three girls descended on my desk like birds landing for bread crumbs.

A wide-eyed blonde pulled up the chair next to me. "Is it true you were with Jessica Wilson and Hudson Gardner at the Walgreens when it was robbed?"

I nodded. Jessica must have been the teenage girl who was with us.

The second girl sat on the corner of my desk. "Did the robber really say the only thing he wanted to steal from you was a kiss, and then"—she waved her fingers dramatically—"and then he kissed you?"

I nodded again.

This made the girls squeal. "I Googled his composite sketch," the third said. "He's a total babe."

"Were you afraid?" the first asked.

"Do you think he'll try to see you again?" the second put in.

"Is Bo upset about it?"

That question I could answer. "Bo and I broke up Friday night."

Now all three girls oohed like they had learned a great secret.

"Good timing," the first one said.

The second girl put her elbow on my desk and rested her chin in her hand. She smiled wistfully. "You must attract the dangerous type."

"I'm going to hang out in convenience stores until I run into him." The third let out a sigh.

The other girls trilled in agreement, then speculated where the bandits might strike next.

My mind drifted back to Hudson. I couldn't help being curious about him, and this was as good a time as any to get information about him. I kept my voice casual. "Hudson was really cool under pressure. Is he always like that?"

The third girl grunted. "No, he's just too sullen to get worked up about death."

Sullen? That description didn't fit. The second girl leaned toward me. "Don't mind Sarah; she had a thing for Hudson once."

"Every girl in school has had a thing for Hudson at *least* once," the third girl—Sarah—said defensively. "But then his mom died a year ago and he went all antisocial."

"He's not antisocial," the first girl said. "He just took it hard. Can you blame him?"

I felt a pang of sympathy for him and wished I hadn't asked. It seemed wrong to hear these girls talk so lightly about his pain.

"We all wanted to help him," Sarah went on, "but he cut everybody out of his life." She twisted her pencil through the ends of her hair. "He used to start for the football team, and he didn't even go out for it this year. He didn't run for student body either, and he was class president freshman and sophomore years. He would have been a sure thing, but it's like he doesn't care about the people at school anymore."

The girls didn't say more because the bell rang and the teacher told them to go to their desks. But I kept thinking about what they said, and I saw Hudson in a new light.

All during the rest of school, girls came up and asked me about the medieval bandits. Everyone wanted to know the details of the robbery. It was strange to have this surge of popularity.

Before long, Bo heard about the kiss. He texted me his opinion about it, but I didn't care. At least he knew I wasn't at home pining for him on Saturday night.

· · ·

After school, I did homework in my room. I kept staring out my new pristine window. It was so clean it looked like nothing was there, like I could lean out into freedom. I couldn't, though. I pulled the curtains shut.

Before long, I heard voices in the kitchen—Nick's and someone else's. I wandered out of my room to get something to eat and to see who was over.

Hudson sat at the table with Nick, their math books spread out in front of them. The sight made me do a double take. Hudson looked so out of place there—Mr. Model Material next to the clutter, dirty dishes, and ordinariness of our kitchen. I stared in surprise and sputtered, "What are you doing here?"

He smiled lazily. "Nice to see you too, Tansy."

It wasn't an unjustified question. Granted, Hudson had told me he was friends with Nick, and suddenly I realized which of Nick's friends had access to a police scanner, but they weren't hang-out-at-each-other's-house friends. Nick's real friends belonged to the computer club. He wasn't on knuckle-bumping terms with the football players.

"We're doing homework," Nick said.

I walked to the fridge, took out an apple, and let my gaze return to Hudson. I knew things about him now—that his mother had died a year ago, that his grief had changed him. But here in my kitchen, I couldn't see anything about him that was vulnerable. He seemed more than confident—at least confident in my guilt. I raised an eyebrow at him. "You came here to spy on me."

Hudson wrote an equation on his paper. "If you're not hiding anything, you have nothing to worry about. I mean, it's not like that band of thugs has ever, say, shown up in your bedroom."

I sent Nick an evil glare.

He shrugged. "You're my sister. I worry about you, especially when the guys you hang out with threaten to cut out your tongue with their swords."

Which meant Hudson had told Nick everything that had happened during the robbery.

"I am not hanging out with them," I said. "I just . . ." But I couldn't explain that I felt responsible for them. That I *was* responsible for them. After all, I had told both Nick and Hudson that it was Robin Hood and the Merry Men and neither believed me. "I'll let you guys finish your homework."

I went back to my room, finished my math assignment, and wrote a long text message to my sister. Kendall thought she was doing drama? Ha.

After an hour and a half, I walked back to the kitchen to throw away my apple core. I hadn't expected Hudson to still be there, and I especially hadn't expected to see him sitting alone at the table doing his homework.

"Where's Nick?" I asked.

"He needed to run to the store to pick out some stuff for his science fair project."

That was odd. I tilted my head at him. "And he left you here by yourself?"

Hudson sent me a look like I should know better than to ask. "Your parents want Nick to make sure you don't go anywhere before they get home from work." He leaned back casually in his chair. "Although that didn't work on Saturday night, did it?"

"Unbelievable," I said. "You're here babysitting me?"

"Nah." He flashed a smile. "I'm here spying on you."

I threw my apple core away and opened the fridge for more food. I needed to eat now because when dinnertime came, I was telling my dad I wasn't hungry and spending the evening in my room. I pulled out last night's enchiladas and took a plate from the cupboard.

Hudson strolled over and leaned against the counter. "So why were those guys in your bedroom Friday night?"

I dished some enchiladas on my plate and didn't answer.

"You're the only lead in the case," he said. "If I tell my dad they were over here, the police will bring you in for questioning. Why don't you make it easier on everybody and tell me what you know."

I put the enchiladas in the microwave and punched in a minute. "Is there some reason you feel the need to be supercop and crack this case?"

"You mean besides the fact that I was robbed at sword-point?"

"You're not even on the police payroll, and I bet you're working harder than the rest of them."

He shook his head. "It's only a matter of time before one of those thugs kills someone. Trust me—everybody down at the station is working overtime."

I watched my plate slowly rotating in the microwave. "I'm doing what I can." I had already called for Chrissy several times today.

"Didn't you learn anything from dating Bo?" Hudson asked. "He pounded your locker today and he would have pounded you too if I hadn't showed up. And I don't care how handsome that Robin guy is. He hurts people. How can you protect him?" He held up a hand in frustration. "How can you be involved with someone like that?"

"I'm not involved with him." I meant I wasn't romantically involved. Which was the truth. One kiss while he was holding me up didn't make us a couple. But apparently the denial counted as a lie. Before I could say another sentence, I caught sight of tiny lights fountaining around my head like a garland of sparklers.

Hudson's mouth dropped open as he stared at me. "How did you do that?"

I put my hand to my head, then jerked it away with an "Ouch!" The sparklers were not only bright but also hot. This was bad. Nothing was burning my head yet, but that could happen next. Was I supposed to stop, drop, and roll, like I was on fire?

Then again, there is only one thing more freakish than having your head unexpectedly ignite with magic sparklers, and that is dropping to your kitchen floor and trying to roll them off your head. I couldn't do that in front of Hudson, and besides, smothering the flames probably wouldn't work to extinguish magic fire.

But how did I get rid of them? I hurried to the bathroom in a walk that was somewhere between a panicked scurry and a don't-fan-the-flames glide.

In the mirror, I saw a wreath of fireworks surrounding my head. Worse yet, a message lit up like wording on a scoreboard: *She's lying!* The disclaimer tromped brightly across my forehead. *She's a blasted liar! She's lying! She's lying!*

"Well, this is wonderful," I said.

Hudson came up behind me. I saw him in the mirror's reflection studying the lights. "Where did that come from?"

I tried to bat the thing off and only succeeded in burning my fingers. What had Chrissy said about the lights? Were they permanent? I couldn't go to school like this.

"You're a 'blasted liar'?" Hudson asked, reading the words.

My fingers stung from touching the sparkler hat, so I turned on the sink and ran them under the cold water. I should have used oven mitts.

Hudson was still staring at me.

"Okay," I said, "maybe I am involved with Robin, but not romantically."

As soon as I finished the sentence, the lights vanished. So the way to get rid of fireworks was to tell the truth. I let out a breath of relief and ran one hand through my hair, checking to see if the fireworks had scorched it. Thankfully, unlike my fingers, my hair was undamaged.

Hudson leaned up against the door frame, his eyebrows furrowed. "So . . . ," he said. "That was the weirdest thing I've ever seen."

The cold water wasn't helping enough. My fingers still throbbed. I walked past Hudson, went to the kitchen, and pulled ice cubes from the freezer. Hudson followed me. While I put the ice cubes in a plastic bag, he said, "I guess I can understand why you don't like talking to the police. The fireworks would be distracting during an interrogation, wouldn't they?"

I put my fingertips onto the bag of ice cubes. "If a fairy asks you to sign a magical contract, think twice about it. That's all I'm saying."

"A fairy," Hudson repeated. He didn't believe me. I could tell he was coming up with other excuses for what he'd seen on my head. He probably thought it was some gag Nick had worked up with his computer-geek friends.

"Look," I told him, "I'll take care of Robin Hood and the Merry Men. Really. Just tell your dad not to shoot any of them before I can work things out. Okay?"

The front door opened and Nick called, "I'm back." He walked into the kitchen holding a bunch of PVC pipes and a sack full of stuff. "I'm going to have one souped-up potato launcher for my project."

I didn't say anything about my fingers or about how Nick had left Hudson in the house to make sure I didn't sneak out.

Nick set his sack down on the table and turned to Hudson. "Hey, thanks for your help . . ." He glanced at me. ". . . With my homework. I think I can take it from here."

"Sure." Hudson glanced at me too and I knew he didn't want to leave yet, not when he hadn't gotten more information from me, but he picked up his books and slipped them into his backpack. "I'd better get home."

Nick walked him to the door and out of my sight. Still, Hudson called to me, "See you later, Tansy!"

Yeah, I bet he would. He'd be tailing me as much as possible from now on. "Good-bye!" I called back.

When Nick walked back into the kitchen, I fixed him with a glare. "You left Hudson here to guard me?"

Nick busied himself picking up his books from the table so he didn't have to look at me. "Mom and Dad asked me to keep an eye on you. I didn't want to break my promise to them." He grabbed his sack, and slipped the handles onto his wrist. "Now I'm going to my room to finish my homework. See? I'm not guarding you." He left before I could say anything else. A moment later, I heard his bedroom door close. I sank down on the kitchen chair and checked my fingers. Tiny white scorched spots had formed on their tips.

"I should have gone with the frogs," I said.

A lyrical voice behind me chimed, "As the saying goes, if you play with fire, you end up with blisters."

I turned around and saw Chrissy.

Chapter 7

This time Chrissy wore a lavender-colored spandex top with a flowing white tutu. Her pink hair was piled up on her head in a bun and held in place with diamond-studded pins. She looked like a ballerina who'd wandered away from *The Nutcracker.*

"Chrissy," I breathed out in relief. "Where have you been?"

She walked toward me and minty-smelling bits of glitter swirled around her. "I've been busy. I told you I was looking for a new job." She glanced at her watch. "I only have a few minutes before I start my tooth fairy shift, but I thought I would pop in and see if you were ready for your next wish."

I stood up, not sure where to start. Now that she was here, the words tumbled out of my mouth in a nearly incoherent jumble. "The police are out looking for Robin Hood. They think he's going to end up killing someone, and I'm afraid they're right. He won't listen to me, and I kept calling for you, but you never came—I thought you said you were going to watch over me."

"I don't need to watch over you the entire time." She pulled a crisp white scroll from a lacy purse and held it up for me to see. "Look, I have the Tansy Sparknotes." She unrolled the scroll far enough for me to read: Tansy Elisabeth Miller Harris: Context, Plot Overview, Analysis of Major Characters, Themes, Motifs, and Symbols.

I gaped at it. My life was not only in print, but in Sparknotes. "That is just wrong."

Chrissy scanned the scroll. "Saturday you cleaned, snuck out of your house, and—oh wow—total make-out session with Robin Hood in Walgreens." She put a hand to her chest. "That's so swoon-worthy."

"No, it wasn't. He was robbing the place at the time."

She let out a wistful sigh. "A highwayman-and-the-lady sort of romance. Those are some of my favorite stories." Smiling, she rerolled the scroll. "So it's going well then?"

I blinked at her in disbelief. "No, Robin Hood is out of control. He keeps holding up stores and stealing things."

Chrissy tilted her head questioningly, as though I weren't making sense. "What did you expect him to do when you wished for him to come here?"

"I didn't mean to wish him here. And I wanted his advice, not his rampages." My fingers started throbbing again. I shoved them back onto the bag of ice. "I thought he was supposed to do good things and help people. In books he was always the hero."

Chrissy slipped the Tansy Sparknotes back into her purse. "Well, you can't believe everything you read. After all, by definition, fiction writers lie for a living."

"But . . ."

Chrissy's wings fluttered in agitation. She looked like a teacher whose students had failed a quiz. "You need to learn how to analyze men better. For example, you might have noticed that in England people often drop the 'g' when saying 'ing,' so if someone's name is Robbing Hood, well, you don't meet many hoods that are upstanding citizens, now do you?"

"Robbing *Hood*? 'Hood,' as in, he's a robbing *hood*lum?" I sat back down on the chair with a thump. "I used a wish to bring a bunch of hoodlums to the city?"

Chrissy gave me a tolerant smile. "Here's a piece of free advice—you probably don't want to use a wish to hang out with Little Red Riding Hood. She's not as innocent as the story makes her sound."

"My wish was a mistake," I said weakly. "You have to send them back." ·

Chrissy smoothed out her skirt, and more minty-smelling glitter tumbled to the floor. "I can't. Remember, all wishes are permanent and binding. You can't undo them just because they didn't make you happy. Magic is sort of like a cell phone contract that way." She glanced at her watch, then back at me. "However, since I'm the caring type of fairy godmother who diligently looks after my charges, and since I still have five minutes left before my shift, I'll have a talk with Robin Hood for you."

She took her wand from her purse, waved it in the direction of my backyard, and Robin Hood and the Merry Men appeared there. They had obviously been sitting somewhere eating, because most of them held food in their hands. Potato chip bags and cereal boxes fell to the ground as the men realized what had happened. Several of them let out shouts and all of them jumped to their feet. Chrissy snapped her fingers and instantly she and I stood outside on my patio in front of them.

I looked around nervously. My parents were due home from work any minute and they wouldn't be thrilled to find Rock Canyon's most wanted hanging out in our backyard. And what if Hudson was still close by somewhere and he heard men yelling? It had only been a couple of minutes since he left my house.

"Good evening, gentlemen," Chrissy chimed. "I want to have a few words with you."

Half of the men drew their swords and watched us apprehensively, but Robin Hood sauntered up to us with a smile. His hat sat on his head at a crooked angle, which somehow made him look carefree and dashing. He even looked cleaner than he had last time. They all did. I wondered if they'd bathed in somebody's pool.

Robin Hood winked at me. "Maid Tansy, how nice to see you again. And who would this goddess of loveliness be?"

Chrissy laughed, a sound like bells ringing. "You, sir, are a rake, but a charming one. I am Tansy's fairy godmother, Chrysanthemum Everstar."

He bowed from the waist. "And I am your humble servant."

Chrissy smiled at him then regarded the Merry Men. She didn't seem concerned that so many gripped their swords. "Tansy is rather distressed at your current occupation. She expected you to be less outlaw and more social worker. Is there any chance you'll reconsider your careers and try something more people-friendly? Perhaps you could put on shows at Disneyland, or . . ." She tapped her wand, thinking. "I hear electrical engineers are in demand."

Several of the Merry Men showed their reaction to her suggestion by spitting on the ground. Which made me glad Chrissy had zapped them into the backyard instead of the house.

Robin Hood bowed again. "I fear I'm set in my ways. When a man is a master of his craft, he doesn't apprentice for another."

Chrissy turned to me and shrugged her slender shoulders. "Well, I did my best. It looks like they want to stay bandits." Her gaze went to her watch. "And now I really have to go or I'll be late. But don't worry. I'll have Clover check in on you later. That is if I can pull him away from his poker games." She wrinkled her nose. "Really, as if he hasn't already lost enough money. You would think he'd find a support group for that or something."

A couple of the Merry Men ran to our cinder-block fence,

jumped up, and hauled themselves up so they could survey the area. "Robin," the first called, "the street lies straight ahead."

"Or," the second man added, "we can see what bounty lies in yonder house."

"Don't!" I said to Robin Hood. "You can't break into my neighbors' homes."

In response to my words, several more of the Merry Men scaled the fence. A couple ran toward the street, and a few dropped into my neighbor's backyard. Robin Hood took my hand and kissed it. "Next time we meet, I would fain linger and refresh my memory about your wishes. As for the present, my men have places to explore." He let go of my hand with a smirk, then strode toward the fence. "Wait up, lads," he called. "I'll lead the way."

I turned to Chrissy, pleading. "You've got to stop them."

Chrissy casually replaced her wand in her purse. "Well, I bet you're glad now that your father installed that alarm system in your house."

Before I could answer, a green puff of smoke appeared in the flower box. Clover materialized, brushing off his green suit. "I'm here," he announced, "and ready to assist you with your magical needs, so you can't tell the UMA I've been slacking off." He glanced over at me. "The lass isn't crying anymore. Things must be going well."

I stared back at him, a wordless protest on my lips. Apparently, he didn't notice the large group of bandits climbing the fence in my backyard. Scary men with swords roaming around your lawn never equaled "things are going well."

Clover straightened his hat. "So then, I'll be in the pub if you need me."

"Wait!" I said. I couldn't let them go. Who knew how long it would be before they checked on me again.

Both paused and looked at me.

"Yes?" Chrissy asked.

I could only think of one thing I could do to fix the Robin Hood problem. Magic had brought them here, so magic had to take them back.

And maybe that was what my fairy godmother was trying to teach me—that I had to take responsibility for my actions instead of waiting for someone else to change things for me. Still, it was hard to force myself to say the words. "I want to make my next wish."

Chrissy pulled her wand back out of her purse. "All right. What is it?"

"I want you to send Robin Hood and his men back to the Middle Ages where they belong."

Instead of being proud of me for sacrificing my second wish, Chrissy let out a huff. "Well, that's a waste of perfectly good magic. Honestly, you ought to make up your mind before you wish for things, but fine, if that's what you want." She turned to Clover. "Assistant, round up Robin Hood and the Merry Men and send them back to Sherwood Forest."

"Me?" he asked indignantly. "That's fairy work."

"I'm late for my shift," she said. "And it's about time you actually assisted, so I'm granting you the magic you'll need." She flicked her wand at him, and a short, stubby wand appeared in his hand. A circle on the top of the wand flashed the number thirteen. "You have thirteen men to find," Chrissy told him, and the next moment, she vanished, leaving nothing but a trail of minty glitter falling to the ground.

Clover let out a sound that was half grumble, half growl, and disappeared too. The Merry Men, however, still circled my yard and climbed the fence.

"Weren't you supposed to . . . ," I started, but as I said the words, a Merry Man vanished. One moment he was climbing the fence; the next, a puff of green smoke appeared in his place. A scraggly man straddling the fence was the next to go, then one who was poking through my parents' shed. Robin Hood noticed the men disappear. His head spun to face me and he took several steps in my direction. "What mischief is this?"

"I'm sending you home," I said.

His blue eyes bore into mine. "You knew I didn't wish for that to happen."

"But *I* wished it. It was a mistake to bring you here."

He stepped closer to me, his hands out in a plea. "I didn't mean to scorn you, Maid Tansy. I beseech you, don't let your disappointment lead you to rash ways." He took hold of my hand and pulled me into an embrace.

His arms wrapped around me, gently surrounding me. I didn't want his affections. What if my dad had come home and happened to look out the sliding glass door while this was happening? Was it possible to be grounded past my graduation date? And yet I didn't try to push Robin Hood away. I already knew how strong he was and besides, Clover was nearby.

Robin Hood leaned toward me, his lips lowering toward mine, then the next moment, he disappeared. The yard was silent and empty. Well, empty except for the discarded chip bags and cereal boxes. I walked around the lawn, picking them up.

I should have been relieved that Robin Hood was gone, and mostly I was, but another part of me felt achingly sad. I had hoped Robin Hood would turn into the hero I'd read about when I was younger. I had wanted it so badly. But maybe heroes were all works of fiction. Maybe in real life, nobody was that noble or self-sacrificing. It was another good reason not to read novels— they set you up for disappointment. Life had enough of that on its own.

I put the trash in the garbage can and went back inside. On the bright side, I wouldn't have to worry about more robberies, or about Hudson spying on me, or about the police hounding me for bandit information.

True, it had been a waste of two perfectly good wishes to ask for Robin Hood to come and then ask for him to go back, but I would make sure I was careful with my last wish. I would ask for something great, something amazing. Something that would make me happy.

• • •

That night after I showered and changed into my pajamas, I sat down on my bed to figure out the best way to phrase my wish. Chrissy, I decided, had been right the first time when she suggested wishing for wealth. If I asked for enough, I could donate it to the library and save Dad and Sandra's jobs—or if they didn't want to work, they wouldn't have to. We could move to some private tropical island. Warm beaches, blue ocean, no nosy police officers poking around. Dad would be happy. He'd finally be glad I was his daughter.

I was hesitant to ask Chrissy for some huge amount of money in my bank account: I'd seen a crime show once that talked about money laundering. I vaguely remembered that banks had to report any large deposits to the government. It might be hard to explain a few billion dollars turning up. And I couldn't very well hide that much money in my bedroom. I could ask for a purse that magically never ran out of money, but if I did, I would worry about it getting lost or stolen.

Asking for the Midas touch would be better because a magic touch was always with you. The story of King Midas, however, didn't end well. Everything he touched turned to gold, including—accidentally—his own daughter.

I needed something more controllable. I combed through the tangles in my hair and said, "Chrissy, I'm ready to make my third wish." I thought it would take her a while to answer, but as soon as the words left my mouth, a flurry of twinkling lights erupted in the air. They grew brighter until Chrissy stepped out of their middle. She wore the same tutu she'd had on earlier, and this time I noticed a name tag over her heart that read *Chrysanthemum*.

She flopped down on my bed and kicked her satin slippers off. "I swear, working for the tooth fairy is the worst job ever." She held out her arm for me to see. A few inches up from her wrist, a broken red circle marked her skin. "Look at this. A boy bit me while I was trying to take his tooth." She leaned her head back on the wall dramatically. "And then my supervisor got all mad at me for turning him into a squid."

"You turned him into a squid?"

"I put him in an aquarium first," Chrissy said. "It's not like there were any piranha in there. Guppies have never hurt anyone."

"You turned someone into a squid?" I asked again.

"Don't say it like that. I turned him back. At the end of my shift. He probably had fun. What child doesn't want to be a squid?" She flourished her hand in my direction. "I bet you wanted to be a squid when you were little."

"Um . . . I wanted to be a mermaid."

"Close enough." She turned her arm over to examine the welt. "This is going to leave a nasty bruise, and the other fairies will never let me live it down. Jade Blossom was all, 'Maybe tomorrow night you can remember that teeth are supposed to go in your purse, not your arm.'" Chrissy rubbed a finger against the wound. "You'd think they'd encourage efficiency at Tooth Fairy, Inc., but no, I got a written reprimand for taking a tooth that wasn't officially underneath a pillow."

Her words didn't make sense. "Where was it?"

She tugged at the lace on her sleeve until it covered the red mark. "The tooth was supposed to come out of that kid three days ago, but he refused to pull it. He was just being stubborn." Chrissy brushed some glitter off her skirt and it drifted to the floor in a minty wave. "I got tired of showing up night after night to see if he'd gotten around to losing it yet. I mean, I have a busy route. He was wasting my time."

I tilted my head. "You didn't pull it out of his mouth, did you?"

She blinked at me innocently. "It was just dangling there."

"Wow," I said. "Somewhere out there is a little boy who will never sleep soundly again."

She fluttered her hand dismissively. "He had fun being a squid. I could tell by the way he was waving his tentacles around." She opened her purse, rummaged through something—I wondered if it was the night's haul of teeth—then pulled out her wand. Her gaze traveled around my room. "I see my assistant decided not to come. Honestly, the things the UMA puts me through."

Still looking around, Chrissy huffed in exasperation. "Belladonna Spritzpetal can claim it's my grades that are keeping me out of Fairy Godmother University, but it's not. It's because I dumped Master Sagewick Goldengill's son. Why else would the UMA give me the same worthless leprechaun for three assignments in a row?"

She tapped her wand angrily against her knee, as though if she flicked it enough times, Clover would appear.

"How come you and Clover don't get along?" I asked.

She hesitated, and I thought she wouldn't tell me, but then she said, "During our first assignment, our teenage charge was being threatened by some neighborhood gangsters. I rounded up the lot of them and told Clover to turn them in to the police." She pursed her lips as if even the memory aggravated her.

"He didn't do it?" I guessed.

"Apparently I should have said I wanted them turned *over* to the police instead of *into* the police. He claimed he didn't understand what I meant." She let out a grunt. "That bit of magic messed up Chicago for years."

"He turned the gangsters into police officers?"

"In my defense, who would have ever thought that using correct grammar would actually come in handy in real life? I mean, nobody pays attention to it during English classes."

My gaze shot to my window. I wasn't sure what I expected to see outside, but I looked anyway. "And you put Clover in charge of sending the Merry Men back in time?"

"Oh, I doubt he messed that up. Even Clover has to get something right every once in a while." She lifted her wand. "So you're ready to make your final wish?"

I nodded, nervous. My carefully planned words jumbled together in my mouth, and I spoke slowly in order to straighten them out. "I want something like the Midas touch, but more controllable. I wish I could create gold, but only when I want to."

Chrissy raised an eyebrow in surprise. "You decided you could buy friends after all?"

"I decided that if I didn't have any, well, at least I can be lonely in a new Porsche."

Chrissy laughed, then stretched her shoulders. "Mortals are so delightfully predictable. It's a wonder they make any of us go to godmother school in the first place. They could just issue us magical ATMs and be done with it. You wouldn't believe the hours of new-invention homework they gave us. Totally worthless. No one ever asks for a better mousetrap." She waved her wand in my direction, and tiny falling stars dropped from the ceiling and surrounded me like wandering butterflies. "Get some sleep," she told me. "You have a big day tomorrow."

Then she and the lights both vanished.

I sat quietly on my bed for a few moments, trying to decide if I felt any different. My fingers felt exactly the same. Ditto for the rest of me. I wished Chrissy had told me how to use my new power before she poofed away. I slipped off the bed, went to my dresser, and picked up a picture of Kendall and me as little girls. Concentrating, I tried to turn the frame to gold.

Nothing happened.

I tried a pencil, a paper clip, and a pair of socks. Still nothing.

But then, Chrissy had said I would have a big day tomorrow, so maybe the gift didn't kick in until then. It was aggravating beyond belief to have to turn off the light and go to bed.

• • •

I slept in. That's the sort of thing that happens when you keep waking up in the middle of the night wondering when tomorrow starts. I knew it didn't start at 12:01 because I got up and tried to change a Snickers bar into gold. It defied all my attempts, so I ate it.

Nick banged on my door in the morning to wake me up. When I didn't answer, he opened the door. He was already dressed. "Your alarm didn't go off because the electricity is out, but you need to hurry, or you'll be late to school." He glanced at his watch. "It's almost seven thirty."

He left, and I staggered out of bed, got ready for school, and went to the kitchen to grab something for breakfast.

Dad and Sandra were in their bathrobes, sitting at the table eating cereal. The library didn't open until nine o'clock, so they always left for work after we'd gone to school. I sat down and poured myself some raisin bran.

"Drink a glass of milk," Sandra said, sliding one to me. "It builds strong bones, and besides, it won't keep long with the power out."

Dad didn't say anything. I wondered if he was going to pretend I didn't exist, like he'd done most of yesterday.

Nick walked to the front door, backpack slung over his shoulder. He opened it, and I waited to hear the door click shut behind him. It didn't happen. Instead, he called out, "Mom, Frank, you'd better come see this."

"What is it?" Sandra asked. Neither she nor Dad moved from the table, but I jumped up and hurried to the front door. *Chrissy is here*, I thought. She must have realized she never gave me directions on how to turn things into gold, and now I'd have to explain her wings to everyone. My thoughts didn't take me further than that. Because it wasn't Chrissy. It wasn't a person at all.

It was the neighborhood. It was gone.

Chapter 8

The street that ran by our house . . . didn't anymore. My neighbors' homes had vanished too. In their place a dirt path wound its way through towering, leafy trees. A brook ran by our yard, and a cylindrical stone building stood next to our garage. Farther down the path, a few cottages poked out of the trees. A couple of the cottages were built of pale gray stone, but the rest were thatch. The scene looked like a storybook picture of the Middle Ages.

"How did those get there?" I asked.

Behind me, I heard the sound of a glass hitting the entryway tile. Milk droplets splashed around my shoes. Sandra gasped. "What happened?"

My father pushed past me to go outside, but Sandra grabbed hold of his bathrobe sleeve. "Don't go out there!"

My father pulled away from her and stepped onto our front porch. He looked around with a stern expression. "This isn't right." His brows furrowed at Nick. "How did this happen?"

Nick held up his hands as though my dad had accused him of hiding the neighborhood. "I didn't do anything. I just opened the door and this was here."

A horrible, sick feeling came over me. This was Chrissy's doing. I didn't know why or what it meant, but it had to be Chrissy's doing. You didn't wake up one day to accidentally find your house transplanted into the Middle Ages.

I cleared my throat uncomfortably. "This might be a good time for me to mention that I have a fairy godmother. Well, she's actually only a *fair* godmother."

My father's eyes narrowed and his mouth pressed into a tight line. "What are you talking about?"

I took a step back from him. This was not the facial expression I'd looked forward to seeing when I told him about my wish. "I didn't ask for this," I said. "I asked for a more controlled version of the Midas touch. I'm supposed to be able to turn things into gold. I don't know why we're here."

All three of them stared at me for a moment, then my father said, "You did what?"

I sighed. I'd heard that question too many times during the last few days. I shut the front door, then calmly told the whole story, even about Robin Hood and using my second wish to send him back to Sherwood Forest. I also told about the lights that circled my head if I lied. When I finished, my father grunted in disbelief. "That's impossible. Fairies and leprechauns don't exist."

"I'm telling you the truth." I pointed to my head. "See? No lights."

My father put his hands on his hips. "There is a logical explanation for this, and it doesn't involve magic."

I put my hands on my hips to match his stance. "I love the way you always listen to me."

Lights ignited around my head, shooting sparks down around my shoulders. It felt like I was wearing a hat made of birthday candles. Nick, Sandra, and my dad all gaped. I knew what they were reading. "See, that was a lie," I said. "Actually, I *don't* love the way you *never* listen to me."

The sparks vanished.

My father walked to the living room couch and sank into it. He rubbed his forehead in bewilderment. Sandra pressed a trembling hand against her lips. "Oh my," she said, and the words sounded lost and lonely, hovering between the four of us.

Nick joined my father, sitting down on the couch with a thud. "What are we supposed to do now?"

That was the question, wasn't it? "Chrissy must have granted me the wrong wish. I'll call her. Sometimes it takes her a while to answer, but eventually she'll come and fix this."

"You're sure it's the wrong wish?" Nick asked. "You didn't ask for this by mistake?"

"I think I would have remembered asking her to drop my house into the Middle Ages." I looked around the room, and called, "Chrissy!"

Nothing happened. Everyone waited for a few moments.

"How long does it take her to answer?" Nick asked.

I shrugged. "Sometimes a few days."

Nick groaned and put his hand over his eyes. Sandra went to the door and locked it. "We'll stay inside. We have food in the pantry, and the water heater is full. Fifty gallons. If we ration it, it should last us for a couple of weeks."

My father didn't move from the couch. "This isn't happening," he said. "This sort of thing doesn't happen."

A small puff of smoke went off on the coffee table, drifting like a green rain cloud over the magazines. When it dispersed, Clover stood on a stack of *National Geographic* magazines. His shabby green jacket had an extra dirt stain or two that he might have picked up while tromping around our yard pursuing the Merry Men.

Dad, Sandra, and Nick stared at the leprechaun in shocked silence.

Clover nodded at me. "Chrissy asked me to check in on you." He put his hands behind his back, taking in the room and my gawking family. "Looks like everything is going well, so I'll be off to the pub."

"Wait!" I knelt down in front of the coffee table to be closer to his eye level. "How can you say things are going well when my house is in the Middle Ages? Why are we here?"

"Oh, that." Clover brushed some dirt off his jacket sleeve. "The last time Chrissy sent someone off to a fairy tale, the lass did nothing but complain about the living conditions. No refrigerators, no soft beds, no comfortable shoes. It was constant whining." Clover gave me a self-satisfied smile. "So now you have your bed and your fridge and you've no reason to blather on about your suffering."

"I didn't wish to be in a fairy tale," I said pointedly. "I wished for the power to change things into gold. And besides, the fridge won't work without electricity."

Clover's brows furrowed at this information. "Ah, well in that case, you'd best go invent some electricity. Isn't that what mortals are best at? Innovation? I'm sure it will take you no time at all."

My hands clenched around the end of the coffee table. The sharp edge bit into my palms. "You need to send us back home."

"Chrissy will send you home," Clover said, straightening his hat. "As soon as your fairy tale is done." And then he vanished.

"Clover, come back!" I reached out and felt through the magazines as though he might be hiding underneath them. The papers rustled an empty protest.

He didn't come back.

My father kept staring at the coffee table in astonishment.

"You were telling the truth." I assumed his astonishment was because of the magic and not because he thought I was incapable of telling the truth.

Nick said, "What fairy tale do you suppose we're in?"

Before anyone could answer, a knock sounded on the door. A booming voice yelled, "In the name of the king, open up!"

Sandra let out a whimper and clutched her throat. My father stood up. His gaze darted around the room, searching for a weapon. Nick and I didn't move. "How many fairy tales have kings?" he asked.

"All of them," I said.

Nick shook his head. "Hansel and Gretel didn't have a king. So on the bright side, our parents won't take us out to the woods to lose us when the food runs out."

My father walked to the door, muttering angrily.

"Don't be so sure about that," I told Nick.

Whoever was at the door banged on it again. "Open up, I say! It's the king's men!"

"The king's men," Nick repeated. "Humpty Dumpty. That's not so bad."

My heart was racing. "Yes, it is. That fairy tale never made sense. Some big egg guy falls off the wall and all the king's horses try to put him back together again? How exactly do horses do that? They have hooves, not fingers. Probably the reason the king's men couldn't put Humpty Dumpty together again was because the horses trampled the pieces first."

Dad put his hand on the deadbolt, but didn't unlock it.

Sandra joined him at the door, nervously shifting her weight. "Kings are usually good in fairy tales, aren't they? They probably just want to know why our house appeared in their village out of the blue."

Dad let out a worried breath, but opened the door. Nick and I went over and peeked around him to see what was happening. Half a dozen men stood on our lawn. Even more sat on

horses on the road. They wore chain mail and red surcoats—
the uniform of the king's men. A boxy carriage sat at the end
of our driveway, but it didn't have windows so I couldn't tell if
anyone was inside.

The knight closest to us had a bushy, black beard and a
crooked nose. He turned a pair of hostile eyes on us. "You are
the miller?"

"The Millers," my father said. I could tell he was surprised a
stranger knew this detail about us.

The man glanced at Nick and nodded. "Millers. Very well."
He gave my father a condescending smile. Several of his teeth
were missing. "And pray tell, are you the selfsame miller who told
patrons of the Bear's Paw Inn that your taxes are too high?"

My father shook his head and put his hand on the doorknob. "No, you're confusing me with someone else. I've never
been to the Bear's Paw Inn."

Several of the knights laughed. Not happy laughter—
taunting laughter.

The bushy-bearded man scoffed. "Everyone's been. I've been
there myself. And what's more, I've heard that when you've had
a few pints, you have quite a lot to say about the king's management of England."

"You're mistaken." My father motioned to our home. "I only
arrived here today."

The bushy-bearded man put one hand on the doorframe.
"This manor is most interesting. Quite a home for a man who
thinks his taxes cut too deeply. You have larger glass windows than the king's palace. How does a humble miller afford
such luxuries?"

Without waiting for my father to answer, the man pushed
his way inside. Several knights followed him.

"The rugs are enormous," one pointed out.

"Behold the furniture," another said incredulously. "Have
you ever seen the likes?"

The rest of the knights pressed past us, peering around in amazement. Several walked into other rooms. I suddenly saw the house from a medieval point of view. Cupboards full of glass dishes in the kitchen. Dressers and closets brimming with clothes. Sandra's necklaces, rings, and earrings sitting in her jewelry box. Robin Hood had said we were all rich in my city. By medieval standards, he was right.

The bearded man let out a snort. "Overtaxed, indeed. To the contrary, it seems you haven't been paying your share."

Our family had gathered closer and closer as the men walked in. Now my father put his arms protectively around Sandra and me. "I'm sorry if I haven't paid enough. You can take whatever you think is fair."

The bearded man's lips thinned into a humorless smile. "Rest assured, we shall. And we shall tell the king of the wealth you've amassed here." He put his hand on the hilt of his sword. "He might wonder if you're a trustworthy subject. So I ask you, do you swear an oath of loyalty to King John?"

King John? I tried to remember my history in order to put us in a time frame. How many King Johns were there in England?

My father hesitated, then said, "Yes, I'm a loyal subject."

"And you are a man of your word?"

"Yes," my father said again.

"You are not one of those foul peasants who still laments King Richard's death?"

Oh no. I could think of only one John who came after a King Richard. "Richard the Lion Heart?" I asked.

The man turned and sneered in my direction. "The Lion Heart. You'd best not let King John hear you speak so. He's king now and his brother's accolades went with him to the grave."

I couldn't breathe. We weren't in a fairy tale at all. We were in the story of Robin Hood. With a bad ending. King Richard had died? I'd always thought he came back to England and overthrew his brother.

I took quick, deep breaths. Why had Chrissy sent me here?

My father's grip on my shoulder stiffened. Apparently he was coming to the same conclusion I'd reached. Clover had said we could go home when the fairy tale ended, but when would that be? At the end of Robin Hood's story?

The bearded man stepped toward me. Two men at his side moved with him, closing in on us menacingly. The bearded man reached out and took hold of a strand of my hair, wrapping it between his gloved fingers. I wanted to push him away, but the swords hanging at the knights' sides made me reconsider. I stood there stiffly, waiting for him to stop.

My father's words came out unsteadily. "Leave my daughter out of this. She has nothing to do with my taxes."

The man didn't let go of my hair. "I've also heard reports of your other boasts. You claim your daughter is the fairest maid in the land—a jewel, a treasure."

I pulled my hair out of the man's grasp. "Trust me, my father has never said any of that."

The man stepped even closer. His voice was soft, like the hiss of a snake. "Oh, but he has. He says you're so talented you can spin straw into gold."

A startled gasp sprang to my lips before I could suppress it. I was in a fairy tale after all: *Rumpelstiltskin*. Somehow the stories had been combined and I was the miller's daughter.

Wow, when Chrissy messed up a wish, she did it in a big way. Not only could I not turn things into gold, but I was now in a fairy tale where the king was going to execute me if I didn't turn a room full of straw into gold thread.

I tried to make the man see reason. "Spinning straw into gold is just a saying, like, 'Every cloud has a silver lining.' Clouds don't really have silver linings, or it would rain money, wouldn't it?"

The man didn't smile at my joke. I pushed on. "Spinning straw into gold is making the best of a bad situation." Like this one. "People can't literally do it. You must know that."

The bearded man narrowed his eyes at me. "Are you calling your father a liar?"

The knights that flanked us drew their swords, which seemed to indicate they actually didn't want more input from me in this conversation.

"If your father lied about your abilities to spin straw into gold, he might have lied about other things too, perchance about his loyalty to King John." The bearded man leaned closer to me. His breath smelled like rotting vegetables. "The penalty for disloyalty is death. So I'll ask of you again, did your father lie when he claimed you could spin straw into gold?"

Sandra let out a sob; an intense, shaking fear lived in that noise.

"He doesn't lie," I said.

The bearded man took hold of my arm. "Then the king would be pleased to see your talents himself. My men shall escort you to the castle forthwith."

The bearded man wrenched me away from my father and pulled me toward the front door.

Sandra let out a wail. My father stepped after me, grabbing hold of my arm. "You can't just take her."

A few of the men advanced toward us, swords drawn, showing that they *could* just take me. I yanked my arm away from my father. "Don't try to stop them. They'll hurt you."

My father followed me anyway. "It's only a fairy tale," he insisted, like that made the weapons less sharp.

The men dragged me out the door. Over my shoulder, I called back, "The fairy tale never says what happens to the miller. I'll be okay. You might not be."

My father stopped following me then. I saw my family for one more moment: Dad, Sandra, and Nick, framed in the outline of the door with stark worry permeating their faces. And then I was hustled into the wooden coach, and one of the king's men slammed the door shut.

The coach was sparse and dark inside, more like a prison than any of the carriages I'd seen in picture books. What light there was came in through several inch-wide gaps in the wall-boards. Two rough-hewn benches sat on either side. No cushions. No backrests. And the wood looked full of slivers. I was glad I'd changed into jeans. At least they offered more protection than my pajamas.

A guard climbed in and sat across from me, smugly resting a knife on his knee. "You will stay seated," he told me. I noticed he was missing several teeth too.

Without warning, the horses moved forward, making the carriage lurch drunkenly down the uneven dirt road. Out of the gaps in the back wall, I watched as my house, so odd-looking next to the wild trees of the forest, grew smaller and then disappeared.

Other houses came into view as we rode—shacks, really. Things made of mud and straw. Homes that a big bad wolf—or at least a severe storm—could blow right over. People came out to watch the carriage go by. The women wore ragged gray dresses and dirty aprons. Children, their feet bare, ran alongside the horses, waving at the procession. I wasn't just a prisoner. I was entertainment.

The guard sat silently, regarding me without pity. I kept looking out through the gaps in the wall, paying attention to every landmark in hopes that if I escaped I'd be able to find my way back to my home.

And then those hopes fizzled. I wouldn't be able to escape. The miller's daughter was trapped in different rooms in the castle for three nights and the only way she kept from being killed was by making bargains with Rumpelstiltskin. That wouldn't be so bad, I supposed. I already knew his name, but part of the fairy tale involved me marrying the king and giving birth to his son.

That was not something I wanted to do, especially since King John was the evil king from Robin Hood's story.

How could Chrissy have sent me here? I asked for the power to create gold, not to go to some fairy tale where a creepy little man spun it for me. Under my breath, I called her name, but she didn't come.

Hours went by. I didn't have a watch and couldn't see the position of the sun, but my stomach told me lunchtime had come and gone a long time ago. Finally, the castle came into view. I saw it during a turn in the road—a sprawling stone castle that peered over a hefty wall. The horses jostled the carriage up to it, then we went through the gates, and stopped in front of the stables. My guard prodded me out of the carriage.

I stepped out into the sunshine, blinking. Before my eyes even adjusted to the light, the man with the bushy beard took my arm and pulled me none too gently across the courtyard.

We went inside the castle and down large drafty hallways. The castle smelled of food, smoke, and something dank and mildewed. Straw was strewn over the floor. I hadn't expected that, but nobody else seemed to think it was unusual. Servants and soldiers came and went without a second glance at the straw, although everyone I passed gawked at me like I was a circus-grade oddity.

I suppose it was strange to see someone wearing jeans and a bright turquoise shirt. No one wore pants here. Even the men wore tunics and leggings. Besides the red surcoats the guards wore, everybody's wardrobes seemed drab and colorless—shades of brown and gray. Had these people even seen the color turquoise before?

The bearded man took me up a set of uneven stone steps. They curved upward in a steep circle without any sort of railing to hang onto. After we'd gone up three floors, he towed me down a dim hallway. Torches hung on the wall, but they only emitted feeble patches of light.

A sentry was posted outside a wooden door. As we walked

toward it, the bearded man said, "Inside your room, a pile of straw and a spindle await you. If the straw isn't spun into gold by morning, the king will assume you refuse to use your talents to help him and he'll sentence you to death for treason. Unless"—he gave me an oily smile—"you want to recant your earlier statement and proclaim that your father lied about your abilities."

What a horrible thing to do to a person—he was making me choose between my life and my father's. I met the man's eyes. "I don't have anything else to say to you."

"Very well." The man gave my arm an extra squeeze. "I'll let the executioner know."

We reached the sentry. I couldn't see his face clearly because his helmet rested low over his eyes, and a long metal piece covered his nose. I could tell he was young though, and his square jaw seemed familiar somehow. I didn't dwell on it. The bearded man opened the door and gestured for me to go inside. "Perhaps the king will have mercy on you," he said, still managing to make the sentence sound like a threat. "Often, the fairer the maid, the more mercy he has."

I gave the man what I hoped was a brave smile and stepped inside the room. The door shut behind me with a thud, and then I heard the scrape of a bar being slid across the door to lock it.

I was a prisoner in a foreign land and time. The thought made my breath catch in my throat. I was not as brave as I wanted.

I glanced around the room. A waist-high pile of straw stood in the middle of the stone floor. Next to it, a lone stool waited. I didn't see a spinning wheel, but something that looked like a wooden top sat on the stool—a hand spindle. Across the room, a narrow, glassless window let in light and fresh air. It was a welcome thing now, but I knew when night came, the shutters on either side of the window wouldn't do much to keep the cold out. Perhaps that was why a couple of dirty blankets lay in the corner. An unlit torch hung on the wall by the door. I supposed they would light that later so I could work through the night.

All in all, the room was a dismal place. I walked to the window and looked out. Down in the courtyard, soldiers came and went out of barracks. A boy drew buckets of water from the well, and a washerwoman scrubbed something in a wooden trough. None of them could help me.

I sat down on the pile of blankets and wrapped my arms around my knees. I didn't want to worry about my family. I had done that the entire coach ride up. But my thoughts slid there anyway. What if any of them were hurt during this fairy tale? What if one of them died? Chrissy had said the effects of my wishes were permanent and binding. And now my family was in danger. No wish was worth that.

I thought about Kendall and my mother. My sister and I texted or called each other nearly every day. It wouldn't take her long to realize we were missing. What would she and my mom do then? I knew with a sinking feeling that they would leave the play to search for us.

My wish had ruined things for Kendall too.

And my mom—in our last conversation, she'd yelled at me about the vandalism, and I had hardly spoken to her. It was such a bad way to leave things between us. I should have told her that I loved her.

A noise at the door caught my attention. Someone was pulling the bolt back. The next moment, the door swung open and the guard stepped inside. He shut the door behind him and stared at me.

That wasn't good. I didn't remember a visit from a guard as being part of the fairy tale. I stood up, trying to read his expression through the shadows of the room. His gaze was stern, penetrating. His sword hung at his side.

I gulped hard. He probably thought he could do anything to

me and no one would care. I was a condemned prisoner, after all. I edged along the wall farther away from him.

He stepped toward me. "Tansy, it *is* you."

I recognized his voice at the same time he stepped into the light. Hudson was standing in front of me.

Chapter 9

I blinked at Hudson, speechless.

He looked me up and down, shaking his head. "I should have known the next time we met you'd be in prison. It's where you always end up, isn't it?"

My eyes swept over him. From his leather boots to the dull shine of his helmet, he looked every bit a medieval man. Well, except that he had straight, white teeth. I walked over to him. "What are you doing here?"

He folded his arms, and his chain mail clinked in an angry rumble. "Do you really not know?"

I reached up and took the helmet off his head. I didn't understand how it was possible, but it was definitely Hudson. His hair was a couple of inches longer than I'd seen it yesterday and it hung in messy strands around his face.

"What are you doing here?" I asked again. I worried, with a sickening panic, that Chrissy had sent the whole school to the Middle Ages. "Why are you one of King John's men?"

"Because I didn't want to be one of Robin Hood's men. But then, you already knew I was more of a stay-on-the-right-side-of-the-law sort of guy." He held a hand out to me. "And you? What brings you to England in the late twelfth century?" His voice was light, but I could tell he wasn't amused by any of this. "Did you come to visit friends or did you just pop in for the fine cuisine?"

I wasn't about to answer his question until he answered mine. "Hudson, really—how did you get here?"

He glared at me and took his helmet back. "Do you remember that day I came over to your house to do homework with Nick?"

"Yeah," I said. "That was yesterday."

"Try three months ago," he said.

"No, I'm pretty sure it was yesterday."

"I've been here for three months, and I have the calluses to prove it." His eyes narrowed as he regarded me. "My father must have looked for me, sent out search teams, put my disappearance on the news . . ."

I shrugged. "Sorry. No one told me you were gone."

He made a grumbling sound in the back of his throat to show his disapproval.

"Time must be different here." I vaguely remembered Clover criticizing Chrissy for not being able to lengthen time. "I only got here this morning. But at any rate, I remember the night." I gestured for him to continue his story.

"After I left your house, I was standing on the sidewalk texting a few people and I heard shouting coming from your backyard. Men shouting." He looked at me to see if I knew what he was talking about.

I felt myself coloring. "Right. I remember that too."

"I walked over to your fence. With those sword-wielding thugs in town, I figured I'd better make sure you and Nick were okay."

"You wanted to catch them, you mean. A rational person would have run away."

Hudson ignored my point. "Before long, the thugs were climbing over your fence." He fixed me with a hard stare. "I won't ask you why they were there, at least not yet. I hid behind one of your bushes and was about to call the police when a leprechaun appeared in front of me, waved a wand in my direction, and the next thing I knew, I was in Sherwood Forest in the year 1199."

I let out a little gasp. "Clover was only supposed to send Robin Hood and the Merry Men back in time."

"Yeah, we figured there had been a mistake when I materialized and someone named Alan A'Dale never showed up."

The dark glare Hudson was shooting in my direction suddenly made sense. "I'm sorry," I said. "I never meant—"

He didn't let me finish. "I know what you meant. Robin Hood told me about your wishes and the fairy godmother you set on unsuspecting people. We had a long talk about it. And when I refused to take a blood oath to join Robin Hood's men, they tied me up, blindfolded me, and left me on the road to town."

I reached out and touched his arm. I'm not sure he even felt it underneath the chain mail. "I'm so sorry, Hudson."

He looked past me as though he hadn't heard my apology. "Before they left me there, they took my shoes and clothes, everything down to my boxers."

I let out another gasp. What could be worse than being tied up and left in your underwear on a road in the Middle Ages? "I'm really, *really* sorry."

"Oh, I wasn't there for long. A group of nuns on a pilgrimage came by and found me."

Being found half-naked by a group of nuns. That would be worse.

"I'm sure my fairy godmother will send you back when she finds out about the mix-up," I said.

He cocked his head like he had his doubts about that. "It's not that I don't enjoy sleeping on straw mattresses and brushing off fleas every morning, but I have a life to get back to in the twenty-first century. So when exactly will that be?"

Hudson suddenly seemed so imposing standing there in his chain mail. I took a step away from him. "I don't know. I've been calling her all morning . . ." I let my voice trail off, feeling miserable. "She might expect me to stay here until I marry King John and have his baby."

Hudson coughed in disbelief. "You wished to be queen?"

"No, it's just that—"

He didn't let me finish. "King John isn't some fairy tale Prince Charming. He's in his thirties and is out of his mind. Literally. If you look deep enough into his eyes, you can read a little sign that says, GONE TO LUNCH. TRY BACK LATER."

"I don't *want* to marry him. I'm not going to if I can help it. I never wished for . . ." It suddenly occurred to me that the best way to get out of this wish was to break the chain of events right at the beginning of the story. If I escaped from the castle now, Rumpelstiltskin wouldn't come, and King John wouldn't want to marry me for my gold.

I took hold of Hudson's hand, trying to make him feel my urgency through his leather glove. "You could help me escape. My entire house was brought here. We could take the things we need and hide out with my family somewhere safe until my fairy godmother sets things straight."

His eyes widened in surprise. "You brought your family here too?"

"I didn't mean to."

He let out a grunt. "Nick barely survived high school PE. How could you send him to a place with wild animals, bandits, and sword-wielding knights?"

"It's not like I asked for this," I said.

Hudson pulled his hand away from mine with an unsympathetic sigh. "What *did* you ask for, Tansy?"

My hand felt small and alone, rejected. Telling him my wish would only intensify that feeling. I hadn't just wished for wealth; I'd wished for *unending* wealth. I'd been greedy.

I turned and walked to the window. The sun blazed high in the sky, but the stone sill was cool to the touch, as though even the sunlight couldn't warm this place.

Hudson followed. He put one hand on the wall and leaned toward me. "I can't imagine that you wished to be imprisoned in the Middle Ages ... although you wished for Robin Hood to come to Rock Canyon and hold up stores, so who knows?"

"I didn't think Robin Hood was going to hold up stores when I wished for him to come."

"Oh. You just wanted some guy with a criminal bent you could make out with in Walgreens?"

"No," I said hotly, "I didn't know that was going to happen either. Wishing for Robin Hood was something I accidentally did when I was complaining about the police. Which, you know," I said, waving a hand in his direction, "sort of makes the whole thing *your* fault since you were the one I was complaining about."

Hudson rolled his eyes.

I wanted to change the subject. "So how did you become one of King John's guards? What happened after a bunch of scandalized nuns found you?"

"They weren't scandalized," he said. "They were very kind. Especially Sister Mary Theresa." The way he said it made me wonder who she was. I imagined her as some young novice who, upon seeing Hudson's broad shoulders in all of their glory, had some serious second thoughts about taking vows.

I raised my eyebrows. "Really? And what did Sister Mary Theresa do?"

"After I was fed and clothed, I was taken to the Sheriff of Nottingham," Hudson said, pointedly leaving out the details I'd asked for. "He didn't hire me because I wasn't good enough with a bow or a sword, but I'm a head taller than most of the people in the Middle Ages, and the castle is always in need of men. He gave me a letter of recommendation and I joined the garrison. I used to have the night shift walking the parapets, but two days ago I was promoted to guarding prisoners. I've been trying to . . ." He surveyed me and then must have thought better of whatever he was going to say because he didn't finish the sentence. "So, now that I've told you my story, tell me yours."

Outside in the courtyard, a young boy was mucking out the stables. A couple of peacocks wandered near the stable door, picking at the ground. It seemed unreal, like a TV show. But it wasn't. It was right outside, and the world I knew was far away in the future. It lay in the seeds of trees that hadn't even sprouted yet.

I wasn't sure if I could trust Hudson, but he was part of my world, and he was also Nick's friend. Those facts made it feel like he was on my side. So I told him the truth. "I wished for a way to change things into gold. It seemed like a nice safe way to make money."

"But?"

"But Chrissy sent me back to the Middle Ages to be the miller's daughter in *Rumpelstiltskin*." I expected Hudson to laugh or tell me I had gotten what I deserved, but his expression stayed serious and intent. Since he didn't comment, I went on. "Clover—that's her leprechaun assistant—says I can go home when I'm through with the fairy tale, but I don't want to marry King John. I mean, I'm seventeen and he's threatening to kill me in the morning. That's not a match I ever envisioned for myself. I think I'm due for a wish refund."

Hudson pondered this. "You don't know much about fairies, do you?"

"I think I could pick one out of a crowd pretty easily."

He shook his head. "People from our time don't understand fairies. Here in the Middle Ages, they're as common as unicorns and dragons—all right, that's still pretty uncommon, but everyone avoids the fay folk. Fairies are mischievous trouble-makers. Your godmother is probably out somewhere right now having a good laugh at your expense."

"No, she's not like that . . ." I was certain he was wrong. Although, now that I thought about it, Chrissy had admitted to turning some random kid into a squid. Maybe this trip was just one step better than waving my tentacles around in an aquarium.

Or several steps worse.

Hudson lowered his voice. "While the nuns took care of me, I told Sister Mary Theresa I was from the future. It took me a while to convince her I wasn't crazy. If anybody here calls you addled, it's not a compliment. But eventually she believed me. Before I came to work at the castle, she sent me to King Richard's old wizard, Bartimaeus the Proud." Hudson cast a glance back at the door, making sure we were still alone. "After Richard died, King John appointed his own wizard. The new wizard broke Bartimaeus's wand and banished him from court. Now he lives in a village ten miles east of here, using what magic he has left to make a living. Bartimaeus and I made a deal. While I work as a castle guard, I'll try to find the thing he needs to repair his wand and when I give it to him, he'll send me home. I can ask if he'll help you and your family too."

This was the first good news I had heard since I'd found myself in the land of the toothless and smelly. I turned from the window to face Hudson. "Really? You'd do that for me?"

"Nick's my friend."

The sentence felt like a rebuff, but I tried not to show it. "What does the wizard need to repair his wand?"

Hudson's eyes swept back to the door. He whispered, "The Gilead."

I didn't know what that was. "The what?"

"It's a plant Bartimaeus enchanted so its sap can fix broken things and heal people. King Richard was supposed to take the

Gilead to France while he fought King Philip, but he thought the journey would kill the plant, so he only took a few cuttings. He figured the cuttings would keep until they were used up, but the magic only lasts for a few months once a branch has been taken from the plant. So Richard died during the siege of Chalus, and King John still has the Gilead somewhere."

"What does it look like?" One thing I'd already noticed about the Middle Ages was that there were way more plants than people.

Hudson held his hands a basketball's width apart. "It's a small, spindly plant with tiny leaves. I've already searched the grounds and most of the castle. It's probably in one of King John's private rooms. I was hoping I would eventually guard those rooms . . ." His words faded off and he smiled. "But in three days you'll be queen, and you'll be able to go wherever you want. It will be easy for you to get it."

The word "queen" landed on my ears with a jarring clank. Other things would also happen when I was queen. Things I didn't want to think about.

I stepped away from Hudson. "You can't ask me to marry some horrible old crazy guy. Why don't you just wait until King John's eating dinner and tell the other guards he asked you to get something from his room."

Hudson shot me a look to let me know I was being unreasonable. "Do you know what would happen if I got caught snooping around the king's rooms? And besides, since when did you get picky about men? I thought you liked the horrible type."

"Just because I dated Bo doesn't make me an idiot."

"Yeah, technically it does."

"No," I said, my hand clenched. "It makes me a person who made a mistake."

"And Robin Hood?"

"I never wanted him as a boyfriend."

"That's not what he says. He says you had a crush on him, and when he spurned you, you sent him back."

"Well, he's not the most reliable source, is he?" I turned away from Hudson and looked out the window again. *Fine.* If he wouldn't help me escape, I'd find a way to do it myself. Before morning, this room would be filled with spools of golden thread. I could braid some of it together and make a rope. After all, it worked with Rapunzel's hair.

That's how you know you're really desperate—when you start making escape plans based on what worked for Rapunzel. Thinking out loud, I said, "How thick would a golden rope have to be to support my weight?"

I shouldn't have thought out loud. Hudson put his hand in front of the windowsill. "Don't you dare escape on my watch, Tansy."

I was about three stories up. The cobblestones on the ground seemed so far away, but what choice did I have? "I'm not doing anything that'll result in me marrying King John and having his baby."

"Okay. Don't." Hudson moved in front of me, blocking the window so I couldn't see past his crimson surcoat. "But don't mess up my plans or do anything that will send me to the stockades. I'm going to make sure there's a guard underneath your window. Don't even think about climbing down it."

"If you escaped with me, they couldn't punish you."

"And if I escaped with you, I couldn't get the Gilead."

"Chrissy will fix things."

He shook his head. "Sorry. I'm placing my bets on the wizard."

I stomped my foot in frustration. "You're trapping me in here?"

"No, you did that with your wish. I'm trying to get us home. If you want to escape, do it sometime when I'm not guarding you." Hudson moved away from the window. "I'd better go so Rumpelstiltskin can come."

Hudson's casual tone irked me even more. "Don't say his name."

"What?"

In a voice so low it was barely more than a hiss, I said, "If he knows that I know his name, he won't ask me for it in a year, will he? That's how I save my baby."

"The baby you're refusing to have?"

"Yes."

"If things go well, neither of us will be here in a year, but fine, my lips are sealed. I'd better go before He-Who-Must-Not-Be-Named comes." Hudson strode back to the door, opened it, then turned and cast me one last glance. My hands were still balled into fists.

"I think you're supposed to be crying," he said and closed the door.

I didn't cry. I took off my shoe and threw it at the door.

• • •

I didn't stay barefoot for long. The stone floor was cold, and it's hard to pace with only one shoe. As I walked around the room, I thought of my family's situation. Hudson was young, strong, and tall even by twenty-first-century standards. Here in the twelfth century where people were naturally shorter, he wasn't having any trouble taking care of himself. But Dad and Sandra were librarians, and Nick was an underweight computer nerd.

These were not stunning recommendations for life in the Middle Ages.

I hoped my family had enough sense to stay barricaded in our house and barter off a few belongings when they needed more food.

As I paced, I sent irritated looks at the door. It was just like Hudson to end up guarding me. He probably thought my stint as the miller's daughter was some sort of divine justice for accidentally sending him here.

I purposely stayed far away from the spindle that sat on the stool. I had the vague fear that Chrissy might have mixed up my wish even more than I'd realized, and if I pricked my finger on the spindle, I would fall into an enchanted hundred-year sleep.

Every once in a while, I went to the window and looked out. Just as Hudson had said, another guard was posted down below.

I wouldn't make the mistake of telling him my plans again. We weren't working together. Even though he told me he wasn't forcing me to marry King John, he might as well have been, since he wouldn't let me escape. See if I helped him find his stupid plant.

I watched the guard below me for a while. Occasionally he glanced up at the window, but mostly he leaned against the castle wall. When the room was full of gold, I could drop a wad of it on his helmet. That ought to knock him out for a while. Then I could climb down a braided rope, bribe a stable-hand into giving me a horse, and sneak out of the courtyard. After I returned to my family, we could hide in the forest until Chrissy showed up to set things right. I would tell her about Hudson. She'd probably be so apologetic for Clover's mistake that she'd grant him a wish before she sent him back home.

I considered what he might wish for and realized I might find myself poofed to some remote spot in the Arctic. I decided to tell Chrissy not to grant him any wishes.

As the day progressed, people came and went in the court-yard. The smell of something cooking reminded me that I hadn't eaten since a few bites at breakfast. Long shadows encompassed most of the room, until only a pale ribbon of light streamed through the window and a chill crept across the floor.

Before it went completely dark, Hudson came in and lit the torch by the door. "I'm not interrupting anything, am I?" he asked.

I had wrapped the blankets around me and was sitting on the pile of straw. "I haven't escaped. You still have job security."

He walked to the window and pulled the shutters closed. "It's best to keep out as much of the night air as you can."

He came toward me and it was only then that I noticed he was carrying something. He held out a large chunk of dark bread, torn in half. "Prisoners don't get dinner, but guards do. I thought you might be hungry."

Part of me wanted to refuse. He was, after all, keeping me prisoner. But I was hungry, and there was no point in turning down his gift. Especially when he was offering me part of his own dinner.

"Thanks." I took the bread from him and bit into it. The bitter taste of rye filled my mouth. I didn't like rye bread, but I was hungry enough that I ate it anyway.

While I ate, a rat came out from the straw and peered at me, perhaps waiting to see if I dropped any crumbs. I gasped and jerked backward. Hudson drew his sword and turned to see what had startled me. When he noticed the rat, he laughed and sheathed his sword. "If you don't like vermin, you chose the wrong place to vacation. They're everywhere." He took a stone from his pocket and tossed it at the rat. The animal darted across the floor and disappeared through a crack in the wall.

I ate quicker, watching the corners of the room for more rats to appear.

Hudson took another rock from his pocket, tossed it casually up in the air, and then caught it. "Any sign of you-know-who?"

"No," I said.

"I told you that you needed to cry. That's part of the story."

"It's hard to get all teary about my impending death when I know someone will come rescue me."

Hudson's voice turned soft, almost lulling. "So what are your new escape plans?"

"I don't have any."

As soon as I said the words, I felt the sparklers flickering around my head. The room instantly became brighter, lit up by my liar's hat.

I shot off of the straw. Some of the sparks landed on the blankets. They were orange embers at first, then darkened into tiny black spots. Luckily none fell on the straw. I took backward steps away from the pile, and sparks streamed around my shoulders onto the stone floor.

Hudson surveyed me calmly. "You shouldn't lie near flammable things."

"I don't have any escape plans." Which was true. I only had some thoughts on the matter. The hat apparently didn't agree. The flames grew stronger.

Hudson squinted at my head, reading the words I knew were lit up and marching across my forehead. "Somehow I don't think that's the truth."

The sparks kept dropping around my feet. I couldn't stand here all night like a human candle. "Okay, maybe I *thought* about escaping. It occurred to me I could drop gold on the guard's head and knock him out."

The hat vanished and the room instantly darkened. In the dimmer torchlight, Hudson smiled. "Thanks for the tip. I'll let the guard know he needs to watch out for heavy, falling objects." He walked to the door. "You're the easiest prisoner I've had to guard yet."

"I'm not speaking to you again. Ever."

He opened the door and stepped outside. "I think you will when you want to go home." Then he shut the door with a final-sounding thud.

He was awful. This whole place was awful. And I was stuck here. Even though I said I couldn't cry, I sat back down on the straw and did just that. I cried in frustration because I was tired, hungry, worried, and apparently not smart enough to remember that when I lied, my head ignited. And now I had no way to escape.

Straw pieces stuck to the blankets and they scratched, but it was too cold not to wrap up. Between my tears and the cold air, I had the sniffles. I needed some tissues, which of course hadn't been invented yet.

A puff of light went off by my side, and I turned, hoping to see Chrissy.

Instead a man stood in front of me.

Chapter 10

Rumpelstiltskin wasn't short and dwarfish like I had expected. He was tall and so painfully thin that if his picture had been on a poster, people would have sent relief money to his country. His stringy brown hair had an unusual tint to it, almost burgundy, and his eyes were deep-set and intense. He wore a golden vest over a flowing white shirt, copper-colored breeches that ended at his knee, and white silk stockings. It was the outfit of the wealthy—but the wealthy of a later time period. I wondered if he knew what century we were in.

He walked toward me, his long legs scissoring across the room. "There, there, don't weep." He held out a handkerchief in his spindly fingers. They reminded me of spiders, of things that scurried off to dark corners.

I took the handkerchief from him. "Thank you."

I wiped my nose, then realized I didn't know what to do with the handkerchief. Certainly Rumpelstiltskin wouldn't want a mucky handkerchief back. But maybe he did. I didn't know what people did before tissues. My history teacher had never covered that sort of thing.

When he didn't reach for it, I kept it in my lap.

"Tell me what distresses you, Mistress Miller." His voice had a deep whispering quality to it, like wind rushing through trees.

I didn't answer. I knew what I should say, but I couldn't speak. Once I did, I would be following the script of this story—sliding toward a destiny I didn't want.

Rumpelstiltskin smiled, which made his cheekbones jut out in sharp contrast to the sunken valleys of his cheeks. "Don't be alarmed at my appearance here. I am your fairy godfather."

"Fairy godfather?" I repeated.

"Aye. No doubt you've heard stories of how fairies some-times appear to worthy young maidens in their time of need." He leaned over and wiped a stray tear from my cheek. "You've been unjustly imprisoned to save your father's life, and you'll forfeit your own unless this straw is changed to gold by morning."

I nodded and shivered.

"I can spin the straw into gold for you if you'll but give me a small token of your trust."

"What do you want?" I asked. In the story, Rumpelstiltskin asked for both a necklace and a ring, but this no longer felt like a children's story. This fairy—the way his eyes hungrily followed my movements—set my nerves on edge. He was dangerous. I could feel it.

Rumpelstiltskin's gaze ran over me and stopped at my neck. He ran one of his fingers along my throat. I tried not to flinch. His finger was cold and smooth. The way snakes feel. "Give me your necklace," he said.

It was a simple gold chain with a heart that my best friend in New York had given to me before I left. I took it off slowly. I didn't have many mementos from my friends and knew I'd never see this one again. "Why does a fairy who can spin straw into gold want a gold necklace?"

He smiled at me with grayish white teeth and plucked the necklace from my hand. "It's merely a token that proves you've agreed to do business with me. The Unified Magical Alliance is particular about such things."

"The Unified Magical Alliance?" Chrissy had talked about them too, but it didn't seem like they should be part of the fairy tale. Did he know I wasn't the real miller's daughter and that this was part of a wish?

Rumpelstiltskin tucked my necklace into his vest pocket. "You need not worry your pretty little head about the Alliance. Rest and let me do the work."

He picked up the spindle from the stool and tossed it aside like it was trash. When he sat down, the largest spinning wheel I had ever seen materialized in front of him.

I watched him from a distance. "Do you know a fairy named Chrysanthemum Everstar?"

He tensed at the name, then picked up a handful of straw and examined it. "The fay folk are many. Quite a few have escaped my notice. Why do you ask?"

He hadn't answered my question, and the way he tensed made me think that he did know her. I could have told him everything—how I was from the future and Chrissy had sent me here mistakenly. But I didn't trust him and didn't want to give him more information than I had to. What sort of person says he's your fairy godfather and then tries to take your baby from you later? It had been a long time since I'd read the fairy tale, but I had a vague recollection that Rumpelstiltskin wanted to eat the child.

Rumpelstiltskin pressed the foot pedal, testing it, and the wheel spun so fast the spokes blurred together. He kept his gaze on me, waiting for me to say how I knew Chrissy.

"She granted me a favor once," I told him, "but it didn't turn out like it was supposed to. I want to talk to her."

Rumpelstiltskin fed some straw into the spindle. It jumped

from his hand like tiny birds landing in their nests. The straw went over the wheel, broken and bumpy, then impossibly turned into a smooth, golden strand on the other side. It looked like liquid light winding around the bobbin.

Rumpelstiltskin motioned to the pile, and a stream of straw swirled onto the spinning wheel. "Did you give this Chrysanthemum Everstar any sort of token for the favor she granted you?"

"Um, no." She had never asked for anything.

"Ah, then it was a gift, not a bargain, and sadly you've no recourse. It does no good to complain about shoddy workmanship if her magic was a present." The corner of his thin lips lifted. "A bargain is binding though. The UMA makes sure of that."

"Oh." I suddenly wished I had read Chrissy's contract more carefully. I also wondered why Rumpelstiltskin didn't give me a contract since his bargains were binding. Perhaps he didn't think I could read.

He stroked the edge of the spinning wheel. "You've no cause to worry about my work though. You'll have nothing but the finest gold when I'm through."

I didn't feel like talking to him any longer so I sat down next to the door. I watched the wheel turning, watched the hypnotic spinning and the torch light winking reflections off the gold.

Rumpelstiltskin sung a low, lilting song as he worked, and I caught snatches of words: "Today do I bake, tomorrow I brew." But these weren't the words I thought about as he spun. It was the phrase he'd said earlier that repeated over and over to the thumping of the foot pedal. *You'll have nothing but the finest gold when I'm through. You'll have nothing. You'll have nothing. You'll have nothing but gold when I'm through.*

Rumpelstiltskin looked over and saw me watching. "The night is far spent," he said. "You must sleep." As though it were a command that I had to obey, I felt exhaustion sweeping over me. I shut my eyes, lay down, and was asleep.

• • •

The next morning, I was awakened by the sound of a voice from the other side of the door. I didn't recognize the speaker. His voice was high-pitched and condescending. "If she is as pretty as you say, perhaps we will stay her execution for a few days, but we doubt we will take a liking to her. That last maiden you brought to our attention—the musical one—we found her dulcimers dull, her vielle vile, and don't even get us started on her gemshorn."

We? Who was talking? I sat up, wiping away strands of hair from my face. Only a few shafts of morning light made their way through the shutter cracks. Everything in the room was dark and muted.

The bolt slid across the door, and I scooted a little bit away.

"We are quite a bit more discerning about women than you are, Haverton, and we have better taste too. We hope you aren't wasting our time again."

The door swung open, letting more light into the room. The bushy-bearded knight strode in with a man who couldn't have been anyone but King John. He wore yellow-and-orange-striped silk robes clasped together at his throat with a doorknob-sized broach. His shoulder-length brown hair was noticeably thin on top or perhaps even absent. He had draped a large section of hair from the back of his head across the top to cover the bald spot and to act as bangs—a medieval version of a bad comb-over.

He surveyed me and his lips puckered sourly. "We thought you said she had golden hair. There's not a speck of gold any-where in it."

Oh. King John talked about himself as "we." Royalty did that sometimes.

Haverton, the bearded knight, nodded. "My apologies, sire. I only meant that she was blond."

King John's lips stayed puckered. "You should learn to speak correctly. Sloppy metaphors lead to confusion and we have quite enough of that in the kingdom already. Don't you recall the time you said the chancellor was casting his pearls before swine?"

Haverton hung his head a bit. "Yes, sire."

"We were nearly trampled by a herd of pigs while we searched their pen."

"I humbly apologize for that again, sire."

"And our green robes still smell like manure." King John flicked his fingers in my direction as though shooing away an insect. "She isn't golden. She is merely a girl dressed in odd clothing. Probably a French spy come here to ferret out our secrets. We should execute her at once for espionage."

I stood up so quickly that I nearly toppled over as I curtsied. "I'm not a French spy, Your Highness. I wouldn't have come here at all except that I was dragged here by your men and—"

King John put up one hand to silence me. "Can you prove you're not French?"

I hesitated, unsure how to do that.

He humphed at my hesitation like it proved my guilt. "Do you speak French?"

"No."

His eyes narrowed. "Do you know how to spell 'rendezvous'?"

"Um, probably not. I've never been great at spelling foreign words."

" 'Hors d'oeuvres'?"

"Why yes, I'd love some."

King John didn't have a sense of humor. He simply stared at me, waiting. I cleared my throat. "No, sire, I don't know how to spell 'hors d'oeuvres,' either."

He gave me another elegant flick of his fingers. "That proves nothing. The French don't know how to spell that word either."

King John turned to Haverton. "We are not impressed with the girl. True, she is pretty, but she doesn't have golden hair and she is a bad speller. We are wondering about your judgment now, Haverton." He shook his head resolutely. "We are not impressed at all."

Then again, it was entirely possible King John kept calling himself "we" because he was referring to the other voices in his head.

Haverton walked to the window. "But, Your Highness, you have not even properly seen the girl." He opened the shutters, and the morning light spilled into the room. Two dozen golden spools shimmered in the sunshine along the back wall.

Both men stared at them. "Wait," King John said. "We have changed our mind. We are quite impressed."

Haverton's jaw dropped in amazement. His gaze shot to mine. "How can this be?" he sputtered. "You spun the straw to gold?"

I figured it was a rhetorical question so I didn't answer. I hadn't actually done it, and I didn't want my liar's hat to go off.

Neither of the men noticed my silence. Haverton paced around the spools, eyeing them in shock. King John dropped to his knees in front of the gold like a man about to pray to the god of greed. As he bent down to examine a spool, his comb-over flopped off the top of his head. It made me feel vaguely like I'd been flashed.

He pulled a shiny thread away from the spool, stroking it like it were a cat, even holding it to his nose and sniffing it. Which made me wonder if gold had a smell.

"She's a lovely maiden," King John said without looking at me. "We are quite smitten, overcome with love, in fact. And now we shall take this gold back to our chamber and get better acquainted."

I was pretty sure he meant he wanted to get better acquainted with the gold and not with me.

With one hand, he tried to pick up a spool. It didn't budge.

He used both hands, with the same result. Either it was very heavy, or he was very weak. Or both. He got to his feet, bent over, and tried again. The spool still didn't lift off the ground. Mostly he just managed to look like he was doing some sort of yellow-and-orange-striped yoga bends.

Haverton took hold of my arm. "How did you do this?"

I couldn't lie, but I wasn't supposed to tell the king about Rumpelstiltskin. At least, in the fairy tale, the miller's daughter never let him know how the straw had been turned to gold— not even when their baby was in danger. And if she hadn't told him, it seemed I shouldn't either.

I stammered out, "This gold is more than my father's share in taxes. You must let me go back to my family now."

Haverton shook his head, but not at me—he didn't give my demand enough notice to refuse it. He was shaking his head at himself. "What a pied ninny I am."

I nodded, then stopped. Maybe that wasn't something I was supposed to agree with.

"I should have known the truth when I saw the riches at your manor," Haverton said. To King John, he said, "Clearly the girl has a magical gift."

King John gave up trying to lift the gold and dropped back to his knees in front of the spool. "Yes, yes, she's charming, but she made the gold too heavy. If we ask our guards to move it, they will rob us blind. They're rogues, every one of them." He took hold of the end of a golden thread and unwound it from the spool. Chortling, he said, "This is how we shall carry it—half a spool at a time."

I tried to pull my arm away from Haverton but he didn't let go. He turned my hand over so it was palm up. "Your hands have no calluses or cracks. The straw didn't even blister them. How did you spin it into gold?"

I didn't answer.

He leaned closer, his foul breath puffing into my face. "The king demands to know."

Actually, the king was humming and winding thread from his thumb to his elbow. It was no wonder, really, that the miller's daughter never told him anything.

Haverton tightened his grip on my arm. "How did you do it?"

Then again, just because the miller's daughter never told the king about Rumpelstiltskin, that didn't mean I shouldn't. Perhaps if I veered from the story script now, I would get a different ending.

Of course, it might be a worse ending. It was hard to judge what King John would do since, at this point, he seemed completely fixated on creating a golden cocoon around his arm. I swallowed hard. "I'll tell you the truth if you promise not to hurt my family."

My answer only made Haverton squeeze my arm harder. "You shall tell me the truth regardless. Now."

I held firm. "My father hasn't lied, spoken treason, or refused to pay taxes."

Haverton pulled me a step closer. "You silly girl, no one cares about your father, but I'll have my men drag him here in shackles if you don't speak at once."

I didn't have a choice. I spoke. "A man appeared in the room last night and told me he was my fairy godfather. He spun the straw into gold so you wouldn't kill me. It wasn't my doing at all, so there's no use keeping me here in the castle. I don't have a magical gift."

Scowling, Haverton let me go. I rubbed my arm where he had squeezed it.

"Haverton!" King John called.

I looked at King John to see his reaction to my confession, but he still wasn't paying attention to me. He had somehow managed to tangle the thread around the broach at his neck and was struggling to free himself, one-handed.

Haverton went to his side, wrestling with the thread to unsnarl it.

"Our heart's love not only made the gold too heavy," King John said, "she made it too unwieldy. She must do better tonight."

"But didn't you hear me?" I asked. "I don't have any magical gifts."

King John smiled warmly. "Your modesty does you credit, my dear. You have a magic godfather and that is gift enough." He held his cocooned hand out to me like he was asking me to dance. "Tonight you shall stay in a bigger room with more straw. When your fairy godfather arrives, you shall beseech him to spin it into lighter gold."

Unable to free the king from the golden tangles, Haverton took out a knife and cut through parts of the thread. This allowed him to slip the bulk of the golden jumble off the king's arm.

King John stretched his fingers. "And if your fairy godfather doesn't appear, my love, well, 'tis no great inconvenience to execute you tomorrow instead of today. We are nothing if not flexible."

I let out a horrified gasp. Despite his terms of endearment, I was still a prisoner with a death sentence. Telling King John the truth hadn't made one bit of difference.

King John walked over and patted my shoulder. "No need to fret," he said cheerfully. "Your fairy godfather won't let you come to harm." He kept patting. "Although one can never tell with fairies. They're such flighty creatures." He put his hand to his chest and chuckled. "Fairies are *flighty* creatures. What witty wordplay."

Haverton laughed along. I didn't.

King John turned to Haverton and eyed me severely. "I say, the maiden has a rather dour temperament."

"You just threatened to kill me," I pointed out.

"Business, my dear." He motioned to Haverton. "We have decided not to carry the gold ourselves, so you must find someone who's trustworthy to move it to our rooms." He paused.

"When we say *our* rooms, we actually mean *my* rooms. None of the gold is to go to *your* room."

Haverton bowed. "As you say, sire."

"Feed the girl and . . ." King John glanced at my jeans and T-shirt disdainfully. "Give her a proper dress to wear." He waved a finger toward my head. "And have one of the chambermaids do something with her hair. It looks like she's slept in a haystack." With that, he turned and walked from the room.

• • •

Two guards took me to the kitchen for some food and watched me from the doorway while I ate. The kitchen was a welcome change. It smelled like spices, and the fireplace not only housed a cauldron, it warmed the room as well. Several servants worked at the long wooden table where I ate, some chopping vegetables, some kneading dough, and a couple plucking chickens.

There's nothing that will dampen your appetite quite like watching someone pull the feathers off a dead bird, but still, I ate. I'd hardly eaten anything the day before.

While I devoured a bowl of porridge, the servants sent suspicious glances in my direction and discussed the dangers of magic.

"Do you recollect old Jonas?"

"Aye, he tangled with a fairy and she turned him into a wolf. Spent the rest of his days in the woods pestering folks that passed by. A mighty nuisance, that one was."

"And remember the tailor and his wife. They wished for a child and a fairy helped them. Their daughter was born as big as a thumb and never grew a stitch bigger."

"Whatever became of poor Thumbelina?"

"Methinks she was blown away in a fierce wind."

"Nay, she was drowned in a rainstorm."

"Nay, 'twas worse than that. Something awful. A cat, perhaps."

I put down the chunk of bread I'd been eating. This was one of the stories my father read to me years ago. I knew the answer. "Thumbelina was captured by a toad but escaped on the back of a swallow and eventually fell in love with a flower-fairy prince and married him."

The servants gasped at my ending and shook their heads sadly. The cook went back to chopping onions. "I told you 'twas awful. Married to a fairy, unlucky chit."

One of the chicken pluckers nodded. "'Tis probably what the first fairy meant to happen all along—that's why she cursed the poor child."

One of the vegetable choppers pointed an onion in my direction. "You best not accept more help from this fairy god-father. Fairies only help themselves, and that's the truth of it."

A dough kneader pounded on her loaf. "But who can afford to offend a fairy? They'll curse you as sure as rain if you do."

Everyone mumbled in agreement and they went back to their work, perhaps considering my hopeless state.

After I finished eating, the guards took me to the chamber-maid's room. I had been hoping for a bath, but only got a basin of warm water, a gritty bar of soap, and a rag to clean myself. The maid washed the straw out of my hair in a bucket of water, and then I dressed in a long blue gown with sleeves so big I could have hidden tubas inside them.

She braided my hair and put it up with ribbons. When she finished, she pronounced me "a marvelous beauty" and gave me a hand mirror to check her work.

I stared at myself as though if I kept watching, my reflection would revert back to the old me, the me from the twenty-first century that had come here wearing jeans and tennis shoes. Instead I saw a fairy-tale maiden with large, worried eyes. I put the mirror down.

The chambermaid left, but I stayed in the room alone, with guards keeping watch outside the door. I was used to the constant noise of the modern world: TVs, iPods, cell phones. The silence felt suffocating. I walked back and forth across the room, wondering if Kendall and my mom knew we were missing yet. I also wondered what Nick and our parents were doing now, and what they'd do if they had to stay here for an entire year like the fairy tale said.

I got to leave the room to eat lunch and dinner with servants— they regaled me with more stories of doomed mortals who'd had the misfortune to come across fairies. And I was allowed to leave the room to visit the garderobes, which were the medieval equivalent of the outhouse. Only they weren't outside of the castle; they were smelly rooms with holes that emptied into some unfortunate place.

When evening came, I was led outside to the barn by a procession of men. Haverton was at the front of the group, carrying a black bag that jingled as he walked. King John's wizard walked next to me. He was a short, stocky man who wore black robes and gripped his wand in front of him like he wanted to poke someone with it.

Hudson stood watch by the barn door. He opened it for us, catching and holding my gaze as the wizard pulled me inside. A few guards poured in after us. Each held a torch, which made me nervous in a barn full of straw. And it was full of straw. Several stacks stood taller than me—great uneven towers staring down at us. A stool sat in the middle of the stacks, looking small and forlorn by comparison. One of the guards set a spindle and a candle next to the stool. Its pale flickering light barely reached me. While I looked around, Haverton came up behind me, took hold of my arm, and clapped a metal band onto my wrist. I let out a startled yelp and pulled away in alarm, but it did no good. I was caught. A long, thick chain connected to the band. This is what Haverton had been carrying in his bag.

I held my hand up angrily, glaring at Haverton. "I've got guards," I protested. "Why are you shackling me?"

Haverton went to a nearby beam, twisted the chain around it, and slid a lock through the links. "The king's orders, m'lady." He bowed slightly when he finished, then slipped the key into his pocket.

The wizard stepped forward then, lifting his wand while he intoned something in Latin. He walked slowly around me and the beam, sprinkling reddish sand onto the floor. When he completed the circle, he tucked his wand back into his robe. "It shall hold her hence," he told Haverton, and without further explanation, he turned and strode out of the barn. The guards followed after him.

I tugged on my chain but I couldn't walk out of the circle—I couldn't even kick the sand with my foot. "What did he do?" I yelled to Haverton. "What does this mean?"

He turned back. " 'Tis nothing to fret about, m'lady—only a bit of magic to keep the fay folk from spiriting you off. They can't cross that line. You'll be safe."

Safe? I was handcuffed and trapped.

Chapter 11

This was what I got for telling the truth about who spun the straw into gold. I would be chained here all night, and even if Chrissy did come, she wouldn't be able to help me.

I sat in the circle for a few minutes, thinking. Perhaps the chain meant there wasn't a guard outside, and if I could find a way out of this cuff, I could escape. I tried to slip my wrist out of the band, then tried to pick the lock using my hair pins. When neither of these worked, I yanked on the chain, hoping it had a weak link somewhere.

I was tugging and rattling the chain so much that I didn't hear the door open, didn't hear Hudson walk over until he said, "They make those strong enough that a horse can't break them. I doubt you'll be able to." He held a torch in one hand. It lit up the area better than the candle that was keeping me company.

I let the chain drop back to the ground and put my hands on my hips, breathing hard. "Do you have a key?"

"No. And I'd be executed if I let you escape. I'm supposed to be guarding you."

I lifted my chin. "Go ahead and ask me what my escape plans are. I don't have any, because it's impossible, and none of this would have happened if you had let me go last night."

He gave me a smirk that reminded me of the one Robin Hood wore. "Sorry, but who am I to mess up your fairy tale? Nice dress, by the way. Fit for a queen. Which reminds me—what do you think of King John now that you've met him?"

"I think if he lived in our day, he would spend his time making tinfoil hats to keep aliens from abducting him." I gave the chain another useless tug. "You know that none of this is my fault. Why won't you help me?"

He leaned up against a post not far from the one I was chained to. "I *am* going to help you. That's why I'm here. I thought we should talk about our plans to find the Gilead."

I tried twisting the chain and then pulling on it. None of the links bent.

Hudson's gaze drifted to the mounds of straw behind me. "The nice thing about having most of the guards either busy shoveling straw in here or sent into the kingdom to buy straw for tonight was that there were fewer men guarding the king's quarters. I actually got to snoop around the king's sitting room. The Gilead wasn't there, so it must be in his bedroom. Probably near his window so it can get some light."

"How nice. I hope his future wife remembers to water it. I'll be someplace else."

"After a royal wedding, everyone will be feasting—except for the kitchen staff who'll be busy serving everyone. I could sneak into his bedroom then and take it."

I stopped pulling on the chain long enough to mull over this possibility. "And we would be able to go home right after that? I wouldn't actually spend a night married to King of the Froot Loops?" Dinner as the queen, I could manage. Anything else, I didn't want to consider.

Hudson rubbed his thumb against his bottom lip, thinking. "Bartimaeus the Proud won't be invited to the wedding. Assuming I can get hold of a horse, it will still take a couple of hours to ride to his village to give him the Gilead. I'm not sure how long it will take him to send us home. We'll probably have to round up your family and come back to the castle for that."

"So the plan is I marry King John so you can get the Gilead, and then you'll ride off and I might never see you again?"

He dipped his chin downward. "You can trust me."

I laughed. I couldn't help myself. "I trusted you in the police station. That worked out real well."

His gaze connected with mine, completely serious. "This is different. We need the Gilead to get home, Tansy."

I yanked the chain again and only succeeded in hurting my wrist. "I don't know how most guys flirt with girls here in the Middle Ages, but King John keeps threatening to kill me. Funny, but I don't find that romantic."

A voice with a distinctly Irish accent came from behind me. "Well, lass, every relationship has its downsides."

I turned around and saw the leprechaun standing eye level in the nearest straw mound. "Clover!" I said with relief. I pulled the chain as far over as I could go in his direction. "Clover, you've got to help me!"

He strolled down the straw, lifting the brim of his hat to better see me. "Technically I'm not allowed to help. I'm just supposed to check up on you." He pulled a pencil and a piece of paper from his breast pocket. "Chrissy even gave me a checklist." He stopped at the bottom of the straw mound and looked me up and down. "Your hair is fashionably done. Check. Wearing a stunning gown. I guess so, if that's the sort of thing you like." He marked it off on the paper, then returned his gaze to my face. "Makeup. Nope. I'd better fix that." He snapped his fingers, but whether anything changed on my face, I couldn't tell.

"Clover, listen to me for a minute."

Clover cocked his head. "I suppose your eye shadow is too bright and Her Excellence of Fairyness wouldn't approve." He let out a grunt. "I'm a full-fledged leprechaun and she's using me as a bloomin' makeup artist." He snapped his fingers again then considered me. "Now the lipstick is too red. We can't have you look like a ruddy barn tart, can we?"

Hudson had been watching us in surprised silence, but now he spoke. "You're the leprechaun that sent me here, aren't you?"

Clover snapped his fingers again. "Better," he said, and made another mark on his paper. "Makeup done. Check." He folded the paper, slipped it into his pocket, then turned his attention to Hudson. "At present, I'm a leprechaun for hire, but I'm not taking new clients until I'm done with this assignment. If you're interested after that, and you have the gold to pay, I can leave you my card. I've started me own business: the You're in Luck Leprechaun Agency."

Hudson put his hands on his hips and narrowed his eyes. "I was outside Tansy's house and you sent me to Sherwood Forest with a gang of thieves."

Now Clover studied him in earnest. "That's because you're one of the Merry Men."

"No, I'm from the twenty-first century and I was just over at Tansy's house doing homework with her brother."

Clover cocked his head, unconcerned. "Well, you seemed merry enough at the time."

"Trust me," Hudson said slowly. "I'm not merry right now."

Clover reached into his jacket pocket and pulled out the short stubby wand Chrissy had given him. The number on the top read "1." He rattled the wand as though this would change the reading. "What a blaggarding mess. This means I left one of the Merry Men in the twenty-first century. Well, that's not going to look good on the assignment evaluation at all." He examined the wand, dissatisfied, and shoved it back into his jacket. "What were you doing hanging about with the Merry Men? Were you trying to trick me?"

"No, I was trying to keep an eye on the suspects until the police arrived." Hudson waved his hand to encompass me in his gesture. "Are you going to fix this mess and send us back?"

"I haven't the magic to send you back," Clover said. "All this means is that now I've got a ruddy lot of paperwork to do, and then I've got to go find a Merry Man. Who knows how long that will take?"

He buttoned his jacket with intent motions like he was about to leave. I moved toward him, forgetting about the chain until it jerked me back. "Clover, this whole wish is a mistake. You can't leave us here. That isn't fair."

Clover shook his head. "Mortals. You have no understanding of magic. You might mistakenly drive your car off a cliff, but mistake or not, you can't undo the damage. When you made your wishes, you took hold of the steering wheel. Where your wishes take you . . . well, that's your business. This fellow has to stay here with the rest of you until the fairy tale ends." Clover took out a pocket watch and squinted at the time. "And speaking of business, I've got to go fill out a 'Mortal in the Wrong Time Period' report sheet."

I knew what to say to keep Clover from leaving. "I'll give you gold."

He looked at me from underneath the brim of his hat. "Gold, you say?"

I nodded. "In a little while this room will be full of gold. King John won't notice if some is missing. If you help us, you can have an entire spool."

Clover walked down the straw mound, stroking his beard. "What sort of help would you be asking for in exchange for a trinket of that sort?"

Hudson came up behind me. He was so close I could smell the scent of smoke from his tunic. Into my ear he whispered,

"Haven't you learned anything? If you're going to ask someone for help, stick to your own species."

I whispered back, "My species has already disappointed me enough."

Hudson leaned closer to me. "You won't trust me, but you'll trust a leprechaun who couldn't tell the difference between a Merry Man and a guy in jeans with a cell phone?"

Clover tilted his head at me. "Do you want to do business or are you going to stand around all night murmuring sweet nothings to each other? Honestly. Mortals and their hormones."

"Business," I said. I knelt down so I could be closer to Clover. "Look, there's got to be some other way to get us home besides completing this fairy tale. I can kiss a frog. I can tap ruby slippers together. But I can't marry a crazy man, stay here for a year, and have his baby. I have things to do in the twenty-first century. Like graduate from high school."

"Oh, you won't miss a year from your time period," Clover said, as though that were my biggest concern. "Chrissy isn't the best at time management, but she can still slow it down a bit. A week here is only an hour back in your own time period. In the twenty-first century, it's still Monday morning on the day you left."

Which explained why Hudson had been here for three months yet I arrived here the morning after he'd been zapped from my house.

And it meant Kendall and my mom didn't know we were gone. They hadn't started worrying yet.

Clover went back to stroking his beard. "There is another way to get you home, but Her Excellence of Fairyness doesn't like me to interfere in her wishes. If I decide to help you, you can't tell her about it."

I nodded eagerly. "I won't."

Above me, Hudson said, "Are you forgetting that you can't lie without flames shooting out of your hair?"

"Not volunteering information is different than lying," I said.

"You're surrounded by straw." Hudson rubbed a hand across his eyes. "I'd better ask the other guards to help me stockpile water buckets. I have a feeling there's a fire in your future."

Clover kept stroking his beard, thinking. "I would have to do a bit of finagling with me poker chums. It wouldn't be easy . . ."

"Please," I whispered. "Please?"

Clover looked at me and sighed. "Mortal girls have a magic all their own. With one imploring eyelash flutter, they have the power to make men do foolish things." Clover gave Hudson a meaningful look. "Be forewarned about that."

I didn't think Hudson needed the warning. He was obviously impervious to my charms, or he would have helped me escape the first night.

"I know of a magic book," Clover said, keeping his voice low. "It's called *The Change Enchantment* and it has the power to change written stories. For two spools of gold, I could get it for you so you can alter the ending of your fairy tale. That way you won't have to marry King John or stay here for a long time."

"What would I have to do in order to finish the fairy tale and get home?"

Clover shrugged. "Just write down the moral of the story at the end of the book."

"The moral of the story?" I repeated. I wasn't quite sure what he meant.

"All fairy tales have a moral," Clover said. "The moral of *The Three Little Pigs* is that hard work pays off in the end. The moral of *Little Red Riding Hood* is that you shouldn't talk to strangers. The moral of *Cinderella* is that men never look at a woman's face long enough to recognize her, so you had better wear distinctive footwear if you want to catch a prince."

"Really?" I asked, then decided I didn't want to talk about Cinderella. "So what's the moral of *Rumpelstiltskin*?"

Clover dipped his miniature chin. "You've got to figure it out yourself, but don't worry, there will be people there to help you."

"Oh," I said. "Right." I could figure it out. And if not, I had a father and stepmother who were librarians and a brainiac stepbrother. They had to know the answer.

"I'll give you *The Change Enchantment* after you give me the spools of gold." Clover walked toward me with his hand outstretched to shake mine, but when he reached the circle of sand, he took a staggering step back. "What kind of foulness is that?"

"King John's wizard put it there," I said. "It's to stop fairies from spiriting me off."

Clover wrinkled his nose and took another step backward. "It also works to keep magical creatures from shaking on a bargain."

I stretched my foot to see if I could push away some of the sand, but I couldn't reach. I turned to Hudson and smiled at him. "Hudson, do you think you could move the sand away?"

He shut his eyes for a moment, thinking. "I'm not sure this is a good idea, Tansy."

He didn't have to tell me why. All day I'd listened to the castle staff tell stories of ill-fated mortals who'd made deals with magical creatures. But there were other stories I remembered my father reading to me when I was young. Stories about good magical creatures. The pixies that helped the cobbler with his shoes. And the fairies who helped Sleeping Beauty after the evil fairy cursed her.

I didn't believe Clover would purposely hurt me. *The Change Enchantment* had to be a good thing if it kept me from having to marry King John. All that was standing between me and a quick trip home was a circle of sand. I turned to Hudson, still on my knees. "Hudson, please."

He hesitated, then let out a long sigh. "So now you're fluttering your imploring eyelashes at me?"

"I'm trying to get us home."

He walked over, handed me his torch, and dropped to his knees near the circle. Taking a cloth bag from his pocket, he scooped up the sand and dropped it inside. He cleared half the circle away, but Clover still wouldn't come near me.

"Mortals are always trying to trap leprechauns," he said, eyeing Hudson warily. "He might redraw the circle around me and then demand me gold."

"Why would I want to steal your gold?" Hudson asked, but he continued to pick up the sand and put it into his bag. "I took all I needed last night."

"You took some of the gold last night?" I asked. *I* hadn't even taken any gold.

"While you were sleeping and no one knew it was there yet, I came in and got some." He scooped up the last of the sand and pulled the drawstring on his bag. "We might need gold later."

When the circle was gone, Clover walked over to me, held out his hand, and shook my pinky. "We've a deal. Two spools of gold for *The Change Enchantment*. I'll come tomorrow for the exchange, you can shorten your story, and Chrissy is none the wiser."

As soon as the words were spoken, the leprechaun disappeared.

Hudson surveyed the ground around me. "I wonder if they'll notice the ring of sand is gone."

"You can put it back now," I said.

"If it keeps the next fairy away and he doesn't spin the straw into gold, you'll be killed in the morning." He picked up a stray clump of sand then took the torch from my hand to get a better look. "Besides, this sand has magical properties. We might be able to use it. I'll find something that looks close enough so Haverton doesn't realize what we've done." Hudson brushed the sand from his fingers, then glanced back at the door. "It's getting late. You'd better start crying so your visitor will come."

I tried. I forced a frown on my lips and blinked my eyes. Nothing happened. Now that I had an agreement with Clover, I was happier than I'd been since I'd been dragged from my home.

Hudson watched me. "I don't think pouting will work. You need some actual tears."

I tried to blink tears into my eyes, and felt so foolish I giggled instead.

Hudson kept watching me. "You know this is serious, right? Your life is on the line."

"I know it; I just can't feel it." I should have taken acting lessons from Kendall. She cried onstage all the time.

Hudson regarded me quietly for another moment. "I wasn't going to tell you this, but maybe I should."

And then he didn't say anything.

I sat up straighter, nervous at the silence. "What?"

"I used some of the gold to pay a messenger to go to the miller's house. I figured your parents would want to know that you're okay and we could start making plans to meet somewhere after I got the Gilead."

More silence. I stood up to better see Hudson's face. "And . . . ?"

His eyes left mine. He looked at the straw mounds for a moment before forcing his gaze back to me. "The messenger returned this evening. Your family isn't there anymore. The house has been ransacked."

I felt like I'd taken a blow to my stomach, like Hudson had hit me with the words instead of whispering them. My family was gone? Our things were ransacked? I tried to extract unsaid things from the shadows of his eyes, the tilt of his head. "Does anyone know what happened? Did the messenger ask the villagers what they'd seen?"

Hudson's voice was low, apologetic. "Maybe they left before your home was robbed, but it doesn't look good. Some said they saw bandits in the village. Your big modern house, the glass windows and curtains ... It must have drawn them there. I'm sorry."

The word "sorry" at the end hurt the most. It seemed so final. Panic erupted inside me. It was hard to breathe. "You're just saying this to make me cry," I said. "It isn't true."

He didn't flinch at my accusation. His voice dropped even lower. "Nick is my friend. I've known him since elementary school." I could see the pain in his eyes, raw and weighted with sympathy. "I'm sorry, Tansy." He held my gaze for a moment more, then turned and walked toward the door.

I tried to follow but was held fast by the chain. It rattled tight, pulling my arm back. "It isn't true!" I called out. "Hudson, come back here!"

He didn't turn around. He didn't even slow down. I saw him clench one hand tight, then he was out the door, and it shut behind him with a bang.

"It isn't true," I whispered to myself, but I knew it was. Hudson had lost his mother; that's why the pain and sympathy had shined in his eyes. He had been through this kind of loss himself.

I sank weakly to the ground. Bandits had ransacked the house. My family had no weapons, no practice defending themselves. My only hope was that they'd gotten away, that they were still alive somewhere. I thought of the contract, how the consequences of magic were permanent and binding. I let out a low wail, put my head in my hands, and cried.

Chapter 12

I had been sitting on the ground for some time, sobbing into my hands, before I looked up and saw Rumpelstiltskin. He wore the same clothes he had worn last night and sat on the stool, resting his foot on one bony knee. His pointed boots made his feet look abnormally thin. Or maybe they *were* abnormally thin, like the rest of him. He regarded me with a smile. "You find yourself in trouble again tonight, Mistress Miller?"

I wiped the tears off my cheeks and tried to compose myself. "My family has disappeared. I don't know if they're all right. Can you help them?"

He gave me a consolatory shrug. "How can I when I have no knowledge of their whereabouts?"

"But can't fairies do that sort of thing? Chrissy could." She had, after all, waved her wand and made Robin Hood and the Merry Men appear in my backyard.

"Even fairies have their limits." Rumpelstiltskin's lips twisted into a bitter sneer. "Some have more limits than others, thanks to the Alliance. And Chrysanthemum Everstar, well, I can scarce believe the Alliance ever gave her a wand. She's more dandelion fluff than fairy. When did you have the misfortune of dealing with her?"

So he did know her. He hadn't admitted to that last night, but this bit of deceit didn't surprise me. I had always known I couldn't trust him. I wasn't about to answer his question. I lowered my head sadly. "It doesn't matter."

He stood up and walked slowly toward me, noting the chain on my arm. "The king has tethered you in a barn and surrounded you with straw. I suppose this is his subtle way of requesting more gold?"

I nodded. "And this time he wants it lighter."

Rumpelstiltskin took my hand from where it had lain across my knee and stroked it between his cold, smooth fingers. I resisted the urge to yank my hand away from his touch.

"I'll spin the straw into gold for you." The stroking of his fingers paused on top of my opal ring. "All I require in payment for my services is your ring. Do we have a bargain?" He caressed the ring, circling the band of gold. I took it off quickly and gave it to him so he'd stop touching me.

Rumpelstiltskin smiled, showing a flash of his gray teeth, then tucked the ring into his breast pocket. Humming, he snapped his fingers, and the large spinning wheel appeared in front of the stool. He sat down, motioned to the straw with one hand, and a stream of it rose from the ground as though it had been picked up by a great wind. It twirled around him for a moment, then dived toward the wheel, wrapping itself where the yarn should go. I watched the wheel spin, watched the blur of pale yellow transform to shining golden string. I had seen it last night, yet it still mesmerized me.

Rumpelstiltskin sang for a little bit, then looked up and saw me watching him. "You're weary. You should sleep." I laid my head down on the ground, exhausted, and heard the whir of the wheel as I drifted off.

I didn't wake up until King John and Haverton came into

the barn. It would have been hard to sleep through King John's laughter. It was high-pitched and gasping. If I hadn't seen the glee on his face as he strolled around counting spools, I might have thought he was choking on air molecules.

He wore a purple tunic and matching purple robe today. I remembered that purple was the color of royalty in the Middle Ages, but modern life had ruined the color for me—he reminded me of Barney the dinosaur. Or maybe the similarity was the way he kept clapping his hands together happily. I sat up and yawned.

Hudson must have come in again during the night and redrawn the anti-fairy ring—although it wasn't the same red sand that had been there before. It looked more like crushed kidney beans.

Dozens of spools were spread across the room—smaller spools, with thinner thread. I supposed because King John had asked for lighter gold. He stopped at several of the spools, admiring them like they were works of art.

"Resplendent! Prodigious!" He knelt down in front of one and stroked it. "We shall name this one Theobald, and he shall sit at the foot of our bed."

Haverton made note of it on a scroll he carried. "I'll have the guards take it there at once, sire."

King John moved onto another spool, patting it lightly. "And this one we shall name Helewise because she is beauteous. Splendiferous."

I was pretty sure he was making up words now, but I nodded in case he was talking to me. Then I motioned to Haverton, pointing to my shackle in hopes he would come unlock it.

He ignored me and followed King John around the room, murmuring in agreement about each spool the king named. Poor Haverton. It must be hard to work for someone who was both crazy and dangerous.

"This one shall be called Engelbert," King John proclaimed.

Engelbert? This was another reason not to marry King John. Our baby would end up with some hideous name, and other children would mock him behind his back.

King John didn't look at me as he strolled around the room. I wasn't sure he even remembered I was there. I hoped I would escape his notice altogether, but when he reached the spool closest to me, he turned and asked, "What would you name this lustrous one?"

I hesitated. I didn't know many names from the Middle Ages. I tried to remember names I'd seen in movies from the time period. "Robert," I finally said.

"Robert?" King John asked disapprovingly.

"Or you could call him Bob for short. Bob the spool."

King John sniffed. "Nonsense. This beauty deserves a name as radiant as she is."

Oh. It was a *she*. Well, that made naming her "Bob" awkward. Instead of trying to come up with a girl's name, I said, "I think you are best suited to name the gold, Your Highness."

He sent me a cold look. Perhaps because I had referred to him as "you" when he kept referring to himself in plural terms.

I tried to fix my sentence. "I mean, you *guys*, are best suited to name the gold . . . *you all*."

His expression didn't change.

I cleared my throat. "I'm sorry, Your Highnesses." His frown increased, so I added another "es" to my already long "Highnesses." I sounded like a snake with a stutter.

"The girl understands nothing about gold," he told me. At least he was *looking* at me, but since he was referring to me as "the girl," maybe he was talking to Haverton. Or maybe he thought I couldn't hear him. It was hard to tell with that whole insanity issue going on. I wasn't sure whether I was supposed to answer.

King John pointed at the spool. "Her name is Alfreda and when we are married, the girl will leave the handling of the gold to us."

I hesitated. "Um, do you mean when you and Alfreda are married?"

King John made clucking noises. "How ludicrous. Of course not. We meant when you and we marry."

"Oh." Unfortunately, *that* part of the fairy tale was happening right on schedule.

He walked over to me, scattering the sand circle with the bottom of his robe. He didn't even glance at it. Instead he gave me a tolerant smile. "We came to tell you the good news ourselves. If you learn to spin the straw into gold, we will marry you tomorrow morning. We know it is a rash decision, impetuous even, but what can we say? We are not ones to dally about when we're in love." He put his hand on his chest. "Romance makes us giddy."

I leaned away from him. "But I already told you—a fairy changed the straw to gold. I can't do it."

He bent down, still smiling. "Yes, but when your fairy godfather comes tonight, you shall ask him to grant you the power to do it yourself. Then you shall spin an entire roomful." King John straightened and took a couple of steps away from me, scattering more of the sand circle. "If you fail, tragically, we will turn you over to the executioner." He tilted his head, considering. "Or if you fail *tragically,* we will turn you over to the executioner." He bestowed another smile on me. "It's where you put the emphasis in the sentence that makes the difference in what is tragic. Call us crazy, but we've always loved grammar."

Without waiting for my reaction, he turned to Haverton. "Take care of the girl. We've a busy day tomorrow. Either a wedding or an execution. Flexibility is our middle name." He walked to the door, brushing up loose pieces of straw with his robes. "And Haverton, do go fetch her family so they can join her in either event." He smiled at me one last time, then went out the door.

· · ·

My third day as King John's guest proceeded much like my second day had. The chambermaid helped me wash and do my hair. I was given another dress, a finer one. It was maroon with a large band of gold brocade on the collar and around the drooping sleeves. I hated it immediately. I no longer liked the color gold.

As soon as I was alone, I called for Clover. He showed up at once, standing on the edge of the wash basin. His outfit was a brighter green than the last one he'd worn. He had on crisp new white stockings and sleek black polished boots. He stepped onto the table with a bounce in his step and surveyed the room.

"Morning, lass." He held a tiny book with a spinning wheel on the cover. "I've got *The Change Enchantment.* Where's me gold?"

"The spools are in the barn. You'll have to zap a couple away."

He let out a disgruntled breath and slapped the book against his thigh. "I can't do that. You have to give me the gold personally. Otherwise, I'm not making a bargain with *you*; I'm stealing from the king. The UMA is picky about these sorts of details."

I inwardly groaned. King John wasn't likely to let me near that gold again. "Can't I just tell you it's okay to take two?"

Clover paced back and forth across the table, glowering at me from beneath his bushy eyebrows. "I already bought new clothes, and I had to grease a few hands to get *The Change Enchantment.* I told the blokes I'd be back with their money today. Why didn't you summon me last night when the gold was done?"

"I fell asleep," I said.

"Well, if you don't want to marry King John, you'd best not fall asleep tonight. Otherwise you'll wake up to the strains of minstrels playing the wedding march." Clover tucked the book into his jacket with more force than was necessary. "A leprechaun can get in a right lot of trouble for not paying his debts. What if the UMA takes away me magic? Then I'll be no better than that ghoul of a fairy you're dealing with now." He looked upward, shaking his head. "Ah, it would just be me luck to end up emaciated in some children's story, scaring tykes before bedtime."

"I'll make sure I don't fall asleep tonight," I said.

"Aye, that's what Sleeping Beauty said before she nodded off. Let's hope you're more reliable."

And with that, he disappeared.

"Wait, come back!" I called. I wanted to ask him if he knew anything about my family. But even though I called several times, he didn't return.

They're okay, I told myself, but if I had said the words out loud, my liar's hat might have gone off. I wasn't sure I believed it.

I slumped over to the window and watched the workers in the courtyard. I saw women drawing water from the well. Men bringing barrels into the castle. A maid hanging out long white tablecloths to dry. I wondered if these were preparations for the wedding feast tomorrow.

The wedding that I still couldn't stop.

All that day, I watched the sun make a relentless path across the sky.

When it was dark, Haverton came, and another procession of guards led me to the barn. The wizard walked ahead of me, muttering and waving his wand as though directing an invisible orchestra. Hudson stood guard at the door. His gaze met mine briefly, and then I was ushered into the barn.

Mountains of straw awaited me. Great walls of it were stacked up to the ceiling. It looked like it might avalanche down and smother us. I regarded it warily, while Haverton chained me to the beam. He tucked the key securely in his pocket, like he'd done last night, but the wizard didn't draw another sand circle around me. He and Haverton had a heated conversation about this. Haverton was sure I would ask my fairy godmother for rescue, not gold, but the wizard insisted that the enchantment couldn't be given to me if I were trapped in the circle away from the fairy.

"Besides," the wizard said, flourishing his long sleeves at Haverton, "why would she ask for escape when she'll be crowned queen in the morning?"

I could have answered that question. In fact, I could have written a five-paragraph essay on the subject that would have impressed my English teacher, but they didn't ask my opinion.

In the end, Haverton relented. He muttered a few threats against my family should I escape, then placed a candle on the ground near the stool and left. The flame flickered apologetically, throwing out only a small circle of light.

I waited for Hudson. He had come inside the last two nights; surely he would come tonight. But the door remained closed. Perhaps King John had ordered so many men to guard the door that he couldn't come in undetected.

I sat down on the ground and thought about my family to make myself cry so Rumpelstiltskin would appear. But the tears didn't come. I had worried so much about them during the day that my eyes felt numb to that pain. Mostly I was just stressed out about falling asleep before I could get gold for Clover.

While I'd been shut up in the castle, I'd tried to figure out what the moral of the *Rumpelstiltskin* story was. When I had heard the story as a little girl, I thought it was that you shouldn't brag about things that weren't true, like the fact that your daughter could spin straw into gold.

That moral didn't seem right, though. My father hadn't been bragging about me. I doubted that was a vice he had a problem with. I had been taken prisoner to the castle because Haverton thought my father criticized the king.

Surely the moral of the story wasn't Don't criticize the king. King John deserved criticism, although I would wait until I was a safe distance away from him to give it.

Perhaps the moral of the story was something along the lines of "If you're innocent, then magical forces will help you. Go ahead and take magical help, even though some of that magical help might later want to eat your baby."

Really, when you think about it, *Rumpelstiltskin* is a horrible story.

I heard a noise behind me and turned, expecting to see Hudson. Instead, Chrissy sat perched on the straw, her hair falling around her shoulders in a river of glossy pink. She wore her tooth fairy uniform and was reading what looked to be a newspaper—except that instead of normal paper, it glowed like a computer screen and the headlines flashed and pulsed. She also had a sort of glow about her, like she carried her own personal sunset with her. A minty smell wafted over to me.

"Chrissy, you're here." Inside me, frustration crashed into relief like competing waves. Relief won out though, toppling and foaming over my other feelings. She had finally come. She could set things right now. I stood up. "Please, you've got to help me."

"I am," she said without taking her eyes from the paper. "At least for the duration of my break. Then it's right back to the wonderful world of swiping teeth from children." She flipped a page in the paper and let out a disgruntled sigh. "Honestly, this moonlighting gig is killing my social life. You'd think there would be more jobs for a fairy with my talent, but apparently art doesn't have to be inspired anymore. Now it's all about the gritty reality of life. Like anyone wants to pay to see that."

I tried to keep my voice calm. "My family is missing."

Her wings swept open, lazily fanning herself, and she flipped another page of her newspaper. "They're fine. Your father packed up his camping gear and they've been running around the forest having a grand time."

I imagined they weren't actually having a grand time, but at least they were alive. My heart had been strung tight in my chest, and now it relaxed a little. "We need to talk about my wish, Chrissy. If you remember, I never wished to be chained up in the Middle Ages or forced into a marriage with a half-mad old man."

"Look at this." She rustled the paper, still staring only at it. "Clover has put a rent-a-leprechaun ad in the classified section." Reading out loud, she said, "Does your event need a little luck? Let an experienced leprechaun host your next wedding, bar mitzvah, or high school reunion. Please, no children's birthday parties. Extra charge for events hosted on St. Patrick's Day." She shook her head. "He is so pathetic."

"You made a mistake, and I—"

"Speaking of pathetic, what are your pathetic numbers these days?" Chrissy folded her paper. As soon as she did, it vanished from her hands.

"I don't know." I gritted my teeth. Frustration was back, and it was the winner now. "I left the pathetic-o-meter at home, and I haven't been back since I was dragged out of there by armed guards threatening to kill either me or my father."

"No problem." Chrissy snapped her fingers, and the blue and yellow disk appeared in her hand. She stared at it. "Hmmm," she said, sounding like a doctor diagnosing a patient. "Your numbers have increased instead of decreasing. When were you yelling at inanimate objects?"

"Chrissy, I wished to be able to turn things into gold. Instead you sent me, my family, and a random guy who was on my street to the twelfth century."

Her gaze shot over to mine. "A random boy got sent here too?" She frowned and let out an irritated huff. "Well, that won't look good on my evaluation."

I held out my shackled hand to her. "Just send us home. Put everything back the way it was before. That's all I want now."

She stood up and brushed stray pieces of straw from her skirt. "I'll send you home when your fairy tale is through. Until then, I'm duty-bound to fulfill your wish. You asked to have the power to change things into gold."

"Right. That's another problem with being in this fairy tale. The miller's daughter never spun anything into gold. It was always Rumpelstiltskin who did it for her."

Chrissy flicked a piece of straw off her sleeve and it fell, fluttering onto the floor. "Nonsense. Rumpelstiltskin gives the miller's daughter the enchantment on the third night. You didn't think she would trade her baby for anything less, did you?"

I felt a prickling sense of dread. That's what King John had demanded—that I get the ability myself. But the original story wasn't that way. "The fairy tale never said she could spin the straw into gold herself."

Chrissy spread her wings out like a butterfly and they shimmered in the darkness of the barn. "I thought after our conversation about Robin Hood's story, you would have learned that you can't trust writers. They're a shiftless and unreliable bunch who spend their time making stuff up. Didn't it ever occur to you that the queen wouldn't want everyone to know she could spin straw into gold? It's bad enough that she had to spin it to get her husband. Can you imagine the friends, relatives, and salesmen who would have come out of the woodwork to pester her? You know what mortals are like."

Chrissy laughed as though she'd forgotten who was standing in front of her. "Of course *you* know. You asked for gold yourself." She shrugged her slender shoulders. "Money is easy to create, but gold is tricky. The leprechaun union has a monopoly on those enchantments. You can't just hand them out. I'm not sure how I would have granted your wish if I hadn't known of a certain leprechaun who lost his gold enchantment in a poker game to a disgraced ex-fairy."

"Ex-fairy?" I asked. "What's that?"

"If a fairy breaks magical laws, the Unified Magical Alliance strips him of his fairy power and locks it up. An ex-fairy still craves magic, though. It's part of our essence, and without it, we shrivel away and eventually die. So ex-fairies are known for stealing magic from anywhere they can take it—from wizards, pixies, unicorns, trolls—and especially other fairies. As you can imagine, ex-fairies aren't invited to many parties." Chrissy smiled airily. "I'd like to see Mistress Berrypond find fault with my methodology on this one. I'm not only granting your wish, I'm taking an enchantment away from an ex-fairy who shouldn't have it in the first place. It's killing two birds with one stone. Except you won't actually be killed. Well, probably not anyway."

"Probably?" I sputtered.

Her wings closed. "I have no control over what happens after you make your wish. Giants, kings, and pirates tend to kidnap things that can produce gold. And Rumpelstiltskin is ruthless. You know what they say, 'An ex-fairy is a vengeful fairy.' "

This didn't make me feel better. "How would I know that anyone says that?"

"Oh. Well, they do." Chrissy checked her watch. "My break's about over."

I held out my hands, trying to keep her from leaving, trying to make her understand. "You can't make me go through with this. I didn't know any of this would happen when I made my wish."

She looked at me benevolently. "Well, that puts you on par with the rest of humanity, doesn't it? Wishes are powerful things. You can't expect them to change the world without changing you too." Her eyes didn't leave mine and she let out a sigh.

I thought she'd taken pity on me and would help me somehow.

Instead, she pulled her wand from her purse and swished it in my direction. "Really, with your fair complexion, you shouldn't go without lipstick." She gave me a satisfied smile, and then the light around her drew in on itself, shrinking into a pinpoint until she disappeared.

I was alone and still chained up, but now I was wearing lipstick.

Stupid fairy.

I tried to walk over and kick the stool, but the chain held me back and I was only able to kick uselessly at some stray strands of straw.

After this brief and pointless flare of temper, I sank down to the floor and glared at the walls. No wonder Chrissy needed extra credit. Her fairy godmother skills were woefully lacking. Which meant I couldn't count on her. I was on my own, grappling with a fate I didn't want. Again.

No, I wasn't completely on my own. Hudson was here. He was trying to help me. I looked to the door, hoping he would come in.

It was easy to conjure up images of Hudson, easy to picture his dark brown eyes and square jaw. Too easy. I made a quick, panicked inventory of my feelings.

Hudson and I were in the same situation, and it had created a bond between us. It was the only reason I wanted to see him so badly right now. It didn't have anything to do with the fact that he was tall and handsome, or that he had an air of confidence about him, a sturdy competence . . . that he was the type of person who could be dropped into a completely different world and still find a way to survive, to get what he needed.

The girls at school had said he was sullen and didn't date anymore, didn't socialize. He clearly didn't want a girlfriend, so he was the last guy I should start getting romantic ideas about.

I forced myself to turn away from the door. I had no guarantee that Hudson would help me get home. He might just use my help to get the Gilead and then go home without me. I couldn't let myself fall for him. Bo had said he loved me, and it hadn't been real. My parents had said they loved each other, and that hadn't

been real either. Romantic love was as unreliable and dangerous as fairy magic and should be avoided at all costs.

I wrapped my arms around my knees and let my chin sink
into the silky material of my dress. Despite the warning to
myself, I still wanted to see Hudson. I watched the closed door
and felt downright needy. I didn't know how to make the emotion stop. How did you take away a longing that lay deep inside—
a longing to love someone else?

Would he come in if I called him? Why wasn't he coming
on his own?

"Hudson . . . ," I whispered. But I didn't call his name. And
he didn't open the door. A single tear rolled down my cheek.
The next moment, I was staring at a pair of pointed leather
boots in front of me.

Rumpelstiltskin had come back.

Chapter 13

I gulped and looked up at Rumpelstiltskin. He bent down and wiped the tear from my cheek, shaking his head slowly. "What a wicked man to treat you thus."

"What?" For a moment I thought he'd peered into my mind and read my thoughts about Hudson. Could fairies do that?

"Giving King John a taste of gold has been akin to giving a wild dog a taste of blood. He won't let go of a fine morsel like you." His sorrowful tone didn't match the glint of pleasure in his eyes. He had wanted King John to make more demands of me.

Rumpelstiltskin's hand was still on my cheek. I stood up so I could step away from him.

He gazed around the room at the towering stacks of straw and tsk-tsked. "He'll have no straw for bedding if he keeps this up. No doubt about it. Does he plan to make you spin every night? What did he tell you?"

"He said I had to get the ability to turn the straw into gold myself, or he would execute me and my family. If I do spin the straw into gold, he'll marry me. I consider the second fate only a little better than the first."

Rumpelstiltskin laughed, but I wasn't joking.

He walked around me with what I imagine was supposed to look like a thoughtful expression on his face. His motion reminded me of the way a shark circled its prey. "Has King John taken your family?"

"No, but he asked Haverton to find them."

Rumpelstiltskin stopped in front of me and pulled a small hand mirror out of his breast pocket. It sat in a decorative frame with such lifelike gold leaves entwined around it that I knew it had to be magic. "I can show you your family, if you'd like." He placed the mirror in my hand. It felt light and warm as though it had been lying in the sun. I looked into it, but instead of seeing my reflection, I only saw smooth blackness.

Rumpelstiltskin leaned over my shoulder. "Say their names, and the glass will show you where they are."

I hesitated. It seemed dangerous to take gifts from Rumpelstiltskin, but I wanted to see my father and Nick and Sandra so badly—to know they were okay. I gripped the warm mirror and said, "Frank Miller." Wherever he was, the others would be too.

The glass fogged with blurry shapes and colors flitting across it; then the picture cleared, grew sharp. And there was my father, his face painted a camouflage green, standing in front of Nick. My father still had the paintbrush in his hand and was painting Nick's face too. A fire must have been going nearby because there was enough light not only to see them, but to see the trees around them.

I hadn't noticed the words that appeared on the bottom of the glass until Rumpelstiltskin read them. "River Bend. That's not far from here. I wonder why they've come so close to the castle."

"Why are they painting their faces?" I asked.

Rumpelstiltskin frowned as though it were of no consequence. "Mortals do such odd things. They're hard to understand, aren't they?" He took the mirror from my hands, and it clouded, then went blank.

I had to fight the urge to snatch it back. I wanted to see my father and Nick again, to try to figure out what they were doing.

"The important thing," Rumpelstiltskin went on, "is that they're alive and safe. Now we must worry about your safety." He leaned so close his breath brushed against my cheek. It smelled of fires and autumn leaves. "I can give you the enchantment that turns things into gold, and then King John will not only spare your life, he'll elevate you to queen. As his wife, you'll be protected and cherished."

Protected and cherished? Rumpelstiltskin had either never met King John, or didn't think I had.

"As fond as I am of you," Rumpelstiltskin went on, "I would hate to part with such a powerful enchantment. I'm not certain what I'd ask for it." He made a show of looking me over. "You have no other jewelry, but after you marry the king, he'll give you many things. You'll have so many treasures, you won't miss one. So, in exchange for giving you my gold enchantment now, I'll come back in a year, and you must consent to give me whatever I choose." He smiled and it sent chills down my spine. "Do we have an agreement?"

That's how it happened then. Rumpelstiltskin had saved the miller's daughter's life twice and asked for trinkets in return. Why wouldn't she have trusted him? Why would she have expected him to ask for her child? I had always thought she cared more about her own life than her baby's. But perhaps selling away your children didn't happen all at once. Perhaps selling your children, your future, just happened one bad decision at a time.

Rumpelstiltskin held out his thin hand to me. "Shall we shake on our bargain, Mistress Miller?"

He was trying to trick me into agreeing to his terms. I felt a surge of anger deeper than this room and this story. He wanted to hurt me and expected me to thank him for it.

I wasn't about to calmly go along with it. As soon as I got *The Change Enchantment* from Clover, I was going back to my day. I wouldn't make any bargains here that could bring Rumpelstiltskin to my future hospital maternity room. This deal would be on my terms.

I shook my head. "No. You want my firstborn child. I'm not going to give him to you."

Rumpelstiltskin drew a sharp breath and took a step backward. I'd surprised him, but he recovered soon enough. A mask of humor came over his face. "Why would you think that? What need do I have of a human child?"

"If you don't want my child, then fine, write it down in a contract. You can have any piece of jewelry you want, but you can't have my children. Ever. I'll make that bargain with you."

His face grew hard, and his lips twitched in anger. "I saved your life twice, and now I offer you untold wealth. You're an ungrateful girl. You care nothing for all I've done for you."

"So I've been told by my parents more than once. You can't guilt me into anything. I've had practice resisting that sort of thing. Go ahead—ask how long my mother was in labor with me." I nodded philosophically. "Eighteen hours. Without painkillers."

He pointed a bony finger at me. "You'll die without my help."

I paced slowly back and forth in front of him. "Are you allowed to buy human children? Does the Alliance know about this?" I had hoped that the name of the Alliance would strike some fear into him. After all, they had stripped him of his fairy powers.

But he laughed, and it was a hollow sound. "When you're queen, you can have as many children as you desire. You'll have none if you die in the morning."

I didn't answer, just kept pacing. The chain rattled dully against the ground as I moved.

He strolled over to one of the straw mounds, his silhouette as sparse as a shadow. He scooped up a handful, muttered something I couldn't hear, and the straw changed to golden sticks in his palm. He held them out to me. "Think of the wealth you'll have. You'll want for nothing."

"Unless I want my firstborn child."

He turned his palm and tipped the golden straw to the ground. "Mistress Miller . . . be reasonable."

It irked me that he kept calling me "Mistress Miller," as though I didn't need an actual name. Mistress Miller was a title that had nothing to do with me. I had never milled anything in my life.

I stopped pacing and folded my arms. "Why do you want a baby anyway?"

"Does it matter? Would you believe me if I told you?" His lips twisted into a suggestion of a grin. "Very well, then. I want to be a father."

He was right. I didn't believe him.

He picked up another piece of straw and twirled it lazily between his fingers. "This child doesn't even exist yet, and you're willing to give your life for it? What an odd species you are." He muttered something and the straw between his fingers turned to gold mid twirl. "Although perhaps it's just you, and not your species. Plenty of your kind discard their own children, don't they? Tell me, did your father let out a peep when the king's men carted you off to the castle to pay for his sins?"

"I told him to let the king's men take me."

Rumpelstiltskin tilted his head in mock understanding. "And he listened to you. How noble."

"My father is a good person," I said.

Rumpelstiltskin ignored my statement. "Besides, maybe your firstborn child will be a girl and thus quite expendable."

I expected him to sneer after saying this, but he didn't. He regarded me as though making a valid point. He not only believed girls were dispensable, he expected me to agree with him. Then I remembered what I had learned in history class about men's attitudes toward women during the Middle Ages. Women were property, without a say in anything. Men wanted sons, and women were just the means of creating them.

No wonder Rumpelstiltskin called me Mistress Miller. He had probably never bothered to learn my name.

Pointedly I said, "I don't think girls are expendable."

"You must think that *you* are expendable if you're not willing to bargain with me. You'll be killed in the morning—you and your family." He tapped the golden straw against his lip, considering the matter. "I wonder how King John will do it."

The mention of my family made me shiver. "My family is safe."

"For the moment, true, but not for long, since I'll tell the guards where they are if you don't agree to my terms. Your family will be easy enough to catch."

My heart banged into my ribs. Rumpelstiltskin had given me the mirror to trick me into revealing my family's location, and I had done it. How could I have been so foolish?

He flipped the straw he'd been twirling. It gleamed for one brief moment in the candlelight, then sank and disappeared into the straw mound. "You may not care about your own life, but are you willing to trade the lives of your entire family for an unborn baby?"

I swallowed hard. I had to make the bargain. My only choice was in the wording. "Fine. If you give me the enchantment so I can turn things into gold, I'll let you have any of my possessions—but you only have a year from this day to ask. Any children I have after the year 1200 are forever out of your reach."

Rumpelstiltskin sauntered over to me. "You think you can put off the wedding night for a year?"

I didn't answer. He laughed again. "Very well. I agree to your terms. You're a fair maiden and I'll wager on King John's impatience." He reached out and took my hand. I felt like I was shaking hands with a skeleton.

Then he stepped away from me and rubbed his bony hands together, not for warmth—in anticipation, to get down to business. "If I still had my wand, I could give you the enchantment that way. As it is, things are more complicated."

He undid the top buttons of his shirt, revealing a pale, sickly chest. Chrissy had a glow about her skin, but Rumpelstiltskin had the pallor of a corpse. He reached under the folds of his shirt, flinched, and yanked something shiny off his skin. As he walked toward me, he held out the object for me to see. It was a golden heart, pulsing in his hand like a living thing.

I stepped backward. "What is that?"

"It's the enchantment. Once I give this to you, only you will be able to take it off again. I wouldn't though—all sorts of folk would try to steal it from you."

I watched the thrumming heart, and took another nervous step backward. "And once I'm wearing it, I'll be able to turn whatever I want into gold?"

"Just touch the object, say its name, and repeat, 'Gold, gold, gold.' Whatever you touch will transform."

"If you could change objects that easily, why did you bother spinning the straw into gold?"

He smiled like it was a foolish question. "Because that's what the king requested. Now then, stay still so I can give you your new heart."

He reached out and put the golden heart on the exposed skin above the collar of my dress. I jolted with shock. The heart was so cold it burned. Rumpelstiltskin moved his hand away, and I expected the heart to fall to the ground. It didn't. It flattened itself and slowly slid downward under the collar of my dress. I could feel the freezing trail it left until it perched directly over my own heart. Then it burrowed into my skin.

I gasped and put my hand to my chest. "It hurts."

"Most things in life do."

It was squeezing my own heart, making it hard to breathe. "How long will the pain last?"

He shrugged. "Does that matter? Now you can have all the gold you want."

I tried to pull it off. Rumpelstiltskin had said I'd be able to take it off. I pried at its edges but it only dug deeper into my skin. "What does gold matter if I can't breathe?" I asked. He didn't answer. I looked up and found I was alone in the room.

The pain was worse now. I sank to the ground, still keeping my hand over my heart. I felt something wet, and when I looked down, I saw blood dotting my hand.

I needed help, magical help. Clover had said he would come when I had gold for him, but I was chained to the beam and couldn't even reach the straw, let alone turn any of it to gold. I pulled at my chain in frustration. It rattled angrily, as though I had woken it from a deep sleep. How could I reach the straw to change it?

But then again, maybe it was better that I couldn't. I grasped hold of the chain. "Chain and shackle, gold, gold, gold!"

The words brought an extra jolt to my heart, and I flinched so hard I nearly missed the transformation. Like an artist painting a bold color across a canvas, a golden color swept across the dull gray of the chains. The chain was denser now and so heavy it weighed my hand down.

I didn't take time to examine it. "Clover!" I called. "I have gold for you!"

The leprechaun appeared near the candle, still wearing his new outfit. He gazed at the mountains of straw surrounding us. "Do you? Where? It looks like you've been slacking off to me."

"Over here." I tried to sit as still as possible. If I didn't move, my heart hurt less.

Clover walked toward me and saw the chain. "Well," he said. "I guess that's what you call being tied to your money, isn't it?"

"The enchantment is squeezing my heart," I told him. "How do I make it stop?"

He grunted and picked up one link of the chain to examine it. "That enchantment was never meant for human folk. Of course it's not going to fit right. But don't worry, the pain will subside in a bit." He glanced over at me, and his attention zeroed in on the bloodstains dotting my dress. "You're too tender-hearted," he said. "It's making you bleed. Try not to feel things so much."

"I don't know how to do that," I said.

Clover let out a sigh. "Women. This is why no one ever puts you in charge of wars, butchering animals, or assembling hockey teams." He held up a link of the chain. "Here, look at this for a bit and it will help. See how it gleams and shimmers? See how smooth it is? Like a sunbeam, it is. Like a sturdy friend. Now doesn't your heart feel better?"

It didn't. But focusing on my objectives did lessen the pain. And my objective now was to get *The Change Enchantment* from Clover and get out of here. I only hoped the book wasn't painful too.

"You can have this entire golden chain and shackle if you'll give me *The Change Enchantment*," I said.

Clover momentarily stopped stroking the chain. "We agreed to trade for two spools of gold."

I lifted my hand, showing him the shackle. "I can't reach the straw. I won't be able to change it until morning when Haverton comes to free me and then they'll probably watch me all day. Who knows how long it will take until I can get some spools for you, and your creditors are waiting."

Clover plucked at his beard, looked back at the mountains of straw, then stroked the chain again. "Very well." He leaned toward me. "But you mustn't tell Chrissy. As far as she knows, I was never here and this story is going exactly as planned." He reached into his jacket and took out the tiny book I'd seen earlier. He placed it in my palm and it grew until it was the size of a picture book. The spinning wheel on the front not only shone like embossed gold, but the wheel turned slowly. A quill pen was attached to the inside cover in a flap. Instead of black ink, I saw a drop of liquid gold at its point.

Clover lowered his voice to a whisper. "Complete the story your own way and write the moral in the back of the book. Once you do that, your fairy tale is done, and Chrissy will have to take the lot of you home." He cast a nervous glance around the room. "And if she doesn't know you changed things, all the better."

"That's it?" I asked.

"Aye," he said, but he wasn't paying attention to me any longer. He took the gold chain in his hands and kissed it. At once the links broke apart. They flew in the air, suspended, and spun into small disks—coins. A black pot appeared below them, and they rained down into it, clinking noisily as they landed.

Clover tipped his hat at me. "I'm off to pay me debts, then see the lads for a bit of poker." And with that, the leprechaun and his pot vanished.

Chapter 14

I rubbed my hand where the handcuff had been. I was free from that at least. I walked over to the candle, wincing. The pain in my chest had subsided but moving made it worse. I eased myself down to sitting position and opened the book. On the first page, written in elaborate script, was a paragraph telling how the miller's daughter had been taken from her home. On the opposite page was a finely painted picture of the events. And I was the girl in the picture.

Time stopped as I stared at the illustration. There I was, captured in an artist's brush strokes, being led to the carriage. My hair flowed around my shoulders in luxurious blond waves that I was sure hadn't been there in the real event, and I wore a brown dress instead of the jeans I'd really had on. Apparently illustrators took liberties with stories too.

In the picture, I was looking over my shoulder at my family. My eyes were wide, frightened, apologetic.

I ran my finger along the page as though I might be able to

rub away the expression. Clover was right. I did feel things too much.

I turned the page. It showed me in the tower room next to the stack of straw, staring at it and weeping. I didn't like seeing myself that way, vulnerable, where any passing reader could see my pain. I flipped to the next page. It was my first meeting with Rumpelstiltskin. I was handing him my necklace as he looked at me hungrily. Who had painted these pictures? How had they known these details? Did the book just magically record them?

I flipped ahead until I reached a picture where I wore a maroon and gold dress and was shaking hands with Rumpelstiltskin—that had happened only moments ago.

I turned the page, holding my breath to see what it would reveal. A picture of me in a wedding dress, a crown upon my head, was fading. For a moment I saw my own eyes staring up at me and then they disappeared, leaving the page blank. I flipped through the rest of the book. It was a series of empty pages. Lines on one side, a framed picture of nothing on the other.

I wanted to hug the book in relief. Instead, I picked up the quill and scribbled down words as fast as they came to me.

The miller's daughter changed the straw into gold, took some with her, and was able to walk out the unlocked door and flee the castle yard altogether. She met up with her family outside the castle walls where they had been safely waiting for her. The king was so happy to have so much gold that he spent the next week counting and admiring it and didn't come after the miller's daughter or her family.

I glanced back at what I'd written. To my horror, it was fading off the page.

"No!" I brought the book closer to my face hoping the words would still exist if I looked at them close up.

But they were gone. What did that mean?

Maybe the words hadn't remained in the book because I hadn't actually done the things I'd written. Maybe I couldn't finish the story by dictating the events. But then, how *did* I finish it? Was there some sort of formula for knowing when a story ended?

I stared at the book.

Who was to say the story wasn't already finished? I was the author. I voted that this was a good place for the story to end. Which meant all I needed was a moral, and we would be back in the twenty-first century.

I put the pen on the top of the page.

The miller's daughter was extremely grateful that she didn't have to marry the horrid king who'd been threatening to kill her, and she learned an important moral: Do not make bargains with magical beings. The End.

The golden ink shimmered in the candlelight, then faded away. I felt sparks of panic igniting inside me. This *had* to work. It was my way home. I just had to get the moral right. Luckily, I had the entire night before King John came for me. I would find the right one.

I sat by the candle and wrote every moral that seemed possible. I tried vague ones: *Good prevails over evil. All that glitters isn't gold.* I tried specific ones: *Fairy men are male chauvinists. Be careful what you wish for if your fairy godmother is more concerned about finding a new job than improving your life.*

I tried my first ideas: *Don't brag about things you can't do. Make sure your father doesn't brag about things you can't do.*

Nothing stuck.

Finally I put down the book and rubbed my eyes. It was useless, and it was late, and there was obviously something that Clover hadn't told me. I called him, knowing even as I did, that he wouldn't come. He was off playing poker and the best I could hope for was that he'd lose quickly and come back for more gold.

I picked up the pen again and wrote: *Poker is a terrible vice.*

Nope. It faded away as soon as I added the period at the end of the sentence.

I would have to escape on my own, and hope that I could figure out the right moral soon. I tucked the pen into its flap, then stood up, stiff from sitting hunched over the book for so long. I walked to the nearest pile of straw, placed my hands on top of it, and whispered, "Straw, gold, gold, gold."

I felt a stab of pain in my chest, as though the power had ripped its way out of my heart, but the transformation was immediate. The straw under my hands was no longer light and prickly. It was a jumble of golden sticks. However, only the straw I'd been touching changed. The rest of it still stood there, unaffected.

At this rate, it would take the entire night and then some to change all the straw.

I really did hope that if King John found the room filled with gold in the morning, he'd be more concerned with guarding, moving, and inventorying it than tracking me down. Could I add measurements to the chant?

I put my hands on a different patch of straw. "Straw mound, gold, gold, gold." The pain was so bad I gasped and shut my eyes, but when I opened them the entire mound had been reduced to a pile of golden twigs.

That was faster. I waited for several minutes until it no longer felt like my heart was beating against razor blades, then walked to the next pile. It was a little bigger than the last and I winced as I put my hands against the coarse straw. I knew what was coming. "Straw mound, gold, gold, gold."

Pain ripped through me as the straw collapsed into a golden heap.

I looked around the room. Seven more mountainous straw piles were pushed against the walls. "I *can't* change it all," I said aloud. "Not even King John needs this much gold." But when the throbbing in my heart subsided, I walked to the next mound, and the next, until half the room was a glittering mess of tangled gold twigs.

Vague sounds filtered in from outside. Faraway commands boomed out from deep, distant voices. I had no idea what it meant. Was it a nighttime guard drill of some sort? I wished whoever was yelling would go to bed. It would be harder to escape if people were running around the courtyard.

I put my hand over my heart. It was no longer bleeding, and the pain was lessening too, or perhaps I was just getting used to it.

I was moving to the sixth mound when the door burst open and Hudson stepped inside. He gripped a large ax in one hand and had a look of grim determination on his face. I froze. It generally isn't good news when ax-wielding men come looking for you. The cynical part of me said: *See, you always go for the wrong guys. He came here to kill you.*

Hudson's gaze went to the beam where I'd been chained and his brows dipped in worry. He scanned the room, taking in the piles of gold, and then saw me. Relief flashed across his face, and he motioned for me to come to him. "We've got to go. The castle is under attack."

"What?" That couldn't be right. That didn't happen in the story.

I grabbed the magic book and the candle. As I hurried toward Hudson, I cast glances at the ax in his hand. "Are they coming in here? Is that why you have an ax?"

"I brought this to cut through your chain. How did you get free?"

"Clover helped me." I didn't say more, and he didn't ask. I ran the rest of the way over to him, ignoring the jabs of pain the motion caused. My mind was focused on the words "under attack." Well, most of my mind was anyway. The sentimental, romantic part was busy gloating over its victory against the cynical part. *He came to rescue you, not kill you,* it said, and then it sighed dramatically.

We reached the door, but he didn't open it. "Who's attacking?" I asked.

"We don't know." Hudson dropped the ax and unsheathed his sword. "Some men put up ladders and were over the wall before the watch could stop them. We can only see a few dozen men outside the wall, but they're good shots and they're keeping the garrison busy."

He opened the door a crack and peered out.

"Where are we going?" I asked. An attack on the castle meant I couldn't escape tonight—not when guards were marching around inside the gates and dangerous men were on the other side.

"We've got to get the Gilead."

He tried to pull me out the door but I resisted. "What?" I asked. "You want to break into King John's bedroom now?"

Hudson let out a frustrated breath. "I left my post to get you, Tansy. Haverton didn't want you freed, but I couldn't leave you chained here while enemies were roaming around. Do you know what they'll do when they find me?" He held a hand out in the direction of the castle. "King John is probably out with the captain of the guard. If you don't want to wait for a wedding, we need to get the Gilead now."

I fingered the magic book in my hand. I hadn't been able to make it work. Maybe it wouldn't. The wizard might be our best bet to get home. "Okay," I said, "let's go."

Scanning the darkness, Hudson led me onto the grounds. I kept pace with him even though each quick step sent shivers of pain into my chest. The candle flame jiggled in my hand, threatening to go out.

I didn't want to go to the castle or be anywhere near King John—not when I knew what the story had planned for me next. It felt like no matter what I did, I couldn't change the fairy tale. I was turning a page and heading right into the wedding dress portion of the book. I would spend my days guarded, turning things into gold while pain jolted my heart because I had an enchantment that was never intended for humans.

I was breathless when we reached the castle guards. Hudson told them that King John had sent for me and they let us through without question. The castle was dim now. The torches hanging on the walls cast shadows that pooled across the corridor floors in crisscrossing circles.

Hudson held on firmly to my arm, so I couldn't make a break for it. I wasn't sure whether that was for show or if he really did worry that I'd have second thoughts about his plan.

A few of the people we passed gave me appraising looks, checking, I suppose, to see what the king's fiancée looked like, but most of the servants ignored us. They were preparing for a full assault, carrying pots of boiling oil and huge stones to throw down on the attackers.

We reached a set of circular stairs. They were in a different part of the castle than the other stairs I'd gone up, but they were identical: jutting stones, no handrail, so narrow we had to go up single file. Hudson went in front, holding the candle up so that light spilled back to me. His long legs strode upward, outpacing me. My breaths came in labored pants and my heart started bleeding again. I knew because I could feel my dress sticking to my chest.

Hudson turned, saw me struggling, and came back. He held out his hand for me, then noticed the blood on my dress. He grabbed hold of my arm as though I might tumble down the stairs if he didn't. "What happened? Were you stabbed? Why didn't you say something?"

Between breaths, I said, "Rumpelstiltskin gave me an enchantment so I could turn things into gold myself. That's where it attached itself." I wiped at the spot. "Apparently I'm too tender-hearted."

He didn't let go of my arm. He kept staring at the spot.

"I'll be fine in a minute." I looked up the stairs. "Probably."

Hudson took hold of my hand and we walked up the stairs slower. He kept checking over his shoulder to see how I was doing.

"What if King John is in his bedroom?" I whispered.

"I'll tell him you were so worried about your safety that you begged me to take you inside the castle. I agreed and then you wanted to see him about something."

"I can't lie."

"Then don't," he said. "*Want* to see King John. Think of something you want to tell him."

Not hard to do. I wanted to tell him I wouldn't marry him. I couldn't say that though.

I thought about it for a few steps then decided I could tell him I had left some of the straw unchanged. People and animals both used it for bedding, so I could ask him if he wanted me to change something else into gold instead.

"What will we do once we have the Gilead?" I asked, half whispering, half panting.

"We'll find a way over the walls."

"During a siege?"

"It's only a small group that's attacking. It will be over soon."

Sooner than morning? "The fairy tale says my wedding is tomorrow."

He glanced back at the book clutched against my side. "Isn't that Clover's *Change Enchantment*? I thought it was supposed to let you alter the ending so you could de-wed-ify tomorrow."

"I've been trying to change the story, but I don't know how." I held the book up to look at it. "I'm not sure this thing is even working."

"Sure it's working." He smiled back at me. "The original story has no mention of the handsome and dashing young guard who saved the miller's daughter from her room on the last night."

"Maybe the author left it out because he was killed tragically by falling down a dangerous staircase. Who built this thing anyway?"

Hudson's breath was hardly even labored. "The stairs were made with defense in mind. People going up can't use their swords in their right hands without banging them into the wall. So in a fight, the person coming down the stairs always has the advantage."

"Great," I said. "We're going up." I nearly stumbled, and his grip on my arm tightened.

He paused to let me catch my breath. I paused to hug the wall and consider all of the things a person could break while falling down the stairs.

Hudson watched my newfound affection for the wall. "You're not afraid of heights, are you?"

"No, I'm fine with heights. It's plunging to my death that worries me."

He gave my hand a squeeze and pulled me slowly up the stairs again. "Just don't look down and don't think about it."

The best way to guarantee that you'll think about something is to have someone tell you *not* to think about it. All I could think about were long, uneven circular steps that went up higher and higher so you could fall farther. "How did you learn that stuff about the stairs being built for defense?" I asked.

"I've been here for three months. You pick things up. I could tell you how they tan leather, forge steel, and salt meat."

"Oh. All I've learned is how to take a bath with two inches of water."

He laughed and I liked the warm sound of it.

Finally, we reached the third story, left the stairwell, and went down a corridor. The hallway was empty, but rows of tapestries hung on the wall. Wild-eyed unicorns and running boars stared at us through embroidered forests. We came to an ornate wooden door. Hudson knocked. "Sire?"

I waited, heart still pounding from the climb, to see if King John would answer.

Please don't be there. I pressed the book to my chest hoping this would magically help the wish come true.

No one answered. Hudson pushed the door open and we slipped inside. It was a sitting room of sorts, perhaps a place where King John met with visitors. We didn't stop in this room, just walked through it to a door on the other side. Hudson knocked on this door as well. "Sire?"

The seconds plodded by. No one answered here either. We crept inside and shut the door behind us.

Hudson held the candle up to better take in the room. The dim light revealed a large canopy bed—the original king size—a few chairs, a couple of small tables, a wooden chest, and dozens of gold spools. They spread out over the floor. One had been unwound and lay draped across a chair. I wondered if it was my old friend Bob the spool.

Hudson and I padded around the room together, searching. I didn't see any plants. We went to the table by the window. It was empty except for a bowl full of coins. I pointed at it. "I suppose that's King John's mad money."

The corner of Hudson's mouth lifted, but he forced back the smile and continued rummaging through things. As the candlelight fell on the gold, each spool shined.

"King John named all of those," I said. "But then, that's not surprising since he's the sort of man who thinks money talks. Probably literally."

Hudson was barely paying attention to what I said. His gaze swept around the room. "It's got to be here. I've looked everywhere else."

"Have you forgotten that King John is insane? He might keep it in his fish pond or his pantry or maybe he set up a little house for it with some friendly shrubbery."

Hudson went back to the table by the window even though

there were clearly no plants sitting on it. "He might be crazy, but he's no fool. The plant is too valuable for him to—" He grunted as if he couldn't believe how stupid he'd been, then bent down and looked under the table. At first I thought King John had thrown a robe down there, but once Hudson pulled the thing out, I realized we hadn't seen the Gilead because we'd been thinking like people from the twenty-first century. In modern homes, you didn't have to worry about keeping plants away from cold, drafty windows.

King John must have put the plant on the table during the day to get some sun, then covered it and moved it underneath the table to protect it during the night.

Hudson took the cover off, revealing a foot-tall bush. It seemed to be mostly twigs, with only a scattering of tiny oval leaves on its branches. Hudson smiled and took a knife from his belt. "There's our ticket home."

He cut a stem from the plant, making it look mournfully unbalanced. King John was bound to realize someone had hacked part of it off the moment he saw it.

Hudson tucked the stem into a pouch at his belt, placed the cover back onto the plant, and then pushed the pot back underneath the table. "I can almost feel the warm shower and taste the pizza. And yes, I do plan to do those things simultaneously."

I was just happy we could leave King John's room. I didn't want to stay in here one second longer than I had to. We hurried out of the bedroom and through the sitting room. Hudson reached for the door handle.

Before he could open it, the door swung open, and King John walked into the room.

Chapter 15

King John's eyes flew wide open and then narrowed as he saw us. He drew his sword in one quick motion—so smoothly that the oil lamp in his other hand didn't even wobble. "What's this?" he growled. "Trespassers?"

I could only grip the book to my chest like a shield and stare in surprise, but Hudson gave him a quick bow. "Sire, your fiancée asked that I take her to you. I thought it was best not to leave her chained up among piles of gold while invaders roam the grounds. I knew you wouldn't want her hurt or kidnapped."

King John lowered his sword, but didn't sheath it. I watched the blade warily.

Certain things shouldn't be mixed together. Crazy people and weapons are two of those things.

Would King John be able to beat Hudson in a sword fight? Hudson was taller, younger, and stronger, but he had only been practicing for a few months.

At the mention of piles of gold, King John turned his attention to me. "Did the fairy give you the enchantment as we instructed?"

When I nodded, an expression of glee bloomed across his face. I wondered if he'd be as excited if I told him I had to trade our firstborn child to get the enchantment.

I wanted to glance at Hudson, to ask him with my eyes what we were supposed to do next. I didn't dare. I couldn't give King John any hint that I knew my guard.

King John put his lamp on a table next to the door, then plucked the book out of my hands. "Is this the enchantment?"

I had to restrain myself from grabbing it back. "No, that's a storybook. The enchantment is attached to my heart."

King John clutched the book, but his gaze traveled to the bodice of my dress. "Ah yes, the heart is the right place for it. Easier to keep track of." He tossed the book onto the table and smiled. "Mother always said we should marry a girl with a heart of gold. How right she was." He still didn't sheath his sword. "Now then, what did you wish to discuss with us? If it is details about the wedding, we can't be bothered. We are currently busy crushing our enemies."

I made sure no lie slipped into my words. "I didn't change all of the straw. I figured the castle might need it and I can turn something else to gold instead. Or if you would rather, I can change the straw." I gave a nervous curtsy. "Forgive me. It was wrong of me to bother you when you're busy crushing enemies."

I made to go but he held his sword across the doorframe, blocking the way. "Do we understand you correctly? You can turn other things to gold?"

Out of the corner of my eye, I caught a glimpse of Hudson. His jaw was clenched, his expression tense. We were still in danger. When King John uncovered the Gilead in the morning, he would know the truth behind our visit tonight. Hudson and I had to escape from the castle before then. But King John

probably wouldn't let me walk out of here now. He'd call Haverton and have him chain me to something else.

No wonder the miller's daughter had to send out servants
to discover Rumpelstiltskin's name. She was probably under
lock and key the rest of her life.

King John leaned toward me, still keeping his sword firmly
across the doorway. "What else can you turn to gold, my dear?"

"I'll show you." I put my hand gingerly on the edge of the
sword and forced a smile at him. "Sword, gold, gold, gold."

My heart gave a little rip of pain and then the silver sheen
on the sword blazed into gold. The next moment the sword
dropped from King John's hand and clanged to the stone floor.
It had become too heavy for him to hold.

Instead of being distressed that he was now weaponless,
King John chortled and knelt on the ground to examine the
sword. "It's sublime," he whispered. "It's exquisite." He caressed
the shining hilt. "We shall have dishes and tables and fountains
of gold. We shall have an entire castle of gold."

He looked up at me, the greed fixed in his eyes. Which was
why he didn't notice Hudson pick up a bottle from the table,
and why he didn't see Hudson swing it toward his head.

"We shall—," King John started. Then the bottle hit him, and
he fell to the ground with a thud.

"—have an immense headache when we awake," Hudson
finished. "Here, help me drag His Majesties into their bedroom."

I took one of King John's arms, Hudson took the other, and
we pulled him across the floor and behind the bed where he
wouldn't be visible. "He won't be out for long," Hudson said,
"and when he comes to, he'll be fit to be tied. So we'd better tie
him up now."

Luckily, it wasn't hard to find string. Golden spools of it were
everywhere. We wound it around his arms and legs. Then Hudson cut part of the bed's canopy and made it into a gag. "That
will buy us a little time," he said.

But I wanted even more time. "I'll weigh him down," I said, grabbing hold of his sleeve. "Shirt, gold, gold, gold."

Nothing happened. I felt no pain. The cloth didn't change. "It didn't work," I said, puzzled.

Hudson cast a nervous glance at the door. "Maybe because you didn't call it by the right name. It's a tunic, not a shirt."

I tried again. "Tunic, gold, gold, gold."

I felt the jolt in my heart and knew it worked even before I saw the cloth transform to metal. I changed his robe, leggings, and boots. It would take him a while to get off the floor while wearing heavy, unbending clothes. And just as long to figure out how to remove the golden clothing from his body.

King John was no longer quite so flexible.

"Wow," Hudson said, helping me to my feet. "When you break off an engagement, you do it in a big way. Remind me never to tick you off."

"You already have ticked me off."

He laughed and took hold of my hand. As we hurried out of the room, I picked up the magic book from the table. We slipped out into the corridor, where Hudson moved to holding my arm instead. It was all for show, I knew, the way he was holding my arm. When people saw us, they were supposed to think he was a guard taking me someplace. But I wanted to hold his hand—for real. I didn't want to feel his coarse leather glove on my sleeve; I wanted to lazily intertwine my fingers with his.

I pushed the thought away. Hudson had as much as said he was only helping me because I was Nick's sister.

While we went down the stairs, Hudson filled me in on the escape plans. "I know where some rope is. We can attach it to a merlon and climb down the back wall."

"A merlon?" I asked. The only Merlin I knew from the Middle Ages was King Arthur's wizard.

"It's the part of the wall that sticks up," he said. "You'll need a disguise—one of the guard uniforms." He glanced at me and sighed. "We'll hope nobody gets too close to you. I can already tell you won't make a very convincing man." Hudson's gaze was straight ahead now, and yet I still felt it on me, appraising me. "Where in the world did you get lipstick from, anyway?" he asked.

"My fairy godmother. She feels makeup is very important."

"Just what we need right now—your lips to be a glossy red." He shot another disgruntled glance at me. "I've never seen anyone with such big eyes."

I do have large eyes. I've always liked them. "What's wrong with them?"

"They're girl eyes," he said. "Princess eyes. I bet if you start singing right now, woodland creatures will come out and help with our escape."

I laughed, and the motion hurt my heart. Still, it felt good to laugh. "And I would accept their help," I said.

When we reached the ground floor, Hudson took hold of my elbow and strode purposefully down the corridors. No one questioned us. Not even when we went outside.

We made our way across the courtyard as quickly as we could, heading toward the guardhouse. Above us on the wall, men yelled things to each other. Archers stood behind the tall parts of the castle wall, then leaned over and quickly shot through the gaps. An occasional arrow flew into the courtyard, its outline momentarily caught in the moonlight, but beyond that I didn't see any evidence of the enemy.

Maybe that should worry me, I thought. How many enemies had slipped through the castle's defenses, and what were they doing now? Surely a couple of dozen men couldn't hope to take over the castle. Were they protesters? Assassins?

Hudson stopped so suddenly I bumped into his back, a wall of chain mail and muscle. "Stay behind me," he whispered.

I didn't know what he'd seen, but I followed his command.

"If they attack, run away."

They? And then I saw four men in front of us, still far away but advancing in our direction. I could make out their silhouettes. One wore strange bulky armor; the other three wore no armor at all, but carried weapons in their hands. Bows drawn. And they'd seen us.

Hudson, even if he'd been good with his sword, couldn't have stopped the men from shooting. And although his armor might have deflected the arrows, I had nothing to protect me.

The men came closer, walking in crouching, soundless steps. Right toward us.

Hudson held his sword at the ready. "Run," he told me.

I didn't move. I couldn't bear to think of him being shot, or worse yet, hacked down in a four against one fight. *It's my fault,* I thought, *because I changed the story. I shouldn't have. I should have married King John, and then, after a year, Hudson could have gone home.*

"Run!" he said again, this time louder.

I turned and ran. I had no idea where I was going, and each step pierced slivers of ice into my heart.

A flashlight beam passed over me—a circle of light I'd seen a thousand times in my century, yet couldn't make sense of here. And then I heard a voice I recognized. My father's. "Tansy!" he called out. "Come back!"

I stopped, breathless, and spun around. My father, impossible as it seemed, was part of the invaders. He had come for me.

He had come for me!

As I ran back to the group, the words repeated in my mind, each an exclamation of joy. I didn't even notice the pain the footsteps brought. The flashlight had been turned off, so I couldn't tell anything about the other men, but I knew they wouldn't hurt me. My father wouldn't have called me back otherwise.

Even though it had been painted a dark green, I recognized

my father's face easily enough. He was the one walking toward me with his hands outstretched.

I threw myself into his arms, gasping. He was here. He was safe.

His bulky armor, I realized, was made up of pans of all sizes that had been tied together over his chest, back, and stomach. He also wore our two-handled pot on his head, secured by—from the minty smell of it—an entire box of dental floss. I could imagine Sandra making this outfit. "You are not going to storm the castle without wearing something safe," she'd probably said.

And he'd undoubtedly complained while putting it on. "All the other invaders will make fun of me."

My father ran his hand over my hair, scanning me the best he could. "Are you all right?"

I nodded. "How did you get here?"

He gestured to the other men and his armor rattled. "With some help."

One of the men was talking to Hudson. The other two still had bows drawn, and were surveying the area. I kept hold of my father's hand, suddenly feeling like a little girl. I pulled him toward Hudson to make introductions. As I drew closer, I recognized the man talking to Hudson.

It was Robin Hood himself.

• • •

Introductions were brief. I told my father that Hudson was from our century, but I didn't have time to explain how he'd gotten here. Hudson and Robin Hood were busy plotting the best way over the walls. Robin wanted to stop in the barn and get sacks full of gold—it was what they had come for—but Hudson convinced him it was better to leave now. I could make them gold when we were safe.

I wondered if they recognized each other. I wouldn't think

Hudson would forget Robin Hood's voice, not after being held up in one century and tied up and left half naked in another, but if Hudson was angry with him, he didn't show it. He told Robin Hood about the guard posts and the best entrances onto the wall. When they had agreed on one, we all scuttled off toward the chosen destination. My father took something out of his pocket and held it to his mouth. It was bigger than a cell phone and made an electronic crackling noise as he whispered into it. "We've found her. We'll let you know when we reach the rendezvous point. Over and out."

"What's that?" I whispered.

"Nick's old walkie-talkies," he said, then held his finger to his lips—the sign to stay quiet.

It was hard to do. I wanted to ask where Nick and Sandra were and how he'd gotten hold of Robin Hood and where we were going next.

Instead I silently followed the procession. Hudson led the way, sword drawn. Robin Hood walked beside him, his leather boots hardly making a sound against the ground. The fighting was going on at the front section of the wall, so we went to the back. Only a handful of guards patrolled on top of the wall back there, and they were mostly looking for an attack from the outside.

When we drew close to a set of stairs that led up the wall, Robin Hood turned back to my father. "Stay with your daughter. We'll give the sign when it's safe."

My father took a large cylinder that had been tied to his side and handed it to Hudson. It was thicker than a baseball bat but only half as long. "Do you know how to use this?" my dad asked.

Hudson nodded.

Then Robin Hood, Hudson, and the other two men took off, running for the stairs. I was still gaping at my dad. My mild-mannered father, who wouldn't even shoot pigeons off our roof, had just handed Hudson some sort of weapon?

I had thought Robin Hood and his band were uncivilized

when they'd been running around my century, brandishing weapons. A week ago, my father and Hudson wouldn't have dreamed of breaking a law, but here in the Middle Ages, my dad had joined forces with bandits and had broken into a castle to rescue me. What's more, Hudson and I had robbed the king and left him bound and gagged in his room.

What a thin coating civilization had. It hadn't taken much to turn us into outlaws.

Once we got home, I was probably in for a lot of stern dinnertime lectures about all of this.

I shivered in the night air, holding the book tightly against my chest. I tried to spot Hudson and the others in the shadows along the top of the wall. "Are Nick and Sandra okay?" I whispered to my dad.

He nodded.

"I'm really sorry about this." It felt strange to be the one saying it, meaning it, begging with those few syllables for some understanding. I had been stingy with my forgiveness over the years, and now I needed it so badly.

He squeezed my hand. "I know. It's okay."

Those words lifted a weight from inside me. And I wasn't sure which made me feel lighter, that he had forgiven me, or that in that moment I had forgiven him for everything too. I squeezed his hand back.

Minutes went by. A distant crash sounded on the wall. I leaned forward, straining to see what it was. Was that the sound chain mail made when it fell violently to the ground? Hudson's chain mail maybe? I didn't have long to worry about it. An owl hooted near the wall.

Dad tugged on my arm. "That's the signal."

We ran to the stairs. Even that short amount of jogging made my heart feel like it had been sliced up and returned to my chest. Then we started to climb. My dad kept turning back and motioning me to speed up.

I pushed myself to keep going and decided the elevator was

man's greatest invention. Better than fire. I put my hand over my heart. It was wet again. It was never going to heal at this rate. And not only had I totally ruined this dress, I would probably ruin every article of clothing I ever put on. How was I supposed to explain that to people? I wouldn't even be able to make it through first-period calculus. *Excuse me, Mr. Rowley, can I go to the bathroom? My heart has ruptured again.*

My dad came down the stairs, took hold of my hand, and pulled me, stumbling, up the next few steps. I didn't see Hudson until he was in front of me. These stairs were wider and Hudson stepped past my dad to me. Without a word of explanation, he picked me up, plunked me over his shoulder, and hauled me the rest of the way up the stairs.

It would have been kind of romantic if my face hadn't been smashed into the back of his chain mail. Plus there weren't any handrails on these stairs either. And worrying about what it would feel like to fall that far kind of sucked all the romance out of the situation.

When we reached the top of the wall, I waited for Hudson to put me down. He didn't. He moved along the wall, half jogging, until we came to Robin Hood and his men. The Merry Men were tying up two guards with . . . I blinked to make sure I was seeing right . . . our bike locks. A strange white coating covered the guards. It looked like their faces and torsos had been frosted.

"Thanks for helping me up the stairs," I told Hudson.

"No problem," he said.

I waited for him to set me down. He didn't.

He and my father whispered to each other about where to go next.

"You can put me down now," I said.

"I'm fine," he said. "You don't weigh much."

"The blood is rushing to my head."

"But at least this way you won't slow us down."

Using my arms to push against his back, I propped my head up. "I can be faster now. Going up stairs is just hard and . . ." I broke off as I got a better look at the white coating on the captured guards. Paint? Or maybe it was foam. "What did you do to those men?"

"We used fire extinguishers."

Dad smiled proudly. "We may not have had any weapons at our house, but that doesn't stop us from improvising."

"Will it hurt them?" I asked.

"Nah," Dad said. "Well, probably not. Besides, this way they won't be flammable for a while."

One of the guards let out a muffled groan, and Robin Hood pointed his sword at him menacingly. The guard fell silent at once. Robin Hood shot Dad an angry look. "This would be easier if you let us dispatch the guards properly."

"We've already gone over this," Dad said. "Killing someone could change history. That could be my great-great-great-grandfather you want to run through."

Robin Hood rolled his eyes and motioned for Will Scarlet to hurry securing the men. "Very well, then. Are we ready to leave this family reunion?"

"Aye," Will said, and stood up.

The next moment, we all jogged along the wall, well, except for me. I bounced against Hudson's shoulder, wishing chain mail weren't quite so hard. The ribbons holding my hair had come loose, making it even harder to see what was going on.

Finally we stopped. I wasn't sure why until Hudson slid me off his shoulder.

Little John had looped a rope around one of the stone merlons. He pulled on the rope, testing the knot's strength. "She'll hold," he said, and to prove it, he hoisted himself over the edge and disappeared.

Robin Hood wrapped a strip of cloth around his palm. "Now the rest of you."

My father pulled a pair of gardening gloves from his pocket and shoved them in my direction. "Put these on. They'll save your hands from rope burn."

I took them and tried not to think about how far down it was, or the fact that I'd always stunk at rope climbing in PE.

My father went next. Even as he flung one leg over the side of the wall, he was giving me directions. "You can do this," he told me. "It's like that rope swing you used to climb when we went to the lake, remember?"

I stared at him bleakly. "We haven't been to the lake since I was in fifth grade."

He took hold of the rope and flung his other leg over the wall. "Has it been that long?" He shook his head to banish that line of thinking. "Just don't let go of the rope." Then he was gone. I held my breath and listened, hoping I didn't hear the sound of him falling.

Hudson nudged me forward. "It's your turn. Don't freeze up, we need to hurry. Oh, and don't scream. It will give away our position."

"I'm not going to scream," I said. I hoisted myself on the wall, grabbed hold of the rope, and prayed that rope climbing was like bike riding and I would remember how to do this. Otherwise my fairy tale would have a very bad ending.

New moral of the story: You should have paid attention in PE class.

My father was nearly to the ground. He had slid down more than climbed down. I meant to climb down. The rope had other ideas. It was hard to get a good grip while wearing gardening gloves. I slid from the moment I let go of the wall. But I didn't scream—except for in my mind, where I was screaming at the top of my lungs and coming up with really colorful curses for fairies.

In less time than I thought, I reached the ground. Little John waved for Dad and me to follow him. As we did, Dad took out the walkie-talkie again. "We're headed toward the rendezvous point. Over and out."

We strode down a hill. No trees grew around the castle walls. They'd been cleared, I supposed, to keep enemies from using them. I felt exposed out in the open grass. "Where are we going?" I asked my father.

"To the road."

It was around front, where the fighting was. This did not seem to be a particularly good point to meet with Nick and Sandra, but I didn't have time to ask about it. Little John was moving fast, and I didn't want to lose sight of him.

Before long, Hudson, Robin Hood, and Will came up behind us. "Good," Little John said. "Now we can hurry."

I *had* been hurrying. Still, I tried to pick up my pace and accomplished a staggering run.

"Are you all right?" Hudson asked, jogging effortlessly beside me.

"If your mother tells you to marry a girl with a heart of gold, she doesn't know what she's talking about." I regretted saying the words as soon as they left my mouth. I had forgotten about Hudson's mother. But if he had a reaction, I didn't see it.

"Do you want me to carry you again?"

"I'm fine," I said. I couldn't elaborate because I was panting too much.

Hudson eyed me, as though waiting for me to collapse, but he didn't say more on the subject.

We reached the front of the castle, making a wide berth in the process to avoid any random arrows shot our way. The attackers had brought their own cover with them. They stood behind wooden walls with tiny slits that let the men shoot arrows from behind them. The walls were movable too. Every few minutes, the attackers skittered sideways or backward to avoid being hit by the rocks that the castle catapulted toward them.

I recognized Nick right away. He was the one with the potato launcher over his shoulder. As I watched, he shot at the castle wall. A cloud of smoke went off where it hit. Obviously, he wasn't shooting potatoes.

The men were too far away for either side to do much damage, but damage wasn't the point. This fight had only been a distraction. Once we were close enough to the road, Robin Hood gave a whistle. The men grabbed hold of their walls and fell back.

I'm not sure whether their retreat gave the castle enough courage to send out knights after them, or whether they had planned to do that anyway, but the castle gate opened and knights on horses thundered toward us.

I let out a gasp. These horses were huge and wearing so much armor that they looked like giant robotic horses. We couldn't outrun them. In a few minutes, they'd be on us.

Chapter 16

I looked around, searching in the dark for the Merry Men's horses. Certainly they hadn't walked here, but I didn't see any sign of animals. I heard the shouts approaching, though. Yells of anger as the knights pounded the ground toward us.

Nick sprinted ahead of me, disappearing down the road into the darkness. I hoped he would get away. I wasn't going to be able to make it as far. I had already run too much and now it felt like not just my heart was bleeding, but my lungs were too.

My pace slowed. Hudson took hold of my arm and pulled me forward. I wanted to ask, What's the point? but didn't. Maybe the point was that you've got to keep trying even when it won't matter. I thought of Kendall and my mom, and my throat felt tight. They would never know what happened to us. That part seemed the worst of all.

New moral of the story: Not all fairy tales end happily ever after.

My father took his walkie-talkie back out of his vest. "We need help fast."

What did he expect Sandra to do against charging knights with battle axes?

Up on the road ahead of us, lights flicked on. Headlights—two sets shooting beams of light into the dark. Nick was driving Dad's truck and Sandra sat behind the wheel of her Honda. As they roared down the bumpy road toward us, the beams of light jumped and swayed, throwing different patches of ground into and out of focus.

I stumbled toward the car, finding more strength than I thought I had. We would make it before the horses reached us.

I heard the Honda's locks unclick, and Sandra called out, "Get in!"

I opened the door and flung myself inside. Hudson crawled in next to me, and four men I only vaguely recognized crammed in as well.

Sandra flipped on the interior light and twisted around to check on me. "Are you okay?"

"Yes." I breathed out, panting too heavily to say more.

"We need more room," Hudson told me, and without more instruction, I got up, he scooted over, and I sat on his lap. He wrapped his arms around my waist and leaned his head against my back, breathing hard from the run. I would have enjoyed the feeling of being snuggled into him if my mind hadn't been so crowded with thoughts of the giant robotic horses and their ax-waving companions.

Well, actually, I enjoyed the feel of his arms around me a little bit anyway.

Three men piled into the front seat next to Sandra. She had opened the trunk so they could crowd in there too. Another set of headlights came on—Nick's old Camry. Dad had climbed into the driver's seat, and that car was weighed down with men too.

Our procession started down the road. We couldn't go very fast. The road was jutted and uneven, making the car shake around like a wild bull trying to throw us.

Sandra's hands gripped the wheel tightly, and she leaned forward in concentration. I couldn't see anything out of the rear window because the trunk was open, but through the side mirror, I saw the knights gaining on us.

"You need to go faster," I told Sandra.

Her voice was a forced calm. "People will fall out if I do."

"People will die if you don't."

She glanced in her mirror. "We've thought this through."

I felt my panic rise. I had just thought this through too and at the end of my thoughts, we all died. It wouldn't take much for the knights' axes to shatter the windows or slash our tires.

They were close now, almost within striking distance.

Then Sandra laid on the horn.

The sharp blare rang through the night, startling the horses. Some horses tried to stop, causing an equestrian pileup, while others bolted away from the car, whinnying and shaking their heads in distress. We continued on, bumping down the road away from them while they regrouped.

After a few minutes, the knights regained control of their horses and charged us again, but the horses were skittish now. We must have seemed like strange creatures to them—so large and noisy. When the knights got close, Sandra blared the horn again. The horses scattered away from us, like they'd done the first time.

The men sitting in the trunk of the car laughed and taunted the knights, something I thought was severely stupid. But the Merry Men understood horses well enough to know the chase was over. The horses could keep up with our speed for a few miles, but they were tiring. Slow car speed is still pretty fast horse speed if both horse and rider are wearing armor.

The knights yelled insults back at us in return, but they didn't try to follow again and we bounced off into the night.

Hudson let out a sigh. I hadn't noticed how tense he was until he relaxed; even his hands went slack in my lap. "Those were trained horses," he said. "At a knight's command, they'll kneel in battle or kick an opponent. I can't believe a car horn scared them off."

Sandra checked her mirror again. She was usually such a cautious driver that, I imagined, even in a medieval forest, she would use her blinkers when she changed directions. "Luckily, those knights never trained their horses not to react to car horns." She eyed him in the mirror for the first time. "You're not one of Robin's men. Who are you?"

We told her, Hudson and I taking turns, although we edited our versions of the story. I said things like "Hudson is Police Chief Gardner's son."

And he said things like "I was an innocent bystander."

I didn't tell Sandra that Hudson tricked me into turning Bo and his friends over to the police. He didn't tell her that I made out with Robin Hood in a convenience store.

She only stopped our stories once. She told Hudson, "I knew your mother from the library board committee. She was a lovely woman."

"Thanks," he said, but his voice sounded flat, or maybe just tired.

Little John peered at me from the front seat. "About you turning things to gold—you're truly able? Your pa promised we'd have gold to spare if we rescued you."

I imagined he did. The Merry Men were mercenaries at heart. They wouldn't have risked the rescue for anything less.

"What do you want me to turn to gold?" I asked.

Little John handed me a pouch from around his waist. I took it in my palm and said, "Little John's pouch, gold, gold, gold." It directly turned into a useless but very shiny pouch. I handed it back to him, and he and the other Merry Men passed it around, admiring it. Then they wanted me to transform every-thing they had on them. I think they would have stripped naked if they'd had the room to undress. Fortunately they didn't.

Finally, after being stuck in the car for way too long with a bunch of men who rarely bathed, we pulled off the main road and onto a narrower one. A few minutes after that, we left the road altogether and went through an opening in the forest where some trees had been cut away.

When the car stopped, I didn't even care where we were. I was just happy that everyone piled out and I could unbend myself and breathe in the fresh forest air.

Robin Hood's men greeted each other, laughing and slapping one another's backs. I ran over to Dad and Nick and gave them hugs, then Sandra came over and we all hugged each other again. It was our first real family moment.

I never expected to feel like part of a family with Sandra, Nick, and Dad. But I did, and I wasn't sure what was odder: that I felt this way or that it had taken me so long to realize a family could expand to include other people.

The Merry Men took cut tree limbs from a nearby pile and laid them across the cars to hide them from the road. Sandra and Dad went to talk to Robin Hood, but Nick stayed with me.

"I'm really sorry about all of this," I told him. "I didn't mean to put you in danger. Has it been awful?"

He patted me on the shoulder. "Nah, actually some good things have come from this."

"Like what?"

"Oh, the way you've made it really easy for me to look like the good child. Because no matter how badly I screw up in the future, at least I've never sent the family to the Middle Ages."

"Thanks," I said. "I feel better now."

"Plus, I got to use my science fair project to attack a castle. Not many people can say that."

I remembered the smoke I'd seen. "What were you shooting out of that launcher?"

"Mostly smoke bombs. And a few explosive potatoes. You'd be surprised what you can do with stump remover, gasoline, and hair spray." He shot a look over at Sandra to make sure she wasn't listening. "Don't tell my mom though. I don't want her to ask me how I knew how to make all that stuff."

Hudson walked over to us, and Nick did a double take. "What are you doing here?"

"Oh, I got dragged on the Tansy Wish Cruise like the rest of you."

Robin Hood let out a whistle to let everyone know it was time to go. He and the Merry Men headed out through the forest. Nick had a flashlight, so Hudson and I stayed close to him. As we walked, Hudson told Nick how Clover had sent him here and what had happened since then. At least most of it.

"You forgot the parts about Sister Mary Theresa," I said.

Hudson smirked. "I didn't forget. I just figured I'd tell Nick those parts later."

Nick chuckled. "A nun. She sounds hot."

Hudson's smirk didn't fade. "Nuns have a heavenly beauty."

Yeah, I bet that's what Hudson was interested in. Heavenly beauty.

Nick shook his head. "Man, you've been here too long. I've seen the women here. They all have greasy hair, smell bad—and dentists haven't been invented yet. Some of them are downright trollish. Really, this place has ruined medieval computer games for me."

Hudson and Nick went on talking. I stayed quiet and listened, envying how easily they got along. Hudson's voice was never measured, never wary, like it was sometimes when he spoke to me.

We kept trudging around bushes and trees until we came to a clearing. Not only was Dad's big blue tent set up, but dozens of small ones—blankets propped up on sticks—were spread around too. More horses than I could count were tethered to nearby trees, sleeping with their heads hanging low. The remains of a fire sat in the middle of the camp, along with a messy pile of logs and tinder. Boxes sat outside our tent with some of our belongings piled in them. My coat lay on top of one box. Bottles of water were stacked in another. My backpack leaned up against a sleeping bag. I hoped someone had thought to bring me a pillow, pajamas, and a toothbrush. These items suddenly seemed like the height of luxury. I realized I might be able to sleep with a real pillow tonight.

Robin Hood strode over to me wearing his usual half smile. "Now then, about our pay . . ."

I sent my sleeping bag a longing look. "Can't it wait until morning?"

He shook his head. "Most of these men are mere villagers who came on this venture on the promise that they would be paid handsomely. They'll want to leave at first light, before the king can send his knights around to enquire if anyone knows aught of the attack."

Which meant the sleeping bag would have to wait.

I ended up changing the tinder from the woodpile. Then Little John chopped the firewood into small chunks and I changed that into gold too. Each time I uttered the chant, pain rippled through my chest. Finally, when everyone had as much gold as they could carry, they let me go to my tent. I walked there with Sandra.

"How did you guys even connect with Robin Hood?" I asked.

She unzipped the door flap. "It's amazing what sort of messages you can pass along when you bribe people with things from the twenty-first century. It makes me wish I had bought the jumbo-sized cinnamon container at Costco. You wouldn't believe what that stuff is worth here."

Inside the tent, a pillow, pajamas, a toothbrush, and toothpaste waited for me. I wanted to cry when I saw them. They were better than gold.

• • •

I was the last one to wake up in the morning. The sun had already risen, and the extra men from last night had left. Only the Merry Men were around, cooking some unidentifiable creatures over the fire. Robin Hood had provided my family with medieval clothes to help us blend in. I put on a stained brown dress that was too short, too wide, and had an odd collar that I didn't believe was ever in style. He said he bought them, but I wondered if he stole them. Perhaps somewhere out there was a short, fat, tasteless peasant woman who was missing her dress.

For our breakfast, Sandra warmed up a couple of cans of hash on a frying pan that lay over the coals. We had no way to make toast, so we put butter in another pan and fried the bread. Frying pans—not just fashionable but functional too.

We still had some leftover fruit from our fridge, and the Merry Men were so eager to have the oranges that Sandra pulled all the wedges apart and handed them out. I hadn't realized oranges were a delicacy in the Middle Ages. It almost made me feel guilty for the way I'd always eaten them without thinking about it.

While we had breakfast, Hudson told my family about the deal he'd made with Bartimaeus.

"Will he be able to send all of us back?" Nick asked.

"Do you think he could send the house too?" Sandra asked.

Dad put a hand on her knee. "That doesn't matter. We can always get a new house. The important thing is to get *us* back."

I wondered if the neighbors had noticed that our house was gone yet. That wasn't the sort of thing we were going to be able to explain very well. When we returned to Rock Canyon, we would probably be known as those bizarre Millers whose house up and disappeared one day. Which was one more thing that would make me stand out as the weird girl at school.

Hudson ate his hash slowly. "Bartimaeus needs the Gilead, so hopefully he'll agree to send us all back."

"How long will it take to get to his village?" Sandra asked, taking small bites of her toast.

"It's about ten miles east from the castle," Hudson said, "but I'm not sure where we are now. How far north did we come last night?"

"About twenty miles," Dad said.

Nick shoveled hash into his mouth. "So that's only thirty miles—less if we can cut across the distance. We could drive that in a couple of hours."

Hudson shook his head. "Most of the roads here are just footpaths. You can't drive cars on them. We only got as far as we did last night because we kept to a road that wagons use to go to market. Besides, King John's men will be watching for your cars now. They know they were used in the attack." He looked up from his plate as though remembering something. "Did the Merry Men go brush away the tire tracks from the road this morning?"

Dad nodded. Apparently they'd discussed those details before, maybe last night while I'd been changing wood into gold. It was odd to hear my father and Hudson talking like equals. Dad usually spoke to Nick's friends with a kind of patronizing tolerance. But Hudson had been here for months. He knew this century better than the rest of us, and my father was listening to what he had to say.

"We should still leave this campsite soon," Hudson said. "Any of the villagers who helped last night could turn us in. Right now I bet King John would pay a lot for Tansy's return."

Probably true. If not to marry me, then to hang me. And he'd probably make me change the gallows to gold before he did.

Dad scooped up some hash onto his bread. "How long would it take to get to Bartimaeus's village on horseback?"

Hudson thought for a moment. "One day if we find good trails and the horses gallop for part of the trip. Two if they walk."

The Merry Men had horses. They were tied among the

trees, munching foliage. Nick glanced in their direction. "Would Robin Hood let us borrow some of his horses?"

"We don't have to make a two-day trip," I reminded everyone. "As soon as I figure out the moral of *Rumpelstiltskin*, the story will be over and my fairy godmother will send us home."

Hudson sighed, giving me the kind of patient look people save for children and the delusional. He had already told my family what he thought of fairy magic. "The story probably doesn't have a moral," he said, "and your leprechaun pal thinks it's hilarious that you're racking your brain to find one."

I ignored him, stood up, and walked over to our boxes.

Dad had included a few books with the supplies. One dealt with outdoor survival, one was about the Middle Ages, and one was a book of fairy tales. My family had read the story of Rumpelstiltskin looking for clues that might help with my rescue. The story hadn't proved useful in that way, but I was glad they had brought it. I sat back down with the book propped open in my lap.

In the pictures, Rumpelstiltskin looked more like a friendly garden gnome than a villain. In fact, the whole story seemed deceptively tame spread out in the pages of this book. But it wasn't a tame story. It was tense and frightening, and I was surprised it hadn't given me nightmares as a child.

"So what's the moral?" I asked.

My family came up with ones I'd already tried: Don't brag about things you can't do. The pure in heart are helped. Good triumphs in the end.

I shook my head at each one. "None of those work."

Nick popped a piece of the fried toast into his mouth. "How about 'Gold makes the world go around.'"

"Or 'Don't let your daughter talk to fairies,'" Dad added.

"'Men will manipulate you to get whatever they want,'" Sandra said.

Dad shot her a disapproving look.

Sandra held her cup with both hands, taking slow sips. "Hey, it works in the context of the story."

I opened my magic book. "Can't hurt to try them."

I turned the pages and drew in a sharp breath. The story didn't end where it had yesterday. On what had been a blank page, there was now a picture of me sneaking up the castle stairs, hand in hand with Hudson. I looked ready to swoon. He looked strong, determined, and glowingly attractive. I flipped over the page. The next painting showed King John holding his sword across the door, blocking the way. I looked totally swoony again. Hudson stood in the background, his chain mail glinting on his broad shoulders. He seemed so toweringly handsome that I wasn't surprised my storybook self was completely smitten.

I glanced over at Hudson. I didn't want to, but somehow I couldn't help myself. I had to see him in real life.

He noticed my stare and stopped eating. "What's wrong?"

I didn't answer, just turned the page. It showed King John, tied up in gold string and weighed down by his gold wardrobe. On the page after that, Hudson carried me across the wall—but not flung over his shoulder, like I'd really been. In the painting he held me in his arms as though I was a new bride going over the threshold. My hair lay gracefully around my shoulders in radiant blond waves. The muscles in his biceps rippled. It could have been the cover of a romance novel.

"What is it?" Hudson asked. He stood up and walked over.

My father, who sat next to me, leaned over and read, "The young guard carried the miller's daughter to the wall where they escaped from the king's men, making their way into the surrounding wilderness. That night they slept under a blanket of stars."

It was the last sentence written on the page, the new end of the story. Dad examined the picture more closely. "Is that supposed to be last night?"

From my other side, Hudson looked at the picture. "How come it doesn't mention anybody else?"

"I don't know," I said. "Artistic license, I guess?"

Nick reached over and took the book from my hands. "Hey," I said, trying to snatch it back. "I'm supposed to write the moral."

"It will help us figure out the moral if we know the story." Nick proceeded to read the entire thing, including the passages about the handsome young guard who came to the miller's daughter's rescue. Nick snorted during those paragraphs, then turned to Hudson. "I think this book seriously has a crush on you."

I blushed. Did the book know I found Hudson attractive, that I had liked the feel of his hand around mine last night? Is that why it had painted him as some romance novel hero?

"So," Nick said, "the new moral of the story would be what? 'Make sure you've got a buff guard to carry you around'?"

I reached for the book again, but Nick still held it away. "No? Okay, I've got the real one. It's 'Always be prepared.'"

"That's the Boy Scout motto," Hudson said, like this automatically disqualified it from being the moral.

"Then what is it?" Nick asked Hudson. "The new part of the story is about you, so you should be able to figure out the moral." He handed the book to Hudson, who flipped through the pages, searching for clues. Or maybe he wasn't searching for clues. Mostly he seemed to be examining the paintings. He looked carefully at the ones of us together. He took in the details, noting the way I held on to his neck while he carried me and the longing that had been painted into my eyes.

I expected him to laugh like Nick had, but he didn't. He lowered the book and looked over at me, examining my eyes in real life. I could barely hold his gaze. It felt like he could see into my mind, like he could open up my thoughts and sort through them. Did he know I had a crush on him? Would it make

things awkward between us now . . . or was it possible that he
liked me too?

I kept my voice casual, unconcerned. "So what do you think
the moral is?"

He paused, keeping his gaze on mine for another moment.
Then he handed the book back. "I wish I knew."

I'm not sure why that answer disappointed me, but it did.

Chapter 17

While everybody else cleaned up breakfast and worked on packing our stuff, I sat by the fire and wrote down morals, starting with the Boy Scout motto.

It did sound like a good moral: Be prepared. If you're going to travel to the Middle Ages, do it with boxes of canned goods, fire extinguishers, and automobiles with loud horns.

Nothing stuck.

Maybe the moral of the story was that magic books are evil and they want to make you suffer. I didn't bother writing that one. There was no point in antagonizing it.

Finally, I put the book down on my lap in disgust. "This should work. We escaped. The story is over."

Only Hudson was listening to me. He was shoving one of our sleeping bags into its sack while Nick and Sandra took down the tent. Dad had gone over to talk to Robin Hood.

I ran a finger over the book cover dismally. "The hero and heroine made a dramatic escape and slept underneath a blanket of stars. That's a good ending."

"It's not even accurate," Hudson said. "You slept in a tent with your family. I slept on a bedroll next to a bunch of outlaws."

"It doesn't have to be accurate," I said. "It just has to be good."

Hudson gave the sleeping bag one last shove, pushing it into its sack. "So the moral of the story is that if you can turn things into gold, you can buy off people to help you do anything you want."

I tapped the pen against my hand. "That doesn't sound like a very good moral for a children's story."

"No," he said. "But it's true, isn't it? And what are you planning on doing with all that wealth now that you've got it?"

I didn't understand his sudden snippiness. Did he think I was going to turn into a King John? That I was going to sit around all day admiring my stash of gold and paying off lackeys to do my bidding?

"I only asked for this enchantment because I wanted money to keep the library open so my dad and Sandra wouldn't lose their jobs."

Hudson let out a laugh like he didn't believe me. "So when we get back home, you're not planning to move to some mansion somewhere and spend your time hobnobbing with the rich and famous?"

I slid the pen back into the book. "You make it sound bad when you put it that way."

He shook his head. "So the moral of the story is about money, isn't it? 'Get as much as you can.'"

And what was wrong with money? I wanted to finally have a say in my own life instead of being pushed around by everyone else's circumstances. I wanted to be able to live whereever I wanted. Money was freedom.

I stood up and brushed the dirt from my dress. "I shouldn't have expected you to understand."

He straightened. "Meaning?"

"Meaning, you've never tried to understand my point of view in anything."

"*I've* never tried to *understand*?" He tossed the sleeping bag into one of the boxes. "I risked my life to rescue you. I carried you along the wall."

"Thanks," I said. "What do you want as payment for that? Just name your price."

He let out a groan. "You know, not everything in life is for sale." Then he turned and headed toward the Merry Men. "I need to help your dad pick out horses."

I watched him go, wondering why he was so upset. I wasn't trying to buy him off; I was being generous. We could all be rich when we made it back home.

I should have gone to help Sandra pack things, but I watched Hudson for another moment. His boots, sword, and chain mail— they looked normal on him now. Normal in a masculine, rugged sort of way. It was hard to imagine him back at Rock Canyon High in jeans and T-shirts. When we returned, would he talk to me in the hallway? Pretend none of this had ever happened? Treat me with the same sullen distance he used with the other girls at school? But then, if I moved to a mansion somewhere in another city, it wouldn't matter. I wouldn't go to school with him anymore.

I didn't like that thought, not after we'd gone through so much together.

I had the sudden desire to yell out to him, "I don't have to move to a mansion. I'd be perfectly happy with my old house if it weren't trashed and stuck in the Middle Ages."

But that was assuming too much. He probably didn't care about seeing me again.

I went and helped Sandra and Nick pack up the boxes. Before we were done, Dad came over, frowning. "Robin Hood says they can't spare any horses because they need them to carry their provisions. He says Hudson should go to the nearest village and buy horses for us. In the meantime, he wants us to drive the cars about ten miles down the road to a better hiding spot. It's less populated there."

Nick grunted as he set the tent bag down. "That's what we get for giving them so much gold. Now they need all their horses to carry it."

Dad rummaged through the supplies, taking a few things out. "They don't even want to let Hudson borrow a horse so he can make it to the village faster. He's still trying to convince them about that."

"Hudson is going to walk?" I asked. I had heard the Merry Men talk about the village this morning. It was six miles up the road.

Dad put a flashlight, matches, and a box of crackers into a pillowcase. "Hudson is the only one of us who knows anything about horses—and he's got a sword. He's the best choice. We've set up a meeting place and I'm giving Hudson one of the walkie-talkies so he'll be able to reach us when he gets close." Dad dropped one of the walkie-talkies into the pillowcase, then added granola bars and a water bottle.

I turned to look at Hudson and Robin Hood. They still stood talking by the horses. From the way Hudson's jaw was set, I didn't think it was going well.

Dad left the pillowcase on the ground and hefted the biggest box onto his shoulder. "Let's pack up the car."

Nick picked up his backpack and the tent bag and followed after him. Sandra grabbed a couple of sleeping bags. When I picked up a box, she shot a look at the Merry Men and motioned for me to stay.

The men were busy wrapping up their gold inside their bedrolls, and they were talking loudly enough that they couldn't hear us. Still, Sandra leaned toward me and whispered, "Someone should guard these supplies until we can lock them in the cars again. We only took them out last night because we needed room to carry the men. These modern things . . ." She ran a hand over a box. "I don't completely trust the Merry Men, so we shouldn't tempt them."

Sandra walked off in the direction of the car and I sat down, trying to find a place on the ground that was less dirty than the rest. Although, really, it didn't matter. My dress was stained enough already.

My gaze drifted over to Hudson and Robin Hood again. I couldn't help but compare them. They were both tall and handsome, but Robin Hood didn't seem nearly as . . . as solid and sturdy as Hudson. I didn't know how else to describe it, and I didn't know why I found it so attractive, but I had felt it every time I'd touched Hudson: that solidness.

Hudson motioned to a horse. Robin Hood wrinkled his nose and said something that made Hudson narrow his eyes. I had wondered last night if Hudson and Robin Hood remembered each other. I could tell now that they did. And since the common enemy was gone, they weren't getting along anymore.

Finally Hudson turned away from Robin Hood and strode back to me, his expression grim.

"Robin Hood wouldn't let you borrow a horse?" I guessed.

"If I ever get back to the twenty-first century, I'm going to write a new book about Robin Hood." He came up with a few titles then, although none that publishers would ever print.

I stood up. "I can pay him for a horse. I'll just change something else into gold."

Hudson sent Robin Hood another withering look. "I offered to buy one, but they already have as much gold as their horses can carry. Right now, they're over there deciding which town they'll go party it up at."

I let out a sigh. "I guess it was too much to expect that they'd give any gold to the poor."

"Oh, they'll be spreading it around at every alehouse and inn they come to," he said. "The poor will get a share."

I handed him the pillowcase with the supplies. "Do you have enough gold to buy horses in the village?" Without giving him time to answer, I added, "I can give you more."

"I have enough." His next sentence came out slowly, thinking out loud. "But it's still tempting to take more."

"It's not a problem." At least it wasn't much of one. I picked
up a handful of acorns from the ground and changed them,
only flinching a little.

I held the acorns out to him. He stared at them, but didn't
take them. After a moment of waiting, I slipped them into his
pocket.

His gaze moved to my eyes. His expression was a mixture
of realization and reproach that I didn't understand. "I let you
change those," he said, "even though I knew it would hurt you."
He shook his head as though he regretted that and looked me
over. "How bad is the pain?"

"It's not bad for little things."

"The whole enchantment is bad." He took an acorn out of
his pocket and turned it over in his hand. It glistened in his
fingers like a piece of jewelry. "Your enchantment unleashes a
powerful dark magic."

"What do you mean?"

"Greed," he said. "If it's doing this to me, what is it doing
to someone like him?" He nodded over at Robin Hood. "It's got to
have occurred to him that his band will have all the money
they want if they don't let you go."

"They wouldn't . . . ," I started, but I didn't finish the sentence. Why *wouldn't* they keep me a prisoner? King John had
been eager enough to do it.

Hudson didn't take his gaze off the Merry Men. Friar Tuck
and Will were shoving each other over some insult, and the rest
of the men were laughing. "I shouldn't leave you with them,"
Hudson said. "You're outnumbered, and your family doesn't have
any real weapons. Why would bandits ever let you go?"

I had left the magic book sitting on top of one of the boxes,
and now I picked it up and held it tightly. Suddenly I worried that
Robin Hood would take it from me. Did he understand what it

was? We had been sitting in two separate groups this morning at breakfast, but some of the men must have overheard us talking about it. If Robin Hood took the book away from me, I couldn't write the moral, and I would be trapped here.

I stepped close to Hudson so he wouldn't have to raise his voice while we talked. No, that wasn't why I stood close. I wanted to be near him, to feel his sturdiness.

Hudson lowered his voice. "When I leave to buy horses, Robin Hood will probably take you somewhere different from the meeting spot and then say I didn't show up. He won't let you leave."

I clasped the book harder. Hudson might be wrong—I hoped he was wrong—but could I take that chance? "We never should have told him I could change things into gold." My gaze swept around the forest and the thick wall of trees that surrounded us. At breakfast, the forest had seemed beautiful, but now this place seemed remote, isolated. "You're right. I can't trust him."

Hudson stared in the direction my family had gone. "Well, at least you're finally listening to me about men."

I rolled my eyes. "I never had a crush on Robin Hood. Bo cured me of thinking bad boys were a good thing." For a moment I worried this would count as a lie and my sparkler hat would go off. Because really, Hudson had cured me of that as much as Bo had. I hurriedly added, "I like more solid men now."

"Solid?" Hudson's eyes slid to mine again. "As opposed to wispy, transparent men?"

I ignored that line of questioning. "Do you have a plan?"

Hudson opened his mouth to speak, then shut it as his gaze shifted over my shoulder.

I turned and saw Little John leading a large brown horse over to us. He was a mountain of a man, with arms like tree trunks. I had noticed this fact before, but now it made me gulp.

Little John stopped when he reached Hudson. "Robin says

I can ride out to the main road with you if you like. Give you a head start to the village."

"No," I said too quickly. I didn't like the thought of Little John and Hudson out in the forest alone. What was to keep Little John from killing Hudson and thereby cutting off one of our ways to return to the twenty-first century?

"No thank you," Hudson said more casually. "I've already had one of your escorts out of the forest and it was quite enough."

Little John grunted. "As you will. But you'd best be on your way. You've a ways to go."

Hudson put his arm around my waist, as calmly as if he'd done it a hundred times before. "True enough. But it's hard for those who are courting to part ways."

Little John's gaze bounced back and forth between us and he made a grumbling noise. Twelfth-century lingo wasn't my strong point, but I was pretty sure Hudson had told Little John I was his girlfriend.

To prove the point, Hudson pulled me closer. I leaned into him, playing along. He smelled of campfire smoke and earth and steel. I was glad for the excuse to lean into him, even if it was an act on his part. "You can stay for a few more minutes, can't you?" I asked.

Hudson smiled down at me. "If that's your wish, I wouldn't think of disappointing you."

Very pretty dialogue. I bet the book would use it for the next page. Little John grunted, then turned and walked back to the others.

When he was out of earshot, I said, "What's your plan?"

Hudson kept his arm around me, and leaned toward my ear as though he were flirting. "As soon as the Merry Men aren't looking, we both leave. You can pretend you're just walking a little ways into the forest to kiss me good-bye. If you're with me, Robin Hood will have to take your family to the meeting place. It's the only way he'll have a chance at more gold. We

won't come back with horses though; we'll come back with the
wizard."

I considered this while Hudson ran his hand across my
back. My skin tingled where he touched it, making it hard to consider much of anything else. "My parents will worry if I take off."

"We'll call them on the walkie-talkie and tell them what we're
doing." His lips brushed against my ear. My knees felt weak.

"The king's men are looking for me," I whispered.

"We'll take back roads." His hand tapped the small of my
back, waiting for my decision.

I pulled my mind away from the curve of his lips and the
depth of his brown eyes. Which was the greater danger—
the king's men or the Merry Men? I tried to think it through
logically, but logic wouldn't stick. Emotion made the decision.
If I left, I was risking my safety, but if I stayed, I was risking my
family's freedom. I couldn't do that to them, not after I had
already put them through so much.

"I'm with you," I said.

Hudson massaged a slow circle on my back, which sent more
tingles radiating up my spine. "The Merry Men won't expect you
to go far. Not with so many of your possessions sitting out in the
open. They know you're guarding them."

I put my head against his chest. His heart beat a slow, steady
rhythm against my cheek. "I can't lie. If I tell them I'm going to
kiss you good-bye, we'll really have to kiss." I glanced up to see
his reaction to that.

He smiled and wound a strand of my hair around his finger.
"I'd be happy to kiss you good-bye."

I inwardly winced at the double meaning. Of course he
would be happy to kiss me good-bye. He probably couldn't wait
to put me and this whole horrible episode behind him.

Which meant when we got back to the right century, I was
not only moving to a mansion, I was moving to a mansion in
Hollywood, so I could have famous actor friends that I would
flaunt when I came back to visit Rock Canyon.

Hudson whispered into my ear, "Tell Robin Hood you don't want anyone going through your supplies while you're saying good-bye to me. Emphasize that. Then they'll be so busy going through your supplies they won't worry about coming after you for a while." He let go of me, and I instantly missed his arms, the security they'd given me.

I was hopeless, really. One minute I was planning on flaunting famous friends in front of Hudson; the next, I missed his arms around me.

New moral of the story: Crushes make no sense.

"We need a horse," I told him. "I'll try to get one."

Hudson had just told me about the power of greed. I might as well use some of it to my benefit. I handed Hudson the book to hold and headed over to Robin Hood.

He stood next to a horse, tying a blanket onto the saddle. When I reached him, he doffed his hat in my direction. "My Lady Tansy?"

I stepped close to him and lowered my voice to a conspiratorial whisper. "I'm going to walk a little ways into the forest with Hudson. I want some privacy to . . ." I let the sentence dangle. "Well, you know how it is when those who are courting have to part." It amazed me, really, how well I could bend sentences into lies without ever actually lying. "Can you make sure your men don't go through our supplies?" I glanced in the direction my family had gone. "And if my time with Hudson takes a while and I'm not here when my family returns, will you tell them not to worry because I'll be back." This was not a lie. I would be back eventually.

Robin Hood put his cap back on his head. "Little John was not telling tales then? You're in love with that knave?"

"What?" I hadn't expected Robin Hood to ask this, and I didn't know what to say.

Robin Hood noticed my hesitation and raised an eyebrow. "My lady does not answer. She is perhaps reflecting on the way she kissed me in yonder twenty-first-century store. She has feelings for me."

I felt my cheeks grow warm. "You were holding me up at sword-point."

He stepped closer and gave me a rakish smile. "You wished me to your bedchamber and begged me not to leave it. Now fate has brought us together again. Are you certain you want to send off that sop of a fellow with anything more than a maidenly wave of your hand?"

"I'm sure, and if I could ask you for one more thing—"

Robin Hood took hold of my arm. "Judge for yourself, Lady Tansy. The man is not trustworthy." He glanced at Hudson again and pursed his lips. "He'll toy with a maiden's affections, then leave her with naught. I can tell."

I bet he could. He had probably done it enough times himself. I pulled my arm away from him. "You told me yourself you weren't ready to stand up with a woman." I'd had no idea what the phrase meant when he said it, so I'd looked it up on the Internet. It meant he didn't want to stand up in front of a priest for a wedding. Like that's why I'd wished for Robin Hood to come—no one in my own century would marry me.

He gave me a dazzling smile. "True, but your fair fingers not only change wood into gold but a man's heart into fire."

No doubt it was the gold part that interested him.

Robin Hood held his hands out, palms up. "Who better than I to keep you out of King John's grasp? I've eluded him for years. Don't bother kissing that fellow farewell. Kiss me hello instead." He put his arms on my shoulders and I worried that he was going to lean down and kiss me in front of everyone— in front of Hudson.

I stepped backward, smiling. "I'll consider your words if you consider mine. Little John offered to ride Hudson partway to the village. If you can spare the horse for a trip to the road, then certainly you can let Hudson take it for a little longer to ride to the village." I gestured to a pile of medium-sized rocks on the ground. "If you do, I'll change those into gold for you."

Robin Hood's blue eyes flickered over the rocks, calculating their potential wealth. The greed was taking hold.

"We have a shovel over there." I pointed at our supplies. "If you can't carry all of the gold now, you can bury some and come back later for it."

He didn't answer, so I stepped closer, putting my hand on his arm. "Please?"

Robin Hood's lips twitched. I could tell he didn't want to grant my request but couldn't help himself. "I suppose we can spare one horse." He turned and made a quick inventory of the horses, then called for Will to bring over a brown mare. "But you'll need to change the extra wood as well."

I didn't think twice about agreeing.

Changing the rocks to gold was more difficult than I thought. "Rock, gold, gold, gold" didn't work. The same thing had happened last night when I'd first tried to change the kindling. I had to figure out what sort of wood it was—oak—and then use that word.

"What sort of rocks are these?" I asked Robin Hood.

"Common forest rocks," he said.

Not a really helpful description.

Hudson came and stood next to me. "Try sandstone, limestone, or granite. It's not volcanic."

Hudson was obviously not only gorgeous and brave but also smart. It sort of made me regret destroying my English grades. I bet Hudson took honors English. I could have been in his class.

It turned out the rocks were limestone. Each change ripped at my heart, but I wouldn't pause to rest. Not for the rocks. Not for the wood.

When I was done, Little John took our shovel, proclaimed the blade to be "wonderful sharp," and began to dig a hole to bury the extra gold.

Hudson helped me to my feet, then took the horse's reins from Will. Wordlessly, we walked together toward the edge of the forest, the horse tromping nonchalantly after us. My heart was still clenched from changing things to gold, and I had to force myself to keep my footsteps steady. Just before we were swallowed up by the forest, I turned and looked over my shoulder. Robin Hood was watching us leave, his arms folded across his chest.

Even with gold at his feet and our provisions unguarded, he wouldn't lose track of time. We wouldn't have long before he figured out what we'd done. Would he come after us?

When we were out of sight, Hudson effortlessly mounted the horse then held his hand down for me. I grabbed it, ignoring the fact that the horse was shifting her weight impatiently as though she didn't welcome another rider.

As soon as I put my foot in the stirrup, Hudson heaved me up in front of him. He pressed his boots to the horse's flanks and she trotted off through the trees.

"Well," he said, "it looks like we're off to see the wizard."

"Let's hope he turns out to be more helpful than the one in Oz."

Hudson took the walkie-talkie out of his pocket and turned it on. Putting it next to his lips, he whispered, "Can you hear me?"

Nothing but static answered him for a few seconds, then my father's voice came over the speaker. "Did you say something?"

"I'm taking Tansy with me. She'll be safer away from Robin Hood. Out."

"What?" Even over the poor connection, my father's alarm was obvious.

I took the walkie-talkie from Hudson's hand. "We're afraid Robin Hood won't let us reconnect otherwise. If you get back to camp before they come looking for us, don't tell them what we've done."

"Where are you?" Dad asked.

But we didn't have time to talk. I scanned the forest ahead

of us, half hoping I'd catch sight of my family through the trees and half hoping I wouldn't. "I love you, Dad. Thank you for everything you've done for me."

It sounded too much like a good-bye. When my father spoke next, his voice rose. "Meet me at the car and we'll talk about this."

Hudson took the walkie-talkie from my hand. "Here's the new plan. We'll bring the wizard back to the meeting place. It will take us at least two days, maybe even four. In two days, turn on your walkie-talkie for five minutes every hour. As soon as we're within range, we'll turn on our walkie-talkie and keep calling until we get ahold of you. Out."

Hudson had barely finished speaking before my father's voice came back over the speaker. "You can't just take off with my daughter. It isn't safe—" He said more, but Hudson turned off the walkie-talkie and put it in the saddlebag.

I wished I'd been able to tell my father I was doing this for him, for the family.

In a few minutes, we reached the main road and Hudson brought the horse to a gallop. We were out in the world by ourselves. Fugitives not only from King John but from Robin Hood as well.

Chapter 18

We passed by the first village we came to. Hudson thought Robin Hood would look for us there. I had only ridden a horse a couple of times—always as part of some tourist trip where the horses gently strolled behind a guide. This was completely different. I spent the entire ride grasping hold of the saddle, the horse's mane, and sometimes Hudson in an effort not to fall off.

Finally, we came to a village Hudson thought was safe, and we bought two fresh horses at an inn. I would have my own horse to ride, which meant it would be easier to stay on, but I would no longer have Hudson's arms around me. Safety versus romance. It was a hard call whether to be happy or not.

We had to wait both for the horses to be saddled up and for the blacksmith to melt down the gold Hudson gave in payment. The innkeeper wanted to make sure it was real. Apparently not many people came through the village with gold acorns. While we waited for the stable boy to ready the horses, we bought provisions—food, blankets, cloaks—and studied the innkeeper's map. At least, Hudson studied the map. I mostly paced near him, nervously checking for either Robin Hood's or King John's men.

The only people who paid extra attention to us though were two barefoot little girls who kept casting adoring looks at Hudson. They even followed us into the stable when we collected our horses. While Hudson put things into his saddlebag, I told him, "You have a fan club."

He glanced in the girls' direction and they erupted in giggles. Hudson winked at them, then turned back to me. "It's only because women love a man in uniform."

I leaned against the stall door. "You're so right. I found those police officers who arrested me irresistible."

Hudson grinned. "You're an exception to many rules." Instead of putting a couple of the apples we'd bought into his saddlebag, he held them out to the girls. "Would you like to feed our horses?"

The youngest girl took an apple but instead of offering it to the horse, she bit into it, devouring it in a few bites. Hudson watched her, then without saying another word, he took the bread and eggs from his saddlebag and gave them to the children. The younger girl grabbed her share, wide-eyed, and ran away, as though Hudson might change his mind and demand it back.

"Beg your pardon," the older girl said. "My sister's too young to say thank you."

I hadn't noticed until then how thin the girl was, how ragged her clothes were. I took the food out of my saddlebag and handed it to her as well. I reached for some gold, but Hudson grabbed my hand and shook his head. "Not that."

The sternness in his face warned me not to argue, so I didn't. I just stood silently by the horses while the girl left and Hudson went to buy more food. I couldn't stop thinking about it, though. After we rode out of the village, I said, "Why didn't you let me give that girl some gold? It probably could have fed her family for a month."

Hudson looped his reins around one hand. "If the village men knew we had enough wealth that we could afford to give gold to children, we wouldn't make it a mile out of town before someone came to rob us. Or kill us. Less chance of reprisal that way."

I looked back in the direction of the village, a sudden chill washing across me. "But the people there were so nice."

"One of the things I've learned here is that when your children are hungry, even nice people do bad things for money."

That thought sat with me for a long time. When I had asked for this ability, not once had I considered the problems of having magical wealth. Now it seemed to put me in danger everywhere I went.

We left on the main road in case someone asked the villagers which way we went, but as soon as we were out of sight, we cut through the forest to a different path. According to the map, in about ten miles, we would reach a river. We needed to travel alongside it for several miles, then cross a bridge and take a road to the wizard's village.

Sunlight streamed through the forest, making the leaves look like jigsaw pieces of a hundred different shades of green. Birds trilled so loudly they nearly drowned out the sound of our horses.

My horse rode almost alongside Hudson's. Close enough that I could peek at his profile without him noticing. His dark eyes were alert, scanning the forest and he looked all the more handsome for his seriousness. No, that wasn't right. He was more handsome when he smiled. He didn't do that enough.

"Did you learn how to ride as a castle guard?" I asked.

"No. My grandparents have a couple of horses." His gaze wandered in my direction and he gave me one of his elusive smiles. "That's the sort of thing you do in hick towns."

I gave him a pointed look. "You're never going to forget that I called Rock Canyon a hick town, are you?"

"Well, you're a New Yorker. You don't know any better."

"New York is a nice place."

"If you like concrete, crowds, and that claustrophobic, closed-in feeling."

I pulled my horse next to his. "Okay, hometowns are off our conversation list. What do you want to talk about next? Oh, and I'm banning anything about computer games or professional sports teams."

"You've got a list of approved conversation topics?"

"It's a long way to the wizard's house and we should get to know each other better."

He tipped his head to the side. "Why? Aren't you going to move to some luxury apartment in New York as soon as we get home?"

My gaze went to his, trying to figure out if he cared or was just curious. I couldn't tell. His eyes were intent and a little bit amused. "Maybe not," I said. "I haven't decided. Besides, you brought up hometowns again. That's off the list. You have to talk about something else."

He shook his head. "This is such a girl thing—talking about what we're going to talk about. With guys, if you've got a question, you ask it."

"Okay," I said, deciding to use the opening he'd given me. "I have a question. Why didn't you go out for football this year?"

His head swung over to me in surprise. "Where did that question come from?"

I fingered my reins. "I asked some girls at school about you. One said you didn't go out for football or student body because you stopped caring about people at school."

He let out a grunt. "How did my personal life get on your approved conversation list?"

"We're doing this the guy way," I reminded him. "I had a question. So is it true?"

He paused and looked out at the forest. "I stopped doing extracurricular things because I have two younger sisters who want to be driven to dance lessons and need help with their homework. I have to be there for them since our mom isn't." He let out an irritated sigh. "I'm assuming you know about my mom too. The gossipy girls at school didn't leave out that part?"

"They said she died over a year ago. That's all."

"She was hit by a drunk driver. Probably a teenager. They never found out who."

Maybe by someone at school, then. I could see how that would make a person feel less social. "I'm sorry."

"Yeah, everybody is sorry. That topic is off the list."

I didn't speak for a few moments. I didn't want to say the wrong thing again.

He looked over at me, and his expression softened. "I didn't mean to snap at you."

He hadn't, really. "It's okay," I said.

He looked out at the forest again, but this time his posture had a tightness about it. "You're lucky, you know—about the whole wish business."

That made me laugh. "I don't feel so lucky right now."

"No, I mean you're lucky that you had three wishes, and all you wanted was a visit from Robin Hood and some gold."

It wasn't all I had wanted, but the point was the same. I didn't ask what he would have wished for. I already knew, and it was off the list.

We spoke about other things. He told me about his sisters, and I told him about Kendall. We talked about what we would do when we got home. I wanted to sleep someplace that was not a barn floor. He wanted to eat a lot of junk food.

But the entire time we spoke, I thought about his wish.

Hours went by. We stopped at another village long enough to feed and water the horses. Once we had eaten and they had rested, we went back to the trail. It was harder to climb back on the horse this time. I had ridden for so long my legs had gone beyond aching. They throbbed, and each bounce in the horse's step made it worse.

I wished I had thought to ask at the last village if I could buy some kind of painkiller. People here must have some sort of herb or something they used. Better yet, I should have thought to take some ibuprofen from my parents' provisions. They had a first-aid kit. I'd seen it next to a box of toilet paper—which was another thing I wished I'd brought. The privy at the last village had something that resembled corn husks.

In order to take my mind off the pain in my legs, I took the magic book out of my saddlebag. I might as well try to think up new morals.

I flipped through the book. A new painting of Hudson and me horseback riding had appeared. Hudson's uniform looked crisp, and his black horse gleamed in the sunlight. I wore a sapphire blue dress with lace sleeves. The painting also showed me wearing some sort of blue bejeweled hat. In reality, I was pretty sure I still had bits of straw entwined in my hair.

The prose read, "The next day the guard and the miller's daughter rode through the forest. Little did she realize the surprise that awaited her."

I caught my breath and turned the page, but it was blank. No painting, no words. "Hudson, you need to see this!"

He looked over his shoulder and I waved the book at him. "It says something is waiting for us. A surprise."

"What?" he asked.

I wasn't sure if he meant "What is waiting for us?" or "What are you talking about?" I waved the book again. "You need to read this."

He halted his horse, and I rode to his side. He took the book and looked at the picture. "Love the dress. You really know how to travel in style."

"Read it."

He did, then flipped the page just as I had. "So what's the surprise?"

"It doesn't say." I glanced around, wishing we hadn't stopped. Anything could be hiding in the forest.

Hudson shut the book and handed it back to me. "Well, there's nothing we can do about it. Besides, it doesn't say the surprise is something bad."

I slipped the book into the saddlebag. "Oh, it's going to be bad. Surprises in stories are always bad. Robin Hood will ambush us or a troll will be waiting under the bridge. Something like that."

Hudson flicked his reins, but his horse had found a patch of grass by the path, and she didn't seem in any hurry to move. Hudson let her eat. "Surprises aren't always bad. It could be the surprise of . . ." His broad shoulders shrugged. " 'She found a patch of wild strawberries and got to eat something besides stale bread.' "

I raised an eyebrow at him. "Have you ever actually read a book?"

He tilted his head at the question. "Have you?"

"Of course I have." My horse wandered a few steps off the path, chomping leaves from a nearby bush. There didn't seem to be a point in pulling her away since Hudson's horse was eating too.

Hudson was still surveying me. "Nick told me you refuse to read books as a way to tick off your dad."

"Well, I used to read a lot, and I distinctly remember that all the surprises in books were bad. This is clearly a problem."

"Clearly," he said with a teasing lift in his voice. He directed his horse farther off the path. She went willingly, stepping over to the next patch of grass. "The horses are tired and hungry, and so am I. We might as well find a place to set up camp for the night."

I didn't move my horse. "That's the last thing we should do. We should keep riding until we're safe."

Hudson dismounted and walked his horse farther away from the path. The mare went, pulling up clumps of grass and chomping them as she went. "We have to set up camp sooner or later," Hudson said. "We might as well do it while it's light. If something is going to surprise us, I'd rather have it happen when I have a fire going."

I groaned but dismounted too. He was right. We couldn't ride until we were safe. No place was safe until we knew what the surprise was.

My legs ached so badly I could only take tiny, awkward steps in Hudson's direction. Eventually he found a spot he liked and turned back to check on me.

He watched my mincing progress. "Saddle sore?"

"Aren't you?"

He took a section of rope and tied his horse to a tree. "I told you, my grandparents have horses. You'll get used to it after a few days."

If my legs didn't break off by then. Hudson walked over and took my horse's reins, murmuring things to her as he led her to a tree. By the time I had winced my way over to help him, he'd already untied our provisions, put them in a pile, and was hefting off his horse's saddle. I hadn't even thought about the saddles and probably would have left them on all night.

I watched him effortlessly swing my saddle off my horse and place it on the ground. "Maybe the moral is 'If you're going to get stuck in the Middle Ages, make sure you bring along a country boy.' They know how to build fires, take care of horses, escape from castles—really, is there anything you can't do?"

"Lots of things." An emotion flashed across his expression

that I recognized but didn't understand. Self-recrimination. Some memory of a time he had failed had surfaced in his mind.

We gathered wood, set out our blankets, and made a small fire that crackled against the growing cold. We sat beside it and ate apples, cheese, and stiff bread. I tried not to keep checking over my shoulder for a surprise. Hudson ate without speaking. Whatever memory I'd brought up, it was still bothering him.

This was the Hudson the girls had told me about at school. The sullen one.

Finally, I got tired of the silence, of the undercurrent of pain that swirled between us. I put my hand on his knee, trying to console him. "Your mom wouldn't want you to be sad about her for this long."

He ripped a piece of bread from his loaf. "She's off the list, Tansy."

"She would want you to have a social life, to be happy."

"What's the point of crossing things off the list if you're still going to bring them up?"

"You've got to let the sadness go."

"Fine," he said with a grunt. "We'll talk about this." He ripped another piece from his loaf, but didn't eat it. "My mom and I got in an argument that night. I told her I was going to a movie with friends but I went to a party instead." He turned the piece of bread over and over in his hand. "When you're the police chief's son, you're not supposed to go to parties where there's drinking. It would look bad if the party got busted. I wasn't trying to undermine my father or the law or anything. I went because my friends were there." He looked straight at the fire, but I knew he wasn't seeing it anymore. He was back in that night. "Somebody called and told my mom where I'd been. When I came home, she was getting off the phone and was really steamed. She went off about how I was supposed to set an example. My friends weren't going to respect the law if I didn't. And I was making my father a laughingstock.

"I told her I wanted to have my own life, and I didn't want to be their son anymore." The rest of the bread in Hudson's hand crumbled under his grip, but he didn't notice it. "She stormed out of the house, and I knew I should go after her. But I didn't. That was the last thing I ever said to her—that I didn't want to be her son."

"You couldn't have known what would happen," I said. "It wasn't your fault."

He still kept his gaze on the fire. "I thought she might be headed to the party to yell at my friend's parents. It wasn't far away, just the next street over. So I called my friend and warned him that his party was about to get busted." His voice wavered, dropped. "My mom was probably hit by someone leaving that party, someone who was drunk and going too fast. Because *I* warned them."

The breath went from my lungs. I didn't know what to say. But Hudson didn't stop, didn't wait for my reaction.

"My father was on duty that night. He was called out along with the paramedics. He didn't know until he got there . . ." Hudson's voice broke off. "He's never forgiven me and I don't blame him."

I took hold of Hudson's hand. "That can't be true. Has he said that?"

"He doesn't have to. I see it in his eyes every time I look at him."

Even though Hudson's hand was stiff and unresponsive in mine, I kept hold of it, pressing it between the palms of my hands as though I could force comfort into his fingers. "He's probably in too much pain to see what you're going through." I intertwined my fingers into his. "Pain makes you blind."

It was true, and yet it wasn't. The pain of my parents' divorce had made me blind to a lot of things, yet here, holding Hudson's hand, I realized that suffering could also make a person see. I could understand a little bit of the crushing weight he felt because I had been crushed myself.

"I should have gone after her," Hudson said.

I slid one arm around his waist and laid my head on his shoulder. I didn't think he would return my hug but he wrapped his arms around me, resting his cheek against the top of my head. "I'll never be able to make it up to him."

"You don't have to," I said. "Your father doesn't want you to carry around this guilt."

Hudson didn't say anything else, but I don't think he believed me. The muscles in his arms and chest were rigid. Neither of us moved, though. We sat there by the fire, arms around each other, while the flames hissed and popped and smoke swirled up into the sky.

Eventually, the tension left him. He let out a deep breath and it drained away. But instead of letting me go, he pulled me closer. As though, after pushing away comfort for so long, he finally wanted it. And I wanted to comfort him. If I lifted my head, I could kiss him. I raised my head and looked into his eyes, trying to read his expression.

He looked back at me with a calm intensity.

I tilted my face to his, then heard an irritated voice behind me say, "There you are! I've been looking for you all over!"

I turned, startled. Chrissy stood behind me.

Chapter 19

She wore a filmy green dress with flowing layers that reminded me of plant leaves. Her hair had changed from pink to blond, and small white flowers were woven through it, making her smell like orange blossoms. She carried something in a blue fuzzy blanket, which she held against her chest and shoulder.

Hudson dropped his arms away from me. "Surprise," he muttered.

Chrissy stepped toward me, eyes blinking to the same fast rhythm that her wings fluttered. "You're supposed to be at the castle. I showed up in my official fairy godmother outfit expecting a wedding, and the whole place was in disarray. King John is furious and threatening anyone and everyone. He sent all the knights scuttling across the kingdom to look for you, and . . ." Her gaze swept over me. "What in the world are you wearing? I specifically told Clover to make sure you wore evening gowns." She made disappointed *tsk*ing noises. "Never trust a leprechaun where fashion is concerned."

"I'm in the middle of the forest," I pointed out. "Why do I need an evening gown?"

With her free hand, Chrissy pulled a wand out of a leafy bag that hung around her shoulder. "Because this is a fairy tale, and my professor gave me a horrible grade after my last assignment when Cinderella's ball gown changed into a bath towel at midnight." She gave a careless shrug. "I did warn her. It wasn't my fault there were people around."

Chrissy swished her wand in my direction. Before I could utter another protest, I was wearing a white gown with silver beading radiating from the bodice like an exploding star. I felt something on my head and reached up to touch it. My hair was up in some sort of bun with a tiara nestled into it.

"Now then," Chrissy said with satisfaction. "We'll need to get you back to the castle for your wedding."

I found my voice then. "No!" I sputtered. "I won't marry King John. I won't." I stood up so quickly that my legs nearly gave out. I had to take a couple of stumbling steps before they would support me.

Chrissy's rosebud pink mouth dropped open. "What's wrong with your legs?"

"I've been riding a horse all day. After I escaped from the castle—"

"You escaped from the castle?" she repeated indignantly. "That's not supposed to happen. You're messing up my fairy tale."

Hudson got to his feet and stood by my side. His voice was calmer than mine, but had a firm insistence to it. "Tansy doesn't want to be the miller's daughter. She wants to go home. We all do."

Chrissy let out a disapproving humph and wrinkled her nose at him. "You're not even part of this fairy tale. Whoever heard of a nameless extra running away with the heroine?"

I reached out and took hold of Hudson's arm, afraid

Chrissy would whisk him away with a dip of her wand. "I want his help."

Chrissy shifted the bundle she carried from one shoulder to the other. "This is most irregular. I put safeguards in place to keep the story from veering off track. You shouldn't have been able to escape from the castle."

I held a hand out to her, pleading. "Please don't send me back to King John. I'm only seventeen. I can't marry some crazy man and have his baby. You've got to see that."

Chrissy's expression softened and she let out an almost motherly sigh. "I was never going to make you have King John's son. That's why I've brought you yours." She moved the bundle from her shoulder and cradled it in her arms, revealing a baby. His eyes were shut in sleep, his lips puckered in an invisible suckle.

"What?" I stammered. "I don't have a son."

She handed me the bundle. He was warm and soft, and he had flower-petal-smooth skin. I held him to me and inhaled his baby-powder scent.

"Well, you don't have a son when you're seventeen," she said. "I went to your future and borrowed him. Now you can tell that awful ex-fairy his name, be through with the story, and go home."

"No . . ." I held the baby back out to her, panic gripping my chest with more fierceness than the golden heart had ever done. My hands trembled, and I had to force myself to look at Chrissy and not the baby. I wanted to stare at his round cheeks, his button nose, and the wispy brown hair that curled at the ends. My baby. My future son.

"Take him back to the twenty-first century. He's not safe here."

Chrissy bent over and kissed his forehead. A puff of silver glitter momentarily twirled around his head. "I know you've never taken care of a child, but it's not that hard. I packed bottles, formula, diapers, and the cutest little outfits you've ever seen." She reached into her purse and pulled out a bag that grew until it was a full-sized, leafy green diaper bag.

In a low voice, Hudson said, "Tansy, you have to tell her what you did."

I didn't need the prompting. The words had already started tumbling out of my mouth. "I traded Clover some gold for a change enchantment. So now the fairy tale doesn't have to end like the real story did. I can't have my own baby here. Rumpelstiltskin will take him."

Chrissy's lips tightened and her wings spanned open sharply. "You *changed* the fairy tale?"

"It seemed like the easiest way to get home."

Chrissy tapped her wand in exasperation. "Well, that's mortal logic for you. Complicate things in the name of simplification." She put one hand on her hip and held the other out, palm up. "Let me see *The Change Enchantment*."

I was still holding the baby, so Hudson got the book and handed it to her. Chrissy opened it, barely glancing through the illustration and text. "Writers," she muttered, then put her wand to the book. "Give me the nonfiction version, please."

At once the paintings changed to actual pictures, moving ones, like paper-thin computer screens. She put her wand back into her purse and flipped through pages, pausing at the one where Clover and I made our bargain. She scowled, then turned the next page and the next, watching the important events of the last two days, until she reached the final page and saw herself peering at the book in the forest beside Hudson and me.

Chrissy let out a dramatic sigh and slammed the book shut. "How am I ever supposed to finish an assignment to the UMA's approval when they keep sending me an assistant who purposely sabotages my efforts?" She gripped the book hard, as though she'd like to throw it. "I'll tell you why he did this. He's ticked off that I'm using the gold enchantment that he lost to

Rumpelstiltskin to complete my assignment. He just can't bear the fact that he doesn't own it anymore."

"It used to be Clover's enchantment?" I asked. The shabby clothes and second job as a party entertainer suddenly made sense. He had lost his ability to make gold. But had Clover really given me *The Change Enchantment* to sabotage me? Would he do that? The thought settled into my stomach like I'd swallowed lead. Weren't there any magical creatures out there that actually helped people? What was going to happen next? Would a unicorn come along and try to impale us?

I glanced down at my baby. I hadn't ever thought much about having children before, but seeing him, holding him, was doing something to me. Emotions gripped me so strongly I couldn't even identify what they were. He was beautiful. Perfect. I didn't want to let him go, and yet the desire I had to protect him outweighed everything else.

I held him out to Chrissy. "You understand why he can't be here. Anything can happen now."

"Yes," she said, clutching the book as proof. "You decided to leave the safety of a plotted story and plunge into the unknown. You might as well have stayed in your old life if you were going to do that. Are you so fond of uncertainty that you had to bring it into your wish too?" Her wings fluttered in agitation, and a wind rushed through the forest as if nature had no choice but to match her mood. The fire blew out. Strands of her hair flailed around her shoulders and bits of leaves swirled at my feet. "I brought your son here because I thought he would be safe within the confines of the fairy tale. You only had to do two simple things when Rumpelstiltskin came for the baby: cry so he offered you a second chance, and then answer his question. His name is Rumpelstiltskin. How hard is that? But now anything can happen. You put your son in danger by choosing this."

I held my baby protectively to my chest, shaking with both fear and anger. "I didn't choose to have a baby in the Middle

Ages. It's your fault he's in danger. You've got to take him back to the right time."

"My fault?" She blinked in indignation. "I granted you three wishes and in return you made a deal with a leprechaun that could lead to magical calamity." She gestured to the baby. "Your son is the key Rumpelstiltskin needs to regain his old powers. It won't matter where I take the baby now. He was here and yours within a year from your agreement. That means Rumpelstiltskin can claim him."

Around us, tree branches shuddered in the wind. The sound of their swishing leaves created a dull, chastising roar. "Do you realize what Rumpelstiltskin will do if he gets his fairy magic back?" Chrissy asked. "He won't be a friend to mortals, I can tell you that. Expect a lot of frozen crops, plagues, and men to mysteriously change into frogs. Meanwhile, the fairies will have to join forces to fight him all over again. As if I don't already have enough to do."

She let out a disgruntled huff and crossed her arms so forcefully she nearly dropped the magic book. The wind ended at the same time as her outburst, and the billowing leaves settled limply back down. "This," she said pointedly, "is precisely why fairies stay away from humans most of the time."

I gaped at her. I could feel Hudson's hand on my arm, warning me to let it go, but I couldn't. "I asked for a way to change things into gold and you threw me, my family, and all of our possessions into the Middle Ages. I have been imprisoned, threatened, shackled, and my house was ransacked. I was forced into a bargain with a creepy ex-fairy, knights are out looking for me in order to force me into a marriage with a crazy old man, and the gold enchantment rips at my heart every time I use it. And now, on top of that, you've put my baby in danger."

Chrissy regarded me evenly. "You know, you're pretty unhappy for someone who got exactly what she wanted."

I gritted my teeth. "I never asked to be part of this fairy tale!"

"But it's what you *wished* for. The trouble is that you didn't really want gold. You wanted a life with no worries, no problems, and the answers to every test before it's given to you."

"Okay," I said. "That sounds good. Give me that instead of this wish."

She flicked my words away with a toss of her manicured nails. "If that's what you wanted, you should have asked to be turned into an encyclopedia." She shook her head patiently. "You wouldn't be happy on a dusty shelf though. Living is more fun. The key to happiness—as any good fairy godmother will tell you—is not to avoid problems, but to overcome them." She took a deep breath, composing herself, then gestured grandly toward the forest. "So off you go on your journey, my little charge. Overcome."

Hudson cocked his head at her in disbelief. "Overcome?"

She ignored him and kept waving her hand at the forest. I looked in the direction she was motioning and then back at her. "It will be dark soon, I have a baby, and there are sword-wielding men out there who want to capture me."

She pulled her wand out of her purse and waved it at the horses. They changed from brown mares into white steeds, fully saddled. "Overcome," she said. "And if you can't overcome, at least learn something meaningful. Otherwise it will be an awful story, and no one will want to read it. You don't want to be responsible for not only giving an ex-fairy his powers back but also ruining a perfectly good fairy tale, do you? Now off you go."

With another flourish of her wand our supplies flew off the ground and repacked themselves onto the horses.

"No one will want to read it?" I repeated. "*That's* what you're worried about?"

Her gaze ran over me and she let out a martyred sigh. "I suppose as long as I'm blowing my magic budget, I ought to fix your legs too. You can't go hobbling around for the rest of the story."

I didn't argue with her about that. She swept her wand in my direction and the pain drained away, until it had completely disappeared.

"Here," Chrissy said, holding out the book. "You should read the next page before you go."

I was holding the baby, so Hudson took the book and opened it so we both could see it. Illustrations covered the pages again, and the latest painting was of Rumpelstiltskin. He held his magic mirror in one hand, a look of dark determination in his eyes. I recognized the background. He stood next to the boxes of supplies at Robin Hood's camp. He must have come not long after I left.

Which meant he was looking for me.

My heart jumped into my throat. My hands trembled.

"Even ex-fairies know the ways of the forest," Chrissy said. "All Rumpelstiltskin needs to do to find you is ask the birds and the trees which way the fair blond maiden went. If you want to keep ahead of him, you need to keep moving. And you," she said, turning to address Hudson, "would do well to stay a nameless extra during this story."

Hudson shut the book with a thud and put his hand on the hilt of his sword. "Rumpelstiltskin had better stay away from us."

Chrissy patted his shoulder tolerantly. "A very noble thought from you, extra-character guard fellow, but fairies—even ex-fairies—can't be killed by the sword. They can only be slain by magic, something you have precious little of." To me she said, "The Alliance may have stripped Rumpelstiltskin of his fairy powers, but over the years, he's picked up plenty of enchantments. He still has enough magic to kill you easily enough." She shook her head as though it couldn't be helped. "Mortals have such a frail grasp on life to begin with. I swear, you're all born with one foot already in heaven." Her voice had risen in frustration and she took a breath to calm herself, then smiled at me benevolently. "What I mean is, be careful. More than your life is riding on the outcome of this fairy tale now. Think of your family, and the mortals who will bear the wrath of an empowered ex-fairy. Think of my *grade*. I can feel it slipping down the alphabet as we speak."

"Your grade?" Hudson asked, but he didn't wait for her to answer. He strode over to untie the horses, mumbling things about fairies as he went.

I stayed where I was. "How is my son the key to Rumpelstiltskin regaining his powers?"

Chrissy's lips twitched into a frown. "The UMA doesn't destroy a fairy's magic; they can only lock it up. Regular locks don't keep out fairies, of course, so the UMA uses magic spells. For example, Sleeping Beauty's enchanted spinning wheel is in a vault with a spell that only lifts for those who know the wheel is there but don't want to use it. I could open the vault right now because I have no desire to use sleep-inducing furniture. The moment I wanted to use it, I would never be able to pry the door open." Her voice slowed. "I wish the UMA had used that spell for Rumpelstiltskin's power. Instead, his vault can only be unlocked by buying love that cannot be bought." She lifted her hand and then let it fall. "He found a way around that spell by buying your son when you thought the baby wouldn't exist."

My arms wrapped protectively around the fuzzy blue blanket. "What will happen to him if Rumpelstiltskin takes him?"

Chrissy's wings slowly slid open, then quickly shut. She didn't answer.

"What happens to my baby?" I asked again.

"Rumpelstiltskin will leave the baby in the vault. And he'll die there."

My legs felt weak. I worried they might give out. One thought pounded through my ears. I couldn't let Rumpelstiltskin take my baby. I couldn't. I had to find a way to prevent it. "Chrissy, please just tell me the moral to this fairy tale. If I write down the moral, we can go home, right?"

Her wings continued their slow fanning. "It's not Rumpel-stiltskin's moral you need; it's the moral of your own story. That's the magic of books. They're never quite the same for any two people. When you read one, you automatically make it your own."

"I've tried every moral I can think of," I said. "Nothing works."

She slid her wand back into her purse. "Well, you need to ask the right question to get the right answer."

"Okay." I tried to keep my voice calm, rational. "I'm pretty sure the right question is, what is the moral of the story?"

She glanced at her watch—a sure sign she was about to leave. "No, the question to ask is, what have I learned?" The light around Chrissy glimmered; she was fading, and I knew in another moment, she'd leave altogether.

I stepped toward her. "Don't go yet."

"Very often," she said, her voice already sounding far away, "the lessons you learn are more important than the things you accomplish."

And then she was gone.

"Lovely," I said out loud. "A very lovely sentiment, unless what you want to accomplish is getting to safety." The baby stretched. He lifted one arm, leaving his hand by his face as he drifted back to sleep. "Or saving your baby's life." His life sud-denly seemed more important than my own.

Hudson walked back over, holding the reins of my horse. "You were right," he said. "That was quite a surprise."

I knew I should be moving, but I felt too shaky to take a single step. I hadn't even wanted to bargain with Rumpelstiltskin when the baby he asked for was only theoretical—when I didn't think it would ever exist anyway. Now I held the baby in my arms. He was mine.

I could identify the emotion that had coursed so forcefully through me from the moment Chrissy placed him in my arms. It was love, stronger than anything I had ever felt before. This feeling was why parents ran into burning buildings to save their children. It was why animals killed to protect their young. It was why my own father had made a deal with bandits and stormed a castle to rescue me. I knew unequivocally that I would do anything for this child. And I had traded him to Rumpelstiltskin for the ability to change things into gold. My voice choked in my throat. "What have I done?"

"It will be all right," Hudson said. "You already know Rumpelstiltskin's name."

This brought me some comfort, but not enough. I had changed the fairy tale. What if I had changed the bargain at the end too? What if he asked a different question?

"At least your fairy godmother gave us fresh horses," Hudson said. "Here, I'll hold the baby while you mount."

"Be careful," I said. "Don't drop him."

Hudson held out his arms. "You can trust me."

He had said the same thing back at the castle, and I had laughed at him. I didn't now. I handed him my son.

On a hunch, I checked the diaper bag, and found what I was looking for—an over-the-shoulder sling to carry the baby in. It took Hudson and me a few moments to figure out how to work it, but then the baby was nestled against my chest, sleeping, and we rode through the forest.

The horses were strong and fast. While the last bit of evening light lingered in the sky, they raced down the path without much urging on our part. In the back of my mind, I could always see Rumpelstiltskin walking through the forest, his thin face scanning the trees. "Which way did she go?" he asked them, and their leaves quaked in my direction.

As soon as we were far enough away, I would write morals until I found the one that brought us home—to a time period that was long beyond the date that Rumpelstiltskin could ask anything from me. I made a mental list of things I had learned.

Magic was dangerous. Greed was dangerous. And my father

loved me enough—Sandra and Nick loved me enough—to risk their lives to rescue me from King John. That was my favorite thing I'd learned.

Another thing I'd learned: despite the fact that I hadn't liked Hudson at first, I liked him a lot now. He was smart, brave, and thoughtful. I had no doubt when we got back to Rock Canyon, he could do anything he wanted in life.

I had also learned that at some point I was going to have a son. As I felt the warmth of his little body against my own, I thought about that responsibility. I wanted to be the best person I could for him. I would make sure I was ready to be a mom, and married, and that the guy I married would be a good father. Someone who was dedicated to me and our son so I wouldn't ever have to raise him by myself.

The thought made my throat tighten. My mother had raised Kendall and me by herself for years, and I hadn't made it any easier for her. I was sorry about that now.

The sun set and the moon rose in the night sky. It was full, but still didn't shed much light. Hudson turned on his flash-light, and held it out in front of him in order to keep the horses moving forward at a walk. When we reached the river, it became a little easier to travel. The ground was smoother, and the water made a dark arrow of a path to follow.

The baby woke up as we went along the riverbank. I had no idea how old he was. He was bigger than a newborn, but whether he was five months or ten, I couldn't tell.

He fussed, squinting his eyes in displeasure. "It's all right," I whispered to him. "I'm here. Mommy's here."

I expected him to dispute that statement with a few wails. After all, I wasn't really his mother. Not yet. But he settled back into me.

He knew my voice, I realized, and I felt incredibly happy at that fact.

We continued riding on. When our horses clattered over

the wooden bridge, the baby woke again, this time opening startled eyes and throwing his arms out in surprise. He cried in indignation, and my whispered assurances weren't enough to soothe him. Was he hungry? If I made up some formula and he didn't want it, then it would be wasted, and I wasn't sure how much food Chrissy had packed for him. I found an empty bottle in the diaper bag and put it to his lips to see if he tried to drink from it, but he just turned his head, arching away.

I felt along his diaper. It was dry.

What else did parents do when babies cried? I didn't know any lullabies, but my dad used to sing "You Are My Sunshine" to me when I was little. It seemed like a parental song, so I sang it.

The baby settled down, watching me with dark eyes and sucking on his fist. Maybe I sang this song to him in the future. Or perhaps my father did.

I only knew the first verse of the song, so I sang it over and over, and thought about how your childhood is with you, even when you don't realize it's there.

I hadn't thought that we would be able to travel very far along the path into the forest. I kept waiting for the flashlight to dim or for Hudson to say he couldn't hold it steady anymore, but we trudged on at a slow pace, and the moon rose higher in the sky.

The pathway finally widened into a real road and then we came to a village. All the huts we passed were dark and shuttered. Some were little more than shacks; others looked like log cabins. A few were made of stone—these were the largest homes.

Hudson rode to a stone house set farther back than the rest. It had a large garden in front and a barn behind the house. The wizard might have been out of favor with the king, but he still seemed to be one of the more wealthy residents of this village.

We dismounted from our horses, tied them to a hitching

post, and walked to the door. Hudson knocked and we waited. I kept my arm around the baby. "Once the wizard's wand is fixed, are you sure there isn't a way he could send us all back home without having to travel the entire way back to meet my family?"

Hudson shook his head. "It's not something he can do long distance. We've got to be near to his wand for the magic to work."

I looked up at the moon and wondered what time it was. One o'clock in the morning? Two? "Do you think he'll be willing to come with us tonight?" I asked.

I could see the exhaustion in Hudson's eyes, but he said, "The sooner we leave, the better chance we'll have of avoiding King John's men. Hopefully Bartimaeus will understand that."

I ran my hand along the bottom of the sling. "We'll have to travel to the meeting place another way so we don't run into Rumpelstiltskin."

"Right." We were both too tired to say more.

A woman in a white nightdress and a cap answered the door. She gave me the impression of a snowman come to life, bulky and pale. She lifted up her brass candleholder to examine us, and sniffed when she noticed Hudson's uniform. "My master has no dealings with King John or his men," she said, "and we've already answered all of your questions."

She went to shut the door, but Hudson put his hand out to stop her. "I'm not one of King John's men. My name is Hudson and your master knows me. I've come on urgent business. Tell him I can give him the Gilead if he'll travel with us to it."

Hudson actually had the Gilead in his pouch, but he'd given me strict instructions on the ride up not to reveal this fact. His reasoning was that if Bartimaeus knew we had the Gilead with us, it would be harder to get him to agree to travel all the way to my family to send them back. But if Bartimaeus went to the camp to get the Gilead and was already there with my family, we'd have a better bargaining position. It wouldn't be much extra trouble to send us back together.

The woman eyed us and humphed, clearly not happy about waking the wizard. "Very well," she said, then shut the door, leaving us outside.

I stared at the door for a moment, not sure if this ended our interview. "Is she going to wake him?"

"She'll get him." Hudson rubbed the back of his neck wearily. "How's the baby doing?"

In the darkness, it was hard to see him, but I could feel the rise and fall of his little chest. "All right, I guess."

We waited. The door opened, and the woman appeared again, this time holding blankets under her arm. "The master says he'll speak with you in the morning."

Hudson squared his shoulders. "Did you tell him who we were?"

"I know who you are well enough." She wagged a finger in my direction. "She's that trollop from the castle who ran away. Don't bother denying it. No other woman would wear such finery. King John's men came through this morning pestering the entire village and searching our homes for you." Her gaze fell on the sling around my shoulder. "Though I can see why you wouldn't marry King John, what with a babe of your own already. Still, you shouldn't have brought danger to our door. What if someone saw you come here?"

Hudson lowered his voice to a harsh whisper. "No one saw us. But you're right, King John's men are looking, and if they find us, your master won't get his Gilead."

She brushed off his words, unconcerned. "They're not out looking at this hour. They're sleeping like God-fearing people ought."

"Then this is the best time to travel."

"Only if you want to break your horse's leg or your neck. My master has no intention of gallivanting about in the night like a common ruffian." She thrust the blankets at Hudson. "You can sleep safe enough in the barn. It has a spell upon it so that none of King John's men may see it. A few days past, they came through and demanded half of everyone's straw. Next they'll be wanting the straw, and my master has horses to feed." She looked at Hudson suspiciously. "You see the barn plainly, don't you?"

"I saw it when we walked up," Hudson said.

She humphed. "No matter. If you're not in the barn in the morning we'll know you're not what you claim." She narrowed her eyes at Hudson. "My master may not be the court wizard anymore, but he still has things that work against those who would do him harm."

Then she slammed the door shut again.

Hudson groaned, then tucked the blankets under his arm and went to retrieve the horses. "Come on," he said. "I guess we're resting for the night after all."

I followed him, casting nervous glances at the street. "Do you think the spell on the barn will work to keep Rumpelstiltskin away too?"

"Don't worry about it," Hudson said.

I wanted to tell him I had every right to be worried, but I didn't. He couldn't change Bartimaeus's mind, and the barn was the safest place to be right now.

We took the horses inside with us. I started to help Hudson unpack the provisions, but he handed me the blankets. "You take care of the baby. I'll take care of the horses."

I spread some straw on the floor and arranged the blankets on top of it. After I'd settled the baby onto our straw bed, I checked the book to see if there was any new information. An illustration of me riding the white horse and cradling the baby had appeared. I smiled at it, this time liking the fact that I'd been painted beautiful and glowing. The baby's angelic face was just barely visible in my arms, but he looked up at me adoringly.

I wrote the things I had learned, and was still writing them when Hudson made his own bed. I was almost glad that the things I'd written about him hadn't stuck, since he looked over my shoulder to read what I'd written. " 'There's no place like home,' " he repeated.

"It worked for Dorothy." The words vanished and I penned another sentence.

Hudson read, " 'Lean on people when you're not strong. They'll be your friends, they'll help you carry on.' Hmm. Are you writing morals or song lyrics?"

"Both," I said.

He didn't comment on the futility of my writing. Instead he reached into his pouch, took out a handful of red sand, and walked around me, sprinkling it onto the blanket. It was only then that I remembered he'd taken the anti-fairy ring that King John's wizard had put around me the second night.

Even if Rumpelstiltskin was able to find the barn, he wouldn't be able to cross the line to take my son. That's what Hudson had meant when he told me not to worry.

"Thank you," I said.

He smiled, then tossed his helmet on the ground near his blankets. "You're welcome."

I turned off the flashlight and put the book down next to me. I was safe and my baby was safe. At least for tonight.

Chapter 20

When I woke up, pale sunlight poked through cracks in the barn window. I reached for the baby and found only empty blankets. He was gone. I sat up in panic, my heart beating so fast the gold heart sent ticks of pain through my torso.

Then I saw Hudson sitting on the haystack feeding him a bottle. I exhaled slowly to calm myself and walked over to them. The baby had his hand wrapped around one of Hudson's fingers and was looking happily at him while he drank. They were a perfect picture of contentment, oblivious to my still-racing pulse.

"You scared me to death, you know. I thought my son was gone."

Hudson smiled at the baby. "I bet real mothers wake up when their children cry."

"I slept through his crying?" I'd only been a mother for one night, and I'd already done something wrong. So much for my intentions to be the perfect parent. I sat down on the straw with a dejected huff.

Hudson's voice softened. "He was mostly just fussing. I'm a light sleeper."

I shifted in the straw to get more comfortable. I wanted to take the baby from Hudson's arms and feed him myself, but at the same time, I was afraid to. He was so small, and I didn't know how. What had Chrissy been thinking to entrust me with a miniature, breakable person?

"What are you going to name him?" Hudson asked.

"In the future? I have no idea."

"I meant now. We have to call him something."

I stroked the baby's tuft of wavy brown hair. He looked over at me, two large brown eyes taking me in. Then he stopped drinking and smiled. The sight of his grin sent my heart skittering. I felt like I'd won a prize.

He made a happy-sounding *umm, umm* noise and went back to drinking.

"How old do you think he is?" I asked.

"Old enough that he eats baby food, because Chrissy packed some of that too." Hudson tilted his head and regarded the baby. "I think he looks like a . . . Remington. Maybe a Colt."

"Aren't those gun names?"

"He's a manly baby. He needs a manly name. How about Stetson?"

"Are you picking names or describing how the West was won?"

Hudson laughed and looked all the more gorgeous for it. His smile lightened his features, made him look approachable, touchable. "You don't have to keep the name in the future, but people will think it's strange if your son doesn't have a name now."

I ran a finger over the baby's hand where tiny dimples puckered his knuckles. "If I call him Stetson now, then I'll start thinking of him as Stetson and when I have him in the future I won't be able to call him anything else."

"What's wrong with that?"

The baby finished his bottle, and Hudson set him upright. He gurgled and reached for me with waving hands. I took him in my arms, not even caring that he spit up a little of the formula. It ran down his chin, reminding me that you were supposed to burp babies after they ate. There were probably dozens more details I didn't know. I pulled a washcloth out of the diaper bag and wiped his face. "How about we call him Junior? After my husband. Whoever that is."

Junior reached up and tried to grab my bottom lip.

"It's not Robin Hood," Hudson said.

I pulled Junior's hand away from my mouth. "I never said it would be."

Hudson leaned back against the straw. "I just mean, you're blond and Robin Hood's blond, so you'd have blond children. Apparently you marry a brunet guy."

"Well, I've always liked brunets." My gaze went to Hudson's brown hair, then quickly fell away. I didn't need to announce, more than I already had, that I found him attractive. After all, I had practically thrown myself at him last night at the campfire. I'd taken his hand, then put my arms around him, and when he hugged me back, I'd tilted my face up to his so he could kiss me.

He hadn't kissed me. Maybe he would have if Chrissy hadn't popped in, but then again, maybe he wouldn't have. He hadn't done anything since then to indicate he wanted to be more than friends. Which made me feel all the more awkward about the way I'd draped myself around him last night.

Thankfully, Hudson didn't seem to notice my furtive hair glancing. He took the Gilead out of his pouch to check on it, then slipped it back.

I patted the baby's back. "What will happen to Junior when we go to our time period?" I asked.

"We'll take him with us."

"But he hasn't been born yet."

"Neither have we, and we're doing fine in this time period. We don't have any other choice."

He was right, I supposed, but it was hard to imagine how that would work out.

In my lap, Junior grabbed at the beads on my dress. When he couldn't move them, he twisted in my arms and reached his arms out to Hudson.

"He likes you," I said in surprise. I had taken his friendliness toward me as proof that he recognized me, but perhaps he was just a happy baby.

Hudson shrugged and took Junior from me. "That's because I fed him. Babies are like stray cats that way."

"Babies are not like stray cats," I said.

Hudson ignored my protest. "Watch. He loves this." He held Junior up above his head, then brought the baby down and blew raspberries on his neck.

Junior's cheeks bunched up into a smile, and he laughed a deep belly laugh that wobbled through his whole body. I watched the two of them, wishing I had a camera. I wanted to keep the moment.

The barn door opened with a creak, and through the halo of the daylight, a man walked inside. I had expected Bartimaeus to be elderly, with a long white beard and a flowing robe. Instead he was clean shaven with black hair that only brushed his shoulders. He was dressed like most of the men I'd seen in the Middle Ages with the exception that his tunic was cleaner and he wore an embroidered belt around his waist. His eyes had a lofty look to them, and his large, hooked nose gave him an imperial air. Hudson had referred to him as "Bartimaeus the Proud," and I could see why he had the name.

He strolled over to us, unsmiling. "You say you have the Gilead?"

"I left it with friends." Hudson handed me the baby and walked over to the wizard. "But things have changed since we made our agreement. A few more of us need to go to the future. We can pay whatever price you'd like in gold."

Bartimaeus tucked his hands behind his back. "Where are these friends?"

"A day's ride if we travel on the main road by carriage." Hudson gestured toward the far corner of the barn, and it was only then that I noticed a carriage standing there. "Two days if we travel on horseback through the back trails. But either way, we need to avoid King John's men."

The wizard looked at me for the first time, regarding me sourly. "Ah yes, they're out searching for a young woman. Tall, blond, and pretty." He said these things like I'd chosen to be tall, blond, and pretty instead of being useful and productive.

Bartimaeus turned his attention back to Hudson. "Why can't you bring the Gilead here?"

Hudson folded his arms. "Unfortunately, circumstances don't permit it."

The wizard continued to look over us with a deepening scowl. "I have no intention of traveling around the countryside for four days. I'm accustomed to sleeping in my own bed and there's hardly a decent inn from here to Derby." He paced in front of us, the sound of straw crunching beneath his feet.

"My apologies," Hudson said. "Do you still want the Gilead?"

Bartimaeus stopped his pacing. "Oh, very well. I'll have the stable boy hitch up the carriage, and we'll find you some less conspicuous clothes." He shot me one last withering glance. "Something that flaunts fewer jewels than the queen of Sheba would wear."

Technically, the beading on my dress wasn't made of jewels, and I had planned on wearing my cloak over the dress, but I didn't turn down the offer. It would be nice to change into something that didn't look like it had come from the evening-gown portion of the Miss America pageant.

"Be ready when the carriage is," he added. "I don't want to waste any more time on you than I have to." With that, Bartimaeus turned on his heel and left the barn.

I rubbed Junior's back through his fuzzy sleeper. "I've thought of a new moral for the story: 'Wizards are a bunch of grumpy old men.'"

"Maybe," Hudson said. "But if he can send us home, I'd vote for naming your baby after him." He reached out and tweaked the baby's chin. "Right, little Bart?"

· · ·

An hour later, the carriage was packed, the horses were ready, and I was wearing a worn brown dress that smelled of onions and garlic—one of the servant's gowns. The wizard had also given me a head-covering wimple to hide my blond hair. "If we see anyone, shrink down so as not to appear so tall," Bartimaeus had told me. I wasn't that tall, but the Middle Ages was populated by short people. Then Bartimaeus had grumbled disapprovingly. "And for mercy's sake, do something so you don't look so pretty."

Personally, I thought the ugly brown dress and wimple did a sufficient enough job of that. The wizard also gave me an outfit for the baby—a beige shirt that was so long it looked like a shapeless dress. Cute baby clothing hadn't been invented yet.

Hudson changed into new clothes too because King John had told his knights that I was traveling with one of his guards. He wore an oversized gray tunic, leggings, and a leather belt. Unlike my wimple and kitchen-staff ensemble, Hudson's outfit somehow looked good on him. It was his broad shoulders. He could make anything look rugged. I had to quell the urge to call him "farm boy," and pretend I was Buttercup from *The Princess Bride*.

But I did let my eyes rest on him a lot.

Before we left, the wizard sprinkled a spicy-smelling liquid on each corner of the carriage. "Don't touch these spots before they dry," he told us. "If you ruin the hiding spell, our enemies will be able to see the carriage." He sent me an especially deep frown. "We can't have that while we carry a fugitive."

I wasn't looking forward to a day-long carriage ride with Bartimaeus and his many complaints, so I was happily surprised when he climbed up to the box seat and announced he was driving. "There are things out in the forest that only a wizard can ward off," he told us in a condescending tone.

Fine. More power to him and more room for us. Junior was already bored with the baby toys in the diaper bag, and I had no idea how I was going to entertain him in a carriage all day.

The answer to this question was soon evident. Junior wanted to play Grab Mommy's Lips. Hudson was coconspirator in the game and kept holding Junior airplane-style, zooming him toward my face.

After we played that for a stretch, Junior moved on to Try to Throw All of the Baby Toys Out the Carriage Window. Then he tried to teethe on the seats. We fed him creamed carrots, which he somehow managed to smear across not only his bib but his entire body. I only had wet wipes to clean him off, which weren't very effective, especially since Junior then decided he wanted to eat them.

By the time he took a bottle and fell asleep that afternoon, I was exhausted. I propped him against the crook of my arm and noticed a smear of carrots near the shoulder of my dress. I tried to clean it off with a wet wipe, one-handed.

"Don't worry about stains," Hudson told me. "I'm sure the book will erase them."

"This dress belongs to the wizard's servant and you know he'll gripe about me getting it dirty." I kept wiping but couldn't manage very well with only one hand. Finally Hudson moved from his seat to mine, took the cloth, and wiped it for me. He was so close now, bent over and touching my shoulder, that my heart skipped a few beats.

He finished, and straightened. "There. Now it blends in with the general brownness of the dress."

"Thanks," I said.

Neither of us said anything else. Hudson didn't go back to his seat. The silence seemed to be waiting for something. Or maybe that was just me.

His eyes were a warm brown, gentle but intense. "You know . . . I never gave you a good-bye kiss."

It was hard to breathe. "Oh. That's right."

"I was supposed to do that so you wouldn't be lying."

"Yeah," I said. Had I actually told Robin Hood that I was going to kiss Hudson, or had I merely implied it? But then, it was better to be safe than sorry.

The suggestion of a smile played on Hudson's lips. "We'd better kiss now so fireworks don't go off around your head."

Fireworks. I nodded. Somehow I couldn't speak anymore.

He leaned toward me gradually, as though giving me time to change my mind. I shut my eyes and let his lips come down on mine.

Hudson wasn't in a hurry to say good-bye. The kiss was slow, caressing. All the bumps of the road and the sway of the carriage seemed to fade away, replaced by the beating of my heart. I didn't remember putting my free hand around his neck, but it was there somehow, twining through his hair. His arm moved from the back of the seat to my shoulders. I liked the feel of his arm around me. I felt enveloped, cared for. When he lifted his head from mine, my mind was spinning.

I blinked at him. "Well, you certainly have a way with good-byes."

He smiled, amused, then moved back to sit across from me. I wondered if he really had only kissed me to make sure no sparks went off around my head. Maybe he hadn't meant to cause the sparks that were now going off inside me.

I waited for him to say something about the kiss, about us. Was he interested, or was he just the type of guy who liked to prove he could turn girls into quivering piles of hormones?

Still smiling, Hudson looked at the baby. "You ought to call him Stetson."

I tried to keep my voice calm, like the kiss hadn't really mattered. "My husband might not appreciate me naming our son after a hat."

"It's not like you're naming him Baseball Cap or Sombrero."

Did he want to be more than friends? Not even that? I wanted to ask, but instead I stared at Junior. He was safe ground. "Can you believe how tiny his fingernails are?"

"They match his tiny fingers."

"His pinky curves in a little," I said, noticing it for the first time. "I've never seen that before."

"It's not so uncommon." Hudson lifted his own hand. "Mine are that way."

As soon as the words were out of his mouth, Hudson's gaze shot to mine.

I stared back at him, suddenly light-headed. The baby had brown, wavy hair and dark brown eyes like Hudson. I felt a blush creep into my cheeks.

Instead of blushing, the coloring dropped from Hudson's face. He clenched his jaw. This was not a good indication that he wanted to be more than friends.

When he at last spoke, it was with marked frustration. "Chrissy said she went to the future and got *your* baby."

I nodded, still blushing.

"But she's your fairy godmother, so she probably didn't want to risk your child. I'm just a nameless extra who's messing up the story. She would have thought it was dramatic justice to take *my* baby instead."

I gulped, finally able to breathe. He hadn't connected the details the same way I had. "You don't think I'm the mother?"

Hudson's gaze swept over the baby. "He doesn't look anything like you, and he loves it when I hold him—he probably recognizes me." Hudson leaned back against his seat, folded his arms, and let out an exasperated breath. "He's my kid, and his name is Stetson."

But I knew he was mine. He had calmed down at the sound of my voice. I wasn't about to relinquish him. "The story is about the miller's daughter. Rumpelstiltskin bought *my* child, not yours. Why would Chrissy have brought the guard's son into the fairy tale?"

Hudson waved a hand in my direction. "You're not actually a miller's daughter. Your father is a librarian. Chrissy is improvising and she doesn't care whose baby she steals for the story. Fairies don't follow rules."

"They must have some rules because they have a magical alliance."

Hudson shook his head. "I don't know why I didn't see it before. He looks just like my baby pictures. Trust me, he's mine."

There was no point in arguing about it. "Fine," I said, wrapping an arm around Junior possessively. "He's *ours*." I meant for the duration of the trip, but Hudson understood what I hadn't meant to say. I could see the realization dawning on his face.

"You think that . . . you and I?" The words hung in the air for a moment.

I didn't answer. I probably blushed again.

Hudson tilted his head back and grinned. He looked like he might break out laughing.

What did that reaction mean? Did he think the idea of us being a couple was funny, that it could never happen?

I sent him a challenging look. "I suppose you're too good to marry me?"

He leaned against the carriage wall, settling in with satisfaction. "Not at all. You're King John's fiancée, the heroine of the story. One day Disney will make a movie about this and then you'll have thousands of little girls toting around lunch boxes with your face on them. Me, I'm only a nameless extra."

"Then why do you look so smug?"

"I'm contemplating telling our kids I met their mother at a police station after she was brought in for questioning."

"That's probably grounds for not marrying you right there. And besides, I'm not positive you're Junior's father. I bet when I go back to New York I'll meet lots of brunet guys with wavy hair and weird pinky fingers."

He leaned forward, checking on the baby. "How is Stetson doing?"

"*Junior* is doing fine."

Hudson tucked the blanket back around him where it had come loose. "I'm never going to live in New York, so that means you must stick around Arizona. A city-girl-finds-her-country-roots sort of thing."

"Maybe you fall so desperately in love with me, you follow me to the city. Country-boy-sheds-his-boots sort of thing."

Hudson rubbed his jaw, considering. "No, you don't want to raise Stetson in some apartment building in a city. A growing boy needs a yard. Trees to climb. Mud to play in—"

"The Empire State Building. Museums and cultural events—"

"A horse."

"Snow."

Hudson opened his mouth to speak and stopped suddenly. A new thought had occurred to him and whatever it was, he didn't like it. "Maybe Chrissy didn't take the baby from the twenty-first century."

"You think she stole some random baby from here that just happens to look like you?"

"Not random. Ours. Maybe this means we never get home.

We'll marry each other here because we're the only ones around who won't think we're crazy when we do modern things. If we made it back to our own century, what are the chances we would even live in the same place back home, let alone get married?"

Judging by his facial expression, not great.

That stung. It was like he was telling me he could only see himself marrying me if I were the last woman on earth— or at least the only woman on earth who knew what dental hygiene was.

He let out a deep breath. "Forget I said that. We shouldn't think about being stuck here. We'll get home."

I couldn't forget he said it. He had been trying to come up with a sensible reason why he would ever marry me.

After that bit of discussion, Hudson changed the subject to contingency plans. He not only wanted to figure out a plan B, he also went over plan C and D and probably would have gone beyond plan Z if there were more letters in the alphabet. He went over what I should do if the carriage were stopped by King John's men, if we were separated, attacked, lost, wounded, captured, or ran out of food. Hudson's face was completely serious during these instructions, and I wondered which fate he was trying to change: being stuck in the Middle Ages, or marrying me because of it.

Chapter 21

We stopped at an inn to eat and hire fresh horses for the rest of the trip. By getting new horses now, Bartimaeus's horses would be rested and waiting for him on the way home. After some deliberation, Bartimaeus decided it would look suspicious if Hudson and I didn't go inside the inn to eat while the horses were being switched. He scoped out the place for king's men, then came back and told us, "When the horses are ready, we'll leave. No dawdling. I have to go oversee things in the stable. Innkeepers are all cheats and scoundrels."

This sort of speech was probably the reason why the wizard was known as Bartimaeus the Proud and not Bartimaeus the Friendly.

After he left, Hudson climbed out of the carriage, then helped me down. He kept hold of my hand when I was on the ground, intertwining my fingers with his. When I looked at him questioningly, he said, "It's part of our cover. You're my wife." I wasn't sure who the cover was for, since no one else was on the street by the stable and no one could see us yet from the inn window. "And," Hudson went on, "this is our son, Stetson."

I didn't move toward the inn. "We should at least choose a name that works in the time period. Edward, or maybe Jacob . . ."

"You are not naming our son after *Twilight* characters."

"They're older names," I pointed out. "I can't help it if they're also good-looking fictional guys."

Hudson shook his head. "Women." To the baby, he said, "Don't worry, I won't let her name you after a vampire." He bent and kissed the top of Junior's head. As Hudson straightened, he hesitated, and looked at me questioningly. Seemingly on a whim, he put his hands on my shoulders, leaned forward, and kissed me too. The pressure of his lips on mine made my heart skid helplessly inside my chest. I shut my eyes and kissed him back, then was angry at myself for acting that way. We weren't a couple. He had never even said he liked me. He thought he would only marry me if he were stuck in the Middle Ages.

I stepped away from him, taking a deep breath to clear my mind. "Okay, just because I might at some point have your baby, it doesn't mean you can kiss me whenever you want."

He smiled, self-satisfied. Whatever his question had been, he thought he knew the answer. Hudson took the baby from my arms and spoke in a hushed tone. "Here's another thing you need to learn about women, Stets. They might pretend to like the bad-boy Robin Hood types, but they can't resist hick-town boys."

"You're so sure about that?" I asked.

He smiled. "You're into me, I can tell."

"I'm not into you," I said hotly. Hotly, because as soon as the words left my lips, sparklers erupted on top of my head.

Hudson looked at them, and a grin spread across his face. The baby cooed and reached out, trying to grab the flaring light. Hudson moved farther away. "Don't touch. Just look at Mommy's pretty liar hat."

He was enjoying this way too much. "Okay," I said. "Maybe I like you a little."

The sparklers dimmed, but didn't go out.

Hudson raised an eyebrow.

"All right," I said, nervously eyeing the area to make sure no one saw us. "I'm into you."

The sparklers died, but I didn't wait around for more commentary. I headed to the inn. Behind me I heard Hudson still talking to the baby. "Yes, we like Mommy's flaming hairdo, don't we?"

Once we reached the inn, Hudson stopped trying to come up with ways to embarrass me. He gave the innkeeper some coins for our meals, and then we sat down on a bench at one of the tables. I held out my hands for the baby. "Do you want me to hold Junior?"

"Junior," Hudson repeated with distaste. He whispered conspiratorially into the baby's ear. "I don't think we should trust your mother where names are concerned. She put you in a dress."

"It's what babies wear here," I said.

Hudson ignored me and kept whispering to the baby. "Don't worry, when we get back to the right century, I'll teach you to play football and drive a pickup truck."

We didn't say more about the future because the innkeeper's daughter came by with our food. She was about my age and cooed happily at the baby until her mother came over and told her to get back to work. But they both stayed for a few more minutes talking to the baby and risking their lips to his grasp.

"You've a fine-looking lad," the innkeeper's wife told us, giving him a pat good-bye.

"Thank you," I said. "His name is Edward." The hat didn't go off. I hadn't lied—at that moment I wanted to name him Edward just for spite.

As soon as the innkeeper's wife was out of earshot, Hudson took the baby from my hands and pointedly started calling him Stetson again.

When we were nearly done eating, I saw two men on horse-back ride past the inn. They wore the red surcoats of King John's men.

Hudson saw them too. He stiffened and handed me the baby. All the lightheartedness in his expression vanished. Before I knew he had done it, he took the pouch that held the Gilead and handed it to me too. "If they come in here, I'll hold them off so you can get to the carriage. Don't let Bartimaeus know you have the Gilead until you reach the others."

Fear swept through me. "No," I whispered. "You can't fight two trained swordsmen. I'll go with them if I have to."

Hudson's eyes connected with mine. "If they take you back to the castle, it won't be for a wedding. King John will throw you into the dungeon and keep Stetson hostage to force you into making gold for the rest of your life. Do you think I'm going to let that happen?"

I could see the men out front. They were nearly to the front door. I held the baby with shaking hands. "We'll find another way. One that doesn't end with you being killed."

"Don't argue with me. Just do what I say."

I would have argued with that, but I saw the pain that flashed across his face—the same pain I'd seen at our camp-fire. He wasn't thinking of the future. He was back in the past on the night he'd lost his mother. It hit me with a sickening *thud* that he didn't want to escape from these men; he wanted redemption—to die heroically. He would act now because he couldn't forgive himself for the way he had acted then.

"Dying here will not bring her back," I said.

Hudson flinched. My words hit home, but he didn't acknowledge them. He stood up. "Let's walk to the door like we've finished our meal."

I stood up to follow, putting my hand on his arm. "Your mother wouldn't want you to do this."

"How can I know what she'd want?" His voice had a bitter edge. "She's dead."

We stared at each other for a moment, then the emotion on his face vanished and he was all practicality again. He took my elbow. "At the first sign of trouble, bolt away from me and run to the carriage." He propelled me forward and we walked toward the door. The baby made happy gurgling sounds and looked at me with his big brown eyes. Hudson's big brown eyes.

"*I* don't want you to do this," I said.

He sighed in frustration, but didn't answer. The door to the inn opened and the knights entered. Hudson nodded to them, the way you might to any stranger you were passing.

They didn't move. In fact, they stopped directly in front of us, sizing me up.

The first was a bear of a man, with a beard and mustache that covered most of his face. His eyes kept running over me. "Is this your wife?"

Hudson put his arm around my waist. "Yes, and the little one is our son."

The man didn't take his eyes off of me. "She's tall and pretty. Is she blond?"

"She's taken," Hudson said with forced humor. "If you're looking for a pretty maid of your own, I can recommend a few in the village." Hudson pulled me to the side, trying to walk around the knight, but the man stepped in front of us again.

He pointed a finger at me. "Are you perchance a miller's daughter?"

I couldn't lie, but I could tell a safer truth. "My father works with books."

"Books?" the man repeated with disbelief. "You mean he's a monk?"

The second man stepped toward Hudson's side. I knew it was a strategic move; if Hudson drew his sword he would have two fronts to fight on. The move also opened up a space I could dart through to get out the door. Hudson nudged my back, and I knew he wanted me to run.

I couldn't. I didn't like Hudson's chances. If anyone was going to sacrifice themselves, it was going to be me. It had to be. This trip to the Middle Ages was my fault.

One of the knights put his hand on the hilt of his sword. In another moment, Hudson would reach for his own. My breath seemed to lodge in my throat. Should I blurt out who I was? Would that stop them from hurting Hudson?

I hadn't heard the innkeeper's wife approaching, but she stepped over to the guards. She addressed them in a cheery voice, as though their swords weren't about to scrape free from their scabbards. "Welcome, gentlemen. Are you here to eat or do you have business with our cobbler?" She looked at their boots, appraisingly. "He does some fine work, this young man. I've known him and his wife since they were no bigger than their own sweet babe." She patted the baby's arm, lovingly. "You won't go amiss with a pair of his boots."

Her speech did the trick. The guards muttered under their breaths about us wasting their time, then walked to the tables and spouted off their order to the innkeeper's wife.

Hudson didn't need to nudge me forward again. I hurried out the door and down the street. I made it to the stables, ahead of Hudson, who kept looking over his shoulder to make sure we weren't being followed.

In front of the carriage, a teenage boy was hitching up the new horses. He hardly took note of us as we climbed inside. I was shaking as I sat down. I moved the curtain a sliver in order to peer out the window. No one had followed us, but I didn't see any sign of the wizard. "Where's Bartimaeus? Do you think he saw the men ride in?"

"From now on," Hudson said, "if I'm jabbing my thumb into your back, that's your cue to run."

"It worked out better this way," I said.

"Only because the innkeeper's wife saved us. You didn't know she was going to do that."

"You're right," I said, giving Hudson the full force of my gaze, "but that's how life is. You never know how it's going to turn out, and you can't plan for everything. You just have to do your best dealing with things as they come and hope people forgive you when you make a mistake."

He grunted and peered out of the window. "That makes a lovely moral. Why don't you write it in the book and see if it sticks?"

I did. I handed the baby to Hudson and got out the book. A new illustration showed Hudson and me traveling in a much nicer carriage, one with cushioned seats and backrests. I wrote the moral on the last page. I thought it would work this time—I *had* learned something important.

It still didn't stick.

A tapping sounded from the door.

Hudson and I looked at each other, but neither of us moved. Enemies weren't supposed to be able to see the carriage, but Bartimaeus wouldn't bother to knock on the door. He would just check to make sure Hudson was inside, then take off. Whether I was there or not was probably optional to the wizard.

"Pardon me," a girl's voice whispered through the door, "but my ma sent me to give you this."

The innkeeper's daughter. I opened the door, and the girl handed me a cloth napkin, folded into a bundle. I could tell by the smell that food was wrapped inside. "You had to leave some of your food on the table," she said. "Ma didn't want you to go hungry."

I took the napkin. "Tell her thank you for helping us."

"Knights," she said in disgust. "They're nothing more than thieves. A few days ago they came through and took half the village's straw. Taxes, indeed." She looked back over her shoulder, then continued. "Now they're bothering our patrons, searching for some maiden who's supposed to marry King John. They'll take every blond woman who can't prove she's not the one." The innkeeper's daughter looked at the wimple covering my hair. Perhaps she guessed what color it was. "You best be careful."

She turned to leave, but I reached out for her. "Wait, I have something for you too. Let me put this food somewhere so I can return your napkin."

I expected Hudson to try to stop me, but he didn't say anything as I pulled a golden acorn from my pocket and wrapped it in the napkin. "Have your mother open this later tonight when the knights are gone. Don't let anyone else see it."

She gave me a questioning look, but thanked me and left.

A minute later, the wizard returned. He opened the door and glared at me. "King John's men are everywhere. From henceforth the woman stays inside the carriage."

He slammed the door.

For once, I agreed with Bartimaeus. I was staying put until we reached the rendezvous point.

Moments later the horses clopped down the street, gently jostling us back and forth. Hudson shifted the curtain to see if anyone followed us. "I hope your gift doesn't come back to bite us. If the knights find out about the golden acorn, they'll know which way we're headed, how we're dressed, and that we've got a baby with us."

He was right, but I didn't regret what I'd done. "What's the point in having this enchantment if I don't help people who deserve it? That's worth the risk, isn't it?"

I didn't think he would agree, but his gaze rested on me and his expression softened. "Yeah. Some things are worth the risk."

It may have been the gentle tone of his voice, or the way his eyes held mine, but I felt he meant *me*, that he was saying I was worth the risk. And the sentence warmed me in a way I hadn't expected.

"You're into me," I said. "I can tell."

He smiled and didn't deny it.

"Of course you might still like Sister Mary Theresa better ..."

"Well, I might if she weren't a nun and about fifty years old." Hudson looked at the ceiling, contemplating the matter. "It's a close call, but you still have all your teeth."

"In that case, I win."

"You win."

I switched benches so I sat next to him, and he put his arm around me. It felt so comfortable. So right. We sat that way for a long time, talking and keeping the baby entertained.

At one point, while Hudson was holding Junior-Edward-Stetson, I said, "Would you forgive him if someday he grows up and goes to the wrong kind of party?"

Hudson nodded. "Yeah."

"Even if he called the party to warn them it was about to be busted?"

He nodded again, slowly this time.

"Your dad still loves you. I think the only person who's not forgiving you is you."

He didn't say anything about that. He just held the baby closer.

A while later when the baby went to sleep, I took out the magic book again. *Some things are worth the risk.* It was a moral. Probably not the one the book wanted, but another one that had written itself onto my heart. It was worth the risk to trust people. And to let people back into your heart. And to love new people.

When Clover first gave me the magic book, I had worried I wouldn't be able to think of a moral for the story. Now I couldn't turn around without bumping into one. They were hanging in the air in front of me, waiting for me to snatch them. Had these truths always been there and I just hadn't ever seen them before?

Some things are worth the risk.

The gold ink glimmered and disappeared. I shut the book

and flicked the cover angrily. "I don't care what you say; I think that's the moral of the story."

The book didn't respond.

"Stupid book." I was talking to inanimate objects again. My pathetic-o-meter numbers were probably skyrocketing. I shut my eyes and tried to think of more morals. I had learned so much I was already brimming with self-realization. What else could I possibly take from this experience? Words tumbled around my mind to the rhythm of the jiggling carriage, and I drifted off to sleep.

• • •

I woke up to Hudson's voice, speaking into the walkie-talkie. "Can you hear me? Out."

I sat up and tried to orient myself. The carriage was going slowly now. Only dim light and cool air drifted through the windows. It was nearly night. The baby sat on Hudson's knee, grabbing for the walkie-talkie, while Hudson held it out of his reach.

I waited to hear if my father would answer Hudson's question. Only static came through the speakers. "Are we to the meeting point?" I asked.

"We're close. We might have to wait for an hour before they respond though."

I knew this. I had been there when Hudson told my father to turn on his walkie-talkie for five minutes every hour. Still, the static filled me with dread. What if something had happened to my family? King John's men had been looking for me. What if they found Robin Hood's camp instead? Would they have killed everyone on the spot for being with bandits?

I didn't want to think about that possibility, but it hovered, uninvited, in my mind.

Then my father's voice came on the line, "Where are you? Are you all right?"

Relief washed over me. He was there.

"We're fine," Hudson said. "We've got the wizard with us."

My father gave Hudson directions to their hiding spot, and then Hudson banged the hilt of his sword against the roof as a signal to Bartimaeus to stop the carriage. Once it halted, Hudson went outside to give directions to the wizard, and I talked to my father on the walkie-talkie. It felt like so much longer than two days since I'd seen him.

"You're all right?" he asked again.

"Yes, and I'm bringing a surprise."

"A good surprise, I hope. I'm not sure how many more bad surprises I can handle."

I held the walkie-talkie away from the baby's curious hands. Would my father consider me showing up to camp with my infant son a good thing or a bad thing? "It's a very cute surprise," I said.

Junior-Stetson-Edward gurgled out a stream of *umba, umba* sounds and reached his chubby fingers toward the walkie-talkie.

"What did you say?" my father asked. "I didn't catch that last part."

I didn't want to explain, so I changed the subject. "It's lucky Hudson got ahold of you right away."

"It wasn't luck," my father said. "I never turned off my walkie-talkie."

I shifted the baby in my arms. "I thought you were supposed to conserve batteries."

"I brought plenty of extras from the house, and I wanted to make sure I heard you whenever you called."

I didn't say anything for a moment. Perhaps I was just over-tired and emotional, but tears filled my eyes. My father had kept the walkie-talkie near him and on, waiting for word from us, waiting for me to come within range.

"Are you still there?" he asked.

"Yes, I'm here." I leaned the walkie-talkie against my cheek. "I'll be back soon. I love you, Dad."

"I love you too," he said.

Hudson climbed back into the carriage, and we trundled down the street again. He told my dad we were on our way, then switched the walkie-talkie off. "When we get to the turnoff, I'll go alone to camp," he said. "The wizard doesn't want to walk into unknown parts of the forest, so he's staying with the carriage. You should stay too. Less temptation for bandits that way." Hudson fingered the walkie-talkie, thinking. "I hope they don't get any ideas about holding your family ransom for more gold."

I didn't want to believe Hudson's suspicions, but it was best to be prepared for the worst. "I'll go with you partway and change some things into gold along the path. You can tell Robin Hood it's my gift to them. Maybe a bird in the hand will be worth two in the bush—at least if it's a big, golden bird."

Hudson nodded. "Good idea. Maybe they'll care more about moving and hiding their new stash than about keeping your family from leaving. And if that doesn't work—we'll ask the wizard to turn them into hedgehogs."

I wasn't sure if Hudson was serious about that, but he got a satisfied look on his face, as though already picturing it.

Eventually, the carriage left the main road and wobbled over bumps and juts until it came to a stop.

I put the baby in his sling, debated for a moment whether it would be safer to leave the magic book in the carriage, then slipped it into the diaper bag and took it with me. I didn't want to risk its safety.

Bartimaeus had suspended some sort of magic lights in front of the horses, but beyond those, the forest was a patchwork of shadows. Hudson and I followed the path into it. He carried his sword in one hand and the flashlight in the other. Since I was going back to the carriage soon, I followed Hudson, holding a candle. I kept my hand in front of the flame to keep it from blowing out.

A night bird called overhead. Bushes rustled. My eyes glanced around the shadows of the forest, looking for King John's men behind every tree we passed. I had to keep reminding myself that people didn't stay out after dark in the Middle Ages. The knights were settled in for the night by now, and besides, if anyone else had been around, we would have seen their lamp-light.

A bird flew from a bush straight at me, startling me so much I let out a gasp. Hudson turned back to check on me. I expected him to tell me not to be so jumpy. Instead, he took my hand and squeezed it. "It's going to be all right. We'll be home soon."

Home. That life seemed like the fairy tale now, and this was the real one. These huge trees and darkness and uncertainty.

A little farther down the path, I saw some rocks that were the right size to turn into gold. They were big enough that it would take some work on the Merry Men's part to move or hide them. As I changed each one, I felt a stab of pain and then the rock's rough surfaces grew smooth underneath my fingertips.

Hudson helped me up when I was done and handed me my candle. "Can you make it back to the carriage?"

I nodded.

He turned to go, but I reached out for his arm. "Be careful. Watch out for bandits."

He smiled. "I will." He dropped a quick kiss on my lips. It was over so soon I didn't have time to think about it.

But as I turned and walked back toward the carriage, I thought about the kiss anyway. It was okay to feel this way about Hudson because things would work out for us. Didn't the baby prove that? I ran my free hand along the sling and the contours of the baby's warm little body.

For the first time in a long time, I let myself hope for good things. When we got home, my family would be closer, happier. Hudson and I would be together—and not in a running-for-our-lives sort of way like the last few days, but in a boyfriend-girlfriend sort of way.

I was wondering how Hudson would break the news to his

father about dating the girl he'd met at the police station, when a gust of wind blew my candle out. I was instantly plunged into darkness.

I reached in the diaper bag for the box of matches. My fingers fumbled nervously through the contents. The sudden darkness reminded me how alone I was.

A noise came from behind me, like twigs breaking.

No need to panic, I told myself, it's another bird or something.

I put the candle in the bend of my arm so I could use both hands to find the matches. I heard another noise, like dry leaves being stepped on. I spun around to face whatever was there, but I couldn't see anything in the darkness.

These sorts of noises had probably been here all along. I just hadn't paid attention to them because I could see. Nothing was in front of me. Nothing was coming closer. Everything would be fine as soon as I lit the candle again.

A clunk sounded in front of me, perhaps a footstep. I took a step backward, and stopped sifting through the diaper bag. I realized I didn't need the candle to see.

"I'm not afraid," I said.

The sparklers went off around my head, illuminating the forest better than the tiny flame had done.

The trees in front of me were clear of any danger, and I relaxed until I heard a voice to my side say, "You're lying about that."

Chapter 22

I spun around. Rumpelstiltskin stood only inches away. His thin lips spread into a smile. "And you *should* be afraid."

I dropped the candle and bolted forward. I needed to escape, to get the baby to safety. I only made it a few steps before Rumpelstiltskin's fingers clutched my arm and pulled me back with more strength than I expected from such bony hands.

"You mustn't run in the dark forest, Mistress Miller," his voice hissed near my ear. "You're bound to hurt yourself that way." He wore a dark cloak that brushed against the ground. A wreath made of twisted, bare branches encircled his head, which made his cheekbones seem even more angular. His eyes looked sunken but every bit as full of the churning darkness they'd held during our other meetings. It struck me as strange that even here in the evening forest, I could see the churning in his eyes.

"Let me go." I tried to pry away his fingers but couldn't budge them.

He grinned at me, amused at my attempts. "I'll let you go when you give me the baby. Then you can go back to creating gold to your heart's content."

I couldn't use strength to get away, so I decided to stall him. If we stayed here long enough, Hudson would come back. He had the anti-fairy sand. Maybe he could use it to free me. "How did you catch up to me so fast?" I asked. "Our horses raced here and no enemies could see the carriage."

"Catch up to you?" Rumpelstiltskin smiled, showing his graying teeth. "Did you think I followed you?" He shook his head, and the wreath let out a scent of decaying wood. "No point in that. Not when I knew you would return to your family eventually. My mirror still shows me where your father is. I waited near his camp and lo, tonight the trees were whispering about a carriage lumbering through. Enemies might not be able to see your carriage, but trees can. I was on my way to your carriage when I found you on the path." He pulled me closer to him. "Now then, give me what you promised."

I shrank back as far as his grip would allow. "We made an agreement for King John's son. I never married him."

With his free hand, Rumpelstiltskin pulled a paper from his cloak. "This is our contract—the very words we shook on." He placed it in my hand, and the paper immediately wrapped itself around my arm like a snake. I tried to shake it off, but it wouldn't let go. Pulsating, it clung to me, then sunk into my skin so the words looked like they had been tattooed onto my arm.

Rumpelstiltskin watched it and laughed. "The contract is binding. You agreed to give me whatever I asked for within the year—including your child." He pointed his long fingers at the sling. "And there he is. Give him to me."

I held onto the sling with my free arm, trying to keep Rumpelstiltskin from taking the baby. In the fairy tale, the queen cried so piteously that Rumpelstiltskin allowed her to guess his name within three days. If she was successful, she could keep the child. I didn't have to force myself into the part. I couldn't bear to think of Rumpelstiltskin taking my baby and leaving him to die alone in a vault. The tears and the fear came in equal measure, making it hard to speak over my sobs. "Please don't take him. I didn't think I would have him when we made our bargain. It isn't his fault." I had nothing to offer Rumpelstiltskin in exchange except my own life. "Take me instead. Please. Please." I couldn't say more. The tears choked my words.

Rumpelstiltskin let go of my arm. "Do not flee again," he said. "I've never hunted down prey like a lion, and what if I discovered I liked it? What would happen to all the innocents that walk through the forest? You don't want that on your conscience, do you?"

I gave a small shake of my head. I couldn't run and hide among the trees, not with sparklers flowing from my head—but I couldn't see without the light. Besides, the trees could tell him where I was anyway.

"Please," I begged. "Give me another chance to keep my baby."

Rumpelstiltskin reached over and ran his bony thumb over my cheek. "Such compelling supplications from a fair maiden." He leaned closer. His eyes were not brown as I had thought before. They were a deep burgundy, like drying blood. "I'm moved," he said. "I won't pretend I'm not." His hand went to my chin, and he cupped it between his cold fingers. "You want a chance to get out of this bargain?"

"Yes," I said hurriedly.

"Perhaps you would like to make some sort of wager?"

"Yes." My hopes rose. This is when he would ask me the question, and I already knew the answer.

He dropped his hand away from my chin and smiled at me. "Do you know how I passed the time while I hid near your father's camp?"

I shook my head, tears still flowing down my cheeks. *I know your name*, I thought. *Ask me so I can save my baby.*

Rumpelstiltskin's voice dropped to a low hum, as though telling me a secret. "I read. Would you like to see what?" He reached into his cloak and pulled out a book. I recognized it with a sick thud to my chest. It was the book of fairy tales my father had brought from our house.

Rumpelstiltskin held the book up, opened to the end of his story. The picture showed the queen smugly holding her baby while the dwarf figure representing Rumpelstiltskin raised a fist in defeated anger.

He snapped the book shut. "Interesting story, though truly I can't imagine myself flying off anywhere on a cooking spoon. Too undignified, really."

I breathed hard. My ears rang with fear. I couldn't speak.

Rumpelstiltskin brandished the book at me. "My fate was already decided by the fay folk. They wrote this story and gave it to you, didn't they? It's instructions on how you were to deal with me."

I shivered and couldn't stop. This wasn't how it was supposed to go. What had I done when I changed the story? What could I do now?

His smile turned to a grimace. "I found their book and I don't intend to follow their script. You already know my name. I won't be tricked into asking you that question. In fact, I won't ask you anything at all." He tossed the book to the ground in disgust. It lay there like a wounded animal, its pages blowing limply in the breeze. "I will make no bargains with you. Give me the babe."

I took a step backward. This was happening too fast. Hudson probably hadn't even reached Robin Hood's camp yet. He wouldn't be able to help me.

"Chrissy!" I called. "Chrissy, help!"

If ever I needed a fairy godmother to show up, it was right now. But there was no sign of her. No glimmering, no fountain of lights.

Rumpelstiltskin rolled his eyes. "By law, she can't interfere with another fairy's bargain. And besides, Chrysanthemum Everstar is only a chit of a fairy anyway." He paused, his gaze sliding around the forest, checking to make sure she really hadn't come. When he saw we were alone, he smiled again. "Fairy girls, like mortal girls, are best suited for growing flowers and having babies. You've done admirably in that regard. I was expecting to have to wait nine months for you to produce an heir. It's so considerate of you to come up with one sooner. Was it dark magic or just incompetent magic that made it so?"

I didn't answer. Rumpelstiltskin had been close enough to my baby that he could have reached into the sling and grabbed him, but he hadn't. Perhaps the spell wouldn't work if Rumpelstiltskin took the baby from someone, perhaps the baby had to be given. I wouldn't do it. "Our contract was made under duress," I told him, taking another step backward, "and technically I didn't give birth to this baby in the time period we agreed on, so the contract isn't valid."

I wiped at the words that clung to my arm. They didn't come off.

"I still have magic," he said. "Enchantments I've taken from trolls and goblins. Did you know trolls can turn things into stone?" He took a step toward me, grinding his graying teeth. "Chrysanthemum may have told you that I can't take the child by force, but that doesn't mean I can't turn you to stone and lift the child from your arms. In fact, I should turn you both to stone and you can keep your babe company for eternity. Either way will break the spell. I bought love that can't be bought. All that's left now is to take the baby to the vault."

To emphasize his threat, Rumpelstiltskin put a hand on a nearby tree and chanted, "Oak tree, stone, stone, stone." Underneath his fingertips, a gray color grew and spread, simultaneously rushing down to the ground and up through the branches.

Rumpelstiltskin dropped his hand without even looking back at the tree to see his stone creation. "I hope you didn't miss the lesson in that example, Mistress Miller."

I nodded, an idea forming in my mind. "Yes, it's a very important lesson—if you happen to be a tree. I suppose that will teach the rest of the shrubbery to tell you what's happening in the forest."

He stepped toward me, his eyes churning with even more ferocity. Anger toward me, anger toward the other fairies. Rage had blinded him. Otherwise he would have understood the warning in the fairy tale when he read it. I was only frustrated for not figuring it out before. Chrissy had hinted at it the last time I'd seen her by warning Hudson to remain a nameless character.

"Enough of this," Rumpelstiltskin roared, and the leaves on the trees around us shook on their branches, sounding like vengeful rattlesnakes. He strode over to me and grabbed hold of my arm. I didn't stop him. At the same time that he said, "Mistress Miller, stone, stone, stone!" I said, "Rumpelstiltskin, gold, gold, gold!"

He let out a sharp breath as though he'd been struck. Where he held on to my arm, I could see his fingers turning to gold.

"My name isn't Mistress Miller," I said. "And you don't know my name or my son's name, so you have no power to turn us to stone." I was infinitely glad right then that I hadn't named the baby.

Rumpelstiltskin shrieked in indignation and tried to pull his hand away from me. He was stuck though—his fingers were an unbendable golden band around my arm. He stared at me, his eyes wide and furious. The gold traveled up his wrist haltingly as he fought the transformation. I couldn't tell how fast it was progressing but I had no doubt he would cut off his own arm if it would do any good.

"The story," he gasped out and looked to where he had thrown the book. "I'll find your name in the story." He waved his free hand and uttered breathless words I couldn't understand. The book flew to him like a tame bird, landing on his outstretched palm. The pages ruffled open in front of him, showing him the text.

"It won't do any good." I couldn't keep some smugness from creeping into my voice. "The only name the fairy tale ever mentions is yours. I guess the writer thought my name didn't matter since women are only here to raise flowers and babies."

Rumpelstiltskin didn't look at me. His eyes sped hungrily across the flipping pages. He grimaced when he reached the end of the story and saw I was right. The heroine was referred to as "the miller's daughter" at the beginning of the story and "the queen" at the end.

No name. Not for me, and not for my baby. Rumpelstiltskin threw the book down and clawed at his chest, as if hoping to halt the gold's progression this way. He only succeeded in ripping off his cloak. It fell to the ground, revealing a golden edge that traveled up his neck. He couldn't stop it. "No!" he screamed, and it rang across the forest, sending the leaves into another rattling chorus.

He was still screaming "No!" when the gold crept onto his face. The word broke off sharply and seemed to fall back, silent, against his lips.

I stared at him for a moment, making sure he wouldn't suddenly open his eyes and shake off his gold coating.

He didn't. He was frozen there, the rage permanently engraved on his twisted face.

Now that my mind was no longer wrapped up in fear, I felt several things at once: the squirming baby in the sling, startled by Rumpelstiltskin's shout; pain—both sharp in my heart from using the gold enchantment and throbbing in my arm from Rumpelstiltskin's unbendable grip; and panic. How was I going to get him off of me? He was solid gold and too heavy to move. I was trapped here. The thought of being stuck alone in the forest with a dead fairy clutching onto me made my skin crawl.

I pulled my arm hard. It didn't budge.

Off in the forest, I saw a bobbing stream of light. The beam of a flashlight. "Tansy!" Hudson called out. He must have heard Rumpelstiltskin's screams. I could tell he was running.

"I'm here!" I yelled back. I watched the beam come closer. He wasn't far away. "And I am so glad you didn't call out my name a minute earlier."

Who would have thought my name could have been used as a tool against me?

The baby let out another cry of protest, and I rubbed his back to calm him, but I, too, was shaking. Not with fear, but with relief. I was foolish, really, not to figure out beforehand that my enchantment could be used as a weapon. It seemed so clear now that in the fairy tale, Rumpelstiltskin had asked the queen if she knew his name not because he wanted to offer her a second chance to keep her baby, but because he knew the queen could change him into a golden statue with one touch. He had asked the question for his own protection.

Hudson came closer. He wasn't alone. My father was just a few paces behind him, along with my family, Robin Hood, and the Merry Men. Flashlights and torches weaved their way through the forest in my direction.

Hudson and my father reached me first. "What happened?" Hudson asked, swiping his beam of light across the fairy's form.

"Rumpelstiltskin tried to kill me—I was so afraid." My liar's hat disappeared at this truth, dimming the area around me. "I turned him to gold and now my arm is stuck."

Both Hudson and my father went to my side but kept their flashlights pointed at the grimacing statue, checking to make sure it didn't move. Hudson tried to wrench my arm out of Rumpelstiltskin's hand, without any better luck than I'd had. My father gave Rumpelstiltskin's fingers a useless tug. "We need something slick." He turned to find Sandra getting closer, and called out to her, "Do you have something slippery to put on Tansy's arm?"

She hurried toward me, breathing hard. "I have some sun-screen and lip balm in my backpack."

While she got it out, Hudson looked at the sling. "How is the baby?"

I checked; he was blinking sleepy eyes up at me. "He's fine."

"What?" my father coughed out. "What baby?"

Hudson shot me an apologetic look. "Sorry, Tansy, I was going to let you break the news to him."

My father's voice rose. "Break what news to me? What baby?" He swept his flashlight beam over me until he saw the sling. In disbelief, he moved the corner of the cloth to get a better view. "Where did you get a baby from?" His voice was full of alarm, as though I might have borrowed the baby from some unsus-pecting villager and forgotten to return him.

Robin Hood had just reached us, and he lifted his hands and took a step away from me. "I but kissed the maid once. Only once."

"Chrissy brought him from my future," I said. "He's mine." I couldn't help smiling at the baby, at his smooth round cheeks and big brown eyes. "Isn't he beautiful?"

Sandra peeked at the baby and immediately started cooing.

My father simply stared at him, stunned. "A baby from your future?" He held up his flashlight for a better look.

Sandra leaned toward the sling. "Oh, Tansy, he's so cute." To my dad she said, "He looks like you, Frank."

The baby reached out, trying to grab the flashlight beam. My dad tilted his head, studying him. "He looks like someone, but I can't put my finger on it ... someone with dark hair ..." My dad stopped speaking, and his gaze zeroed in on Hudson. "Huh," he said, and his eyes narrowed. "This baby had better not show up for quite some time in the future."

Which goes to show you that your parents can embarrass you in any situation.

Nick wasn't a lot better. While Sandra spread sunscreen on

my arm, he smirked at Hudson and said, "Dude," then shook
his head a lot.

Robin Hood walked around Rumpelstiltskin, surveying him
from head to toe. "You didn't jest when you said Tansy had
a golden present for us." He held his torch up to see Rumpelstiltskin's face better. "But why did she form it in such a hideous shape? Can you imagine us dragging this thing through
a village to a blacksmith?" He held his torch directly under
Rumpelstiltskin's twisted lips. "It would frighten children and
put chickens off laying."

I gestured down the path. "The gold for you is back there." I
let my gaze slide back to Rumpelstiltskin's frozen, twisted face.
"This isn't a present. It was a fairy who tried to kill me."

Robin Hood's eyes widened in surprise. "Your magic is strong
enough to destroy fairies?" He took a couple of uneasy steps
away from me. "My lady will remember that although I held
up several stores in her village, I have always been her humble
servant."

His nervousness made me smile. I didn't clarify that Rumpelstiltskin had only been an *ex*-fairy. It wouldn't hurt Robin
Hood to worry about getting on my bad side.

He gave me a deep bow. "By your leave, my men and I will
retrieve the gold you say is by yonder tree." He turned and hurried into the forest and the Merry Men followed.

Once my arm was coated with sunscreen, I tried pulling it
out of Rumpelstiltskin's grasp. It didn't work. "My hand is starting to feel like it's going to explode," I said. "Is there some way
to cut this off?"

Nick fingered Rumpelstiltskin's grip. "Not with the tools
we have."

Hudson took hold of my arm and pulled with no better
results. "Maybe the wizard can do something. I'll go get him."
Without waiting for my response, he turned and jogged down
the trail in the direction of the carriage.

I didn't know if my arm could make it until Hudson came back with the wizard—and I also doubted the wizard would willingly help me, but I knew who might. "Clover!" I called, and didn't bother explaining to my parents why I was yelling out random plant names. "Clover, I need your help. I can pay you in gold."

The leprechaun appeared, standing on Rumpelstiltskin's shoulder. He wore a different green jacket with olive-toned embroidered leaves and a matching bowler on top of his head. He looped his fingers behind his belt. "Gold, you say?"

My father held his flashlight up so Clover looked like he was standing in the middle of a spotlight. "Is that the same leprechaun we saw before?"

I didn't bother answering. I needed Clover's help, but I wasn't sure he would help me if he realized that was what he was doing. I had to make it seem like I was offering him another bargain. "Clover, if you tell me what moral to write in the magic book, you can have this golden statue."

Clover rubbed his beard in consideration. "Statue, eh? Looks an awful lot like that ghoul of an ex-fairy, Rumpelstilskabob."

"He's a statue now, and worth his weight in gold. Think how rich you'll be."

Clover kept rubbing his beard. " 'Tis a precious lot of gold, but it would be bad luck to play poker with coins made from an ex-fairy. And none of the shops would take it—can you see me tipping a waitress with part of a megalomaniac ex-fairy?"

I tugged uselessly at my arm. "Then I'll change something else to gold for you if you'll just help get this thing off of me."

"Help you?" Clover pulled the brim of his hat down farther on his eyes. "I gave you *The Change Enchantment* to help you and got in a ripe lot of trouble from Chrysanthemum. She wrote me up for interfering in your story. All in a snit, she was." He raised one of his tiny fingers at me, shaking it. "You weren't supposed to tell her about it."

My hand was throbbing. I could feel my pulse drumming in my arm like a hammer. "Well, it wasn't much of a bargain for me. The enchantment didn't work. I wrote every moral I could think of, but none of them took us home."

"Did you wait until the story ended before you went scribbling morals down?"

"The story never ended," I said. "It just kept adding new pages."

He flicked his hand in my direction. "Well, that's your problem then. If you had read books, you would know that you had to face the villain before the story could finish." Clover tapped his foot against Rumpelstiltskin's shoulder and it made a metallic clang. "As for the moral of Rumpelstiltskin, I already told it to you. It's that you've got to figure things out yourself, but you shouldn't worry because there will be folks to help you—in this case, me, seeing as you didn't figure out the moral by yourself. Even though I told it to you." He leaned backward on his heels in a self-satisfied manner. "When you get out your pen next, you could sum it up by saying, 'Humans need leprechauns to save their sorry britches.'"

It didn't seem like a very good moral, but I didn't argue. If it would get us home, I'd write it word for word.

Clover tilted the brim of his hat. "I suppose I can use this gold to pay me union dues to the UMA. It's enough to last a couple of centuries. And they'll be stuck with the lot of it as nobody else will want tainted currency." Clover chuckled happily. "Serves them right for making me Chrysanthemum Everstar's glorified errand boy."

Clover was still smiling when he disappeared from Rumpelstiltskin's shoulder. The next moment, a wave of fissures spread through the statue. The metal cracked like ice breaking and crumbled to the ground in a rush of gold coins.

I rubbed my freed arm and watched the pile of coins shine in the flashlight beams. And then the pile disappeared too. The only trace that Rumpelstiltskin had ever been there was a heap of clothes and the pins-and-needles sensation in my hand as the blood rushed back into it.

Dad held his flashlight to my arm, examining the bruised skin. "Are you okay?"

I nodded.

Sandra gave me a sideways hug so she didn't squish the baby, then checked on him again. This involved more ooohing on her part. He reached out for her, and she took him out of the sling, cooing as she held him. I took the book out of the diaper bag and flipped through the pages. New illustrations had been added. My showdown in the forest with Rumpelstiltskin lay on one page. On the next, he was a hideous gold statue. The last picture showed Hudson standing by my side and my family hugging me. It read, "And the miller's daughter lived happily ever after. The end."

Even though my family was reading the book over my shoulder, I called out, "It ended! I live happily ever after." This sentence brought me a ridiculous amount of relief—like the book had put a stamp of approval on my life. I was going to live happily ever after.

I pulled out the pen but didn't put it to the paper. "I'll wait for Hudson to come back."

"Start it now," my father said, "and you can write the last bit when he returns."

Nick nodded. "Yeah, save the part about people needing leprechauns to save their britches until he gets here. I'm sure he'll want to know what the real moral of the story was."

I sat down on the ground and spread the book out in my lap. "I should have known all along it would be a biased moral."

I didn't start writing until I saw Hudson running back down the trail. He slowed to a walk when he saw the statue was gone. "What happened to our buddy Rumple?"

"Clover took him," I said. "He's going to use the gold to pay his UMA dues for the next century or two."

"Ah." Hudson drew a couple of deep breaths and walked over to me. "Greed pays off again."

"There's another good moral from the story," Nick said.

I finished writing the sentence Clover had told me, but like the others, it faded from the book. I gripped the pen hard, then threw it onto the open page. "No!" I yelled.

Alarmed, Hudson took the book from my hands. He read the last page and looked at me quizzically. "You didn't want to live happily ever after?"

"Not that. Clover told me the moral of the story and it still didn't work."

Nick shook his head and glanced at the book. "So much for leprechauns saving our sorry britches."

I suppressed a frustrated scream. Nothing worked. What sort of awful enchanted book was this?

Hudson helped me up and handed the book back to me. "Let's hope the wizard's magic works better."

Chapter 23

Another light came bobbing up the trail toward us—the wizard hurrying, but not running. He slowed when he saw me. "Where is this statue you said entrapped the girl? What sort of trickery are you up to?"

"No trickery," Hudson said. "I told you the truth. A leprechaun took the statue away because it was made of gold, but you can look at the mark on Tansy's arm if you don't believe me."

I didn't expect the wizard to actually care about the proof, but he strode over to me. I showed him the mark on my forearm. It was deep red, almost purple, and my arm was swollen. He wrinkled his nose, then turned back to Hudson. "Very well. Let's conduct our business directly. Where is the Gilead?"

Hudson opened the pouch at his waist and pulled out the branch. "You can have it if you promise to send everyone here back to our time period. We can pay you gold for your extra trouble."

The wizard pursed his lips. "Our bargain was for one person. No more."

Hudson motioned to my family. "All of us need to go home. We don't belong here."

"Do you know how much effort, how much magic, that would entail?" The wizard held up a finger. "One person. Choose whomever you desire."

I didn't want to hear this, not after we'd been through so much. "Please," I said, but Bartimaeus probably didn't even hear me. Hudson was talking again.

"It has to be all of us," he said.

My dad stepped forward. "If you help us, we'll give you the things we brought with us from our day—walkie-talkies, flashlights, watches, first-aid kits . . ."

Perhaps the wizard might have been interested if he had known what any of these items were, but he didn't bother to ask. He shook his head as though we couldn't possibly have anything worthwhile.

Sandra walked over to him, still carrying the baby. "Think how you would feel if your own family were stranded in the wrong time. Wouldn't you want someone to help them?"

A moth flew by the wizard's oil lamp, and he batted it away. "That is precisely why I have no family. They're simply more people who need something from you. Annoying insects." I wasn't sure whether he meant families or the moth that was still circling his lamp. "The mosquitoes will be out next." He swung his hand through the air as though swiping away an incoming swarm and glared at Hudson. "Choose who will go, or our bargain is over."

Hudson turned to me, his dark eyes pained. He was going to say good-bye to me now; he was leaving. The realization caused a spike of pain in my heart that rivaled the stab of the enchantment. I wanted to tell Hudson it was okay, that I wouldn't blame him for going and leaving the rest of us here. I couldn't do it, though. My throat felt tight at the thought of never seeing him again.

"Well," I said, trying to keep my voice light, "it turns out 'happily ever after' isn't all it's cracked up to be."

He walked over and took hold of my hand. I didn't want this moment of kindness. It felt like a consolation prize. I couldn't pull my hand away, though. Suddenly I wanted to cling to him and was afraid I wouldn't be able to let go.

"Should we send Stetson back?" he asked.

"What?" It hadn't been what I expected him to say. I couldn't process it. He wasn't leaving?

"We could send Stetson back to our day. He'd be safer there—with modern medicine and better food . . ."

Emotions swirled inside me. Hudson wanted to stay with me. He had chosen the baby to go back instead of himself. But where exactly would we send Stetson? Who would take care of him? I couldn't send him to the void of the future and never know if he was all right or not. I shook my head. "He belongs with me."

Hudson nodded then turned to my family. "Nick, do you want to go?"

Nick looked at Sandra and my dad. "Not without the rest of my family."

My dad put his arm around Sandra. "We go as a family or not at all."

Tears welled in Sandra's eyes, but she didn't let them fall. "We'll make do in this century if we have to."

Hudson turned back to the wizard, keeping the branch close. "If you want the Gilead, it has to be all of us."

The wizard grunted, and a sneer curled his upper lip. "You've wasted enough of my time. When you decide who to send, you'll find me in the carriage. But be quick about it. Once the horses are rested, I'll leave." He turned so quickly that his cloak spun around his feet, and he stalked off down the trail to the carriage.

My father rubbed the three-day beard on his chin and glanced over at Hudson. "Are you sure you want to stay? Your family is back in the twenty-first century."

Sandra shushed my father, but he ignored her. "Hudson shouldn't give up his trip home without thinking about it."

Hudson fingered the Gilead, turning it over in his hand. "I'm beginning to wonder if this plant might be more useful than a trip back home. Just imagine the things we might need to fix: leaky roofs, swords, broken arms . . ."

Hearts, I thought. Could the Gilead fix the gold enchantment that hurt my heart so badly? Could it fix the sadness I felt about never seeing my mother or sister again? Could it fix Hudson's pain?

Hudson raised his voice as though talking to someone besides those of us standing on the trail. "We might even be able to make some good changes to the Middle Ages. With twenty-first-century knowledge, unlimited wealth, and a bit of magic to fix things, we'll be able to accomplish anything we want."

I realized what he was doing and raised my voice too. "Right—we could raise armies, create new countries. Do you think the fairies will mind if we take over, say, Belgium?"

Chrissy popped up in front of me, her wand visible in her crossed arms. Her glow lit the area so brightly that the flashlight beams seemed to dim. She wore modern clothes again: a white miniskirt, a polka-dot blue halter top, and rhinestone-embedded flip-flops. A pair of white sunglasses sat atop her deep blue hair, and a purse with pictures of little beach umbrellas hung from her shoulder. "It's not nice to threaten fairies," she told Hudson and me pointedly. "I was going to come talk to you just as soon as my pedicure was over. Look—" She put out her foot to show us her toenails. All but one were painted baby blue with fluffy white clouds swirling all over them. "I had to leave before my last toe was done. I suppose Belgium can thank me later."

"The story is over," I said. "You said you would take us back to our time period."

She sniffed and tossed her hair off one shoulder with a hand that featured the same blue-polish-with-clouds manicure. "In the original contract, I was to take you back once Tansy defeated Rumpelstiltskin, but as you pointed out, you changed things.

Now you'll get back when Tansy writes down the moral of the new story in the magic book."

She looked at me and sighed in exasperation. "Really, the outfits you keep showing up in. My ball-gown professor would fail me for that dress alone." She flourished her wand in my direction, and my brown dress turned into a slim-fitting golden evening gown.

I ignored the change, picked up the magic book, and showed it to her. "I wrote down the moral that Clover told me to. It still didn't work."

Chrissy took the book and flipped through the pages, checking on the story since she'd seen it last. "He probably told you the moral of the story is that leprechauns are awesome, didn't he?"

I nodded. "Something like that."

She rolled her eyes. "That's the moral he takes from every story, but this isn't his story. It's yours, Tansy. You need to write *your* moral." She reached the page where I turned Rumpelstiltskin into a golden statue, and a smirk stole across her lips. "That's what he gets for underestimating women. I bet he wishes he'd gone off on that cooking spoon now."

She handed me back the book, but I could only grip it in frustration. "I already wrote every moral I could think of."

She tilted her chin down. "Yes, but you wrote them before the fairy tale was finished. For a moral to be accurate, you need to know how the story ends." She waved a hand at me. "Now then, what did you learn?"

So much that I couldn't answer right away. It seemed I had learned more in the last few days than I'd learned in all the years before. My family and Hudson were staring at me, waiting for some gem of wisdom to fall from my lips. Instead, I fingered the pen.

Chrissy's wings spanned open and then fluttered impatiently. "You may have, for example, been paying attention when I told you that the lessons you learn in life are more important than the things you accomplish, or you may remember when I told you that you can't expect wishes to change the world without them changing you too, or that I pointed out that the purpose of life was not to avoid problems, but to overcome them. Those might have stuck in your mind if you weren't currently—" She snapped her fingers and the pathetic-o-meter appeared in her hand. Her eyebrows rose in surprise when she read my numbers. "Oh, look. Now you're only 34 percent pathetic." She flashed the disk at me so I could see it. "That's quite good, really. Mortals are always at least 33 percent pathetic—it's just your nature. It's the reason you like rap music and keep bringing low-rise jeans back into style." She tucked the pathetic-o-meter into her purse. "Anyway, what have you learned from all this?"

I put the pen to the paper, and a single gold dot leaked from the pen, waiting to be turned into a thought. "Do I need to write down everything, or just one thing?"

"One thing will do."

Robin Hood and the Merry Men came back to the trail then. I heard someone say, "Where is that light coming from?"

Little John stopped in his tracks. "Be wary, lads, it's the self-same fairy who snatched us back and forth between centuries."

"Should we flee?" Will asked.

Chrissy flicked her wand and a gust of wind rushed in their direction, blowing off a hat or two. "If I wanted to do you harm," she said loudly, "it wouldn't matter where you ran to. You might as well come out, be gentlemen, and offer me proper homage." To me she said, "Fairies own the forest in the twelfth century. It's like, you know, being royalty."

The Merry Men shuffled forward. Robin Hood took the lead. When he reached Chrissy, he took off his hat and bowed deeply. "We have no gifts to offer such a fair one as yourself, but will gladly give you the homage of our praise."

"I accept praise," Chrissy said, smiling benevolently at him. "And sonnets will do."

"Sonnets," Robin Hood repeated without enthusiasm. He

glanced back at the Merry Men, who didn't look much happier about the request. "We shall confer and compose one forthwith." They all fell back a little ways away from us, whispering among themselves.

Nick put his hands on his hips. "Come on, Tansy, write something so we can go home. You don't really want to be around to hear poetry from twelfth-century bandits, do you?"

Still, I hesitated. "I'll be able to change things to gold when I go home?"

She nodded. "The gold enchantment is yours until you take it off."

"Will the book—*The Change Enchantment*—will it still work when I get home?"

She nodded again. "But you'll have no need of magic then to change your future. It isn't set in stone or book or by any spell. You can make whatever you want of your own future."

Part of me knew this had always been the case. I'd been told the same thing by adults for years, but I'd always been concentrating on the past so intently that I'd never noticed my future, wide and endless in front of me. Now the kaleidoscope of possibilities hit me. I could do anything I wanted. Fate had unchained me.

I glanced back at the Merry Men. Robin Hood was shaking his head. "You can't stick 'gorgeous' at the end of a stanza. Nothing rhymes with it."

Friar Tuck frowned. "Poor us."

Will added, "More fuss."

Little John grumbled. "Boar pus."

Robin Hood waved their words away. "Do you want to be turned into something filthy like mushrooms?"

I leaned toward Chrissy. "Can I give *The Change Enchantment* to Robin Hood when I'm done with it? He didn't like how his story ended."

Chrissy smiled at the idea. "If that's what you want to do with it."

"Good," I said. "Can you send my family home first, and I'll stay for a few minutes and explain things to Robin Hood?"

"Sure," she said, even though neither my father nor Hudson looked pleased about my staying behind for a few minutes.

I turned back to the book and held it up a bit, suddenly too shy to let anyone see the moral I had chosen for the story. I wrote the words, wishing I could have thought up some really elegant phrase to say what I was feeling, but everyone was waiting and I'd never been very poetic or profound.

I placed a period at the end of the sentence and watched to see if the words disappeared. They didn't. They glowed as though I had written them with fire, blazing so brightly that I had to shut my eyes.

When I opened them, my family was gone and Robin Hood stood in front of me. He looked at Chrissy in surprise and frustration. "I have not yet finished composing your sonnet."

"Relax," she said. "I brought you over because Tansy wants to give you something."

I shut the book. The spinning wheel on the cover still spun in a way that shouldn't have been possible for an embossed illustration. "This is *The Change Enchantment*. If you accept it, then you'll be able to change your story. Your ending won't have to be like the one in the novel I gave you. I don't know if it will be better or worse, but it will be yours." I held the book out to him. "Do you want it?"

He hesitated, then slowly took the book from my hand. "I'm not sure whether it is wisdom or folly, but yes, I want it."

The spinning wheel vanished from the cover, and a green feathered hat appeared. He flipped open the first page. It showed a painting of Robin Hood, rugged and handsome, surveying the forest. He read the text under the picture. "Robin Hood was wise and generous." He nodded. "Quite true. And . . ." He peered at the picture more closely. "I cut a dashing figure in that tunic. I will have to procure one like it."

"You're quite wealthy now," I told him. "You could help the

villagers around Sherwood Forest if you wanted. You could be the Robin Hood so many generations will love—or now that we've changed things, your story could disappear from my culture altogether. Someone has to love you enough to record your good deeds for posterity."

Robin Hood flipped to the next page of the book. It was another picture of him. "It does seem a pity to disappoint future generations, doesn't it?"

"And just think, somewhere along the line you'll probably get to meet a very pretty woman named Maid Marian."

He chuckled, then swept a hand toward Chrissy and me. "If she is half as fetching as either of you, my dear ladies, I shall deem myself a fortunate man."

Chrissy let out a tinkling laugh. "That is quite enough poetry from you. You may return to your men." He smiled, bowed, and walked back to the Merry Men with the book tucked under his arm.

"Now to get you back home—" Chrissy raised her wand.

I held up a hand to stop her. "Wait, there's something else I want to talk to you about." I had been thinking about this since I walked into the forest. I would only have one chance to ask.

Chrissy paused, her wand still lifted. "What?"

"This gold enchantment I have is valuable, even to the magical community, isn't it?"

She nodded. "Like I said, the leprechaun union has a monopoly on them."

"I propose a trade. I'll give you the gold enchantment if you let me make a detour through time on the way home."

Chrissy lowered her wand, tapping it against the palm of her hand as she considered my proposal. "And what sort of thing would you be doing while you made your detour?"

"I want to save Hudson's mother."

She let out a patient sigh. "You realize that if you alter the outcome of that event, it will have a ripple effect on the events around it. Anything and everything could change when you get home. Hudson will still have his old memories, but his alternate self—the self he would have been if his mother hadn't died—will have lived a completely different life during the last year. He'll have no memory of that life. And he'll most likely have another girlfriend. Nothing will have stopped his alternate self from being social over the last year. Do you really want that?"

I had to think about this for several moments. She was right. If I changed that one event, Hudson's life would be completely different. What if he liked his alternate life and alternate girlfriend better? Would that still be worth it?

"Will it change Stetson's future?" I asked. "Will he still be born?"

Chrissy's wings opened, shimmering with a light all their own. "Maybe. Right now, the baby is at your house with your family. I was going to let you say good-bye to him before I sent him back to the future. But if you change things too drastically, he might have no future to return to."

I pondered this, already missing his dimpled cheeks and toothless grin. "Then I'll keep Stetson with me in the present day. Can I do that?"

Chrissy put her fingers to her temple and let out a small groan. "Do you have any idea of the paperwork involved in permanently transferring a mortal to—"

I didn't let her finish. "I got rid of an evil ex-fairy—one who didn't like you or the Alliance. Just think what he might have done if—"

"Oh, all right." She let out a begrudging huff. "But only because fairies don't like being indebted to mortals. It's unnatural. And embarrassing." She held a hand out to me in a conciliatory gesture. "If Stetson wouldn't exist in the future, he can stay with you in your present. That's the only consequence I'll be able to adjust for you, though. If things are worse off because of your efforts—if Hudson doesn't care about you anymore, you'll have to live with it. The only thing I can guarantee that won't have changed are your wishes and their consequences. Magic is beyond the grasp of time."

I hesitated then, doubts chipping away my resolve. Who was I to play with time?

Then I thought of the pain in Hudson's eyes when he talked about that night, the guilt and responsibility that weighed on him. What was the point of having the enchantment, I had asked earlier, if I didn't use it to help people? Hudson had told me some things were worth the risk. This was one of those things.

"I have to try to save her," I said. It meant saving a part of Hudson. "I just need to do one more thing first." I knelt down beside the diaper bag and used the enchantment for a last time to turn the things inside to gold. Dad and Sandra would need it to buy new furniture, cars, and everything else my wish had ruined.

As I thought about how my wishes had gone, more doubts filled my mind. What if Chrissy somehow messed this up?

Then I pushed the worries away. This wasn't a wish; it was a business deal. Rumpelstiltskin had told me mortals had recourse with the Alliance if a business deal with a fairy wasn't performed correctly.

When I was done creating gold diapers, formula, and toys, I stood up. Chrissy held her palm out to me. In an official-sounding voice, she said, "Give me the enchantment and your request will be granted."

I took hold of the edges of the gold heart that pulsed over my own. It was attached to my chest so tightly that I was afraid I would tear away a huge chunk of skin when I pulled it off. But it came off with only a little tug. My own heart immediately felt better, lighter. My lungs could finally expand fully.

I put the still-beating heart in Chrissy's hand, and it

transformed from a heart into a gold apple. She smiled at it, satisfied, and slipped it into her purse. "I'm totally going to gloat to Clover about having his enchantment. It serves him right for making deals behind my back."

Her voice faded, and a dizzying array of lights went off around me. It felt like soda bubbles were fizzing past me. When they cleared, I wasn't in the forest any longer. I stood on a modern street back in Rock Canyon—I could tell by the stucco houses, the hot evening air, and the cacti and palm trees perched in the lawns.

Chrissy leaned over my shoulder, pointing far down the street. "Hudson's house is that one. His mother is about to come out."

And then Chrissy vanished.

The door opened. A tall woman with Hudson's brown hair stepped out. Even from a distance, I could tell she slammed the door behind her. She strode across her lawn and went down the sidewalk heading in my direction. Her gaze was down, her expression furious. She didn't see me. She wasn't paying attention to anything around her.

I glanced back at Hudson's house. It sat silently behind a manicured lawn. Hudson was inside right now, thinking he should go after his mother. But he wouldn't.

She came closer, her pace fast, and I felt awkward standing in the middle of the sidewalk wearing an evening gown and baby sling. I took off the sling and shoved it into the diaper bag that sat at my feet. Which only made me marginally more normal. I still had the evening gown and diaper bag.

Hudson's mother glanced up long enough to see me. She was pretty in a motherly sort of way. Her hair and makeup were still done at this late hour, and she wore a crisp tailored blouse. She struck me as the type who would run the PTO, be on all sorts of committees, and make sure her family ate nutritious dinners.

"Mrs. Gardner?" I called to her.

She paused, looked at me more closely, and stopped altogether. Surprise flitted across her large, brown eyes. Hudson's eyes. Stetson's eyes.

"Mrs. Gardner?" I asked again. "Can I talk to you for a minute?"

Her gaze ran over me. "Do we know each other?"

"I'm one of Hudson's friends. I wanted to talk to you about the party tonight."

Her lips thinned into a tight line. "You were there too? I didn't know it was a formal event."

"You need to know that Hudson is sorry. He wasn't trying to undermine his father, or the law, or set a bad example. He went to the party because his friends were there, and he didn't consider the consequences. He wants you to come back home so you can talk about it."

Her eyebrows rose and she scrutinized me for a moment. "How do you know that?"

I couldn't tell her we had chatted about it in the twelfth century, but I didn't want to risk lying. Chrissy had said the liar's hat would only be in effect until my wishes were fulfilled, but I wasn't sure if this trip counted as part of my wishes. "Cell phones are wonderful things," I said.

Mrs. Gardner looked around the street, as though she might see Hudson. "Why didn't he tell me any of this himself?"

"Sometimes it's hard to say those sorts of things, and then it's too late."

She put one hand on her hip, drumming her fingers against her pants. "He realized I'm going down to the party to break it up, didn't he? He doesn't want me to embarrass him in front of his friends. Well, you can tell him he'll be a lot more embarrassed if his father breaks it up and hauls his friends off to the station."

She moved to go past me, and I reached out, brushing my

fingertips against her arm. "Please, go back to the house and talk to him. He loves you. He would be so devastated if anything happened to you."

She stopped and tilted her head at me. "If anything happened to me? What exactly are they doing at this party?"

I hadn't expected changing history to be quite this hard. My words came out too fast and emotional. "Call your husband about the party if you want, but go back and talk to Hudson." I stopped and held out a pleading hand. "You're his mother. He needs you."

I saw the break in her anger. It slid away from her, taking the tension in her expression with it. She ran a hand through her hair, then looked back at the house. "Okay," she said, "I'll talk to him." She turned to me, putting on a polite smile. "It was nice of you to come out and talk to me, uh . . ."

She was waiting for me to tell her my name, and I couldn't lie, but I hesitated, not wanting to impact the future more than I already had. "Tansy," I said. "But don't tell him you talked with me. I wouldn't want him to . . ." *Tell you he doesn't know anyone named Tansy.*

She nodded. "It will stay between us."

She looked like she was about to say more, but a car barreled down the street, tires screeching as it turned onto the street next to us. It went up on the sidewalk and across a corner of the lawn as it made the turn. I let out a slow breath. Mrs. Gardner would have been there if she hadn't stopped to talk to me.

She watched the car and reached into her pocket for her cell phone. As she punched in the number, she shook her head. "This is why those parties are a bad idea. That guy is going to hurt somebody. Did you get the license plate number?"

I hadn't been looking, but I knew it anyway. NDSTRCT. It was Bo's brother's car. I had recognized Bo in the driver's seat.

I gave her the license plate letters, feeling both sick and relieved. Had Bo even realized what he'd done that night? How could he have lived with himself if he had known? I wasn't sure whether to feel angry or sorry for him.

Mrs. Gardner's phone call connected. She was no longer looking at me, but down the street where Bo had turned. She gave her husband the information and told him about the party. I was glad she wasn't looking at me because I saw lights spinning around me, coming in close, and then I stood in my family room.

Chapter 24

The room wasn't like it had been before our trip to the Middle Ages. The furniture and curtains were gone, and the carpet had been pulled up, as though someone tried to take it but realized it was too big and heavy to move. Clutter lay everywhere. Books, pencils, electronics, canned food. Apparently the thieves hadn't known what to make of a lot of our modern things.

I was definitely back on our street. Through the bare windows of the living room, sunshine poured in. I could see the paved road, the neighbors' houses, the streetlamps standing sentry over the sidewalks. Sandra held Stetson in her arms, gently bouncing him on her hip. I caught sight of my dad in the hallway, checking the rest of the house.

The desk in the family room was gone, but the computer sat on the floor, still plugged in. Nick was bringing up an Internet page. Hudson, sitting next to him, looked at me wryly. "Did you say your good-byes to Robin Hood?"

"I did. And he was very grateful for the chance to change his destiny."

"Oh really? How grateful?"

Nick jiggled the mouse in an attempt to hurry along the computer. "She couldn't have gotten in much trouble. She was only there about ten seconds longer than we were."

"Yeah, but that's probably twenty minutes in Middle Ages time," Hudson said, and he looked considerably less certain about my ability to stay out of trouble for that long.

I needed to tell Hudson what I'd done, but I couldn't just blurt out that I had changed his whole last year. What would he think about stepping into a completely different life now?

I would break the news to him carefully.

"Um," I said, but didn't get any further.

Sandra walked over to me and gave me a hug. "Thank goodness you made it back. Now I can stop worrying and start cleaning."

She handed the baby to me, and he grabbed hold of my neck eagerly, clearly not knowing what to make of this strange, empty place.

"When is Chrissy going to take Stetson back to the future?" Sandra asked.

I held Stetson so his head rested against my cheek. His hair felt like silk against my skin. "I don't know."

Sandra gave him a kiss on the back of the head. "I'm glad we had the chance to spend some time with him."

I wondered if she would be as glad if she knew he might have to stay here.

The computer screen popped up, and Nick said, "It's last Monday morning at 7:03 a.m. We didn't even miss a day of school. If we hurried now, we could make it on time."

"Except that all your clothes are gone," Dad said, coming into the room. "The dressers, the beds—everything was taken."

Nick gestured to his dirt-splattered tunic. "We can't go anywhere like this. How are we going to shop for new clothes?"

Dad rubbed the back of his neck. "Especially since we left our cars in the Middle Ages."

Hudson stood up. "I can't wait to find new clothes. I need to call my dad now. He's probably been looking for me all night. What am I going to tell him?" He took a step toward the kitchen and then turned back to us, snapping his fingers. "I've got our story: the police have been searching for Robin Hood—I mean, the medieval bandits. We'll tell the police that they broke in here, took our clothes, made us dress in their medieval stuff, and then held us hostage while they cleaned out this place. They only just left, and now we're alerting the authorities."

"Why did they make us dress in medieval clothes?" Sandra asked. Her eyes were wide at the prospect of having to know facts about this story. She wasn't used to lying.

Hudson held out a hand as though grasping at the air for details. "They're some sort of revolutionary group that's trying to bring back the feudal system. They stole your cars, and we heard them saying they're driving to California and then flying back to England. That way, the police will stop working over-time to look for them in town." His glance slid over me, and his lips twitched in dissatisfaction. "Well, the bandits made all of us wear their medieval clothes except for Tansy, who was clearly on her way to the Oscars when the bandits broke in."

"Hey," I said. "It's not my fault Chrissy was in charge of my wardrobe."

Nick regarded me. "They made Tansy put on an old prom dress because that's the sort of gown befitting a maiden."

Sandra bit her lip. "You think the police will buy any of that?"

Hudson nodded. "The Merry Men stole silverware from the Village Inn and a nose ring from a store clerk. They set a prece-dent for weird behavior."

He strode toward the kitchen, and I called out, "What about your hair?"

"What about it?" he asked.

"How are you going to explain that it's a couple of inches longer than it was yesterday?"

Hudson stopped in his tracks and ran a hand through his hair.

Sandra headed to the hallway. "Let me see if we still have the haircutting scissors."

Hudson followed her, rubbing his hand against his cheek. "I should shave too."

Dad went with them. "I think we still have some razors. I'll show you where."

For the next few minutes, Hudson, Nick, and Dad shaved. After that, Sandra trimmed Hudson's hair. Thankfully, the haircutting scissors were in a black plastic box that the thieves hadn't found interesting enough to take. I stood near the bathroom door with Stetson, watching Hudson's hair flutter to the ground.

"I need to talk to you in private when you have a minute," I said. I kept my voice casual so I didn't lead him into asking a lot of questions.

"Right." His gaze went to the baby and he smiled. "When is Chrissy going to send Stetson to the future?"

I shrugged. Every minute that ticked by made me worry a little more. Perhaps she hadn't come because Stetson no longer existed in the future. Had I changed things that much?

From the living room, Dad called out, "Tansy, how are we supposed to move this?"

Oh. The diaper bag. I went to go talk to him. When I reached the family room, Dad and Nick were fingering through the bag. Dad took out a bright gold bottle. "Why did you change this stuff? The police are going to wonder why we have golden baby toys, diapers, and wet wipes in a place thieves just left."

"I gave the enchantment back to Chrissy," I said. "But I wanted to have some gold first. I didn't know the police would be checking it. Sorry."

Dad stared at me in surprise. "After all the trouble you went through to get the enchantment, you gave it back to Chrissy? Why?"

"It put all of us in danger during the Middle Ages," I said. "I didn't know if the danger would stop once we got back home. Chrissy said that kings, giants, and pirates come after you if you can produce gold. Besides, the enchantment was never meant for humans, so it hurt my heart. And," I added more quietly, "I traded it for something Hudson needed."

"Ahh," Nick said, like the last sentence explained everything.

My father sighed and turned the gold bottle over in his hands. "You're probably right. Unending wealth might have its downsides. All those servants getting in the way. The car insurance rates on our Cadillacs." He let out another sigh. "I sure hope Hudson appreciates whatever you got him."

"I hope so too," I said.

Nick picked up a gold pacifier. "Gold is worth thousands of dollars a pound. We still have a pretty good fortune here."

"The bag is too heavy to move," Dad said. "We'll have to take it piece by piece to the safe in my closet. That way, the police won't see it."

I helped Dad and Nick move a few of the lighter items. It was hard for me to carry much while I was toting around a baby.

When I went to check on Hudson, he was done with his haircut and was on the phone. I didn't have to listen for long to figure out it was someone at the police station. He was giving a description of our cars and their destination.

Which meant the police would be here soon and I would have even less of a chance of speaking to Hudson privately.

When he hung up, I said, "I need to talk to you about something."

"Right. In a minute." He walked toward the family room. "Where is everybody? We need to go over our story to make sure we get it straight."

"They're moving gold from the diaper bag into my dad's safe."

"What?" he asked, but we reached the family room and he saw what was happening. He went to help, shaking his head at me as he did. "You know, if you could have waited until after the police left to create ducky-shaped treasures, it would have made things easier."

I followed after him. "That's what I wanted to talk to you about."

"Gold?" he asked, and the way he said it sounded like it was the last thing he wanted to talk about.

"Not gold specifically. I want to tell you what happened after you guys came back home."

"Oh, Robin Hood then." He sounded even less thrilled by this subject.

"No, not Robin Hood either."

Hudson picked up the last of the gold items, a pair of booties, and headed toward my father's room with everybody else. He motioned for me to come with them. "We can talk later; we need to go over our story before the police get here." Loudly enough for everybody to hear, he said, "Okay, last night while your parents made dinner, Nick and I were sitting at the table doing homework. The doorbell rang and you went and opened the door without looking through the peephole first."

"Oh, I get to be an idiot."

"No, you're just the trusting sort. The medieval bandits pushed their way inside with their swords drawn. They made us change clothes, then held us at sword-point in the kitchen while they robbed your house. We already know what Robin Hood and the Merry Men look like, so we shouldn't have any problems giving descriptions."

We had reached the closet. While my dad tried to make everything fit into the safe, Hudson went on describing details of our night. He ended with, "Stetson will be Sandra's nephew that she's babysitting. We have to hope he doesn't vanish during the investigation, because, yeah, there's no good way to explain that."

I looked at Hudson impatiently. "Now can we talk for a minute?"

"Sure."

The two of us headed back to the family room while Nick and Sandra stayed behind to help Dad. I stroked Stetson's back and tried to think of the best way to break the news to Hudson. "Well . . . ," I said, and didn't say anything else for a moment.

He tilted his head, trying to read my expression. "Is this about you moving to some luxury apartment in New York?"

"No, it's about your wish."

"What wish?"

"The wish you would have made." It was the wrong place to start. He looked at me like he had no idea what I was talking about. I tried again. "You see, after the rest of you left, I made a deal with Chrissy—"

He didn't let me finish. "*You what?*"

"It worked out well," I said. "At least I think it did. I'm not really sure yet."

He let out a groan and put his hand over his eyes. "Tansy, Chrissy made a mess of your wishes. Haven't you had enough near-death experiences?"

I didn't answer. We were in the family room, and I could see a police car pulling up in front of the house.

"What deal did you make?" he asked.

I still didn't answer. How could I tell him what I'd done and why I did it when he was glaring at me?

"You said it was my wish," he said. "How am I involved? What's going to happen?"

The doorbell rang. The police were here. Hudson turned to me, waiting for my answer.

This might be it, I realized—the reason Hudson and I didn't

get together in the future. He was mad at me for interfering in his life, for making changes without consulting him.

"I changed the past," I said.

"Right. You gave Robin Hood *The Change Enchantment.*"

"No, I mean, *your* past."

He gave me a puzzled look. "What? My past in the Middle Ages?"

There was a knock at the door, and then a man's voice called, "Hudson?"

Hudson turned away from me. "That's my dad. I've got to let him in."

He walked to the door and as soon as he opened it, his father stepped inside. He was tall, like Hudson, with streaks of gray coloring his hair. His features were sharp, imposing even, but his eyes softened when he saw his son. "Hudson," he called with relief and gave him a hug. "You're all right? Everyone is okay?"

Hudson nodded.

His father kept his hand on Hudson's shoulder. "Don't worry, son. We'll get the men that did this."

Well, the police chief was probably going to be disappointed in that regard.

Hudson's father kept patting his shoulder as though he didn't want to let go. "I've never seen your mom so worried. We were calling people half the night looking for you."

"Mom?" Hudson repeated.

"I already called her. She's on her way."

Hudson turned to me, but he didn't speak.

"*That* past," I said.

Hudson paled and then flushed. He turned back to his dad. "Mom is coming?" He didn't sound like he believed it.

Mr. Gardner smiled wearily. "I know, I know. Neither of us will get a word in edgewise about the robbery until she's had her say, but I couldn't let her keep worrying about you."

Hudson gazed through the living room window, where a car had screeched to a stop in front of the house.

"There she is now," the police chief said.

Hudson walked to the door slower than I expected. I think he was in shock. He opened the door as she reached the front step. Without a word, he threw his arms around her.

She had plenty to say, but I didn't hear what. It was all murmured into his chest. After a minute, the two walked back into the house. She held on to his arm with one hand and brushed tears from her face with her other. "I just knew something bad had happened to you. I was so afraid I'd never see you again. You can't imagine."

His eyes didn't leave her. "Yes, I can."

"Oh, of course you can." She turned and hugged him again. "I'm so sorry for what you've been through."

He blinked and hugged her back, burying his face into her hair. He was trembling. When he looked up, I saw the gratitude in his eyes.

I smiled. He was happy, for now at least. I hoped he remembered this moment when he found out he had no real memories of the last year.

Sandra, Nick, and my dad came into the room. "Are the police here?" Dad asked.

Mrs. Gardner stepped toward them. "Are you folks all right?"

"Yes," Sandra said, and then stopped suddenly when she saw who was speaking. Sandra drew in a gasp, her head tilted back in astonishment, and she fainted. She would have hit the floor if Nick hadn't caught her. He eased her down to the ground and fanned her face with his hand.

Mrs. Gardner pressed her lips together and motioned to her husband. "Dear, you'd better call the paramedics."

"No, no, we're fine," Dad stuttered, but he was looking strangely at Mrs. Gardner too. I had forgotten that Dad and Sandra knew Mrs. Gardner and knew she had died a year ago. Still staring at her, Dad said, "We're all fine . . . I think." He strode over to the window and looked out as though checking to see if the rest of the world was the same.

"Hmmm," Mrs. Gardner said, watching him. To her husband she mouthed, "Make the call."

While he did, the rest of us congregated around Sandra. Dad came over, although he kept a good distance away from Mrs. Gardner. She knelt down by Sandra, took her hand, and tapped it gently. "Can you hear me?"

"It's probably delayed shock," Nick said. "I'm sure she'll be fine."

Sandra blinked open her eyes, took in Mrs. Gardner, and let out a startled scream.

"It's okay," I told Sandra. "I can explain everything"—I glanced at Mrs. Gardner—"at a later time."

Sandra's gaze ricocheted between Mrs. Gardner and me, and at last she seemed to understand. She let out several quick breaths. "You traded . . . ," she gasped out, ". . . for Hudson."

"Right," I said.

When Mrs. Gardner looked at me questioningly, I shrugged and whispered, "It's the shock. I'm humoring her."

My dad's eyes widened and he said, "Oh—ooooh!" And I knew he understood too.

Sandra took a few more deep breaths and pulled herself to a sitting position. She put her free hand on her chest. "I'm fine now," she said weakly.

"Good." Mrs. Gardner looked Sandra over carefully before she let go of her hand. "Don't try to get up yet. If you need anything, have one of your children . . ." Her gaze narrowed in on my face. Then her mouth opened in surprise. "You're Tansy, aren't you?" To Sandra she said, "I didn't know Tansy was your daughter."

"You've met?" Sandra asked.

"Yes, last year . . ." And then, as though she just realized it, she added, "I think you were wearing that same dress."

I forced a smile. "Weird coincidence."

Her gaze fell to Stetson. "And who is this darling baby?"

"My nephew," Sandra said quickly.

"Well, isn't he the cutest thing." Mrs. Gardner bent down for a closer look. "He reminds me of Hudson when he was a baby."

Another weird coincidence I was not going to comment on.

Hudson apparently didn't want to comment either. He went and talked with his father, repeating the story of what the bandits had done.

Over the next few minutes, more police officers came, along with paramedics. I was glad the golden heart was gone because I wasn't sure how I would have explained it to the guy who listened to my heart and lungs with his stethoscope. We were examined and questioned while the police roamed around taking pictures for their report. As they were packing up to go, Mrs. Gardner came over to talk to Sandra again.

"I feel so awful that you lost so much," she said. "What can I do to help?"

"We didn't lose anything that can't be replaced." Sandra glanced around the nearly empty room. "And on the bright side, it just got a lot easier to pack for our move."

Mrs. Gardner's eyebrows dipped. "What move?" Before Sandra could answer, Mrs. Gardner put a consoling hand on Sandra's shoulder. "You're not going to let this robbery make you move, are you? Rock Canyon is still a safe city, and the library needs you. Don't tell me I went through all that work to keep the branch open for nothing."

"All that work . . . ," Sandra repeated.

"I had to practically browbeat the mayor," Mrs. Gardner said.

"The branch is staying open?" Sandra asked.

Mrs. Gardner pursed her lips and cocked her head. "The paramedics checked you out, right?"

Sandra let out a happy gasp. "That's wonderful . . . I mean about the branch. I mean, of course we won't move. Thank you so much for working to keep it open."

"Well, we all do our part to help the community," Mrs. Gardner said, still eyeing her as though she might faint again.

I smiled. I hadn't needed gold to save Dad's and Sandra's jobs after all. I'd only needed Mrs. Gardner.

Hudson left not long after that. His mother looped her arm possessively through his and said, "I don't know about you, but I need to go home and sleep."

He hesitated, said, "Just a second," and walked over to me. He took one of Stetson's hands in his and whispered, "See you in a while, kid." Then Hudson smiled at me. "I'll call you later."

Mrs. Gardner had strolled over to us. "Speaking of calling girls"—she took his arm again and they turned toward the door—"your girlfriend texted me twice last night and once this morning asking about you. You'd better call her."

Over his shoulder, Hudson shot me an alarmed look.

I shrugged. What else could I do? Everything had changed for him, and now he had to figure out what was going on in his new life. I just hoped there was room for me.

Chapter 25

One of Sandra's friends brought over clothes for us. They were guys' shorts and T-shirts, but it felt great to take showers and change into something clean. My parents got rental cars and went shopping. It took several trips to get the basics: food, clothes, mattresses, bedding, baby things. I got a short nap, but spent most of the day cleaning up the house and taking care of Stetson.

I picked up the scattered books and stacked most of them against the family room wall. The rest I took to my bedroom. It was about time I got caught up on my reading.

Nick looked up information on the Internet about Robin Hood—he was still a folklore hero. Then he looked up King John—he married a thirteen-year-old girl not long after we left. Which was utterly creepy.

Reading out loud, Nick said, " 'In 1216, while retreating from a French invasion, the baggage train that carried King John's treasures, including the crown jewels, was lost in a marshy area by an unexpected incoming tide. This dealt John a terrible blow, which affected his health and state of mind.'"

"His state of mind?" I repeated. "The only state in his mind seceded from that union a long time ago."

"'King John died soon after that. His reign has traditionally been characterized as one of the most disastrous in English history.'"

Well, historians got some things right.

Nick nodded thoughtfully. "His treasure sank, and he died a broken man. There's a moral in that."

"Yep," I said. "Keep your wealth in lighter stuff like stocks and bonds."

I spent a lot of time walking Stetson around or giving him objects that he would gum for a few minutes and then toss across the room. Chrissy still hadn't come to get him. I knew what that meant. Or at least thought I did. It was possible that Chrissy was out getting another pedicure. She'd never been a punctual fairy godmother.

By the time we finished dinner that night, I was convinced she wasn't coming. Not only did Hudson and I have no future, but now I had to be a teenage mother. How was I going to explain that to people—especially to oh, say, my mother and sister?

I was so discouraged that I went to my room, put Stetson on a baby blanket on the floor, and lay down beside him. I stroked his forehead, willing him to sleep so I could too. If I slept, I wouldn't cry.

I heard the doorbell ring, but didn't think much of it. Some of Sandra and Dad's friends had been dropping things off— old dressers, extra chairs—all day.

I waited to hear Dad's voice greeting whoever had come. Instead I heard Hudson's voice in my doorway. "I wonder why Chrissy hasn't sent Stetson home yet."

I didn't answer. I didn't want to tell Hudson about that part of my bargain.

He walked into the room. He wore a pair of faded blue jeans and a form-fitting T-shirt that showed off his broad shoulders. His hair was clean and shiny. I had forgotten how good he looked in this century. I couldn't take my eyes off him.

"I brought you something." Hudson held out a jar of water containing the Gilead. It was suspended in the water by a frame-work of popsicle sticks over the opening. He walked past me and set it on my windowsill. "I cut off the end of the stem and put root starter on it. I don't know if it will work, but if it does we can plant it."

"Do you think it will be magical here too?"

He shrugged. "I hope so. It would be nice to have something that could fix things. Illness, broken bones—I wonder if it works on computers."

I only wanted to fix one thing right now.

Stetson gurgled in a very unsleepy way when he saw Hudson, and then flung his teething ring across the blanket. I picked up another toy and handed it to him. "So how are things at home now that your mom is back?"

Hudson turned and leaned against my windowsill. "You say that so casually, like she was gone on a business trip." He tilted his head, examining me. "What did you give to Chrissy in exchange for changing my past?"

"The gold enchantment."

"You gave up your luxury apartment in New York?"

"Well, Stetson needs a yard to run around in . . . cacti to climb . . . whatever it is you do in hick towns."

I had expected Hudson to smile, but he didn't. His expression stayed serious. "I don't know how to thank you, Tansy. I can't *ever* make it up to you."

He'd said the same thing about his mother's death—that no matter what he did, he couldn't make it up to his father.

"You don't have to make it up to me," I said. "I just want you to be happy." I looked at him more closely. "You are happy, aren't you?"

"Yeah." He smiled then, a warm and easy grin that I hadn't seen very often. "After we got home, I talked to my mom for three hours straight. I couldn't stop. She fell asleep on the couch while I was talking. And even after that, I sat there watching her to make sure she didn't disappear."

"That's sweet."

"It didn't take her long to figure out that I can't remember a lot of things—like who my girlfriend is and that I'm on some student-body committee that's planning the homecoming dance. And I'm a linebacker this year . . ." He ran a hand through his hair. "I've got games soon, and I don't know any of the plays."

"You could tell people that one of the bandits hit your head and say it's amnesia."

"I wish I had thought of that at the beginning. Mom thinks it's post-traumatic stress disorder. She's got me scheduled for a doctor tomorrow."

"Well, you've got your excuse then."

Hudson left the windowsill and walked the length of my room. His smile vanished. "While my mom was sleeping, I checked my e-mails, text messages, that sort of stuff—so I'd know a little bit about what I did over the year."

I waited for him to say more. He didn't. He paced back the other way.

"So who's your girlfriend?" I asked.

He gave a short laugh and looked at the ceiling. "I'm embarrassed to tell you."

"Why? Is she an idiot or something?"

"Yeah, pretty much." He paused, then said, "Donna Hatch."

"Oh." I didn't know much about her except she was a cheerleader and beautiful and had an entourage following her around in the hallways.

"You know, in my real last year, she never talked to me after

I dropped out of football. She didn't even tell me she was sorry about my mom or try to reach out to me—and now she's my girlfriend."

"Apparently the person you would have been had no taste."

He kept pacing. "It seems like everything I did and said over the last year was stupid and shallow. The girl I dated before Donna—I dumped her in an e-mail. What kind of jerk does that?"

"You wouldn't. I mean you wouldn't *now*." I sat up straighter. "Wait a minute, did you come here in person to dump me?"

He stopped walking and turned to me. "No, I'm not dumping you. I'm two-timing Donna until I can dump her later tonight." He ran his hand through his hair again and went back to pacing. "See, I really am a jerk. I just didn't realize it until all this happened and I got a good look at myself."

I stood up, took hold of his hand, and made him sit down beside me so he would stop pacing. "You're not a jerk. You're someone who has learned a lot over the last year. That's not a bad thing, is it? You don't have to be that other person. You can keep what you've learned."

He squeezed my hand. "I'm keeping you. I know that much." He leaned toward me and brushed a strand of hair away from my face. "Speaking of two-timing, I'll have to show you some of the messages you and I sent to each other. They were downright flirty."

That made me smile. "You and I sent flirty messages to each other?"

"Yeah, apparently I started going over to your house to see Nick a lot after you moved in. And you were pretty nice to me, considering you're still dating Bo."

I stopped smiling. "I'm what?"

"The library isn't closing. He never took you to vandalize city hall."

I tilted my head back and groaned. "What am I going to tell

him when I break up with him? I'm dumping him because I know if we ever did vandalize a building, he'd leave me to face the cops alone?"

"You'll think of something." Hudson leaned closer and gave me a look that sent shivers racing down my back. "I'll help you come up with some reasons right now."

Before I could build on that sentiment, a frenzy of sparklers went off in the middle of the room. Chrissy stepped out of them, smiling happily. She wore a tight floral dress, a Hawaiian lei, and a pair of green sunglasses. "I've been celebrating our success by throwing a luau." She moved her sunglasses to the top of her head. "I see you've been celebrating by . . . sitting on the carpet. How nice."

She bent down, picked up Stetson, then dropped a kiss on his forehead that sent a swirl of glitter flowing around him. Her voice softened into a lullaby tone. "I need to get you back to your own time period before your mommy notices you're gone." She snapped her fingers and the baby blanket rose from the floor and floated to her hand. She tucked it around him and looked at me. "You don't need to worry, by the way. After you have him, you can just remember he was fine through the whole adventure. There's no need to put all those anti-magical charms around his crib like you're going to do in a few years."

Chrissy was right. Even though my trip through the Middle Ages had turned out fine, I knew that in the future, I would still try to stop her from taking him. I would be every bit the overprotective mother.

Hudson and I both stood up. Chrissy turned the baby so he faced me. "Say good-bye for now. You'll meet him again later."

I hadn't imagined saying good-bye was going to be so hard. After all, it was only temporary, and I was sending him to myself, an older me who loved him and could take care of him better. I stroked his hand and memorized his features: the dark lashes, the smooth skin, the full cheeks, and tiny parted lips. I kissed his head and felt a lump well in my throat. "Make sure you tell the future me that the baby went and came back, so I can stop worrying about him being taken."

"I will," she said reluctantly. "Although I can imagine what a fun conversation that's going to be. You've got an entire bookshelf in your house devoted to magical creatures and how to overcome each one. That's a little paranoid, don't you think, considering how well everything turned out?" Chrissy tucked the blanket around Stetson. "I bet you won't even let him put teeth under his pillow for the tooth fairy."

She was probably right about that too. I wouldn't want to risk him being turned into a squid. I didn't say this though.

Chrissy turned to Hudson. "For someone who wasn't even supposed to be in Rumpelstiltskin's story, you did quite a bit. Do you want to say good-bye too?"

Hudson brushed his fingertips against the baby's dark hair. "Take care, Stets. No more time-traveling around." He leaned over and kissed the top of the baby's head, then returned his attention to Chrissy. "Am I in the story later on?"

Chrissy smiled, an enigmatic expression that reminded me of Mona Lisa's famous one. "You'll have to find out for yourself. I'm not one to ruin endings." She let out a satisfied sigh, and held the baby to her shoulder. "If this doesn't get me into Fairy Godmother University, I don't know what will. I mean, how many other applicants have rid the Middle Ages of Rumpelstiltskin during their projects? Not Belladonna Spritzpetal. Let's see her brag about being at the top of the class now." Chrissy slipped her sunglasses over her eyes. Lights flickered around her like a convention of lightning bugs circling for a landing. "It's been a pleasure doing magic with you," she chimed out, and then she and the baby vanished.

In the place where she'd stood, a thin book lay on the carpet. It was, I saw at once, a picture book retelling of *Rumpelstiltskin*.

Like I would ever want to read *that* story again. I ignored it, opening the card that sat on top of it instead. But Hudson picked up the book and flipped through the pages.

Meanwhile, I read the card out loud.

To Tansy, I thought you'd enjoy a copy of the real story to read to your children. Remember, heroines are always beautiful!

I turned the card over, but there wasn't anything on the other side. "I'm not sure if that last bit was a compliment or instructions."

Hudson was only half paying attention to me. He had turned to the end of the story and was reading. I peered over his shoulder to see what he was looking at and blushed. The moral was there on the last page in my own handwriting. "Give me the book." I reached for it, but Hudson effortlessly held it away from me.

"Hudson," I said, making another grab for the book. "That's private."

"Morals are meant to be shared." He held me away for another moment, reading, then grinned and handed me the book. "I like this one."

I shut the book, but it didn't matter. In my mind, I could still see the sentences I'd written, framed on the page.

It's better to love people than wealth. I love Dad, Mom, Kendall, Sandra, Nick, baby Stetson, and especially Hudson. I wouldn't trade them for a mountain of gold.

"I love the word 'especially,'" he said. "And I love the person who wrote it." Then he bent over to kiss me.

From the Honorable Master Sagewick Goldengill
To the Department of Fairy Advancement

To the Esteemed Department,

I am in receipt of student Chrysanthemum Everstar's extra-credit report and have reviewed it thoroughly. Although I give Miss Everstar high marks for her part in eliminating that menace of an ex-fairy, Rumpelstiltskin, it has not escaped the UMA's notice that were it not for some swift action by the mortal, Tansy Miller Harris, Rumpelstiltskin would have regained his full powers and undoubtedly wreaked havoc on both the human and fairy realms.

As the UMA is strictly against unleashing vengeful ex-fairies on society, they have insisted I turn down Miss Everstar's current application to Godmother University. It did not help matters that Clover T. Bloomsbottle has already paid the next hundred years' union dues with coins made from the cursed ex-fairy. None of the receptionists will go near it.

However, we think Miss Everstar shows impressive potential. Please have Madame Bellwings give her another assignment.

Yours austerely,
Sagewick Goldengill